The Convent House

by

Margo Carey

Watcher Clan, Book One

Cover Art by *Kristian Norris*

The Wild Rose Press, Inc.
PO Box 708
Adams Basin, NY 14410-0708
Visit us at www.thewildrosepress.com

Publishing History
First Edition, 2024
Trade Paperback ISBN 978-1-5092-5666-2
Digital ISBN 978-1-5092-5667-9

Watcher Clan, Book One
Published in the United States of America

Dedication

To my friend, Reba, who always believed in me and my writing. I wish you were here to see this.

Author Note

A special thanks to my writing buds: Michelle Caffrey, Robert Erickson, Beverly Jackson, Glenn Erik Miller, Dianne Herlihy, Lisa Pais, and Rachel Jylkka-Tesler.

Chapter One

Finished! Alexandra Ryan scooped up the document from the printer beside her desk and hurried off to complete the more substantial duplication. Her boss wanted it *now* for a last-minute conference.

An edgy hum filled the office as she wound her way between the cubicles. Not the usual Friday morning vibrations, but something more intense—secretaries ignoring their coffee to tap out those last sentences on their keyboards. Sounds of shuffling—chairs, papers, and files—replaced the normal morning conversation.

Executives from corporate were in the building.

The nervous chorus followed the rapid click of her heels to the copy room where she slid to a stop. Damn! Someone was ahead of her. Alex sighed, leaned against the wall, and shifted the papers in her arms. The small space held only the main copier and a long table with various office-related instruments: staplers, tape, scissors, and a large paper cutter. The seemingly unending hiss of completed sheets continued as she examined the dingy ceiling tiles and empty, beige walls. The dismal sight only added to her annoyance. She hated these corporate ambushes that put everyone under pressure.

Finally, the last page covered the pile. She marched forward then stopped. The woman had more. Alex pursed her lips, backed up, and peeked at the clock. Oh,

God. The meeting would start in a few minutes. Perspiration trickled down the back of her neck. Was the air conditioning even working in this room?

"Excuse me," she said. "Do you think I could sneak in before you do that?" She indicated her burden. "This is for a meeting that starts in five minutes."

The woman scowled. "So is this."

Alex's boss would not be happy, but this position, like all the others, was temporary. Her assignment at this company would end in a few days. Still, she needed a good report. Lately, she'd had a few. . . *problems* on a couple of her jobs.

When the swish of paper stopped this time, the woman gathered up both stacks. She nodded to Alex, who did the same as she placed the forty-five page presentation on the table. Now to try and figure out this model. They were all different.

She punched in the code for her department, then found the proper tray. Good. *Single-sided to double.* Check. *Color copies.* Done. *Twenty-five.* Okay. That wasn't hard. She pressed *Start*, and the machine snatched the first page. The steady tick, as the report slipped through, eased her mind until she glanced at the lighted choices. *Stapled* wasn't one of them.

Panic gripped her as the machine continued to churn. She punched *Stop*. When nothing happened, she hit it again. Time was against her. If she had to hand-staple the packets, she'd be late. Once more, she banged the red button. No change. Even though she knew it was pointless, she tried pressing random switches.

A sudden urge to strangle this artificial monster consumed her. Powerless to do anything about the situation, she clenched her teeth and squeezed the gray beast's sides. An unnerving sense of retribution clouded her mind. Heat filled her palms, and the tips of her fingers buzzed and snapped like static electricity. She snatched her hands away. An ominous sizzle followed. The rustle of printed sheets ceased. All the lights flashed, then died. Not good.

There must be something she could do. Maybe unplug it and wait a minute. While she searched for the cord, the ailing copier shuddered and made a last moan.

A quick glance revealed an empty room. The solution might lie inside, so she released the top to poke around. Seconds later, the sharp stink of burning wires invaded her nose. *Oh Lord, what have I done?* The smell made her gag. She backed away, then looked on in horror as smoke rose from the back. Someone behind her yelled, "Get out of here. It's on fire!"

Alarms screamed, and the scent of noxious fumes followed her as she joined the queue of annoyed people trooping outside to greet the fire department. Trembling, she looked at her hands. What was going on with her? She needed help.

How could she explain what happened?

Moreover, who would believe her?

****

That night, when the phone rang, she checked the ID and knew what it meant. Her whole being screamed to ignore it, but that would only postpone the inevitable. She answered her boss's call.

"Hi, Ellen. What's up?"

"Hi, Alex. I heard about the fire today."

She couldn't speak. Her insides cramped.

"I know you're a good worker, but the company's security cameras showed you poking around inside the copier at the time of the fire. The CEO is not happy. My temp agency can't survive with bad reviews. This is the third time something unpleasant has occurred in relation to you. I'm sorry. I have to let you go."

Alex hung up and squeezed her eyes shut, the sound of her panicky heartbeat clamoring in her ears. What could she do? She was almost twenty-five, and her life was a mess. She needed the work. She couldn't survive on the few freelance articles she published.

The short-term jobs were perfect. They paid well, and no one got too close. There were other agencies, but she needed a good reference. Maybe if she called back tomorrow, Ellen would take pity on her and forget to mention the problems in Alex's referral.

For the past month, every time she'd been annoyed, weird things had happened. At one office, some jerk patted her behind in the break room, and her hot coffee splashed all over him, but she hadn't done it on purpose. Then there were the odd prickly sensations she'd been having in her hands. She hugged herself. What was the matter with her? Was she losing her mind?

****

The next day, Alex went through the bills on her desk. The new landlord had almost doubled the rent. Her final check from the temp agency would help cover one more month, but that was it. Even if she had a decent job, she'd be in trouble.

Her stomach churned as she rubbed the back of her neck and paced the tiny apartment. A good walk in the fresh air would help relieve the tension. At eight a.m., although the Phoenix sun baked her shoulders, the atmosphere still retained some of last night's cool. As she strode along, enticing scents from her favorite coffee shop called to her, but she could no longer afford the luxury. She ran her fingers through her shoulder-length chestnut waves as she passed Betty's Hair Boutique—out of the question now, too. Ah, well. She could go for a while without a cut.

By the time she reached Fong's Market, she was winded. She paused, glanced in the window, and saw her reflection. A young woman stared back at her, medium height, okay figure, and no indication that her existence was on life support.

When she returned to her apartment, she stopped to examine the cozy living room filled with gently used furniture. The tan leather sofa and chair she'd found online, her parents' TV and stand, and the round, wooden dining set. Her gaze paused at each of the watercolors she'd discovered at yard sales. She'd been comfortable here. What would she do with all the furniture if she lost this place?

Time to check her options. An Internet search for jobs and apartments wasn't encouraging. Rents were high everywhere, and the employment market was slim. An invisible vise squeezed her head. She needed someplace to think. Time to visit her parents.

Since she'd had to get rid of her old clunker when the price of repairs and gas became too much, she'd learned to rely on public transportation. At the end of a comfortable, air-conditioned bus ride, she stepped out into the now-intense summer heat for a ten-minute walk. Before long, she had to take a swig from her water bottle. The drought hadn't been kind to a few gardens along the way. Though the wilted plants made her sad, the homes with native succulents cheered her. They thrived in this weather.

By the time she reached the cemetery, her feet squished in her sneakers, her tank top was soaked, and her hair under the baseball cap was plastered to her head.

Inside the gate, she paused, as usual, to admire the well-kept grounds and read the names carved in granite. A sense of peace reached out to her in the quiet solitude. She slowed her steps, took a deep drink, and gazed across the sea of stone. All those lives that had burned bright then winked out. Some, like her parents, too young. After a few minutes, she stopped in the shade of a large Arizona Ash. Her mother had paid extra for this spot when Dad had died, but it was beautiful and cool. She took a long swallow from her bottle, used the last of the liquid to rub along the back of her neck, then filled the empty from a nearby spigot to give her parents' plants a drink.

With a sigh, she settled on the ground in her usual place across from the pink stone, legs crossed and fingers playing with strands of grass. Her chest ached as she focused on the inscriptions. *Daniel J Ryan. Cecile M Ryan.* Since she'd been unable to part with her mother's ashes, she'd added the words, *Together in Heaven.* It had been almost a year since her father died, but only six months since her mom's sudden death. The pain was still fresh.

"I miss you both so much. I wish I could talk to you. Something's happening to me. I'm terrified, and I don't know what to do. I don't have anyone to turn to."

She'd been close to her mother. Sitting here today, she imagined the warmth of her mother's embrace, her voice telling Alex everything would be all right.

A gruff voice startled her. "You always talk to dead people? They ever talk back?"

She twisted to her knees and tried to see the man's face, but the dappled sun peeking through the leaves made it difficult. A sense of danger slid through her. She pushed up off the ground. "Who are you? What do you want?"

She was able to see him now. Shaved head and dark, pock-marked cheeks. Close-set, watery eyes framed his long, bent nose. A dark, cloudy aura clung to him. Although he looked to be in his forties, his body was wiry. His face held a nasty sneer. In a deceptively friendly tone, he said, "I want you to come with me. Now."

"That's ridiculous. Get away from me."

Her insides screamed at her to run. She threw her plastic bottle at him and sped off. She took a quick peek behind her. He was fast.

She dodged gravestones, looking for anyone. The cemetery was deserted at this time of day, but she cried out for help. When she chanced another glance behind, she didn't see him. In a panic, she whipped her head around. Dear God. He was ahead of her on the road.

She swerved, going farther into the graveyard. Her chest hurt, and it was hard to breathe. She wasn't used to the exercise, and the heat was a killer. Footsteps pounded behind her. The fence loomed ahead. She had nowhere to go.

She tried to scream again, but she couldn't get enough breath. He caught up to her. His grip bit into her arm as he swung her around. He was panting, too, but that didn't stop him from holding up a big, shiny knife. "You want to live?" He huffed out. "Come with me."

He let go of her arm and motioned toward the gate. "Let's go."

Anger mixed with fear bubbled up inside her. A voice whispered in her head. *I'm here, sweetheart.* Heat surged in her chest. The warmth traveled down her arms and ended with a hot crackling in her fingers. Strength flowed through her body. Without thinking, fingers spread wide, she shoved her hands at him and yelled, "No!"

The man flew backward, his face contorted with fear. She gasped as his body crashed into a life-sized marble angel. He hit the ground and didn't move.

Silence, broken by the occasional sound of traffic in the distance, surrounded her. She started to shake, then stared at her hands. What had she done? Time to leave. One last look at her attacker, then she scrambled away.

The trip to the bus stop was agonizing. She half-walked and half-ran, wheezing like a losing prizefighter, and each time she checked behind her, she staggered.

By the time she made it to her destination, sweat poured down her face. After one more peek behind her, she swallowed. No one. Safe for now. The two other people waiting at the covered bench moved away from her.

She couldn't think straight. The police. She had to call them. She took out her phone but paused. She'd sent the man flying. Oh, God. What if he was dead? How could she explain that? People already thought she was strange. They'd never believe her. She worried about it all the way home.

The familiar neighborhood with its typical morning traffic and friendly faces eased her fear. Even if he was still alive, he would never find her here. As she turned her key in the lock, goose bumps broke out along her arms. The hairs on the back of her neck flared. Someone was watching. Icy fingers worked their way down her back, and she swung her head in all directions. Nothing suspicious in the immediate vicinity, but she rushed inside her apartment, slammed the door, and threw the deadbolt. She knew her emotions were frayed, and she had every right to be suspicious after this morning, but she didn't want to descend into paranoia. Still, the feeling persisted, and she peeked out the window. The sharp ring of the phone startled her. Though the number was unfamiliar, she sensed she should answer it.

"Hello?"

"Hello. My name is Bree Brendani. I'm looking for my sister, Cecile Brendani Ryan."

Alex slumped down on the sofa. Her hand shook, and her throat tightened. Mom had been an only child.

Chapter Two

Alex stared at the cellphone screen. Was this a cruel joke? "I'm not sure what you're trying to pull. Cecile Ryan had no siblings. Don't call again."

Before she pressed the red button, she sensed a note of desperation. "Please don't hang up. I can't explain how, but I'm certain I have the right person. Are you acquainted with CeCe Ryan?"

She wanted to scream. How was this person connected to her mother? Words failed her, so she ended the call.

The minute she cut her off, she wished she hadn't. The tone of the caller's voice was familiar. When realization dawned, Alex sat up straight. The woman sounded like her mom.

Emotions warred inside her. Anger at the caller for her lies, yet at the same time, a secret wish she'd spoken the truth. She replayed the conversation in her mind. The speaker knew her mom's nickname. Her voice had the same resonance as Mom's. Could her story be true? *Were we related?*

No. Of course not. Her mother would never have hidden something as important as family.

Alex shook off the sense of longing and loss resurrected by the phone call. She ached to speak to someone she trusted. For a moment, she considered Stefan, her former boyfriend. The idea of his strong arms holding her, protecting her, made her reach out to call him. With a start, she snapped out of the fantasy. There was no more Stefan. She'd finally come to her senses when her mother became ill. Unless the subject was about him, Stefan was an emotional cipher. He was never there to comfort her or consider her feelings. Even in bed, her needs had been unimportant. Breaking up with him had been the one thing she'd done right.

No family, no guy, no close friends, and a man with a knife after her. How had she become so isolated? She frowned. Daddy's death. Grief had pulled her away from everyone except Mom. Then, six months later, her mother contracted a disease that killed her in less than a week. Alex had fallen apart. Unable to work, she hid at home. Grief therapy and antidepressants pulled her from the darkness and helped her get back to work. She even tried going clubbing with women from the office until the weird buzzing began in her hands.

While she worried about her present situation, the doorbell rang. She jerked toward the sound. Strength leached from her bones. Chills squeezed her spine and stole the power from her lungs. *Had he found her?*

Her gaze darted around the room. What to do? Move. She forced herself to retrieve her phone. She'd escape through the back. Halfway there, a voice entered her mind. *Don't be afraid. I just want to talk about my sister.*

She gave her head a shake. The voice must have come from outside. Alex gaped at her cell. *I didn't give her my address.* How did she get here? Her mind spun. As she tried to focus, a loud voice from out front said, "I phoned a few minutes ago. Please speak to me."

Alex sidled to the window and peeked out. A

middle-aged female stood there. With the morning's attack uppermost in her mind, she let her senses speak to her. A neutral aura surrounded the woman, and Alex sensed no hint of danger. The person on her doorstep wasn't a threat. She breathed out her fear and shook off the stinging anxiety that had begun to pulse in her hands. Curious now, she decided it wouldn't hurt to listen.

When she opened the door, her visitor gasped and touched her chest. "You look just like her. Where's CeCe?"

The question hit Alex like a punch. She glared at the impostor, cradled her stomach, and choked out the answer. "Mom's dead."

The woman's green eyes widened in shock, and pain radiated from her features. Alex stared in confusion at a face eerily like her mother's—late forties, same eye shape and distinctive cheekbones.

Although she wasn't ready to trust yet, she sensed no harm, and her intuition had always guided her. More than anything, she craved answers, but she didn't want to invite a stranger into her home.

"I'm sorry. I have no idea who you are, but if you want to talk, I'll meet you in ten minutes at the coffee shop down the street."

"Of course." Her visitor sighed and turned to leave. Alex watched the slim figure trudge along the sidewalk, head bowed.

Alone again, she paced the living room. Anger pulsed in her voice as she sputtered to the air. "What's going on, Mom? Who was that person?"

A warm breeze touched her shoulders, then wrapped around her like a loving hug. *Everything will be all right, sweetheart.*

She peered around in a panic. Her mother's voice. Again.

****

By the time she arrived at Java Sensations, she'd relaxed. More curious than anything, she sat down and vowed to keep an open mind.

Her companion had also composed herself. "I'm glad you agreed to talk to me. I realize my presence must be quite a shock, and I'm sorry for that. I only wish my sister was here to introduce us. I believe now that she called out to her family in her last moments. We were aware of trouble when the Brendani signature exploded into the ether. For CeCe to drop her protective shield after so many years meant the situation was dire. Though we feared the worst, hope resurfaced with the emergence of the latest energy spikes." She shook her head and gazed at her hands. "We were hoping…"

Alex stared in astonishment. Shielding and energy spikes? This woman was clearly deranged, but something about her struck a chord. If Alex lowered her lashes and gazed at Bree, she could almost see her mother.

She continued to gape, then remembered her manners. "I, um. I owe you an apology for the hang-up. When you mentioned my mother, it just…I was at her grave earlier."

"I'm so sorry." She touched Alex's hand. "Let me introduce myself. I'm your aunt Bree."

In that moment of contact, something happened. A rush of familiarity swept through her. An awareness as if her soul recognized and accepted one of its own. This person looked right. She even sounded right. As crazy as it seemed, Alex recognized her blood and knew Bree was her aunt.

"I think this might help." Bree opened her purse and took out a photograph.

A fist closed about Alex's chest as she examined the picture. Two young women laughing at the camera. Her mother. Probably about seventeen. Beside her, the woman who claimed to be her mother's sister. As alike as any siblings could be.

Mom had lied to her.

Time to accept the truth. Her throat tight, she explained about her mother's illness and her father's accident.

Bree's voice deepened with anguish. "We had no idea what happened after she left. Never realized she had a child." With a heavy sigh, she said, "I don't even know your name."

"It's Alexandra Ryan. Alex."

"I'm glad to meet you, Alex. Tell me, do you have anyone else here close to you?"

A bout of loneliness threatened to overwhelm her. "No."

Bree squeezed her hand. "You're part of a big family now: aunts, uncles, and cousins. You'll never be alone again."

A tiny seed of hope sprouted in her soul. Family? An end to her isolation? "Where do you live?"

"Newport, Rhode Island."

Her fantasy crashed. All the way across the country? Even if she wanted, she couldn't go. No money for a plane ticket or even a bus ride. "I...I can't."

"You can. I'm here to help. You're a Brendani and my niece."

Much as she wanted answers, an image of the

incident that morning tormented her. She'd just met her aunt. How could she tell her she thought she'd killed a man?

"I can't afford to move."

With a flick of her hand, Bree dismissed the concern. "Money isn't a problem. Your family has plenty. Don't let that concern you anymore."

She caught her breath. Her aunt's offer seemed like the answer to all her problems. She yearned to tell someone. For a moment, she dared hope, but the memory of a body lying against a gravestone squashed her dreams.

The secret was eating away at her. Though the truth was unbelievable, even terrifying, she needed relief. With a glance around, she sighed. This wasn't the place. Instead, she focused on another issue.

"I'll need to find an apartment."

"Don't be silly. You'll stay with the family. There's plenty of room. What do you say? Come home with me. I'll take care of everything."

She sat back and regarded this woman. A stranger. For a moment her trust wavered, but instinct kicked in. She sensed love and truth, and, with her life crashing around her, she'd be a fool to dismiss this opportunity.

"It's all so sudden. Give me some time to consider it."

Bree nodded. "I understand." Then, with a penetrating stare, she said, "I have one question."

Here it comes. There's always a catch. Alex saw the lovely life Bree had described vanish.

"What's happening with these energy bursts?"

Alex's gut twisted as she contemplated the answer to her aunt's question.

Chapter Three

Bree's query reignited pangs of doubt in her chest. The coffee shop wasn't the place to discuss this. Instead of answering her aunt's question about the energy bursts, she said she needed time to process all she'd learned. Although Bree frowned at her response, she said she understood.

All the way to her apartment, uncomfortable thoughts chased through her head. Why had her mother distanced herself from her relatives? For Alex, the idea of family, people who might welcome her, sounded like a dream, although the prospect of meeting and living with strangers played havoc on her nerves. Would they accept her? Was she making a mistake?

A rumble from her stomach reminded her of the time and propelled her into her compact kitchen to forage for lunch. The pickings were pretty slim in the fridge, but she scored an apple, a piece of lettuce, half a tomato, and leftover chicken salad. An old but still soft sesame roll completed the menu. With her sandwich and a glass of iced tea, she sat to ponder her situation. Since her mother's death, her life had been as colorless as her plain kitchen cabinets. The addition of red accents had brightened the whole room. Maybe moving to Newport might do the same for her.

She ran her finger along the small oak table, a yard-sale find, and smiled as she glanced around at various treasures she'd acquired to brighten her refuge. She'd have to leave most of them here. The trio of painted bud vases, a gift from her mother, caught her eye. Each had a face at the top, so she'd named them: Rosie, Violet, and Petunia.

She winked at them. "Don't worry, girls. You're coming with me."

After she ate and cleaned up, she walked around to catalog her belongings. Whether she went to Newport or stayed here, she had to leave this apartment, the cocoon that had sheltered her in her grief. She might as well choose the items she'd like to keep. There weren't a lot. Some books, her computer, and important papers. Her clothes and a few precious tokens of her parents.

The furnishings posed a problem. Storage was too expensive. Her only option was to leave them. With no income and no hope of remaining in this apartment, she had no choice. At least, if she went to Newport, she'd have a place to stay until she could afford to move out.

One part of the earlier conversation troubled her. She'd be dependent on an unknown family across the country. Despite her concern, she liked her new aunt, although Bree's last words made her cringe. She'd sensed Alex's, what did she call them, energy bursts? Then implied it was a family trait. That had to be wrong. Other than reading auras, her mother had been normal. Hadn't she?

The question haunted her for the rest of the afternoon as she inventoried her possessions. Later, while she sat on the sofa speculating, the sun set, and shadows crept across the floor. Sparks of cold teased her neck. The deep twilight reminded her of her assailant at the cemetery, and she hurried to turn on lights and check the locks on the doors and windows.

She hadn't mentioned the attack to Bree because she wasn't sure how to explain it, but she wanted her aunt's advice, and, if she was honest, her sympathy and her protection.

A bout of depression settled in as she glanced around her bedroom. It had been difficult to match the navy-blue and rose print of her spread with drapes, but the indigo she'd found worked well. The small desk below her window held her laptop. She grabbed it and settled back in bed against her pillows.

"Now, let's see what the Internet has on you." Moments later, information on the Brendanis of Newport, Rhode Island, appeared. By the time she was ready to sleep, she'd discovered a lot about her family.

****

The warm kiss of morning teased her skin, and Alex raised her arms in a comfortable stretch. She'd made up her mind. The online information she discovered last night about her mother's family helped ease some of her trepidation. Her relatives seemed to be upstanding citizens, and the photos all bore a resemblance to her mom.

A little before ten a.m., Bree called to invite Alex out to a trendy restaurant for lunch. Alex was pleased and headed to the meeting with a sense of adventure and a lightness of heart she'd never thought to feel again. She was no longer alone.

They enjoyed a tasty meal of grilled shrimp and salad followed by cautious "getting to know you" small talk. They shied away from painful topics and centered on Alex's college days and what she might like to do in Newport. By the end of their discussion, Alex felt comfortable enough to bring her aunt back to her apartment.

At the front door, a quiver of unease surfaced, but she banished it. No matter what she'd been told, Alex believed Bree.

Once inside, she was certain her aunt would bring up the troublesome energy bursts again. To forestall the questions, she said, "I'm ready for a cup of tea. Would you like one?"

"Sounds good to me," Bree said and followed her into the cheery kitchen. Her aunt took a seat and glanced around. "Nice decor."

"Thank you."

Alex put the kettle on and grabbed two mugs. "I'd offer you coffee, but my Keurig died." Damn! She'd brought up the subject herself. Might as well give in and admit her aberration. "I've been having trouble with electrical appliances lately."

"Really?" Bree said, eyebrows raised. "Like what?"

"Crazy things. I fried a pencil sharpener, and then…" She lifted her shoulders and frowned. "I set fire to a copier."

Her aunt leaned her arms on the table. "How old are you?"

Alex turned off the burner on the stove and glared at Bree. "What has that got to do with anything?"

"Please. When will you be twenty-five?"

Alex snapped her mouth shut, biting her lip in the process. How did she know?

Bree tilted her head and sighed. "It's soon, isn't it? Your mother never told you about the transformation?"

Alex's nails dug into her palms at the implied insult to her mother. "What are you talking about?"

"I'm going to explain. Please let me finish before you interrupt. Okay?"

Though her back remained rigid, she said, "Fine."

"Our family is gifted with psychic powers." She held up her hand as Alex opened her mouth. "The bulk of these gifts come to us on our twenty-fifth birthday. Those of us in Newport have grown up knowing about our talent and learned to control any outbursts."

Alex's muscles tightened. She felt like she'd fallen into a foreign universe full of hidden snares.

"Please listen. I'm not insane. You've been experiencing small pulses of your power. You must have been terrified. Why don't you tell me about it?"

Frightening images of the last few days flitted through her head. Although she found it difficult to believe her problems were connected to her newfound heritage, she decided to see where this would lead.

"Nothing extraordinary. The pencil sharpener sparked before it went quiet. It was probably ready to die." She looked at Bree and continued. "The coffee maker. Again, it was old, and with the copy machine, I pushed too many buttons and the stupid thing caught on fire."

Bree nodded as she listened to the story.

Alex challenged her aunt. "If I had this so-called power, why would I destroy things?"

"How were you feeling at the time of each episode?"

Alex frowned. What did that have to do with anything. "You sound like a therapist."

Bree grinned. "Actually, I am, but please, indulge me."

She thought back. "I was furious with the sharpener. It kept breaking the pencil tip."

Just before she made her coffee, she'd opened the rent increase letter. "I guess I was ticked off and maybe frightened when I touched the Keurig." She paused, and heat crept up her neck. "When the copier wouldn't stop printing, I…wanted to kill it."

Bree nodded as if Alex's statements were the most normal thing in the world. "The surges occur when you're angry or upset. That makes sense. You're unconsciously calling for help. Did you have an upwelling of hot energy as you touched the machines?"

Stunned by her aunt's uncanny knowledge and easy acceptance of the situation, Alex spread her fingers out and examined them. "My hands. They heated up, and my fingers sort of buzzed, but it was much worse with the man at the cemetery. The heat in my chest expanded and moved down my arm." An image of him hitting the stone made her shudder.

"What man?" her aunt yelped.

Rats. She hadn't meant to say that. She scowled. "Nothing."

Bree grabbed Alex's hands. "What happened? That must have been the heavy shock that jolted me yesterday."

Goose bumps peppered Alex's skin. Could her aunt tune in to the insane things she was experiencing?

She sucked in a breath. "How…"

Bree interrupted her. "We've all experienced that. Tell me everything. I'm here for you. You're not alone anymore."

Relief washed through her, cleansing away the anxiety. She let go of the fear and peered at her aunt. "I think I killed him."

"Whatever happened was not your fault. Your

instinct for survival took over, and your gift protected you. It's okay. Tell me."

At the sound of Bree's soothing voice, Alex spat out the whole horrid episode. She didn't realize she was trembling until Bree came over and rubbed her back.

"You did the right thing, Alex. He was going to hurt you. It's time to come home now. To the safety of your family. He may not have been working alone."

Oh, God. She'd never thought of that. Her whole body began to shake.

****

That night, while Alex informed the landlord of her decision to vacate, Bree booked their flights for Thursday morning. Alex wanted to shriek, "Not enough time." Too much was happening, too fast. Only three days to discard the remnants of her existence in Phoenix. The memory of the hovering danger burned into her mind. She understood and accepted the necessity for speed. She intended to survive. Her insides churned as she planned her departure. Everything she couldn't take would go to the Salvation Army. So many memories tied up in those possessions.

With so much to do, she found herself too busy to grieve the loss of all that was familiar. The last night, though, with everything done, she walked through the empty apartment clutching her mother's urn and wept. She'd bring her mother with her, but she hadn't dared to visit Dad's grave in case someone recognized her. She hated leaving like a fugitive on the run.

Before she had a chance to rethink her decision, Thursday morning arrived, and she was sitting on a plane, spilling more of her life story to her new aunt.

Chapter Four

During the ride from Rhode Island's Green Airport, Bree acted as a tour guide. Alex saw signs for places like Warwick, East Greenwich, and North Kingstown, before they sailed over two high bridges. Even in the fading light, Alex realized the water far below was different than the winding rivers and lakes in Arizona, but she was too tired to appreciate Narragansett Bay.

When they reached her family's home, the strain of the long day threatened to engulf her. To fight the fatigue, she stepped out of the car, stretched, closed her eyes, and took a deep breath. She was surprised and pleased at the cool, salty breeze that greeted her. Turning to the house, her gaze traveled up the weathered shingles to its third-floor dormers.

With each new revelation about her mother, a bitter knot grew in her chest. This house, sisters, and magic? *Who were you, Mom?*

The ornate door swung open, and a small blonde woman rushed over and clutched Alex in a big hug. "I'm so glad you're home," the woman said. "Bree was right. You look just like CeCe. You must be tired and hungry."

Alex instinctively went stiff. Relatives or not, she didn't know these people.

Bree's sharp voice cut in. "Franki. For crying out loud, will you let her get into the house?"

Suitcases in tow, they entered a large hallway with

wainscoting topped by creamy walls and colorful artwork.

"I figured you missed dinner, so I made some stew," Franki said.

She led them to the kitchen at the end of the hall where the delicious beefy scent and tantalizing aroma of baked bread made Alex's stomach grumble. Place settings covered the big, round oak table situated next to the windows. A golden roll peeked out of a covered basket. Dinner simmered on the stove across the room, and Alex noticed a tin of muffins on the island in the middle.

Mouth-watering smells, a safe space, soft lighting, and warm colors ticked all of Alex's *family* buttons. For just a minute, as she listened to her aunts chattering, she pretended her mother was there.

Franki kept up a cheery discourse throughout the meal. Alex merely nodded as she tucked into the food. Chunks of beef, potatoes, and vegetables. It had been a long time since she'd had this kind of cooking. The awareness of her loss dimmed her pleasure. She passed on dessert. With a full stomach, her body craved sleep. Her eyelids kept closing.

"You're exhausted, honey. I'll take you up to your room," Franki said. She pointed to the muffins. "I made those for tomorrow morning. Come down whenever and help yourself. No need for formality here."

Although Bree had promised to assuage Alex's curiosity about their *psychic* family, Alex was too tired to pursue that tonight. The sudden introduction to a new heritage and social status threatened to overwhelm her. Tomorrow was time enough. She said good night to Bree and followed Franki up a beautifully carved staircase.

Her aunt stopped at a door and said, "We thought you'd like to be in your mother's old room."

She sucked in her breath and choked. "What?"

"I'm sorry," Franki said as she patted her back. "Is it too much?"

Alex composed herself, sniffed, and tossed her head in denial. "No. Not at all. I love that I'll be in her room. It's just that—I said goodbye to all the familiar things—everything that reminded me of Mom. I-I didn't expect to find her here."

"We're right down the hall if you want us. The bath is through that door beyond the bed. I think you'll find everything you need." Then she enfolded Alex in her arms. "We're here for you."

Alex relaxed and patted her aunt's back. She'd have to get used to Franki's hugs. They were a part of her loving nature. "Thank you, Aunt Franki."

"Aunty is fine." She tilted her head and smiled. "We're not formal around here."

Alex wanted to laugh. Proper she could take, but the psychic, magical stuff? The thought made her crazy.

****

She leaned against the closed door and surveyed the proof of her mother's hidden life. With a sense of betrayal, she took it all in. *Mom's room.* Cecile Brendani—not an only child but one of three sisters and a brother. The woman she'd known her whole life was a lie.

She absorbed the imposing layout. A queen-size bed, a fireplace, and the seating arrangement—a small sofa and chair—by the window. As she walked around, running her fingers along the backs of the light leather furniture, her chest tightened with anger for her mother's enormous deceit. The one person she'd trusted without question. The urge to run churned in her gut. Any avenue to escape the pain. Then she noticed a picture on the mantel. Three young girls. She wandered over and picked it up.

A sense of longing eased her annoyance as she recognized her mother. She ran her fingers over the smooth surface, and a sigh escaped. Here was proof. Tears threatened, and she collapsed onto the sofa.

The photo was a formal portrait of the three Brendani sisters posed on a bench. Her mother must have been ten or eleven at the time it was done. Alex's mood lightened as she recognized each of the girls. Even at that age, the sisters possessed the traits that carried into their adult life.

Bree, the oldest, sat up straight, hands in her lap, looking pleased. Franki, blonde hair curling around her face, had a dreamy look in her eyes. Alex's mother's hands rested on her knees, and a mischievous smirk played on her face. She could almost read her mother's mind—she'd sit for the picture, but the minute the photographer said, "Good," she'd be gone.

Although she didn't understand why her mother had kept this life secret, Alex had to believe she had a good reason. With that thought, her irritation, like water sliding over oil, disappeared. Whoever Mom had been before didn't matter. She'd shown Alex nothing but love.

Instead of resorting to judgment, Alex decided to go with trust. She replaced the photograph and speculated about a young Cecile. What had she been like?

A smile slipped out. She'd never seen pictures of her mother as a young girl. In her mind, she imagined her, full of fun, jumping and tumbling all over the bed. Had she been messy, tossing her toys and clothes everywhere?

Intrigued now, she scouted the room, eager for anything else that might reveal an insight into her mother's life.

A closet the size of her old bathroom held extra blankets and pillows. She inhaled, hoping to find her mother's spicy scent, but was disappointed as the aroma of lavender touched her nose. About to close the door, she caught sight of an object way up on a shelf in the corner. She lifted herself up onto her tippy toes and reached for it. Her fingers connected with something soft, and she tugged. A brown, cuddly teddy bear fell off, tumbling onto her head. It must have been her mother's. Black eyes stared at her, quizzically she thought, and a faded red bow encircled his neck.

"Well, hello there, fella. Thanks for dropping in." He reminded her of her old teddy bear who she'd named Sashi. A chuckle slipped out as she remembered why. When her mother would kiss her good night, she'd intone a Navajo blessing, "*Wankan tanka kici un*, May the Great Spirit Bless you." Then she'd add, "And you, too, *shash yázhí*," using the Navajo words for little bear. Alex, unable to pronounce it, called her teddy, Sashi.

She felt years slip away as she cuddled the soft stuffed animal and placed him on the bed. "You can sleep with me, tonight." Then she opened her suitcase to pull out an oversized tee shirt.

The bathroom was roomy and well-equipped with a separate shower, a long, marble vanity, and an enclosed toilet. As she brushed her teeth, she stared into the mirror. Her thoughts became fuzzy. She shook her head, then closed her eyes and leaned on the counter. When she opened them again, she saw a hazy face in the glass. It might have been herself as a teenager with a ponytail, but as the details came into focus, they were wrong. The green eyes seemed right, but the hair wasn't as dark as hers, and the mouth was too wide. She gasped. Not her smile, but one she recognized as belonging to a young Cecile Brendani.

Before she could react, a dizzying wave engulfed her. She leaned over, praying she wouldn't pass out. When the vertigo receded, she peeked at the reflection once more. The phantom face was gone. She leaned her head against the mirror. Emotion overload. She needed rest.

Her former upbeat mood quashed, she busied herself putting away her clothes.

With a heavy heart, she placed her mother's urn on the bedside table and cuddled the teddy bear. "Was that you at the cemetery, Mom? Have you been trying to contact me? I'm in your old bedroom. Please, speak to me."

In desperation, her voice rose. "Mom? Where are you? Give me a sign that you can hear me." She tried to concentrate, but the room remained silent.

After a while, she yawned and lay down, but sleep refused to come. Too many questions and worries. The open window across the room called to her. Curtains billowed out like ghostly dancers, and she slid the silky material back.

Light from the almost full moon filtered through the clouds and sent changing shadows across the land that fired up her imagination. She focused on the familiar spirals on the ground.

The discovery lightened her mood as she recalled

the day her mother told her they were going to walk a labyrinth. Seven-year-old Alex had hopped up and down, clapping her hands in expectation of a maze like she'd seen on TV where tall hedges and countless dead ends dared you to escape. The real thing proved a huge disappointment. Her mother brought her to a part of the desert to show her small rocks laid out in boring circles. No traps. No place to hide. It looked like a drawing, but instead of crayons, someone had fashioned the picture with stones. She'd been so disenchanted.

Years later, she'd understood that in ancient times, labyrinths were considered sacred. Today, labyrinths served as a form of meditation and self-enlightenment. A sudden urge to walk the hallowed circle stirred her, but it was too late to go out now.

Off in the distance, the blue-gray sky accentuated the darker landscape below. A light breeze played around the bushes along the grass, and, to the left, almost black against the night, branches swayed along the tree line.

She leaned against the window sash to enjoy the pungent scents of flowers and salty air. Her comfort vanished, however, when one of the shadows moved. The motion had nothing to do with the wind. Someone was out there. She checked the clock on the mantel. Almost midnight. Who would be out that late?

A stray breeze swept in the window and seemed to wrap itself around her, an almost purposeful touch. Goose bumps rose on her arms. Uneasy, she backed away and tried to settle the swelling disquiet inside her.

Chapter Five

Before she opened her eyes the next morning, the scent of lavender alerted her to her altered circumstances. This was her mother's room, and Alex now lived with the family her parents had denied. Had her father known about them? The soft satiny sheets crumpled in her fists as she called out, "Why?"

A lie, all of it. She closed her eyes. There must have been a good reason.

As her sense of faithlessness abated, she sighed and placed her hand on the smooth, cool surface of the metal urn next to her bed, all she had left of her mom. "I don't understand."

The trill of birdsong and the faraway kiss of waves against the shore caught her attention. The answers she sought weren't here. Time to confront the day. People to meet. Questions to ask.

The warm air ruffling the curtains decided her wardrobe choice: navy shorts and a flowery cotton top. Familiar rituals helped center her: applying dusky rose lipstick and pulling a brush through her hair. Handmade Navajo earrings completed her outfit.

As she gazed out the window, a sudden memory intruded. A figure lurking there. Fingers of ice caressed her neck. With an effort, she slowed her breathing. It must have been someone in the family. She'd ask her aunts.

****

The welcome smell of coffee pulled her toward the kitchen. In the light of day, the Brendani home was impressive. Last night, she'd used the word, mansion, drawing a short laugh from Bree. "No honey, not quite. I'll take you for a ride down Bellevue Avenue to feast your eyes on *summer cottages* that far outshine this place."

No matter what her aunt said, this house was extraordinary. Her parents' three-bedroom apartment in Arizona had been tiny in comparison.

Today, Alex poked her head into a few of the huge rooms and marveled: crown molding, ceiling-high bookcases, windows that would take days to clean, and vibrant Persian rugs.

She peeked over her shoulder like an intruder afraid of being caught before she headed to the kitchen where she found the black gold she'd been smelling. The first sip slid down her throat and warmed both her insides and her mood. She savored the strong brew and gravitated toward the French doors that overlooked the backyard. *Hmm, more like a private park.*

Her steps guided her outside where she soaked up the atmosphere. Bree had said the property stretched down to the Sakonnet River, and this was a perfect day for a walk.

After a final sip of her coffee, she placed the cup on a table and followed the heady floral scents to the garden. She'd only taken a few steps along the well-worn trail, when it occurred to her that her mother must have walked here. Alex's hand touched the ever-present pain in her chest before she whispered into the breeze, "I'm following in your footsteps. Can you see me?"

Side trails led to flowers whose names she didn't know. Every few seconds, she'd lean in to touch or smell. Her spirits soared. Too soon, the colorful denizens gave way to the labyrinth's circuitous path, but she wasn't disappointed. Enchantment reached out to her. When her mother had introduced Alex to the maze-like spirals, she'd breathed into her ear, "Labyrinths are magical places."

No wonder her mother loved them—she grew up with one. As she drifted along the path, Alex had an immediate sense of her mom, right down to her spicy perfume. She closed her eyes, pictured her face, and slowed her steps to imagine walking with her. The sun warmed her back as she stooped to examine the rounded beach stones outlining the route. With heightened awareness, she became sensitive to the sharp cries of the gulls overhead, the clicking of nearby insects, and the slight tang of salt in the air. She no longer felt alone.

An ever-decreasing circle led her to the center where a plain stone bench dominated the space. She noticed names chiseled down its sides, some sort of memorial. A closer look revealed two names: Gabriella and Katrina Brendani. The gentle breeze teased the dark waves around her shoulders, and she lifted her face to catch its cool breath. Her mother was right. Labyrinths were mystical. As her tension slid away for the first time in weeks, a sense of peace settled over her.

Beautiful, isn't it?

Alex jumped. Had she heard that or imagined it? She spun around the center space, but there was no one in sight.

I'm sorry. Did I startle you?

"What?" Alex asked as she twisted around. "Where

are you? I can't see you."

Oh dear. I'm your grandmother. Everyone visits me here. Didn't they tell you?

Alex's muscles tightened. She wondered how fast she could make it back to the house.

Don't be afraid. I won't hurt you.

A stinging cold swarmed around her shoulders and arms like an army of angry ants. She'd always believed in spirits but never communicated with any. This whole spectral voice idea made her doubt her sanity. First her mother—now her grandmother? Overwhelmed by a bizarre and frightening week, she dropped down onto the bench. Her trepidation fought with curiosity, however, and her sense of humor poked in. What do you say to a ghost?

"I-I guess I'm pleased to meet you?"

A little light laugh that might have been the rustle of leaves swirled around her.

You are such a novice, my dear. Never mind. My daughters will take care of that. Your mother is worried about you. She's not very strong yet, but now that she doesn't have to watch over you in Arizona, she's opened herself to the ether, and I have her back.

"My mother? Is my mother here? Can I speak to her?"

I'm sorry, my dear, that's not possible. She needs to rest.

"Please. I'm talking to you, aren't I?"

Yes darling, but that's because my ashes are buried right under your feet.

Alex leaped off the bench so fast she almost fell. Another unworldly chuckle swirled around her.

Don't be alarmed, dear. You can't hurt me.

An unsettling concern that she'd lost her mind prompted her to take a step toward the path.

Are you leaving?

"I-I do need to get back."

I've so enjoyed meeting you. You're very much like your mother. Come back often to visit me.

With no idea where to direct her response, Alex settled on the ground. It seemed as good a spot as any. She strained to sound casual but failed. "Goodbye, Grandmother. I'm glad to meet you."

Call me Kitty, dear. Everyone does.

Oh boy, she thought, *Kitty?* She retraced her steps along the gravel path as the incredible truths attached to her mother's family circled around her like a never-ending maze. She was so engrossed in worry about her sanity, she nearly missed a turn. That stopped her. She didn't want to step across any stones. She'd laughed when her mother told her about the bad-luck gremlins. They allowed humans to walk along their paths but became angry if any strayed across the stone barriers. After chatting with the ghost of her grandmother, her idea of reality shifted, and she wasn't taking any chances. She made sure to watch her step.

On her way back to the house, Alex saw someone on the back porch and squinted. A young woman with long, honey-colored hair. Bree had mentioned a cousin, Lia. It must be her. A quick stab of nerves slowed her steps. Meeting new people meant trying to fit in, an art she'd never quite mastered. Since her mother died, she'd avoided getting close to anyone.

The golden eyes of the yellow tabby on Lia's lap regarded her as she approached.

"Good morning, Alex. Welcome to the family. I'm

Lia." Her voice took on a cooing sound. "And this is Annie."

"Hi, Lia, and hello to you, Annie." Alex gave the purring cat a little scratch on the back of her head.

Curiosity burned in Lia's eyes. "How did you like our labyrinth?"

"It's beautiful. You're so lucky to have it in your yard."

"I'm glad you can appreciate it." Lia paused and gave her a considering glance. "Did you notice anything unusual?"

Alex had planned to keep the details of her visit with Kitty a secret but changed her mind. "I was surprised to find our grandmother buried there."

The color in Lia's green eyes deepened as she leaned forward. "So, you met her? Your powers must be coming back."

Heat crept up Alex's cheeks, and she looked away. Everyone else knew all about her, but she still didn't understand.

Lia softened her voice. "It's okay. We all talk to her. The labyrinth tends to magnify our gifts." Lia patted the seat next to her. "Come on. Sit here with Annie and me for a while. I'll give you the lowdown on the family."

Alex hesitated, wanting to flee to her room and process all she'd learned. "I should get back and finish unpacking." A small fib.

Lia gave her an inviting smile. "I promise I won't bite."

Alex had been a little off balance since she'd left home. Now, instead of giving in to her apprehension, she decided to take Lia at her word. "Okay." She sat down. "I have a question."

"Shoot."

"How many people live here?"

"Alive or dead?"

"What?" Lia's answer struck like a punch.

"Well, there's Kitty in the labyrinth." She stopped and looked over at Alex. "Wait. Do you want to count all the ghosts?"

"No!"

Lia blinked at the force of Alex's near shout. "Fine. You've met Aunt Bree and my mother."

"Yes."

"My father, James Ferguson, and Cousin Tony, he's a Brendani, also live here. You'll meet them tonight."

Alex wondered how all these people could live together in the same house. She nodded as she tried to count. "So, there are six of us." She gave a tentative smile. "Not including the ghosts."

Lia nodded and looked down at her wrist. "Whoa, I've got to get ready for work. We can finish this conversation later." She transferred Annie to Alex's lap and disappeared inside.

Alex scratched the cat's soft fur and grimaced. "How many ghosts?"

Annie looked up at her and purred.

With the cat in her lap, the soothing rhythm of the rocker, and the quiet vista, her angst diminished. She closed her eyes and let her thoughts drift. The why of her mother's actions bothered her. She intended to get answers, but unless problems arose with the family, she'd act as if she belonged. With that idea in mind, she decided to poke around downstairs. The cat gave her an imperious glare and twitched her tail when Alex put her down and went inside.

Chapter Six

A while later, Bree found her in the den, immersed in a book. "Getting hungry?"

She stretched her neck and checked the grandfather clock. "Is it lunchtime already?"

Bree grinned. "It is. Come into the kitchen."

This was the first time in days she'd been able to relax. Thanks to the world of fantasy, she'd forgotten her problems for a couple of hours.

Before joining her aunts, she used the lavatory. While she rubbed the lavender-scented soap into her hands, she remembered the person in the shadows the night before. Although she was certain the figure was a family member, she wanted to mention it to her aunts. After the morning's events, she wasn't surprised it had slipped her mind. It was difficult enough trying to get a handle on a group of strangers in a different time zone without having a morning chat with a ghost. She shook her head as she dried her hands and wondered how much more there was to learn.

Franki smiled at her. "How are you doing, honey? Getting yourself acclimated?"

Alex appreciated the time they'd given her to sort out her tangled emotions. "Yes. Thank you."

As they ate, Bree asked about Alex's morning, and Alex told them about her trip to the labyrinth and her introduction to her grandmother.

"A bit of a shock?" Bree asked.

Alex's hand flew to her chest. "She scared me to death."

Franki rolled her eyes and tugged at the gold loop in her ear. "Mother tends to have that effect on people. I hope you were careful to stay on the path."

"Oh, yes. Mom explained about labyrinths. I was surprised to see it from my window last night." Alex's smile dimmed. "That reminds me. I may be paranoid after what happened at the cemetery, but I thought I saw someone out there." She lifted her hands in the air. "It was kind of late, so I wondered."

Bree popped a raspberry in her mouth and sat up. "How late?"

"After midnight."

Franki's hand brushed the air, making her bracelets sing. "Lia's a night owl. She spends a lot of time outside."

"I'm sure that's it," Bree said. "Enjoy your afternoon. Tonight, you'll meet the rest of the family."

"Wait a minute. You promised to answer questions about our powers. Now would be a great time."

After a deep breath, Bree said, "You're right. We might as well start. I wish your mother had better prepared you for this."

Even though she felt cheated by her mother's choices, she didn't appreciate Bree's attitude. "My mother took very good care of me. She taught me to read auras so I could protect myself."

Franki's soft voice broke in. "Your mother never envisioned her illness." Speaking more to herself than to Alex she said, "I know how hard it must have been for CeCe after Danny died. If only she'd called us then."

Surprised, Alex said, "You knew my father?"

"Of course," Bree said. "He dated your mother for over a year, although CeCe kept it secret for months. We all liked Danny." A momentary frown crossed her face as she finished. "Though we all understood we should stay with our own kind, you can't choose who you love."

"In ten days, you'll come into your full powers," Bree said. "You're right about answers. It's time we began."

****

Afternoon sun warmed the muted colors of Bree's office. Alex gravitated to a blue-cushioned window seat. The view took in a trellised garden that Alex hadn't seen before. "Those roses are beautiful," she said with a sigh. "Mom loved them."

"I know. If you go out there, you'll find the garden is dedicated to CeCe. We were heartbroken when she left."

The love in Bree's words made her smile. Curious about her aunt, she examined the office. A sand-colored sofa and chair flanked the stone fireplace, and Bree's desk sat in the corner. Rather austere, like its owner, it held a few books supported by brass bookends, a crystal paperweight, and a large desk calendar.

Alex tilted her head to study two watercolor paintings that adorned the walls, one a raging sea, the other a riot of flowers. She walked over to get a closer look.

"Those were painted by your Aunt Franki. She's quite well-known in Newport art circles."

"They're stunning." She found the explosion of crashing waves exciting. The Internet articles had mentioned Franki was an artist, but Alex hadn't realized the scope of her aunt's talent.

The wall behind Bree's desk held certificates and degrees in the name of Gabrielle Marie Brendani. Her aunt had said she was a therapist. Alex grinned. Abnormal Psychology seemed like a perfect choice for someone in a strange, psychic family.

Bree, who'd remained silent while Alex wandered around, spoke. "I like that you inspect your surroundings. That's good. Never take anything at face value. Always question." She sat in the chair while Alex settled on the sofa. "You've made excellent progress in your transition here. I'm sure you'll do as well accepting your destiny."

Every time Alex got comfortable, her aunt threw out some dire pronouncement. She looked at her empty coffee cup wishing for some liquid for her parched throat.

"Before we begin, would you do something for me?"

"Sure."

"I want you to use your mind to move the statue on that table." She held up her hand. "Wait a minute." She snatched up her phone and a tablet from the nearby desk. "I can't have you frying my electronics."

Guilt bubbled up as she remembered the copier fire, then a spurt of outrage. She hadn't done those things on purpose.

"Remember your fear and anger from the attack. Now, pull in those emotions, and concentrate on pushing the figurine like you did that man."

Alex didn't want to relive it, but Bree's insistence brought it all back.

"Please try. It's very important."

Biting her lip, she gave an uncertain glance at Bree and then at the statue. She flexed her fingers, inhaled, and closed her eyes to focus on her former helplessness and rage. When the terrible feelings bubbled up, a tingling sensation vibrated through her arm, she shoved out her hand. "Move!"

For a second nothing happened, and then the small sculpture gave a tipsy wobble.

Bree let out a sigh. "I was afraid of that. The magic at the cemetery wasn't you. Somehow CeCe tapped into your powers."

Alex opened her mouth and stared at her aunt. "My mother helped me?"

"I believe so," Bree said. "Clearly, you don't have this gift yet."

Alex shook her head and stared at her hands. First a vicious attack and then saved by what—her mother's spirit using Alex's body? Last year, her biggest worry had centered on securing a job at the library.

"What did you feel? Anything like your previous experiences?"

"No. Nothing like before. Just a little buzz in my fingers."

"I'm sure you're unconsciously calling to your power for help. The fear and the proximity to your birthday are overcoming any constraints CeCe applied."

"Constraints? I don't understand."

"She bound your gifts, so they couldn't sneak out. We'll deal with that when we can. Right now, why don't I give you some history before you meet everyone tonight?"

"Are you deliberately keeping information from me?"

"No. We're waiting for the answers from your mother. Kitty will let us know right away."

Alex shook her head. Her aunt spoke as if ghostly communication was normal. With a curl to her lip, she said, "Of course," and then settled into a comfortable position. "I can't wait to hear the family story."

Bree raised an eyebrow. "I realize this is all new to you, but try to suspend your disbelief. The story goes back to the 1400s when our ancestors came to America from Scotland."

"I thought we were Italian."

"We are. We can discuss that later."

Alex shifted in her seat. So much mystery.

"They traveled down the coast from Nova Scotia and ended up in Newport. Of course, the city of Newport didn't exist then." Bree paused for a moment. "What do you know about the Knights Templar?"

Alex searched her mind. "Weren't they, like, Crusaders?"

A pleased smile lightened Bree's face. "Very good. The Templars, our forebears, played a huge part in the crusades."

"They're my ancestors?"

Bree nodded and settled back in her chair to continue. "Circumstances conspired against them, and they were forced to relinquish their true identities and travel in secret. There's a lot more to the story, but that will suffice for now. We can thank the Templars for our gifts."

Bree paused. "Most of our powers lie dormant until our twenty-fifth birthday. Until that time, we develop and strengthen the precursors to our gift with guidance from family members. Young children can often use short energy bursts and sometimes levitate small objects. These differ in relation to a person's latent gifts. The teenage years with all the hormones and experimentation sometimes pose a problem. But, by that time, most of us have learned not to expose our secret."

Bree's long sigh made Alex wonder about the ones who didn't learn. As her aunt continued, she interrupted her.

"You're saying my mother did something to me so that wouldn't happen?"

"For your own protection. Parents use a temporary spell while young children are in school, so no one will suspect the truth. I'm guessing CeCe somehow strengthened the incantation." Bree shook her head. "Her gifts must have been strong. Each person's powers are unique. That's why we can't predict what yours will be." She leaned forward a bit. "I understand this is difficult for you, and you really don't know any of us, but try to accept that we care for you. You're family."

"What about the Templars? What kind of powers did they have? Why doesn't history record anything about them?"

"Only a few, nine to be exact, received the gifts. I'll tell you about that later."

"I thought they took vows of celibacy."

"They did, but after they discovered the secrets of Solomon and received their special gifts, they needed to pass them on. The few who inherited the powers vowed to use them to protect the innocents."

"Who?"

Bree stood up. "Why don't we pick up this conversation tomorrow? Time to get ready for tonight's dinner."

Alex had more questions but agreed to wait.

"I forgot," Bree said. "We usually dress for special family dinners. If you don't have anything with you, Lia will lend you something. You're about the same size."

With those words, Alex's ego took a hit. Her wardrobe couldn't compete with that of her rich relatives, and she'd never fit into Lia's things. She didn't have the curves.

****

The meet and greet was scheduled for six p.m. Fluttery sensations tortured her. What kind of family insists on *dressing* for dinner?

While she showered, she searched her memory for anything unusual about her mother or their life in Arizona. Her parents had been ordinary. No witchy magic. The only difference had been after her father's death when her mom fell into a period of depression and withdrawal. She'd paid little attention to Alex who, with her own heartache, needed her mother even more.

Questions churned. If Mom had powers, how could she give them up? It would be so much fun to have some cool tricks other than frying electrical equipment. Despite her aunt's assurance her gifts would materialize, she had serious doubts. She massaged her temples. Yeesh! Nothing made sense.

Lia arrived with an armful of dresses. "I thought you might like to choose, and I figured, by now, you'd need a friendly face." Lia looked gorgeous in a short, emerald frock that matched her eyes.

"Do I ever. I feel like I've walked into an alternate dimension."

"I can only imagine. Accept that you're special and embrace it. It's an incredible gift."

How could Lia understand what she was going through? She'd had these talents her whole life. "I tried to move a statue earlier." She frowned. "It wobbled."

Lia chuckled. "Don't be discouraged. Most people can't do that."

"Thank you for letting me borrow an outfit." She settled on a full-skirted, sleeveless dress with splashes of sapphire. "Is everybody in the family psychic?"

"Hmm. Well, everyone but my father."

"Doesn't he mind being the odd man out, the only one without powers?"

"No. He's very comfortable with who he is and, for the most part, ignores the antics of his strange family."

Chapter Seven

Alex paused for a deep breath before entering the living room. A quick observation showed only a few people, including two she'd already met. She exhaled. Not too bad.

Bree reclined in a chair. An older gentleman stood near Franki, and a young man leaned against a bookcase. Alex walked in, head held high, and suppressed a powerful urge to flee. She could handle this. The fact they all lived under the same roof amazed her. Then a bizarre thought brought a smile to her lips. *I wonder if they have any relatives locked away in the attic.*

Her aunts looked beautiful tonight. At forty-six, her mother was the youngest, and Bree, the oldest, at fifty. Alex had also learned that Lia, with all her sophistication, was only two years older than her.

A wispy blue dress accentuated Franki's blonde curls. Beside her husband James' tall, lean frame, she looked like a child. James' pale blue eyes crinkled as he patted his daughter Lia's face and placed a quick kiss on Alex's cheek. "Welcome home, Alex."

Aunt Bree also seemed much younger in a chic green number that showed off great legs.

Lia introduced Alex to their cousin, Tony, whose dark good looks harked back to his Italian heritage. Everyone Alex had met in the family so far had either excellent genes or a skilled plastic surgeon.

"The famous Alex," Tony said. With a formal bow, he took her hand and kissed it. "Nice to meet you, Cuz."

She grinned. "Why thank you, kind sir." She might enjoy herself tonight after all.

Then Lia spoke up. "Alex visited the labyrinth today." She continued in a triumphant voice. "She saw Kitty."

Horrified, Alex jumped in. "No." Her sharp retort drew the attention of the room. People sat, frozen in place, some with glasses in mid-air, as they waited.

Lia frowned. "You said you did."

Alex shook her head as she faced the startled group. "I didn't *see* anything." She squirmed. "I only heard her."

Franki's voice floated across the room. "All that will change after your birthday a little over a week away." To no one in particular, she said, "What day does the fourth fall on?"

"Your birthday's on the fourth of July?" Tony said. "How cool is that? Fireworks for the big day. We should have a party."

Lia seconded the idea, and the aunts began to plan a huge event. When a commotion heralded the arrival of more people, Alex shuddered.

"Sal," Bree said. "This is CeCe's daughter Alex." To Alex she said, "My brother Sal and his wife Pamela."

Over six feet tall with dark, thinning hair, Uncle Sal exuded an air of authority that made Alex nervous until he smiled. His eyes shone with kindness. "Welcome to the family."

As she experienced the warmth and acceptance in the room, the ball of tension in her chest dissolved. Her newest uncle surprised her with a big hug before holding her at arm's length. "I can see the Toselli genes. CeCe took after Mother, and you resemble her. The eyes are darker, and you have more freckles, but the face is hers."

His words called up images of her mother, who should be here with her tonight, and Alex blinked to discourage any tears.

When the conversation drifted toward the weekend plans, Lia chimed in. "Tony and I can take Alex to Newport tonight, and maybe dinner tomorrow night. What do you think?" she asked Tony.

"Sure," he said. "Count me in for tonight, but I've got plans for Saturday."

A trip to Newport sounded great to Alex, but not tonight. Too many changes in a short time. A week ago, she'd had a job, an apartment, and a normal, if lonely, life. Then she'd come into some kind of power, been attacked, and discovered new relatives. Most of yesterday had been spent on a plane. She needed rest.

A refusal was on her lips, but Uncle Sal spoke up. "Disturbing information came to my attention today. A couple of tourists near Touro Park claim to have observed lights at the Stone Mill in the wee hours of the morning. I'm sure it must be kids but, still, disconcerting. Let's keep our ears open."

No one else said anything, and they moved to the dining room. She glanced around the table in awe. She'd always envied her classmates with their large families. Now she had aunts, uncles, and cousins. Oh yes, and Kitty, her grandmother, who happened to be a ghost.

After dessert, she tried to plead exhaustion and opt out of the trip to Newport, but Tony refused to accept her excuse. Hand over his heart, he said, "It's my sworn duty to make sure you're properly introduced to the Newport scene."

****

Less than an hour later, Tony dropped Alex and Lia off at a wharf leading to Newport Harbor. "Do a little sightseeing while I park the car."

On this warm Friday night, downtown Newport was jumping. Lia and Alex ambled along one of the entrance lanes to the water. Dozens of shops bunched together flaunting extravagant window displays with everything from fudge to lingerie. The enticing scent of freshly baked cookies flavored the air. Nearer the harbor, shops gave way to restaurants. A never-ending stream of people swarmed around them. Lia grabbed Alex's arm to keep her moving.

At the end of the wharf, expensive yachts preened. Beyond it all, the dark water reigned. Intermittent lights from phantom crafts weaving through stationary boats gave the scene a mystical aura.

Lia tapped her on the shoulder. "Tony said he'll meet us out front."

Fascinated with her surroundings, Alex paused for a last peek around.

"We'll come back another time. I promise."

Tony waited on the sidewalk to lead them to his favorite night spot, the Scottish Pub.

For months after her mom died, Alex's grief kept her isolated, away from her friends. She'd spent most of her time, other than work, in bed, but tonight she vowed to keep up with her cousins. She hid a small yawn as she followed them into the welcome cool of the busy club. Tony yelled in her ear over the raucous din. "What do you want to drink?"

"A ginger ale would be great."

He frowned. "Come on, Cuz, this is a party."

"That's all I want." This first night out was like an experiment. A chance to learn about her cousins and their lifestyle. Add alcohol, and her observations would be off. More importantly, she needed to be on guard. She didn't want another electrical display.

The look in Tony's eyes told her it would be a long night. He headed off to get their drinks. The place was jumping. No available tables, so they followed Tony to the other end of the room and found standing room at the bar. Tight but doable.

Bright tartans, bagpipes, and instruments called Scottish Smallpipes covered the walls on either side of the gleaming mahogany bar. Her ears vibrated to the beat of the music blasting from overhead speakers.

An intriguing mix of people in outfits that ranged from cutoffs to fancy dress surrounded them unlike nightspots back home, where most preferred boots, jeans, and cowboy hats.

When Tony handed her a drink, she took a sip and coughed. Oh yeah. He got her what she wanted, all right, loaded with vodka. As she pushed it away, Tony put his hand on her shoulder. "I'd like you to meet someone."

Alex looked up to see the bartender.

"This is my friend, Nick. Nick, meet Alex, my brand-new cousin, fresh from the wilds of Arizona."

Damn. These people knew how to pick their bartenders. The guy had the requisite biceps and deep-blue eyes to go with his wavy dark hair. This Newport scene might be worth getting into.

Nick shook her hand and winked. "Let me fix that drink. Minus the vodka?" She nodded. "Thanks."

He flashed her a killer grin. "Any time."

Sensing a promise in his smile, Alex geared up for a

little flirting. Before she could implement her plan, however, he'd moved on to other customers. His sudden departure disappointed her. She liked the twinkle of laughter in his eyes. As Alex sipped her ginger ale, Lia headed to the dance floor with a good-looking guy. A few minutes later, her persuasive cousin Tony coaxed her out after them.

While they danced, she laughed over funny stories of failed conquests, although she found it difficult to believe Tony had any trouble with women.

He'd found them a table, and as the night wore on, he and Lia's friend took turns buying rounds. The guys showed the effects, but Lia seemed fine. Curious, Alex said, "Doesn't alcohol bother you?"

Lia's eyes lit up as she leaned in. "Nick takes care of the designated drivers."

Alex stopped peeking at the time when the man, himself, appeared at the table and smiled at her. "My shift is over. Care to dance?"

The song was a slow one, and when Nick held her close, she sighed and inhaled his spicy scent. The warmth from his breath on her ear sent a thrill along her nerve endings, and the movement of his thumb against her spine drove her crazy. She leaned into him and wondered about girlfriends. His whispered words cut a hole in her budding fantasy. "Make sure Tony doesn't drive home."

"What?" This was about Tony?

"He's had too much to drink."

"Well, Lia could . . ."

Nick gave a sharp headshake. "She'll take care of the other one. You'll have to drive Tony."

The dance ended, and Alex fumed as they walked

back to the table. Heat flooded her face. He must think her a fool for flirting with him. What the hell? He could have told her at the start why he asked her to dance instead of pretending to be interested.

Out of the corner of her eye, she saw him nod to the server who brought over the drinks. He placed a hand on Tony's shoulder. "Sorry to do this, my friend, but I have to cut you off."

Tony's smile evaporated. His nose flared as he squinted and shrugged off Nick's hand. "What the fuck?" Tony tasted the drink and spit it out. "Soda!"

When Tony pounded his fist on the table, Alex flinched, but Lia's face showed no surprise. A moment later, though, when her cousin swept his hand in the direction of an empty chair, and it crashed into the wall, Lia grabbed his arm. "Enough."

Alex's heart thundered in her chest. She recoiled from Tony's anger as heat welled up inside her. A tingle in her fingers grew into a strong buzz. By the time she recognized the sensation, it was too late. A light on the wall exploded with a loud pop.

Tony snapped his gaze toward it. "I didn't do that." He wrenched his arm away from Lia, spit out a few more angry epithets, and surged out of his seat.

Alex peered around. People were staring. Lia's face looked thunderous as she stood up. "Come on. We're leaving."

If Lia was furious with Tony for using his powers in public, what would she say about the broken bulb?

Outside, though, Lia mentioned nothing about magic. She convinced Tony to let Alex drive. Although he agreed, Alex wasn't thrilled. The idea of being alone with Tony in the car made her cringe. His whole countenance had changed from jovial host to snarling malcontent. She whispered to Lia. "I don't even know where I'm going, and Tony's pissed. What if he uses magic in the car?"

"Everything's fine now. He won't cause any more trouble."

Alex swallowed and traipsed after Tony. Her hand shook as she started the car. A sidelong glance at her cousin revealed a deep scowl. Although he never said a word, she could feel the force of his rage swirling around them. A troubling thought occurred to her. This car was filled with electronic gear, and if her emotions exploded like they had at the bar, they'd be in trouble.

She pulled her hands away from the wheel. Time to deal with her angry cousin. Straightening her shoulders, she turned to glare at Tony. "Hey, *Cuz*. Keep your annoyance to yourself. You're making me nervous, and when I get upset, things happen. If you don't want me to fry this car like I did the light in the bar, cool it."

His eyes widened, and he grinned. "That was you? Not bad. Why did you do it?"

"No idea. I can't control it. Only happens when I'm anxious or scared."

"Bummer." He chuckled. "Don't worry about me. I'm fine. I'd never hurt anybody."

Tony's return to good humor banished her concern. She shook out her hands and moved into traffic. "Glad to hear it."

While they drove, he discussed some of his own magic faux pas. Alex shook her head. A strange end to a disastrous evening. First, the embarrassment with Nick, then Tony's outburst, and her own reaction. Now she was driving a strange car down a darkened road with her inebriated cousin.

She sent a silent blast to her mother. *Why didn't you warn me?*

****

A huge yawn stretched her face as they arrived at the Brendani home. After an emotionally tiring day, she needed her bed. She slipped inside, crept up the wide staircase, and made it back to the comfort of her room without encountering anyone.

While she changed, her thoughts strayed to the buff bartender at the pub. The memory of Nick's strong arms made her lick her lips. He was definitely hot. Too bad he was so full of himself. Then she remembered the broken light. Tomorrow, she'd offer to pay for it. Her thoughts wandered back to Nick. What if he discovered her powers? Would he be impressed? She snorted. More likely he'd run off screaming. Damn! She hadn't contemplated her love life. Any normal guy would consider her a freak.

Concerned about future liaisons, she drifted to the window where the cool breeze calmed her. Moonlight brushed a little enchantment over the setting. Her gaze swept the grounds. Everything seemed quiet. To her left, she caught the reflection of a window whose house remained hidden beyond the trees. She hadn't noticed it before since huge plots of land surrounded the homes here.

Another yawn convinced her to go to bed, but as she turned away, a bright flash grabbed her attention. She peered at the house again. Had someone turned on a light? No. Darkness still reigned, but something had changed. For a minute, the air seemed to tremble. An unnerving sensation—a slight disturbance in the atmosphere—connected with a force inside her.

She tried to dismiss it, but the feeling remained, as if a hand reached out for her. She pulled away from the window and chided herself for being so dramatic.

Still, she couldn't shake the curious urge to leave her room and walk over to the house. She'd taken a step toward her door when an immediate sense of unease swept over her.

Stay away!

Had she thought that, or did someone say it? "Mom?"

She strained to hear more. In the silence, she shook her head and looked at the door. *What was I thinking?* She turned back to the room, speaking out loud as if to a child. "You're losing it, lady. Go to bed."

Chapter Eight

Alex let the hot water beat down on her as she tried to clear her mind from the disturbing flashes that had haunted her slumber the night before. Sharp pictures, one after the other, replayed in her head like a fractured video: a woman's eyes round with terror, a child's scream, and a splash of red on a lemon-yellow carpet.

She had no idea what it meant, and she didn't care. She wanted it out of her head. The soothing spray eased her anxiety.

Nightmares were probably normal considering her life had been completely uprooted, and someone had tried to kidnap her. It would take time to adapt.

The house remained quiet as she headed downstairs to the kitchen. With a cup of coffee in hand, she went out to the back porch and settled into a cushioned chair. Warm air greeted her, and she relished the peace and comfort of the secluded grounds.

The slight scrape of the screen door and Bree's voice startled her. "Good morning, Alex. Enjoying yourself?"

She nodded. "Mm. I love the sense of serenity out here."

Bree took a seat beside her. "You look a little tired. Up late last night?"

She chuckled. "I'm not used to being up past ten p.m. Last night took more out of me than I thought." A brief picture of Tony's actions from the night before flitted through her mind. His anger had scared her.

"Don't worry about your cousin. He'd never hurt you."

Alex snapped her head up. Her aunt had read her thoughts.

Bree spoke again. "Yes, I can read minds. It's one of my gifts. I don't make a habit of it, though. I did it this morning to demonstrate my special talent. We all excel at something."

Alex's face must have mirrored her horror because Bree patted her hand. "It's all right. I'll teach you how to guard against any intrusion into your mind. In the meantime, I promise not to read you again."

Goose bumps peppered the back of her neck. Her breath hitched, and she pulled away from her aunt. Her hand shook as she picked up her coffee.

Bree stood. "I've cleared my calendar, and I'm ready to work with you."

"What kind of work?"

"On your powers. We'll try to pinpoint what they are."

"We know I destroy things." She frowned. "Last night I zapped a light."

Bree nodded as if she knew about the incident. Someone must have told her.

"Can you help me stop doing that?" Alex asked.

"It's one of the things we'll work on. That and what you did at the cemetery."

Alex sucked in a breath. That had only been last week. "Okay, I'm going to need another cup of coffee."

"I'm afraid that's decaf. We seldom have caffeine. That and alcohol tend to flatten our powers. From now on, please abstain from both."

"Do you mind if I get a refill before we begin?"

"Of course not."

Alex didn't need another cup of coffee; she wanted time to process her aunt's revelations. She didn't like someone sneaking into her head.

Bree followed her into the kitchen. "How did you like Newport?"

Alex remembered the thrill as she'd walked along the busy dock. "I loved it. A continuous flow of people and intriguing shops. I'd have been happy to sit on a bench all night and watch." Alex, who'd been interested in a career in the writing field before her father's death, grinned at her aunt. "I'd like to go back with my notebook and pull together an article to submit online. I have lots of ideas."

"Good. A worthy pursuit." Bree led Alex to her office at the front of the house.

Conscious of her aunt's ability, Alex tried to monitor her thoughts. She slid to a stop as the idea hit her.

"Something wrong?"

"Are my thoughts open to everyone here?"

"No. That's my gift, but some of the Stuarts have the ability."

About to ask who the Stuarts were, another possibility jumped into her head. "Wait a minute. What about my mother?"

"I don't know for certain. It's probable."

Crap! A flush crept up her face. "You need to teach me how to keep people out of my mind."

****

Alex finished her coffee and made herself comfortable on the sofa in Bree's office as her aunt spoke.

"Let's talk about the Brendani gifts. We'll begin with me. My main talent, as you've discovered, is mind reading. I can also direct, up to a point, someone's thoughts, which gives me some control over a person's actions. I've had to calm down some patients before their anger gained control."

"Wait a minute. You mean you spy on your patients?"

Bree looked offended. "Of course not. I use my powers to protect myself. I'm sure you've noticed that certain people or situations give you an uncomfortable feeling which makes you shy away from them."

"Doesn't everyone?"

"To a certain degree, but we're more sensitive to danger."

"What if others try to read my mind? You promised to teach me to protect myself."

"I will—once you learn to control your gifts."

"But . . .?"

"We'll work on it."

Alex pursed her lips but kept quiet. There was so much to learn.

"As for my patients, I sense the minute I'm threatened. Sometimes, all I need to do is plant a thought in someone's mind to defuse that threat."

While Alex accepted the explanation, Bree went on. "Your Uncle Sal can manipulate inanimate objects. It's quite impressive. He could move everything in this room, including the sofa with you on it."

Alex clutched the cushion beneath her. "What about my mom? What kind of powers did she have?"

Bree's smile cracked. Her gaze dropped to her hands in her lap. "Your mother left home before she came into her full gifts." Seeming to shake herself, her aunt looked up with a half grin. "CeCe loved to pull pranks. Well, we all did, but your mother had the best ideas. We drove Kitty crazy playing with our gifts. CeCe's powers were the strongest, so she got into the most trouble. At one birthday party, when it came time to blow out the candles, she used a small energy burst and blew the cake off the table." Bree laughed. "Mother wanted to kill her."

Alex smiled. She could imagine what her mother had been like, but talk of her mother's former life still hurt.

Her aunt's gaze drifted away as if peering into the past. When she looked back, her expression had softened. "Sometimes, when we were young, we'd get into arguments with each other because your mother would know a secret of ours. Franki and I accused each other of telling CeCe. But no one had told her. We found out later that every now and then, she'd get flashes into our minds. My own talents didn't begin to develop until months later than my baby sister's. Everyone's gift is different. Once we start to work with you, it won't take long to discover what you have. Later we'll talk about our responsibilities to our ancestors. Did Lia tell you she's a healer?"

The idea of Lia soothing the sick made her grin. Her cousin seemed more like a sexy witch than a potion maker. "No."

Bree shifted in her chair and cleared her throat. "There's something else I have to tell you."

Alarms buzzed in Alex's head, and she straightened in her seat.

"You know Kitty has been in contact with your mother?"

Alex nodded.

"Together, they figured out what happened to CeCe."

"She had a blood disease," Alex said.

"Not exactly." She paused, and something dark flashed in her eyes. She rubbed her hand along the back of her neck. "The infection that took your mother's life wasn't produced by her body."

"Where did it come from?"

Bree leaned in and placed her hand over Alex's. "Kitty should have known the moment your mother entered her realm, but she didn't. We sensed the burst of energy and worried for CeCe, but Kitty couldn't find her. The reason is now clear. Someone placed a spell on your mother that bound her to her remains. Black magic. Someone deliberately set out to kill your mother and keep her family in the dark."

Alex, who now sat huddled on the sofa, had trouble finding her next breath. Her insides felt like they'd been shot through with hot and cold liquid. She couldn't fathom it. Her mother had been murdered? "I think I'm going to be sick."

Bree jumped up and opened a door beside the fireplace. Alex made it to the toilet, seconds before losing her breakfast.

Bree handed her a wet facecloth. "We've done enough for now." She looked at the clock. "Take some time for yourself, maybe lay down."

Alex, unable to speak, nodded. A couple of over-the-counter pain meds and a soft bed sounded like a great idea. She spent the next few hours in her room with one pillow under her head and another clutched against her chest. She'd known in her gut something was wrong with her mother's death, but she'd never suspected murder.

By the time Franki tapped on her door, she'd accepted all she'd learned. What she didn't understand was the motive. Why would someone want her mother dead? A chill seeped through her. Did the same person want to kill her?

Chapter Nine

Bree looked up as Alex entered the kitchen. "I hope you feel better. I packed lunch for us to take to Franki's studio."

Despite the shattering knowledge of her mother's murder, Alex managed to tweak out a tiny grin. "I'm much better, thank you."

"Good." Bree started for the door and stopped. "Franki says she wants strawberries. Would you grab some of those on the table?"

With a puzzled frown, Alex looked toward the phone. It hadn't rung. How could her aunt know what Franki wanted?

Bree chuckled. "No, we don't need telephones to communicate. We use telepathy."

Alex opened and closed her mouth. Maybe she'd lost her mind and was sitting somewhere in an asylum. With a sigh, she gathered up the fruit and followed her aunt to Franki's aerie above the garage.

Her aunt welcomed them in an un-Franki-like outfit—denim shorts and an old shirt that looked like it belonged to Uncle James. The oversize blouse, decorated with dabs of paint, made her look like a child playing dress-up. Except for a couple of escaped curls, a bright scarf held her blonde hair in place.

"This is my hideaway," she said as she gestured to the room. "Make yourself at home."

The bright and airy atmosphere of Franki's studio had a soothing effect. Light streamed in from three sides, and the view rocked. An off-white sofa with colorful pillows faced the water where peaks of froth blew across the river's surface. A perfect retreat.

Next to her, Franki gave a contented sigh. "I love it here. It helps me work through my troubles better than any counselor." She grinned and looked toward her sister. "Don't tell Bree I said that."

Alex turned to survey the room. "I've never seen an artist's workspace. This is delightful."

Several easels were positioned about the area, and Alex smelled the mingled aromas of paint and some sort of cleaning solution. She stared in amazement at the number of canvasses stacked against the walls.

Franki led her toward a simple wooden table in the corner covered with a colorful splash of cloth. "We can check out the rest later. Let's eat."

Her aunts had planned a relaxing and festive afternoon. For Alex, lunch amid this vibrant chaos reminded her of the picnics she'd enjoyed with her parents. Bree and Franki swapped happy memories. Alex swung her head back and forth between them, clinging to every word as they talked about life with their baby sister.

At one point, Franki brought over a photo album and showed Alex photos of her mother laughing with her sisters at the house, the beach, and shops in Newport. As her fingers traced the outline of her mother's face under the smooth plastic cover, a lump formed in her throat. She decided to pose the question that had nagged at her since she'd met Bree. "Why did she leave?"

After an uncomfortable pause, Franki nodded at

Bree who said, "There wasn't anything terrible. No anger. No recriminations. She fell in love. She met your father and lost her heart. But . . ."

Franki jumped in. "You see, Alex, your father wasn't one of us, had no idea what we were like. Your mother wanted a normal life. No gifts. No watchers. No inherited responsibilities. She couldn't have that here, so she left, cut her ties, and moved. We tried to find her, but she shielded herself. We were all devastated. We loved our baby sister." Franki wiped her eyes and stood up.

Alex, unable to speak, simply nodded.

Bree blew her nose. "Why don't you show Alex some of your paintings?"

"Good idea." Taking Alex by the hand, Franki led her around the room to examine different canvases.

Alex pointed to a haunting image of a beach whose stark beauty included empty sand dunes and one lonely scrub pine. "I love this one."

"That's Third Beach. We'll have to take you there."

She turned to another. "Who's the woman on the bench in the labyrinth? She seems so sad."

The look Franki gave Bree should have prepared her. "That's Kitty, your grandmother."

"You did this before she died?"

"No. I finished it a few days ago."

"Why would you paint your mother with such a sad expression?"

"That was when she found out her daughter was gone."

Bree interceded before Alex could speak.

"*Vision* is your aunt's special gift. She sees what others can't. You've met your grandmother's spirit. You spoke to her. Franki can see her."

Alex considered the picture of her grandmother. So different than how she'd pictured her. Although Kitty's sunny hair matched Franki's, her features, long thin nose, and high cheekbones, resembled Alex and her mother. The image of her grandmother's forlorn figure had deepened her own pain. Too many emotions, too fast. She moved away from her aunts and stopped at the side window. It faced a forested area.

Beyond the trees, parts of a house caught her attention. It must be the same one she'd seen last night, but the structure was closer here. As she focused on the bit of window winking back at her, an uncomfortable foreboding plucked at her nerves. She remembered how it affected her the night before and shivered.

"What is it?" Franki said.

Alex tried to shake it off, but the anxiety lingered. "That house. I don't like it. It creeps me out. It upset me last night."

"Why?" Bree's voice in her ear made her jump. "Did something happen?"

Alex turned away from the house and lifted her shoulders. "There wasn't much. I was looking out the window, and I thought I saw a burst of light, but I can't be sure." She paused and hugged herself. "That's when I sensed it, like an unsettled movement in the air as if the house was watching me."

As she finished her account, she realized that the house did have an odd effect on her. Even today, she'd been drawn to it. She'd never had such strange emotions about an inanimate object. What was happening to her?

Bree's face paled, and she turned to her sister. "I don't like the sound of this."

"Nor do I," Franki said.

Her aunt's worried tone scared Alex. "Why?"

Bree took her niece's arm, ignoring the question, and spoke to her sister. "We've got to get to work. We don't have much time. See if Kitty can contact CeCe. I need to find out how to break that binding spell. Immediately."

****

"Hurry up."

Alex almost tripped on the bluestone path between the garage and the house as she adjusted her pace to keep up with her aunt's power walk. What was it with that house? Both aunts had freaked out after she'd mentioned it.

When she tossed that question out to Bree's back, her aunt kept plodding forward like a soldier on a mission. Alex gave up and followed her to her office.

The door hadn't finished closing when Bree waved her to the sofa. Before Alex could ask anything, Bree fired a question at her. "Now, Alex, what can you do?"

"Huh?" Alex eyed the door, trying to suppress the urge to bolt. One minute her aunts had been laughing and reminiscing, the next all weird and worried.

"Psychically. What have you been able to do?"

"Not much." She looked away from Bree. "Mom taught me to read auras, although it doesn't work here. I mean, I see something, but it's sort of neutral."

Bree's voice came out as scolding. "That's because we're shielded."

"What?"

Bree paused to explain. "Each of us can shield our thoughts from others. When that shield is in place, the aura has nothing to work with and so appears, as you say, neutral. When you meet someone like that, question their motives. Now, tell me. Do you have any other unnatural abilities—like seeing ghosts?"

Alex paused before she answered. "I can't see ghosts, and I've never spoken to any before my grandmother, but I've always been aware of their presence. And, as you said earlier, I'm pretty good at picking up harmful intentions."

"Yes, your mother always sensed things. Her gifts were stronger than the rest of ours. That was the sad part. When your mother left here, she had a great deal of power. I can only imagine what happened to her on her twenty-fifth birthday. The Watcher Clan missed her so much."

Alex's ears perked up at the words, and she started to speak. "Watcher . . ."

Bree waved her hand. "Not now. Can you move objects?" She put her hand to her head. "Oh no, we tried that. Can you read minds?"

Alex inhaled to suppress a screech of aggravation at her aunt's overbearing attitude. "Sometimes I know what people are thinking. Not their exact thoughts but I get a general idea."

"What about healing? Have you ever touched someone and helped them heal?"

Alex shook her head, and Bree went on trying to discover any other abnormal powers her niece might possess, but nothing came up other than the baffling electrical charges.

Listening to her aunt's barrage of bizarre questions was like being caught in a strong vortex. When the probe ended, she slumped back against the sofa.

Bree's concentration was elsewhere, but not for long. Her attention refocused on Alex. "Kitty just relayed the information I need to break your mother's spell. It shouldn't be difficult since the magic's lifespan is almost up."

"You can speak to Kitty?"

"Of course. We all use telepathy. Now, lean back on the sofa and relax. This won't hurt a bit."

Her heart stuttered at Bree's words. Instead of relaxing, she froze.

Bree softened her voice. "It's all right. Your mother gave Kitty this spell so we could help you. She invoked it while you slept, but we don't have that advantage. You'll be fine. I'll place my hands on either side of your head and say a few words to release the spell. You won't feel anything. I promise. Can you trust me?"

The question made her pause. Could she? The new life she'd been thrust into was frightening. She still held reservations about her relatives, especially Bree, whose dictates sometimes seemed harsh, but Mom had given Kitty the words to undo the spell. She looked into her aunt's eyes, so like her mother's. Time to lower her defenses.

"All right." Alex took in a few deep breaths, leaned back on the sofa, and envisioned her safe place. The sight of the heavy, carved door soothed her. Its smooth, brass handle, like an old friend, invited her into a peaceful retreat. She opened it in her mind and walked through. A fresh cool breeze washed over her and dissolved the turmoil in her head. At the same time, the soothing warmth of Bree's hands, and the rhythmic hum of her aunt's voice gave her comfort.

"You can open your eyes now."

When she raised her eyelids, everything seemed different. She was still in the same room with her aunt, but the atmosphere had changed. She felt like she'd awakened from a long sleep. The room was brighter, and her mind seemed clearer than it had been for a long time. She sat up, aware of a new confidence. "Wow. I feel different, more alive." Her previous concern about her lack of psychic skills subsided. She somehow knew she'd succeed.

"Good. It must have worked. That fresh energy is the release of your inherited talents. That's where we'll have to begin."

Chapter Ten

The office door opened, and Franki sailed in, the song of her bracelets tinkling in the air. She'd changed into white capris and a turquoise blouse.

Bree nodded to her sister. "Let's start, shall we?"

A mixture of trepidation and excitement assailed Alex as she encountered Bree's no-nonsense attitude.

"We'll begin with mind reading. Since that seemed to be one of your mother's talents, let's find out if you inherited it. I want you to concentrate on my thoughts. Shut out everything else and picture my mind opening to you. Use your will to push through and read what's there."

When nervous, Alex sometimes resorted to humor. Before considering her words, she gave Bree a crooked grin and said, "I already know what you're thinking."

Bree, who'd been leaning forward as she spoke, sat back and gave Alex a wide-eyed stare. "You do?"

"Yes. You want me to succeed."

Bree's lips compressed. "Please do as I asked."

Alex's face burned. She wished Bree would lighten up. Alex pulled herself together and tried to get centered. She closed her eyes, pictured her aunt's face, and attempted to see into her mind. Tiny sounds around her heightened: the ticking of the clock and the sigh of a cushion as someone moved, but nothing from her aunt. She took a cleansing breath and urged her powers to work. This time, she looked at her aunt and willed Bree's thoughts to unfold. Nothing. Alex let her breath out in a whoosh. Her attempts failed. "I can't do it."

She didn't need psychic powers to read Bree's facial expression. Her aunt's eyes flared as she spoke. "You're not trying hard enough. Push yourself."

The snap, almost disgust, in Bree's voice hurt. Alex wanted to yell, "How do you expect me to focus while you sit there judging me?" Instead, she returned her aunt's glare, clamped her teeth shut, and tightened her whole body. She used her power as a battering ram to force her way in. When that didn't work, she stopped. Anger made it more difficult. She had to clear her mind. She visited her calm place and found, to her surprise, that she didn't have to go through the door for release. The minute she expressed the desire, peace was there.

More centered, she tried again. This time she stared into her aunt's eyes and sought to move beyond them into her secret recesses. Alex envisioned a small pathway that led to Bree's CPU—the central processing unit with all her aunt's information. Alex's confidence soared as she sensed Bree's essence, but instead of information, she encountered a red brick barrier. She released a loud sigh and opened her eyes. "Sorry. It just won't work."

"What do you mean, it won't work? I felt your presence."

Weary and confused, Alex's voice came out in a whine. "All I saw was a wall."

"Excellent."

"Excellent? That I couldn't read your mind?"

Satisfaction radiated across Bree's face. "But you could, Alex. I shielded myself with a brick wall. That's what you saw."

Franki, who'd stayed quiet until then, muttered to her sister. "Why would you ask her to read you and then close yourself up?"

"I wanted to see what she could do against a block. She did well. I could feel her move around and check the perimeter."

"You could have warned her."

Bree frowned at her sister. "We don't have time for niceties."

"Come on, Bree, you can't just steamroll over her."

With an iron glare, Bree shook her finger at Franki. "A week from Monday Alex receives her gifts. We don't have any time."

Franki huffed and tugged at her hair but said no more.

Bree continued, "Okay. Franki, open your mind." To Alex, she said, "Read your aunt."

Alex tried to object. "I don't want to snoop through Aunt Franki's mind."

Bree responded like a drill sergeant, "This isn't a matter of morality. We're trying to keep you alive. Concentrate on Franki."

Alex held back an angry reply. If Bree read her mind now, she wouldn't be pleased.

Alex focused on Franki's sweet face, took a deep breath, and pictured her aunt's mind opening like petals on a flower. This time, she found it easier to infiltrate, but her vision seemed disorganized. Although a sense of love enveloped her, she couldn't understand the words in front of her. It was like looking at parts of an unfinished crossword puzzle. She shook her head and stopped the probe.

"Did it work?" Bree asked.

"Sort of."

Franki looked confused. "You were there. I felt you."

"I got in, but I couldn't make sense of what was there."

"Of course," Bree said, raising her hands in mock surrender. "I forgot. It's like learning a new language. Don't get upset. Sometimes all you need to do is wait for a few seconds until your own brain can sort it out. Try again."

She popped into her quiet place before reentering the confusion of her aunt's mind. This time, the few words she saw made little sense. She gave Bree a nervous glance and spoke to Franki. "I can't have gotten it right."

"Don't worry, honey. It just takes time."

"I'm sure I'm wrong."

Franki's soft voice reassured her. "That's all right. What did you see?"

Alex didn't dare look at Bree. She took a deep breath. "Okay. Here it is: 'I'm sorry, honey. It's tough. I hate Bree.' " Alex ducked her head on the last sentence as if fearing a blow.

Franki burst out laughing, and Bree's lips curved into a broad grin.

Still chuckling, Franki told Alex that she'd missed some of her thoughts. "Want to try once more? It takes practice."

This time Alex stayed in Franki's mind, and the pieces of the message finally fell into place. *I'm so sorry we've put you through this, honey. Bree's being tough on you because she cares. I hate to say it, but Bree's right.*

"Thank you, Aunt Franki. You don't know how

much I wish I didn't have to do this."

Bree clapped her hands. "Good. You succeeded. This skill will become easier to control with practice."

When Alex realized what she'd done, her heart gave a little skip. She could read minds.

"Very good, honey." Franki's beaming smile, so like her mother's, tugged at her heart. Alex had also noticed that, while unshielded, her Aunt Franki had the most beautiful aura.

Amid the elation over her success, she noticed her wrist. "Oh, no!"

"What's the matter?" Bree said, with a worried glance.

"My scar. It's bright red."

Bree let out a chuckle that earned a scowl from Alex. "It isn't funny."

"That's not a scar, Alex."

"Yes, it is. I got it when I was a baby."

Bree held out her left wrist, and Franki followed suit. They had the same tiny cross on their skin. Franki's was faint, but Bree's gleamed a bright pink.

"It's the mark of our Clan, the Templar Cross. We're all born with it. It brightens when we use our powers. I'm sure if you had looked at your wrist after you sent that man flying, it would have glowed like it is now."

"But my mother didn't have one."

"She did, Alex."

It hurt to learn how much her mother had kept from her. She pursed her lips and gave the sofa a whack. "My whole life was a lie."

Franki squeezed her hand. "That's not true. Your mother wanted you to have the luxury of a normal childhood. And don't forget your father. What would he have done if he'd seen you use your gifts?"

"That's right," Bree said. "Your mother had to protect you."

Alex knew her mother had loved her, but still…

Franki clapped her hands. "That's enough for now. It's time for a breather."

"Wait a minute." Alex looked at Bree. "What's this about a Clan?"

"We're part of a group of Templar descendants called the Watcher Clan. We'll explain all that later. For now, just be grateful we're not alone." Bree stood up and stretched. "Now, let's have a break. Then we can try to explore your other gifts."

****

Alex had to suppress a groan as she realized how much strain her mind and body had endured. What she craved was rest and time alone but settled for a short reprieve. While they sipped decaf tea and nibbled warm muffins on the back porch, Bree and Franki chatted about mundane things: a shopping trip to Newport, an afternoon at the beach, Franki's latest painting. It proved to be just enough to pull Alex back into the real world. She straightened her shoulders. "Okay. Let's go."

The exercise began with a few pointers about mind reading from Bree. "Whenever you delve into someone's brain, you must cover your psychic tracks. Don't let anyone trace you. Should you encounter a shield, reenforce your own, and get out right away."

"I don't understand. How would anyone know I was there?"

"You'll immediately perceive an encroachment, like a tiny worm wriggling in the corner of your mind. It won't take long for you to recognize an intruder."

Franki nodded. "Although most who are aware of your presence won't be able to follow your trail, those who can are dangerous. For instance, practitioners of the dark arts. With someone like that, you need every safeguard you have."

Cold invaded her body, and her temporary euphoria evaporated. Her voice became a whisper. "Like the one who killed my mother?"

Bree's shoulders slumped, and Franki's face filled with grief. "I'm sorry. I shouldn't have mentioned that."

Alex corralled the pain, tucked it away, and fixed her attention on mastering her talents. For the rest of the afternoon, she worked on her mind-reading skills: how to enter someone's mind, understand what she found, and get out safely.

"Okay," Bree said, "you're picking it up fast. What you need is practice. Now, let's talk about the ethics involved."

Alex's eyes widened. Could she get into trouble using her gift? Her imagination conjured up a large room with people in long black robes pointing at her.

"No need to worry about Alex," Franki said.

"Nevertheless, it's our duty to explain it all. I've contacted Rosemary, and she's on her way to perform the ceremony."

To Alex, she said, "The Templars gifted us to protect innocents from those who seek to hurt them. We must also take care to cause no harm when we use our own talents. It is paramount that we keep our abilities hidden. You'll need to swear to that before we move on."

Alex thought she was kidding until she saw her aunts' expectant faces waiting for her. "You're serious?"

"Of course," Bree said.

Franki nodded.

"Okay. I swear I won't use my gifts for anything but good."

"Save that for Rosemary," Bree said.

"Who?"

"Our Clan leader. She'll be here in a few minutes. We might as well talk about telepathy while we wait."

Oh right, don't take a minute to breathe.

As an instructor, Bree proved relentless. She insisted that the only method of communication for the rest of the lesson would be telepathy.

"I can't do that."

Bree's answer was a heavy sigh, and a voice tinged with exasperation. "I'm going to teach you."

Alex arched her back, stretched her neck, and chanced a peek at the clock. Less than two hours had passed. She turned to her aunt for guidance, but Bree sat there staring at her. Unsure what they wanted, Alex shifted in her seat and played with the rings on her fingers. She sat up as she felt a fluttering around her temples. Oh great. A headache. The slight quiver became a whisper in her head. Her aunt's voice. Bree's lips stretched in a broad smile as Alex gaped at her. The pulsing began again. This time, she discerned words. *I can see that you hear me. Now, it's your turn. Answer me.*

Alex opened her mouth, then stopped at Bree's smirk. Feeling foolish, Alex formed her ideas and sent them, then waited for the answer. When there was no acknowledgment from Bree, she tilted her head in a question. Her aunt shook her head. Alex pinched her lips together and prepared to try again.

A knock on the door interrupted her. An older

woman with a regal bearing walked in. Her hair, the color of butter, was swept into a bun. She smiled at Alex. "I'm Rosemary Stuart. Welcome home."

"Thank you."

"I'm sorry your mother isn't here with you." She surveyed Alex. "You're very much like her."

Alex had never considered the resemblance until she'd seen the photos of her mother as a young woman.

Bree interrupted Rosemary. "Let's get started. Alex has so much to learn. We're teaching her telepathy."

Bree walked over to a wall cabinet, unlocked it, and withdrew an enormous book that looked old. "It's a bit cliche, Alex, but this is the Brendani family bible. Each member of our Clan has sworn a pledge to protect their Templar heritage on this precious tome."

Alex studied the odd figure embedded in the dark leather. Two Crusaders on a horse.

Rosemary brushed her fingers across the cover and nodded to Alex. "It's a pleasure to induct CeCe's daughter into our sacred Clan. Ordinarily, all our members are present to welcome the neophyte, but these are unusual circumstances. Please place your hand on the Templar symbol."

Alex complied, and Rosemary's fingers covered her own. A sense of belonging surged within her as Rosemary intoned each sentence of the Templar Clan Oath. When she said, "Do you, Alexandra Ryan, daughter of the original nine, accept the responsibility to safeguard your powers, defend our heritage, and protect the innocent?"

Alex smiled and, infused with pride, said, "I do."

"Alexandra Ryan, born of Cecile Brendani, and part of a proud lineage that goes back to the beginning on the

Temple of Solomon Mount, you are now one with the Ancient Clan of the Knights Templar."

After a few brief congratulatory hugs, Bree reminded them of the telepathy exercises.

"I'll leave you to your studies," Rosemary said. "What did you choose as your transfer image?"

"What?"

Rosemary raised an eyebrow at Bree, but Franki jumped in. "It's been so long since we've done this, and we've been under so much strain—we forgot."

Rosemary, old enough to be Alex's grandmother, took Alex's hand and laughed. "I think age is catching up to your aunts."

Alex enjoyed seeing the flush that slid up Bree's neck. Rosemary winked at Alex. "When we learn to transmit information, we use a special image that tells our brain we want to send a message. Mine is the old pipe my dear Da used to smoke."

Franki's bracelets tinkled as she fluttered her hand. "I chose an angel."

Bree said hers was the Templar cross.

Before she left, Rosemary said, "Find something that's dear to your heart. Keep me updated."

Alex must have looked nervous because both aunts assured her this form of communication would become as routine as speaking out loud. "After a while, you won't have to use a picture at all," Franki said.

Alex, who wasn't sure that would ever happen, sought to find her image. As her tired mind sifted through possibilities, her gaze rested on the gorgeous flowers beyond the windows—Mom's garden. That was it. She'd use a yellow rose, her mother's favorite. She nodded to her aunt. "All set."

Bree sent her a message. *Envision your image and the person you want to contact, then send.*

Alex placed a mental yellow rose in her mind and guided her thoughts toward the place where she'd *heard* Bree's words.

How do I do this? Do I just think it to you?

You did it.

Whoa, it worked. Before she could congratulate herself, another little quiver alerted her. Franki's voice. She was sending her kudos. Alex directed her thanks through the same spot where she'd received Franki's message.

You're welcome, Franki sent back.

Though thrilled with her progress, Alex had a question. Forgetting herself, she spoke out loud. "How do I contact someone when no one has sent me a message? I won't know where to put my answer if I don't have something to follow."

Bree turned her head and looked out the window as if Alex hadn't spoken. What a hard-ass, Alex thought and immediately regretted it, praying Bree hadn't read her mind. She reined in her temper and repeated the question using her telepathy.

Much better, Bree said. *Your psyche now understands that when your image appears, you want to send a message, and your gift takes over.*

Holding an image of both her aunts and her symbol in her mind, Alex sent a question. *Can I call two people at once?*

Franki gave her a quick hug, and Bree patted her shoulder. Fatigued but exhilarated, Alex rejoiced at her growing skill and had to stifle a giggle. She yearned to show off her powers to someone else. Mom. She'd always been so proud of her daughter.

When Bree reminded her of the attempted abduction, her enthusiasm over her success waned. "Believe me, whoever wants you hasn't given up. We still have a lot to do. You need to be ready."

After a grueling afternoon, a knock on the door made a welcome interruption. Lia poked her head in. One look at Alex and she opened the door wide and put her hands on her hips. "Do you want to kill her before she reaches her birthday?"

Alex sent her a telepathic thank you.

Lia responded with a smile. "Well, you're welcome." She looked from her aunt to her mother. "Looks like you've made good progress. Can she please come to dinner?"

Bree looked at the time. "Lord, Alex. You must be exhausted. Of course, we can take a break. Why don't we start again after we eat?"

"Not tonight, Aunt Bree. I'm taking Alex to dine in Newport, and then she can get to bed early. If you wear her out, you'll get nothing from her tomorrow."

Bree looked ready to explode; Lia reached over and touched her arm. "Aunty, I promise I'll work with her while we're out. It'll be good practice for her."

To Alex's surprise, Bree's expression softened, and she relented.

Lia linked arms with Alex and steered her toward the stairs. "Lia, I love you. Thank you so much. Another minute and I would have screamed. How did you calm her down?"

"That's what healers do."

Chapter Eleven

As Lia maneuvered the car through the crowded Newport streets, Alex moaned. "I don't think there's an empty parking spot anywhere."

"Not to worry. I'll use my magic."

Alex widened her eyes. "You can do that?"

"Watch me."

A few minutes later, Lia took a left and pulled into an underground garage. When the attendant stopped her, she tweaked her fingers at him, and he let her in.

"Oh my God, did you—like—mesmerize him?"

Lia burst out laughing. "That was my friend, Chuck. I work here. The Chandler Regency Arms is one of the Brendani properties."

"You mean it belongs to Uncle Sal?"

"All of us. Our family has real estate holdings all over Rhode Island."

Alex blinked and tried to take in this latest disclosure. "So, you don't have to work?"

"Wouldn't that be nice? No. We do have a trust that takes care of the house, furnishings, property, and various other expenses like food and transportation." Lia opened her door, and said, over her shoulder, "It also gives each of us a small allowance."

"Seriously?" Alex had trouble finding the door handle and lurched out of the car. She caught up to Lia on the street. "Does that include me?"

"Yup. Once you set up an account, you'll receive a deposit every month."

Relieved she wouldn't be penniless, Alex stared at the impressive brick front of the hotel. "The place is huge. What do you do there?"

"I'm a concierge agent. Daddy's the manager."

Alex wondered if the family business was the reason her mother had gotten into real estate.

During their stroll along the street, Lia gave Alex a little of the town's history. "Newport was once a huge Navy town, and yachting, always a favorite pastime, attracted the America's Cup races and many world visitors." As they walked past an architectural mishmash of buildings catering to retail and food-related businesses, Lia spread her hands. "These days, it's mainly tourism."

Alex was delighted when they turned into Bannister's Wharf, the same lively thoroughfare they'd visited last night. She tried to take it all in and bumped into a man standing in front of her. He hadn't seen her because his attention was riveted on a woman whose large purse hung against her back.

"Excuse me," Alex said.

He glared at her, then moved over to slouch against a pole. His actions put her senses on high alert. Late twenties, she guessed, with longish dark hair. He returned his attention to the woman. *He wants her bag.* She could warn the woman, but maybe she should peek into his mind first. She'd be in and out in an instant.

Focusing on his face, she opened to read him. Voices exploded in her mind. The noise threatened to tear off her head. It took all she had, not to cry out. She didn't realize she'd gone down to one knee until rough asphalt scraped her skin. Lia appeared beside her. She cradled Alex's head. "What's the matter?"

"Too many voices."

Lia's voice sharpened. "Close the channel."

Under her cousin's ministrations, the agony lessened. Alex followed Lia's directions. The pain dissolved. She took hold of a hand helping her to stand and found the other end attached to the thief. She jerked away from him.

He persisted. "Are you all right? Do you need help? I'm a doctor."

Next to him, with her arm around his waist, was the woman Alex had pinpointed as his victim. Oh hell, some intuition. "No. Thank you, I'm much better."

"Let's go, honey," the woman said as she nudged him. "I want to see…"

Her voice faded as they walked away. Embarrassed, Alex tried to explain what she'd done. Lia squeezed her arm. "Don't try that in a crowd until you learn how to protect yourself. We'll work on that later."

"Believe me I won't."

They turned into a restaurant called The Candy Store. Delicious aromas and animated chatter followed them to their table in an open porch area. The sound of water slapping against boats intermingled with bits of conversation and the clatter of silverware and dishes. Alex leaned her head out over the rail and inhaled the night air.

"Hey." Lia snapped her fingers. "What do you want to drink?"

Alex dragged her attention back to the waitress long enough to order a ginger ale. Lia, who'd ordered wine, raised her eyebrows at Alex's order.

"Bree asked me to abstain while I'm training."

Lia nodded. "Smart."

The dining room had an old-time yachting flavor. Colorful photos of sailing vessels and wooden half hulls of famous yachts covered the walls. Lia explained that the restaurant had been popular when Newport hosted the America's Cup trials between 1958 and 1983.

Alex settled back into the lime green canvas chair and grinned. "This place is amazing."

Lia's eyes sparkled. "I knew you'd like it." She leaned her elbow on the table and put her chin in her hand. "Tell me about today."

Alex paused, remembering the incredible events. "It began at your mother's studio. Her paintings are awesome. You must be so proud of her."

"I am." A small chuckle escaped. "She tried to teach me to paint, but I had no talent and even less desire to learn."

Alex's shoulders drooped, and her voice lost its vitality. "I'll never understand how my mother could have hidden her powers from me."

"I'm surprised she was able to keep you in the dark about your own abilities," Lia said. "Even though she bound them, something must have come through. Didn't you feel a little different from your friends?"

Alex laughed. "I did, but not for the reasons you might imagine. I was always a loner, more concerned about my studies than people. I spent a lot of time with my books. Sometimes I'd write, making up strange little stories." She paused and tilted her head. "After learning about my family, maybe they weren't so strange."

"What about guys, boyfriends?"

"Oh yeah." She frowned. "I must give out a

submissive vibe. My needs were never met by any of the guys I dated. Then, after Mom died, I didn't care."

Lia touched her arm. "Well, we'll have to change that. I'll teach you my mad controlling skills. You'll have men begging. So, what was the rest of your life like?"

Alex examined her previous comfortable, often boring, existence. "Dad's work in sales left us alone, sometimes for weeks at a time, but we had a good life. After I graduated with a bachelor's degree in English, I got a job in a local library. I enjoyed it until I screwed it up."

"How?"

"I was showing a film on dinosaurs when something happened. I thought one of them…" She stopped, unable to meet Lia's eyes.

Lia took her hand. "It's okay, Alex."

"It's just embarrassing. I jumped back and said, 'Look out.' The children were frightened, and another staff member came over to stop the movie. They asked me if I took drugs, then let me go."

"Has that happened to you before?"

"Once, at a special Egyptian exhibit when I was about six, we were looking at a depiction of the inside of a burial place, and I asked my mother why the man was putting a loaf of bread on the table. There hadn't been anyone in the picture, and Mom escorted me outside saying I had a vivid imagination."

"Sounds like one of your gifts."

By the time the waitress brought their salads, Alex had given Lia a glimpse into the lives of the Ryans.

Lia nodded. "It makes sense that your mother was interested in native spirit rituals." Then she surprised

Alex when she revealed that she'd always wished she had a sister. "I did have Tony and Nick. They were two years older than me, and they never wanted to play dolls or dress up. Most of the time they'd go off and leave me alone. I never had close friends outside of the Clan." Again, she reached for Alex's hand. "But now that you're here, I'm not so lonely."

Her words elicited a rush of warmth. "I'm glad to have you, too."

"Okay. I promised Aunt Bree that I'd work with you while we were out tonight. You game?"

Alex remembered the pain of her foray into mind-reading earlier and shook her head. She stabbed a cucumber spear and took a bite. "No. There was too much pain when I tried it earlier."

Lia seemed to tune out Alex's words as she looked over the crowd. "We'll work in this small porch area. It won't hurt. I promise. Just read a couple of people here."

Alex's voice dropped to a dramatic whisper. "There are too many. Besides, it's not right. I did it earlier because I was sure that woman was in danger."

"You're not doing it to harm anyone, and you need to hone your skills in order to protect potential victims."

Alex frowned and twisted a piece of hair around her finger.

"Don't worry. If you get into trouble, I'm right here," Lia said. "First, set boundaries. Make a mental image of a wall around the table you're interested in and then focus on the person you plan to read."

Alex wanted to refuse, but this was a perfect opportunity to practice her skills. "Okay, but you better have my back."

Lia grinned. "Why don't you try with the group next

to us?"

As she spoke, Lia covered Alex's hand with her own. A calming wave moved up her arm then spread throughout her body. She sent Lia a silent thank you, then turned her attention to the people at the table where a buxom woman held court. The others sat and listened with obvious rapt attention.

Alex quieted her mind, formed her barriers, and concentrated on one person. A smattering of voices crowded into her head. She stopped. "Too many people."

"Clear them out of your head and concentrate on your subject," Lia instructed. "Hold your target in your mind and open their thoughts. You'll do fine. It just takes practice."

Alex took a steadying breath, tuned out everything else in the room, and formed an imaginary tunnel to the woman she'd chosen. She soon discovered that the placid face belied churning emotions. Not a surprise after seeing her aura. Dark and muddy, it indicated resentment and jealousy.

I wish someone would tell Ruthie to stuff it. She's been going on about herself all night, and I'm sick to death of it.

Ewww, Alex thought, that explains her cloudy essence. She blinked and looked around the room. Oh, Lord. She could poke into the minds of any of these people.

"Alex?"

She snapped out of it and turned back to Lia. "I can't believe I can do it—that I am doing it."

"I know, honey. It's a dangerous power, but you won't hurt anyone with it. It's okay."

Alex twisted around, worried her ability might be

transparent, and that someone would yell at her for the intrusion.

"Were you able to read someone?"

Excitement bubbled up as she nodded and reported what she'd overheard.

Lia's lips twitched. "Same table; try the skinny guy sitting next to the speaker."

Again, Alex concentrated but forgot to put up the walls and immediately had to slam her mental channel shut. She gave Lia a weak smile.

"Don't give up yet," Lia said. "Try again."

This time Alex set the boundaries before directing her attention to her quarry. With his aura tight against his body, she recognized the guy had no confidence in himself at all.

Oh, God, please don't let Stacie say anything to Ruthie. We don't need a scene here at the table.

Alex tried to downplay her feeling of triumph as she spilled out her reading to her cousin.

The waitress arrived then with their food, and Lia had to wait until she left them alone with their meal. "That's wonderful, Alex. Aunt Bree couldn't have done better. You targeted one person in a group and singled out their thoughts. I can't wait to see what you'll be like after your birthday."

Excited flutters tickled her chest. It was only nine days away. "What happens on my birthday? Does a lightning bolt streak down from the sky? Do I light up and start speaking in tongues? Am I suddenly omnipotent?"

Lia smirked. "No, smart-ass. Nothing like that." She took a bite of her fish, chewed, and swallowed. "For me, I noticed that I felt different. I could sense the heightened power. One day my cousin, Maria, and her five-year-old twin daughters were at the house. Vada cut herself, and Tessa ran up to tell her mother. I went over to Vada. She had a small nick on her finger, but it bled a lot. I took her hand, held the injured digit inside my palm, and concentrated. When I opened my hand, the bleeding had stopped, and the cut was beginning to close. I'd already been able to heal with herbs, but now I could do it by touch." With a big grin, Lia smacked Alex's arm. "Don't worry. You'll be a Mutt soon."

"A what?" Alex said.

Lia chuckled. "A nickname for those who go through the Mutatis. Haven't got a clue who came up with it." Before Alex could ask, Lia said, "Mutatis means *change* in Latin. That's what we call the transfer of our remaining powers."

It sounded painful. "Will it hurt?"

"Of course not. You'll have weird sensations for a minute, but then you'll be fine. Don't worry, we'll be there for you."

Alex grinned. "So, Aunt Bree is a Mutt."

Lia's eyes lit up, and her lips twitched. "Yes, but don't ever call her that." After a quick sip of her wine, she continued. "As for the actual sensations, I can't say. It's different with everybody." She reached across the table to Alex. "I wish I'd been able to help your mother."

"You might have if she'd let you know." Alex paused and then whispered, "Of course, she had no idea there was a healer in her family."

Cold anger flashed in Lia's eyes. "I couldn't have done anything against dark magic, but we might have found someone to help."

Alex looked down and noticed the red on her wrist.

She held it out to Lia. "Does your scar get this bright?"

"That's right. You wouldn't have seen that until you used your gifts. Yes, mine lights up like a beacon. It reminds me I'm not alone."

Over decaf coffees, Lia asked if Alex had any employment ideas.

"I'd like to continue my writing." At Lia's look of surprise, Alex explained. "I've sold some pieces to newspapers and magazines. I want to introduce myself to people in this area. In the meantime, I do copy for some web pages and blogs."

"Excellent idea. Aunt Bree's acquainted with the editor of the local rag, and my mother's name should open a few doors. It'll be fun to see you in print. I'll check with the marketing director for the hotel and see if he might have any thoughts."

After dinner, Lia suggested Alex poke around the shops while she got the car. "I'll take my time and pick you up outside the parking lot. About twenty minutes?"

"Cool."

"If you have any trouble, contact me by telepathy."

****

Alex dawdled for a bit until a colorful display in the window of a jewelry store caught her eye. When she slipped inside, it seemed as if everyone else had the same idea. Dismayed by the crush of people, she turned to leave, but a delicate coral necklace beckoned to her. Another minute or two wouldn't hurt. She edged her way to the counter to examine the rose-like pendant.

When she leaned in for a closer look, though, a prickly sensation began to crawl up the back of her neck. Certain someone was staring at her, she spun around. Too many customers. Concerned about the uncomfortable tingles, she remembered her new skill. Maybe she could use it here. With a tiny thrill, she placed the word, *threat*, in her head and opened her mind. All she found was a glut of unrelated snippets—*nice prices, hot in here, Cindy would love...*

This time, Alex cut off the babble before injuring herself. She dismissed the necklace, made a quick exit, and cast a glance over her shoulder. No one followed. Still spooked, she hurried toward the garage and joined a group of people waiting for the light to change. For a moment she considered crossing against the light, but a gnawing sense of unease stopped her.

When the light changed, she stepped off the curb and anxiety morphed into fear. The word *danger* flashed in her head. She jumped back onto the curb seconds before a black car streaked by.

A woman rushed up to her side. "Oh my God! Are you okay? That car almost hit you. Did you see how fast that fool was going?" The woman became indignant. "He ran the red light."

The sound of a horn distracted her. Lia waited across the street. Her cousin gave one more toot and waved. Alex checked the street before she rushed over. She whipped open the passenger door and flopped down in the seat. "Whoa!"

"What's up?"

"I almost got hit by a car. If I hadn't jumped back to the curb, you'd be picking up pieces of me all over Newport."

"I'll bet that was the same jerk who almost hit me in the garage. He must have been drunk. Lucky you saw him."

"That's just it. I didn't see him. An icy jolt alerted

me, and I reacted."

****

Bree met them in the entrance hall when they returned. "How was dinner?"

Lia winked at Alex before she answered her aunt. "We had a very interesting night. First, Alex is amazing. She was able to read two people at the same table as easily as listening to a conversation."

Bree's eyes widened. "That's wonderful." She nodded to Alex. "You never realized you could do that?"

"I never tried. I don't even like knowing the drift of people's thoughts."

The noise of Lia's foot tapping against the floor brought an indulgent grin to Bree's lips. "Yes, Lia?"

"We did have some trouble later."

Bree's smile collapsed. "What sort?"

Lia recounted their ordeal when the black car streamed toward her in the garage and almost hit Alex on the street. "He probably had too much to drink."

"I'd like to believe that, but I can't take any chances. I want you both to avoid any situations where you're alone. If we must, we'll find members of the Clan to stay with you."

Before either woman could disagree, Bree walked away, saying over her shoulder, "Good night, girls. I have things to do. I've got to send out the latest developments to the Clan."

Alex turned to Lia. "When will I get to meet this Clan?"

"Let's hope not for a long time," Lia said. "They only gather when there's trouble."

Chapter Twelve

The morning air had begun to warm when Lia joined Alex on the back porch. "How can you get up so early?" She rubbed her eyes. "I heard you leave your room hours ago."

Alex had to smile. Lia was a night owl. While Alex climbed the stairs to her bedroom the night before, Lia went out to the greenhouse to work with her plants.

"I've had breakfast, chatted with our gra—Kitty, and made a pot of coffee. Decaf."

Lia shook her head. "My usual choice is high test, but after that car last night, I'd better play it safe. Let me get a cup, and I'll give you an official tour of the grounds."

"Sounds good, but we'd better hurry before Bree comes looking for me to start another brutal round of lessons."

Lia returned with her cup. "Come on. The pool's this way."

They walked across the patio and around to the side of the house, past a massive growth of rhododendrons, to a swimming area surrounded by stone pavers.

"It's huge," Alex said.

"Great for exercise if you're into that sort of thing, and it's heated." She pointed to a small structure behind them. "The changing rooms and showers are back there."

Alex gazed at the clear blue water and smiled. "I

can't wait to try it." But her words hung in the air. Lia had moved on. Alex had to break into a short run to catch up to her.

Near the edge of the property, Lia stopped and gestured toward a shed with an attached greenhouse. "This is where you'll usually find me. I take care of my special plants here. Sometimes I come in to block out the world. It's my haven."

The tidy structure housed rows of greenery and what looked like laboratory equipment. "What do you do here?" Alex asked.

Lia waved her hand in the air. "This and that. I'm interested in plant biology." She showed Alex some experimental cuttings before they moved on.

They skirted a Victorian gazebo on their way to the river. Alex admired the intricate design: white pillars, lacy edging, and a rooftop cupola.

As they stood on the beach along the Sakonnet River, Lia became more animated. "I love living close to the water. Rhode Island Sound is right around the corner." She did a sudden twirl, holding onto her arms. "It's best during a storm. The water gets whipped into a seething mass, then lashes out and explodes against the rocks." Excitement tinged her voice. "Standing out here with the wind and the crashing waves, I'm part of the elemental drama."

Alex laughed. "You sound like Mother Nature."

"Don't make light of it, Alex. Your perspective will change once you're a Mutt."

They left the rocky shore and headed toward the other side of the property beyond the garage. "You've got to get back before Bree sends out a search party," Lia said, "but I wanted to take you by the house next door.

Have you seen it up close?"

Alex rubbed her hands on her arms. "No, and I'm not sure I want to. It bothers me."

"That's good. It makes all of us uncomfortable."

Lia poked her way through an overgrown path flanked by bushes and trees. Alex kept checking behind her, afraid she might lose her way. They stopped at a metal gate, and Lia stepped aside for Alex to see. The pitted iron and rust of a once regal barrier told the story of age and willful neglect. Trees, weeds, and tall grasses surrounded the structure.

Alex gaped at the sad towering hulk. It must have been majestic in its day. Ordinarily, she'd grieve the slow decay of a grand old home, but sorrow wasn't the emotion claiming her.

An unnatural chill took hold of her as she gazed at the broken windows, sagging gables, and moldy stone walls. The clinging intrusion of the thick, twisted vines gave the appearance of a mythical creature strangling its prey. The canopy of trees shut out the sun and created a shadowy monstrosity that promised trouble to anyone foolish enough to enter.

"Ugly, isn't it?"

Lia's voice in the unnatural silence startled Alex, but she agreed. "It's awful."

"I wish they'd knock it to the ground."

Surprised at the venom in her cousin's voice, Alex whispered, "Couldn't the owner fix it up and sell it?"

"She hasn't told you?"

"What?"

Lia gave a quick peek over her shoulder toward the well-kept lawn of the sprawling Georgian behind them, then paused for a moment as if trying to decide what to say. After a few seconds, she flipped her hand in the air. "Oh, what the hell, you'll find out anyway. After all, you are one of the owners."

Alex swung her head back to the menacing facade whose filthy windows stared at her. "Me?"

Lia began to fidget. "I shouldn't have said anything. We better get back to the house."

Alex reached out to stop her cousin. "Wait a minute. What do you mean I'm one of the owners? What's the story? Give."

"This property belongs to us and the Stuarts who live on the other side, but that's something Aunt Bree will have to explain. It's complicated. Family business."

"In case you haven't noticed, we're related."

Alex experienced a sudden surge of resentment at the woman who took her privileged life for granted, but Lia ignored her and turned to leave. Alex tripped in her hurry to catch up and get away from the unsettling property. Why did that decaying ruin upset everyone?

She recalled her aunts' reaction when she told them about the flash she'd seen. Bree had dragged her back to the office. No more was said about the house. "I knew that woman was hiding something yesterday," she muttered under her breath.

****

Bree sat on the porch, waiting. "Been exploring, have we?"

Lia took advantage of her aunt's focus on her cousin to make her departure.

Alex spared an angry look toward Lia's retreating form, then concentrated on the tips of her sneakers, like a little kid who'd done something wrong. "Good morning, Aunt Bree."

"I'm surprised you wanted to get near that place after the way you reacted to it yesterday. Was it any better up close?"

Anger replaced guilt. She peered straight into Bree's eyes. "Lia said we own that place."

"Is that a question?"

She'd had enough of Bree's bullying and squared her shoulders. "Yes."

Her aunt stood up and let out a deep breath. "Why don't we talk in my office?"

Alex followed her aunt to the front of the house. The warmth of the furnishings in the room reached out to her. The sight of her mother's garden outside the window nudged her conscience. Should she have mentioned going to the house? Ridiculous. No one had told her to stay away from the place. What was the big deal? Why shouldn't she be interested?

Bree's voice broke into her musings. "You must consider it odd I neglected to tell you the history, but, with only eight days left until your birthday, I'd rather work on your skills." She pointed to the sofa. "I'll give you the short version. Please contain your curiosity until next week. Do you think you can do that?"

"It depends."

Bree sat back in her chair, tapped her hands on the arms, and began. "Fair enough. The house was built by a man named Swenson in 1899. He'd hoped to be near the New Yorkers on Bellevue Avenue, but they didn't like the way he'd made his money. No one would sell him property near the privileged few. He settled for land along the Sakonnet River.

"It cost him next to nothing. He used the best materials and furnishings for his home, envisioning, I'm sure, extravagant parties. The result was a lavish twenty-room mansion, but the Newport elite refused to acknowledge him. From all accounts, though, he was happy. I've often wondered how his poor wife and baby fared in that isolation. There wasn't a soul for miles."

"Was he our relative?"

"No." Bree paused, and a pained expression crossed her face. "The poor things didn't have to endure the solitude for very long. A little over a year after they moved into the house, they were all murdered."

Something ugly twisted inside Alex's chest.

"The property sat idle for almost a year. Then in 1904 your great, great grandfather, Teobaldo Brendani, purchased this lot, and the Stuarts acquired the land on the other side. The Swenson property is owned by both families."

Questions churned within her, but before Alex could speak, Bree held up her hand. "You've met Rosemary Stuart. We share ownership and responsibility of the property for the Templars. I can't get into all that now. You'll have to wait. The reason we live here on either side of a crumbling mausoleum is more important. We're here because the house is tainted." For a minute, she closed her eyes then opened them again. "That's not right. The house isn't the real problem. It's the land under it. I don't know how else to put it, Alex. The place is guarded by an evil that has survived for centuries."

Alex had to force her mouth shut. Her aunt's explanation sounded like the beginning of a horror movie. All it needed was eerie music. She swallowed. No wonder her mother had never mentioned her past.

"I'm sorry if I've upset you, but it's part of your heritage. Brendanis and Stuarts have been here to oversee the building for more than a century. We use our powers to guard the land and make sure nothing ever escapes again. We leave it intact because we don't want to disturb whatever dwells below."

Bree stood up as if that was all she had to say. Alex blinked. "That's it? You're going to leave me hanging?"

"There's more, but what I've told you is the basic story. Even Kitty and a few others who've passed help keep the property secure. You're part of that heritage now and, as such, have the responsibility to stand with us to protect innocents from that hellhole. Your mother refused to drag her husband and child into it and left." She leaned toward Alex. "I hope you don't leave before you hear our story. We need you. And, I must admit, we love having a part of CeCe home again."

At that moment, running away seemed like the sensible option. Power, responsibility, and evil? She shivered. Amid her fear, though, Alex had a surprising revelation. Somewhere along the way, she'd become fond of the strange relatives she'd begun to trust. She believed Bree's tough exterior masked a caring heart and didn't want to let her down. "Let's get started."

"Good. We'll work on psychokinesis."

Alex whipped her head up. "Huh?"

"Moving objects with your mind. It's an invaluable skill if you're threatened."

An image of Tony knocking over the chair at the Scottish Pub flashed through her head. Though his actions had frightened her, she'd also been impressed. She coveted that skill, but its acquisition was more difficult than she thought.

A small wooden bird resisted her efforts. Bree insisted she use her gift. "See it as a mass of molecules to be transferred from one spot to another. Then picture yourself gathering the parts and placing them where you want."

As she spoke, her aunt reached out as if to enclose something and then snapped her hand shut.

Bree's explanation didn't make much sense. All Alex saw was a painted piece of wood. A half dozen tries later, Alex stopped her exertions and reached inside herself. She remembered how she'd moved through those people's minds last evening. This time, she probed the bird to find its essence. Bit by bit, the wood transformed. Small groups of shapes appeared. Without thinking, she reached her arm out to grab them. A foolish mistake. She quickly dropped her hand, glad Bree didn't comment. She wondered if she'd ever have the natural ability she'd seen in her cousins. She forced herself to concentrate and created an image of the bundled atoms in her hand. It worked. She had them. But, when she tried to move her prize, the tiny shapes trickled out of her grasp. The result was an odd wobbling of the bird.

Alex stomped her foot. "I give up. It doesn't work. I'm trying, but I can't do it."

"Calm down. It never works the first time. It takes practice. Keep at it."

Instead of screaming, Alex shook off her exasperation and tried again to move the stupid bird.

More than an hour and a few mini tantrums later, she gained control of the elusive molecules and moved them. Thrilled with her success, she punched out her fist. "Yes!" But when she noticed that the carving had moved less than an inch, she slammed her hand on the desk.

"That's it," Bree said. "Time for a break. Let's have lunch."

During the brief respite, Alex brought her lunch outside and once again explored the idea of escape. This time, though, the memory of a man with a knife changed her mind.

****

When they returned to the office, Bree had a new lesson. "Your life might someday depend on your ability to stop or deflect a projectile headed for you." Bree indicated the paperweight on her desk. "I'm going to send this crystal straight at you. Use your powers to keep it away."

The glass piece began to slide toward Alex. Panicked, she yelled, "Wait. How do I stop it?"

"Pay attention. Center your mind on blocking the object. Picture a wall holding it back. Don't let it get by."

Perspiration dripped from her forehead as she clenched her teeth to halt its progress. She imagined a barrier, but the rounded glass ball kept moving. Her muscles ached as she tensed up trying to hold back the glass.

She couldn't keep it up. Her concentration slipped, and the crystal ball went crashing to the floor. Bree's startled face and the crystal shards at their feet were too much, and Alex held her head in her hands. "I'm sorry. I couldn't block it."

Her aunt patted Alex's back. "It's all right. I've pushed you too hard. We've been at this for hours. It's time to stop."

"But your beautiful crystal."

"Don't worry about that. I can get another paperweight. Why don't you go relax for a while, take a swim before dinner?"

Feeling like an untalented wimp, Alex headed to her

room. A swim in the pool sounded good. The idea of leaving her problems behind and cutting through the smooth blue water dissolved some of the stress. As she imagined the sensation, her muscles began to loosen.

****

The cool June air gave Alex pause. She worried it might be a little nippy for swimming but hoped the heated pool would make up for that. After testing the temperature with her toe, she dove in. The liquid resistance of the warm water helped to work out all her aggravations. She swam a few laps and then ducked and rolled in weightless bliss, laughing like a child without a care.

"Enjoying yourself?"

Alex was so startled she swallowed some water and started coughing.

"Whoa. Everything okay? You going to make it?"

She swam to the side of the pool and looked up at the man who'd disturbed her. She had to squint in the sun. His eyes hid behind an expensive pair of sunglasses, but he had a great big grin on his face, apparently enjoying her predicament.

She was embarrassed and aware of her skimpy bikini. "Who are you?"

He squatted down to her level. "We met the other night. Don't you remember? Nick?"

"The bartender?"

He looked like he wanted to laugh. "Right, the bartender."

Furious at being caught acting like a child, she remembered her attempted flirtation with him on Friday night. Wishing he'd take that grin off his face, she used her frostiest voice. "What are you doing here?"

"I'm visiting."

Alex swam to the end of the pool intending to dry off and cover up. When she got there, however, Nick met her, his eyes lingering on her practically naked body. His frank appraisal sent heat through her. When he held her towel out to her, she snatched it away with a grudging, "Thanks."

"If I'd known the pool would be occupied, I'd have brought my suit."

He wanted a reaction from her, and she tried, without success, to bite her tongue. "Maybe your *friend*, Tony, will lend you one."

She'd put a not-so-subtle emphasis on the word, friend.

That didn't bother Nick, though. "Wouldn't be any fun if there's no one to swim with."

Alex wrapped the soft white towel a little tighter around her. The wind was cool on her wet body. With a slight toss of her head, she strode toward the changing area. She'd had enough swimming for one day.

Nick was still there when she came out, but he wasn't alone. He and Aunt Bree sat at a table in deep conversation. They didn't notice her until she started to walk by.

"Alex."

"Hi, Aunt Bree."

"Did you enjoy your swim?"

Alex sent a quick look at Nick. Damn, he was still smiling. "The water was wonderful."

Her aunt patted the seat next to her. "Come, sit for a minute. I believe you know Nick."

"We've met."

"Good. I wondered if you might like to go into town

105

tomorrow and see about some freelance writing. Nick's acquainted with a lot of the people you need to meet. I've asked him to escort you."

Anger surged, and she could feel her eyes narrow as she looked from her aunt to Nick. Sure, he knew them. He probably served them all at the pub. How had this man conned her aunt, and what was his agenda?

She softened her voice and said, "That's awfully nice of Nick."

He'd taken off his sunglasses, and his blue eyes danced as he spoke. "No problem. It's the least I can do for the family."

Alex shot him a glare. The man was enjoying her discomfort. "I wouldn't think of putting you out. I'm sure I'll have no trouble contacting the right people."

Bree's eyebrows shot up at her niece's tone of voice. "Alex, dear, I'd feel much better if Nick accompanied you. After that car the other night, I'm concerned."

Nick sat up and dropped the grin. "What car?"

Alex jumped in. "Nothing for you to worry about." She hoped her aunt wouldn't say anymore. No dice. Bree blabbed the whole story.

When she finished, Nick reacted as if he had the right to be worried. "What do you remember about the car?"

Alex didn't try to disguise her anger. "Nothing, I was too busy leaping out of the way."

"Nice try. What do you remember?"

Alex stopped and looked at Nick. Really looked. His aura was neutral, and now that she paid attention, she sensed an underlying power. He'd caught her lie. "Who are you?"

Bree put her hand on Alex's arm. "Oh Alex, I'm

sorry. I thought you knew."

Nick, on the receiving end of a nasty glare from Bree, looked away.

"He's Rosemary's grandson and like an adopted child to us." She pursed her lips in his direction. "And he's also a terrible tease. Now, Alex, what aren't you telling us? Nick's very good at detecting lies."

Alex had to swallow her anger at the man's deception. Glaring at him, she said, "It's not much. The car was black, going way too fast for the area, and it had tinted windows."

Nick leaned his arms on the table. "That's it?"

Alex paused.

"What else?" he persisted. "Any small detail might help."

"As the car passed by, I detected a sense of hatred. I'm not sure where the emotion was aimed."

Nick frowned at Bree. "I agree with you. It's disturbing."

He pushed back his chair and glanced at Alex. "I'll pick you up tomorrow at ten."

As he strode off, Alex's gaze wandered after her arrogant neighbor. Suppressing a satisfied sigh, she smiled. Broad shoulders, well-muscled thighs, and a very nice butt. A tingle of excitement replaced her anger. Tomorrow should prove interesting.

Chapter Thirteen

Alex checked the bedroom mirror one more time, smoothed her skirt, and fiddled with her hair. *Did it say professional?*

With a frown at her reflection, she refused to acknowledge that her anxiety might have anything to do with Nick Stuart, their irritating neighbor. "He won't care what I look like." After a final flick of her hair, she went downstairs.

In the quiet of the kitchen, she finished her breakfast and reflected on her new normal. This afternoon she'd be practicing psychic skills with her aunt while communicating through telepathy. Hard to believe that a short time ago she'd been fired and worried about finding an affordable place to live. Now, ten days later, she was living on the opposite coast, part of a large, influential family, and her future would not include financial worries.

Since she'd arrived in Newport, she'd unlocked awesome powers. On the other hand, she also owned part of a mansion that apparently housed an ancient horror. For a minute, she worried if these new psychic powers were worth the danger they seemed to generate.

"Hey, you ready?"

Damn! There he was. The aggravating man looked wonderful. Even as he pushed her buttons, she could appreciate the tousled black hair over magnetic blue eyes, his strong chin, and his tight jeans. She looked at the clock. "You're early."

"I made an appointment for ten a.m. with a friend of mine who works for a local magazine."

Ooh. She could have blown her whole first impression. "You said you'd pick me up at ten, not make an appointment for that time. What if I hadn't been ready?"

As his gaze raked over her, a slow grin crossed his face. "You look ready enough to me."

While she fumed, her aunts walked in. She opened her mouth to say she'd be back later, but they ignored her to speak to Nick. The way they treated him made her bristle even more. The man could do no wrong in their eyes. She grabbed her portfolio and followed the golden boy outside.

His ride surprised her. As she curled into the soft leather of the high-end red sportscar, a quick peek at his face told her he expected adulation. Still ticked off that he'd let her believe he was a casual pal of Tony's, she couldn't resist a taunt. "Kind of an expensive car for a bartender."

He grinned. "I get good tips."

Before Alex had the chance to answer, Nick stepped on the gas and her head whipped back against the headrest. In a juvenile attempt to impress, he laid rubber down the driveway. Alex wondered how often he had to buy new tires.

She'd wanted to make a good first impression with the magazine staff today, but riding in a convertible with the top down didn't bode well for her image. Despite all attempts to hold it in place, by the time they reached the office, her hair resembled a fright wig.

She pulled down the visor mirror and moaned. "Look at this. It's a mess."

"It doesn't look so bad. I'll tell him I had the top down. Let's go."

Alex stayed seated as she tried to drag her fingers through the bird's nest. Nick bounced around tapping his finger against the door, but Alex paid no attention until she was finished. She ignored his extended hand and pulled herself up from the seat.

"Fine," he said. "Have it your way. You missed a spot in the back."

Alex cursed him under her breath as she tried to catch up while scrambling to smooth her unruly hair.

The receptionist asked them to have a seat. Nick grabbed a magazine while Alex continued poking at her snarls.

When a guy with wavy blond hair accentuated by a deep tan walked toward them a few minutes later, Alex sat up straight. His blue-striped short-sleeve shirt showed off strong arms, and snug-fitting khaki slacks emphasized his well-muscled legs. She figured he must work out. He looked like he belonged on the cover of his own magazine. "You must be Nick and Alex," he said. "I'm Hunter Davis."

As everyone shook hands, Hunter spoke to Nick. "Your friend, Doug, wanted me to apologize for him. He had pressing business issues and asked me to step in."

Alex saw annoyance cross Nick's face before he pulled out his *good ole boy* voice. "Hey, no problem. I didn't give Doug much of a heads-up."

When Hunter started to lead Alex to his office, Nick said, "So, Hunter, I haven't seen you around town. You new here?"

Hunter turned. "As a matter of fact, I am. I moved up here from Florida." He turned his back on Nick and smiled at Alex. "I couldn't take another one of those hot summers."

Alex liked the singular attention, his making her feel welcome as if she were an important client.

They entered a neat black and chrome office. The few items on his desk sat in perfect order, and the top of his waist-high bookcase held three tightly aligned piles of paper.

Once they were seated, Hunter steepled his fingers and got right to the point. "I understand you're interested in writing for us."

His gaze traveled from her face to her crisp, sleeveless navy blouse, down to the white skirt that almost reached her crossed knee and ended with the thin red straps covering the foot she tried to keep quiet. The look in his eyes said he liked what he saw.

"As a freelancer, I'm always looking for new markets, and since I live here now, I'd like to acquire local clients." Alex handed him her portfolio. "I've had articles published in magazines, newspapers, and online. I'm also a contributor to a few websites." She didn't mention that had been over a year ago.

While Hunter leafed through the folder, Alex had a chance to study him. He had an interesting face, strong chin, full lips, a Roman nose, long lashes, and brown eyes. Most blonds had blue eyes.

When a few more minutes passed, Alex worried that he might not like her work. Maybe, she should peek into his mind. A picture of her Aunt Bree's face flashed in front of her, and she gave a little shiver. No. She'd never misuse her powers, no matter how much she wanted to.

He leaned back and perused the information. When he sat up and put the folio on his desk, he was all business. "These are good. I like your writing style. It would fit in well with our magazine. Did you have any specific plans for pieces you'd like to submit?"

Alex began to outline a couple of ideas she'd had. While she elaborated, Hunter came around to lean against his desk in front of her. When she finished, he beamed. "It sounds like you have the skills we want. I'd enjoy having you as one of my writers. You'd report directly to me. I'm sure we can work well together."

Alex strove for a professional demeanor. "That sounds perfect."

When he walked Alex out to the reception area, he said, "We should discuss this further over lunch."

His offer surprised her, but before she could respond, Nick interrupted. "I couldn't help overhearing. I'm afraid Alex is busy for lunch today."

Alex shot daggers at him but pulled her features into a pleasant smile for Hunter whose calculating glance seemed to be assessing Nick. Ignoring Mr. Nick Stuart, she leaned toward Hunter. "I'd love to discuss this further with you. Perhaps tomorrow?"

Hunter's eyes lit up. "Tomorrow for lunch it is. I'll pick you up."

Alex gave him the address, and he shook her hand, holding it longer than necessary. A warm flush suffused her body as she followed Nick out of the office.

****

After they got in the car, Alex let Nick know what she thought of his macho control. "In the future, I'd appreciate it if you didn't make decisions for me. I'm capable of making my own choices."

Nick slammed the car into gear. "Look, Bree asked me to show you around the town to get you acclimated. I planned to do that, have lunch, then take you home. If you'd rather go home now, that's fine."

Alex didn't want to miss out on a chance to see more of Newport, and now that she didn't care what she looked like, she could enjoy the convertible and the warm wind in her face. "Oh no. After you canceled Hunter's lunch plans? You owe me."

He mumbled something about having a talk with his editor friend and peeled out of the parking lot.

Alex ignored Nick's childish antics and continued to ruminate about Hunter. What luck. Not only did he appreciate her work, but he'd flirted with her. She recalled how well those slacks hugged his hips and long legs. She wouldn't mind getting to know him better.

As part of the tour, Nick drove the length of Aquidneck Island. Sounding like a travel guide, he gave her a geographical picture of the area. "The Sakonnet River flows along the east side, and Narragansett Bay hugs the west."

Alex delighted in panoramic glimpses of the deep blue waters of the bay.

After Nick found a parking spot downtown, he led them to familiar territory, the wharf where she and Lia had dined. Nick gave a brief description of Newport's history along the way. "Newport was quite the Navy town in its day."

Alex, here for the third time, wanted to window shop. Fascinated by the colorful merchandise, she didn't notice Nick stop until she barreled into him. She was so embarrassed, she wanted to kick herself. "Sorry."

His amused look grated on her as he said, "I know

there's a lot to see, but we don't have time right now. Bree will be expecting us back after lunch."

"Right." At the sound of her aunt's name, her enthusiasm died.

Nick pointed to a roped-off area of the dock that had tables and a bar. "Would you like to eat outside?"

Her spirits lifted again. "Sounds good to me."

While they waited for their food, Nick entertained her with stories of Goat Island on the other side of Newport Harbor. "You see the fancy hotel?"

She nodded.

"That was the station where our modern-day torpedo was perfected."

Alex managed to look impressed, although she didn't care much about weapons. "I've never seen so many boats together at one time."

Nick gave a short laugh. "I don't suppose you see that in Phoenix."

"What we have there is a natural beauty that leaves a mark on your soul. I miss it every day."

Nick covered Alex's hand. "I'm sorry you had to lose your home as well as your mother."

The sunlight hitting Nick's eyes gave them a deep-blue glow, and a lock of his dark hair tumbled over his forehead. She stared at his lips which, for once, weren't grinning. Nick, sitting there without his teasing and take-over attitude, almost took her breath away. Deeply touched, she whispered, "Thank you."

"Hey Alex, Nick." Tony ambled toward them. "I heard you were having lunch. Figured you'd be here. Have you ordered yet? I'll join you."

The mood was broken, and Nick became his old smart-ass self. "Yo, bro, the jailer let you out?"

Tony pulled out a chair and sat down. "I waited until he had his back turned and made my escape."

"Good for you."

"Hey, Cuz, looking good. You two doing the tourist thing?"

She told Tony about their morning. "I'll be with Bree this afternoon."

He grimaced. "Good luck with that. She's a worse taskmaster than my father. I don't envy you."

Tony left first. In the short time he'd been with them, he'd consumed three drinks. When he left, his gait was unsteady. Alex remembered the other night. "Does he have to drive back to work?"

Nick shook his head. "They have an office down the street." He said no more, but Alex noticed the worry in his eyes.

On the way home, he took a detour to show Alex the ten-mile drive. She couldn't help the "oohs" and "ahs" that escaped each time they'd round another bend. Her excitement centered not on the impressive homes, but on the spectacular coastal landscape that surrounded them. Houses clung to tall cliffs that rose from the ocean. Small inlets worked their way around massive boulders leading to placid bits of blue water. With the sun kissing the waves in flashing sparks, the tang of salt in the air, and the wind's greedy tentacles snatching at her hair, Alex felt invincible.

The afternoon with Nick had been so much fun, beginning with lunch on the waterfront and ending with an exhilarating convertible ride along Newport's amazing coastline. After such a heady experience, the trip along the Brendani driveway was anticlimactic. She was a little sad when they pulled up in front of the house.

He parked the car, looked over at Alex, and burst out laughing.

Resentment bubbled up again. "What?"

He let out another whoop. "Your hair."

Alex slammed down the visor and stared into the mirror, horrified at the vision before her. Clown-like spikes rose from her head. It looked like she'd touched a live wire. Then the humor of the situation sank in, and she began to laugh. If she'd tried, she couldn't have made her hair look more ridiculous. As her laughter subsided, she remembered something else that cracked her up. In between giggles, she said, "Should I tell Aunt Bree this is what happened when I plugged into my powers?"

Nick burst into laughter again while Alex had tears in her eyes as she pictured her stern aunt's reaction. She attempted to pull her hair back into place while Nick got out to open her door. With a disarming grin, he said, "If I were you, I'd sneak in and do a quick repair job before you see Bree."

Alex couldn't remember when she'd had such a good laugh. "Thanks, Nick. That was fun."

He tipped his finger against his own mussed-up hair in a small salute. "Glad to have been of service."

****

Bree's voice invaded her mind as Alex stood in the bathroom trying to fix her hair. Startled, she knocked the hot dryer against her head. "Ow!" Practicing telepathy with her aunt was one thing; using it to communicate was a different story.

When Alex didn't answer right away, Bree resent her invitation for Alex to join her in her office.

Sorry, Aunt Bree. I'll be there as soon as I dry my hair.

Okay!

All of a sudden, she was embarrassed to be standing naked in the bathroom and wrapped herself in a towel. She was pretty sure her aunt couldn't see her, but in this house, she figured anything was possible.

Fifteen minutes later, with her hair still damp, Alex sat in Bree's office.

"How did your appointment go this morning?"

When Alex told her about Hunter Davis, Bree tilted her head. "I thought Nicky's friend's name was Doug?"

"He was busy. I'm going to lunch with Hunter tomorrow to discuss my writing."

"What did Nicky say about that?"

Alex stiffened at Bree's words. "Why should he have anything to say?"

Bree softened her tone. "Sorry, Alex. I worry about you. Your emotions have undergone tremendous upheavals in the last few months. I was hoping Nicky's clear head would help you better assess situations."

Alex accepted the explanation but hated being treated like a child. "He didn't seem too keen on the idea, but he didn't say I shouldn't go. For crying out loud, Hunter has a responsible job at the magazine. We're going to lunch, not some secret rendezvous."

Bree's expression said that she didn't like the idea any more than Nick had, but she conceded, "Fine. Make sure you're careful. Remember if you get into any trouble, use telepathy to call us for help. It's too close to your birthday to take any chances."

"What chances?"

Bree's eyes narrowed as she placed her hands on her hips. "Alex. Pay attention. I told you unscrupulous people seek to take control of you. We can't let that happen. You're too important. You must be vigilant. Don't accept anyone you don't know. Now let's begin the practice."

Alex said nothing but felt less like a family member and more like an asset to be used for her talents.

They worked on moving objects, then blocking their movement until almost six in the evening. It took her a mere thirty-five minutes to move the bird. Blocking Bree's new brass paperweight, however, still needed a little work.

Although she'd gotten more comfortable with her emerging skills, she still considered herself a worker bee whose worth was what it could contribute to the hive. She wondered how much more skillful she'd be after her birthday and grinned. Seven more days!

Chapter Fourteen

The next morning, she couldn't stop smiling. She had a lunch date with Hunter.

Lia caught up with her downstairs and did everything but beg her to take a picture of Hunter on her cell and send it to her. "Or better yet, let me know where you'll be lunching."

Alex had no intention of sharing Hunter with her cousin. He was gorgeous and he appreciated her talent. A heat wave had descended on Newport. The sultry air lay heavy around Alex as she headed to the labyrinth to visit her grandmother.

Good morning, Alex. Where have you been?

"Sorry, Kitty. With so many new people and places, time got away from me." As Alex spoke, she looked around, hoping no one could see her talking to the air.

Laughter tinged Kitty's voice. *You can speak to me through telepathy.*

Alex perked up. *That's right. I forgot.*

Met a young man, I hear.

Alex hugged herself. *I'm having lunch with him today.*

Bring him in here so I can meet him.

Alex gasped and forgot to use telepathy. "I can't have him meet a ghost. He'll think I'm crazy."

Oh, don't be dense. I won't talk to him. I just want to see him up close.

The absurdity of dragging a potential boyfriend out here so her grandmother's ghost could give her approval made Alex smile. *I'll do that, Grandmother.*

Kitty.

Okay, Kitty. If he ever visits, I'll have him walk the labyrinth with me. I'll see you later.

I expect to see you soon, young lady.

Yes, Gr...Kitty.

On her way out of the labyrinth, Alex met Lia coming in. "Kitty's got you trained now?"

"She makes me feel guilty if I don't visit her."

Lia's eyes held a mischievous glint. "Ready for your lunch with your handsome editor?"

A little giggle slipped out. "He is so easy on the eyes."

"Well, have fun."

Alex focused her mind on an image of Hunter and forgot where she was. She stepped backward.

"Look out!" Lia grabbed for her but not in time. Alex had stepped across the stones marking the swirling path. "Now you've done it."

"Done what?"

Lia pointed to the ground. "Crossed over the rock-lined boundary and pissed off the gremlins who guard it. You better be very careful. They'll be after you for the next twenty-four hours."

Alex gave a half-hearted laugh. "Oh, so now I'll have itty bitty munchkins chasing me around?"

"It isn't funny. You won't be able to see them, but they'll make your life miserable. You might want to cancel your date this afternoon."

"Oh, come on."

"Okay. Don't say I didn't warn you."

On her way back to the house, Alex wondered about Lia's warning. She'd read stories about superstitions associated with labyrinths, but those were old myths. Sure, this labyrinth did seem to have a little bit of magic, but it couldn't be that dangerous.

As she strode toward the house, swinging her hands by her side, she brushed against a bush and cut herself on a thorn. "Ouch." Blood began to seep from the scratch. Before she could worry about that, she stumbled and fell, crying out as her knee hit the dirt.

"Oh, my God." She stood up and peered all around her and then at her feet. Nothing. Not a gremlin in sight, although what the little monsters looked like, she had no idea. Taking another nervous scan, she wiped off the dirt and headed back to the house, grateful there were no other accidents. With a relieved breath, she opened the door and fell into the kitchen.

"My, my, Alexandra, a little clumsy this morning?"

She jumped up and brushed her knees. "What are you doing here?"

Nick sat at the kitchen table, legs sprawled out in front of him with a cup of coffee in his hand. He tilted his head, blue eyes sparkling, and raised his eyebrows. "And in a nasty mood."

Alex wanted to throw something at him. She'd been all set to have a quiet breakfast. Now she'd have to put up with Nick's smart mouth. "If you must know, I strayed across the labyrinth border. You might want to stay away from me today."

Nick's forehead wrinkled as he sat up. "That's a potent place. I'd be careful if I were you."

"No kidding."

While reaching for a muffin, Alex poured herself a

cup of decaf from the designated carafe. Almost instantly, hot coffee spilled over her hand. "Ow. Damn."

Nick's blue eyes held laughter, and he had a silly grin on his face that emphasized the slight cleft in his chin. "Maybe you'd better go back to bed."

Lia walked in the back door as Alex was running water over the burn. "Problems?" She looked at the reddening spot and shook her head. "Here, let me fix this." She took Alex's hand in hers.

A comforting warmth soothed Alex's pain. When she looked down, the skin was clear. "That's amazing. Thank you." Alex hated to admit it, but she was going to have to cancel her date with Hunter. She didn't want to hurt herself or endanger Hunter, but more than anything, she didn't want to look like a dippy klutz.

After she announced her decision, Nick looked way too pleased, so she elected to make her call to Hunter from the den where she wouldn't have an audience.

"Well, if it isn't my favorite writer." Hunter's voice reminded her of the smooth flow of creamy hot fudge.

Fiery sparks spread through her belly. "Isn't that a coincidence? You happen to be my favorite editor." She hated to destroy this intimate moment, but she couldn't let Hunter see her like this. Damn gremlins. "I'm afraid I have to cancel our lunch today."

"Oh, no."

The disappointment in his voice delighted her. She hoped it didn't show in her response. "I'm sorry. I've come down with a bug. I'm sure it's temporary."

"That's too bad, Alex. I had a little surprise planned for us. We'll have to postpone it. You want to try for tomorrow?"

Nerves had her pacing around the room. "Tomorrow

sounds fine. Oh!" She tumbled butt-first over the ottoman.

The crash and her cry brought Nick from the other room. "Are you all right?"

As Nick started over to help her, she pulled herself off the floor in a flood of embarrassment. She'd completely forgotten about the phone in her hand until she heard Hunter's voice.

"Alex, what's going on?"

"Sorry, Hunter, I tripped." She was mortified and wanted to get off the phone as soon as possible. "Tomorrow for lunch would be perfect. Thanks so much for understanding. Bye."

The blue in Nick's eyes deepened as he crossed his arms and leaned against the door frame, seeming to enjoy her predicament.

Attempting to recapture some dignity, Alex sniped, "I still don't understand why you're here."

Nick pulled a sorrowful face. "Well, ma'am, the Brendanis graciously let me visit their home as long as I use the back door."

"Funny. Don't you ever work?"

"Sometimes."

They were interrupted by Aunt Bree. "Oh, there you are, Alex. I asked Nick to come over and help you with your powers. You'll need to get a handle on them before Monday." She turned to Nick. "Thank you so much, Nicky."

He leaned over and kissed her cheek. "I'm here for you any time you need me, Aunty, but I don't think today will be a good day to work with Alexandra."

At the sound of her given name, Alex grimaced. Everything he said seemed to grate on her nerves. And what was that with his calling Bree, Aunty? They weren't related.

Surprise showed on Bree's face. "Why? What's happened?"

Nick grinned at Alex before turning back to Bree. "Seems she crossed over a labyrinth boundary this morning."

Bree reached out to Alex, putting a hand on her arm. "That's not good. Those gremlins can be nasty. You'd best be very careful."

Nick barked out a short laugh. "She's already found that out."

Bree's hand went to her hip as she glared at Nick. "Seems to me that someone else I know didn't take the power of the gremlins seriously."

Nick stopped laughing, contemplated the carpet, and rubbed his arm as Bree continued. "I remember a ten-year-old who laughed at the gremlins and jumped over the boundary to see what would happen." She turned to Alex. "He wound up with a broken arm."

Alex's expression lightened, and she sent a smirk Nick's way. She could have kissed Bree. "Sounds like a good day for a swim."

Bree pursed her lips in a worried frown. "You'd better go with her, Nicky, to make sure she doesn't drown."

****

Nick had already begun to swim by the time Alex arrived at the pool. Somehow, she'd missed the open changing-room door, banged into it, and landed on the ground. Her poor knees were a patchwork of scabs.

At the pool, Alex stared at Nick whose strong quick strokes propelled him through the water. She remembered the feel of those arms around her when they danced on Friday night and watched fascinated as muscles rippled along his back.

"Are you going to stand there all day and watch, or are you going to join me?"

Quick heat suffused Alex's face. The man was so irritating. She took off her robe, dove in, and tried to ignore him as she swam her first lap. At one point, however, when his voice popped into her head, she sucked in a breath along with pool water and started to choke.

Alexandra? Are you all right?

Seconds later, strong arms wrapped around her, and she was pulled to safety. "Okay, just breathe."

She tried to wrestle away from him and hurled an angry accusation. "You entered my mind."

"I wasn't trying to read your thoughts. I was speaking to you through telepathy. We all do that."

Her heart stilled for a moment. "Are you saying you could see what I'm thinking if you wanted to?"

He shrugged. "If I tried. You haven't set up a shield yet."

"Bree said we'd have to wait until I got a handle on my powers." Alex wanted the protection now. She didn't want anyone in her head. Maybe she could con Nick into assisting her. She hated to ask him for a favor. He was so full of himself. "Nick?"

"Yes?"

She paused, inhaled, then spit it out. "Would you help me with my shield, today?"

He looked a little surprised. "If that's what you want, I'd be happy to work with you."

The realization he still had his arms around her

surprised and pleased her. *Oh, damn!* She hoped he couldn't see that. "I'd like to get out of the water, please."

He let her go. She pulled on her robe and sat on the chaise. Unfortunately, she missed the middle, hit the edge, and tumbled to the ground. Furious, she looked up at the hand he extended. "You'd better not laugh."

He didn't make a sound, but his eyes lit up, and his lips kept twitching.

Once settled, with the sun warming her exposed skin, Alex looked at Nick. In a grudging tone, she said, "Thank you for doing this for me."

He raised one brow. "Nicely put. You're welcome."

She had to bite her lips to keep from telling him to go to hell.

"After a while, securing your shield will be automatic. Until you get used to it, you'll have to practice every day, all day long. Once you learn, it might be helpful if you asked those around you with the gift to try to read your mind whenever they're in your presence."

She sat up straight. "How many others can do that?"

"Bree, my grandmother, and me. You can ask any of us to help you."

Telepathy was one thing, but she didn't want people inside her mind. Alex started to object, but a dive-bombing bee made a swipe at her head.

She ducked, and her attacker disappeared. When she looked over at Nick, she cringed. His narrowed eyes and taut lips scared her. "What's wrong?"

"Sorry." He was back to his smiling self. "I had to persuade that bee to move along. He was all set to sting you. I'm sure he was sent by the labyrinth imps."

She peered at him through her eyelashes. "You can

talk to bees?"

Nick raised an eyebrow and spoke in an old-time villainy voice. "Ah, my dear Alexandra, I can be very persuasive."

"Why are there gremlins in the labyrinth?"

"My mother told me they were there to keep children from playing in the sacred circles."

"Couldn't you persuade them to leave me alone?"

"Sorry. I can't influence what I can't see."

"Why do I have to let people peer into my mind?"

"It's the only way to recognize an intrusion," he said. "You'll get a crawling sensation that gives you an instant alert; then, you can strengthen your shields to protect yourself."

They spent the rest of the morning working on Alex's shields. She'd decided to use a wall. Most of the Clan kept their shield in place all the time rather than build it when there was trouble. Alex had to be content with learning to construct it one rock at a time.

Nick received her permission to try and read her mind. She immediately envisioned a heavy barrier built of rocks. "There!" she said.

By that time, though, Nick had breached her defenses. He said, "You can't just imagine it. You have to build it. See the rocks fitting into place."

She tried again, but he was faster. "You need to make it like that." He snapped his fingers.

After working on it for a while, she began to improve. With the next intrusion, she pictured the construction moving much faster. She wasn't quick enough to keep Nick out, but he congratulated her on her progress and gave suggestions on how to increase her speed.

They stopped when it was time for lunch and headed back to the house. Nick caught Alex twice before her feet became tangled in small vines. She took extra care stepping into the kitchen. When she turned for Nick's approval, her blouse caught on the door handle and ripped. He broke out in a shout of laughter that made her want to scream.

Franki checked out the ruined blouse. "Don't let it bother you, Alex. Those gremlins love listening to your anger."

Aunt Bree poured her an iced tea. "Nick tells us that you've done well with your shields. That's wonderful. Maybe later you'd let us try to probe?" The look Alex turned on her must have been piteous because Bree relented. "Of course, you're tired. We'll wait until you're feeling up to it."

A fly had been headed for Alex as she opened her mouth to sip her tea. Before she could react, it stopped, turned around, and flew away.

She grinned. "Thanks, Nick."

"My pleasure, Alexandra."

Franki and Bree exchanged quizzical glances.

****

After lunch, Nick suggested he take Alex on another tour of Newport. This way she could familiarize herself with the general layout and rest from the morning's efforts, while he tried to keep her safe from troublesome tormentors.

Since Nick seemed genuinely concerned for her welfare, she accepted. She put her hair up in a ponytail, threw on a red jersey and white shorts, and met him in the driveway. Although she'd only lost her balance once as she was dressing, she'd broken her fingernail when she hit the wall.

As the car pulled away from the house, she leaned back and let the wind take her hair. With a suppressed grin, she looked over at Nick. "This car is so impractical." She paused until he frowned, and then she laughed. "But it is so much fun."

There it was. Nick's smile. She loved how it deepened the little dent in his chin and lit up his face. Sometime during the morning, Alex had accepted that he was one of the good guys. She'd never tell him, though. Then a familiar squiggle slid through her mind. That bastard! Too late, she put up her shields.

"So, you think I'm a good guy?"

"Not anymore."

He laughed and drove a little faster.

During the trip, Nick pointed out some of Newport's historic spots, beginning on Bellevue Avenue. "Over on the left, you'll see the Newport Art Museum. They have a couple of Franki's paintings. On the right is Touro Park. You see that stone tower? It's got quite a history and mysterious origins. Some claims have it as old as 1004 AD. Ask Bree to tell you about it sometime. Our ancestors built it."

Alex missed the next few sights, wondering what ancestors they had in common. As they passed the church where John Kennedy and Jacqueline Bouvier were married, she asked him about the tower. "What did you mean by our ancestors?"

"More people are coming around to the realization that the Knights Templar, our ancestors, built what they call the Old Stone Mill."

"Wait a minute. Are you and I related?"

Nick leered at her. "Worried about incest?"

She hit his shoulder. "Stop it. I'd just like to figure out who I am."

A few seconds went by before he answered. "Don't worry. We're not relatives. I'm from the Scots side, and you're from the Italian." He looked at his watch. "Do you mind if I stop at the club for a minute?"

Alex remembered that was where he worked. "Fine with me."

Nick held Alex's arm as she tripped her way up the sidewalk to the front entry of the Scottish Pub. The inside was cool and dark. A few people sat at the bar.

"How's it going, Ted?"

"No problems, Mr. Stuart."

"Good."

Nick started to lead Alex behind the bar, but she held back. Something seemed off. "Why did he call you Mr. Stuart?"

"That's my name?"

"I know that but . . ."

They stood before a door, and he pulled out a key to unlock it. When he ushered her into a fancy office, she bristled. He'd lied to her again. The tone of her voice could have frozen water. "I suppose you're the owner?"

Nick seemed at a surprising loss for words. Alex raised one hand and began ticking off on her fingers. "Let's see. First, you tell me you're a bartender, but you're not. Then you tell me you're a friend of Tony, and you turn out to be part of the Clan. Now, I find out you own the club?"

He slipped his hands into his pockets, glanced at the floor, and cleared his throat. "I do bartend some nights."

Alex rolled her eyes.

"I guess I should have told you."

"Ya think?"

"Look, Alexandra, you were a stranger to me, and I like my privacy."

"Stop calling me that. My name is Alex."

"Your name is Alexandra."

Alex turned to leave, caught her foot, and fell against his bookcase, knocking something fragile to the floor. It broke into dozens of pieces, and Alex fell right on top of them. She cried out as she felt the glass tear into her.

Nick rushed over to her. "Uh-oh. This doesn't look good."

Sharp pain radiated up from both butt and thigh. "It hurts like hell. I'd like to get my hands on those rotten gremlins. When I get my powers, they'll be first on my list."

"Sorry, Alexandra, that's not the way it works. You're not allowed to use your powers to do harm, only for protection." Nick had been looking through his desk and came back with bandages. "Hold still while I take these out."

Alex let out a loud yelp.

"Quiet. My staff will think I'm hurting you."

"You are."

"Don't move. There's a lot of blood. A couple of these are deep. I can slow the bleeding, but we need Lia." He paused. "She'll be here in a few minutes. The hotel is down the street."

Lia's voice rang out in Alex's mind. *Don't worry, Alex, I'm on my way.*

Her vision blurred, and she was a little unsteady. She wanted to sit down, but the placement of the cuts prevented that.

"Here, lean on me."

She flashed him a nasty look.

"I'm sorry I didn't tell you the truth. I figured Lia or Tony would say something, and then, when I stopped by the pool, you were so cute trying to protect your family."

"Cute! For all I knew, you were some kind of scam artist. Not funny."

A few minutes later, the uncomfortable silence was broken by Lia's arrival. "Okay, honey, let me see." Her cousin's touch brought warmth and then a lessening of pain as she spoke to Nick. "Good job staunching the blood." After about fifteen minutes, Lia patted Alex's shoulder. "Better?"

"Much better. Thanks again."

A quick grin. "I'll bet you'll never cross a labyrinth border again."

"You've got that right."

"The cuts will be a little tender for the next day or so. Nick, you ought to get her home where she can stay out of trouble, and she needs to get out of those bloody shorts. I'm going to rest here for a minute and then get back to work. Lucky, the hotel's not far."

Alex leaned over her cousin. "You don't look well."

A slight chuckle escaped. "I'll be good in a minute. Sometimes the healing depletes my strength. No big deal."

Nick took Alex's arm. "Come on. Lia's fine, and I want to get you back before anything else happens."

On the ride home, Nick was careful to avoid bumps in the road. Though her pain had lessened, Alex was grateful for his consideration. When he pulled up in front of the house and tried to help her out of the car, she pulled away, saying, "I can make it," and then smacked her hand against the car door.

"Oh yeah, you're doing great." Nick took her arm and guided her into the house. When he placed her in Bree's hands, he said, "She's not safe anywhere."

"If you didn't have breakable things all around your office . . ."

He raised an eyebrow and smirked. "Goodbye, Alexandra."

As he turned to leave, she wondered how someone who looked so good could be so mean. When the telltale twisting in her head alerted her, she hurried to put up her shield. A shout of laughter and a wink told her she'd been too late.

Chapter Fifteen

One of the aunts stayed with her for the rest of the day. Lia had the evening shift.

Alex used their time for questions. "What was it like, growing up knowing you and everyone around you were special?"

"I didn't realize I was different until I went to school. My mother told me ours was a unique family secret. If I ever told anyone, she'd find out, and I'd lose my gifts forever. Of course, she also used a binding spell to ensure I couldn't use my abilities."

"Like what my mother did to me?"

Lia laughed. "Nothing that strong. Mom's spells had a short lifespan. I do remember a girl hurt herself at recess. I told her if I had the right herbs, I could fix her. She made fun of me. That's the first time I wondered if I might be different."

"You must have been lonely."

"You'd think so, but no. Tony and Nick were always there. They were pretty good to me when they weren't teasing. The worst was the day I followed them to the Convent House. We weren't supposed to go anywhere near it, but I wasn't afraid with the boys around. When I got there, they had disappeared, but I heard a low moaning sound. The gate wasn't locked then, and I squeezed inside and whispered Tony's name. The weird sound came again and scared me. I spun around to take off, and Nick leaped out of the bushes with a yell. I screamed and ran all the way home."

"He's so mean."

Lia snorted. "It worked better than any punishment. I never went there again."

Alex rubbed her arms. "That place makes my skin crawl. Why do you call it the Convent House?"

"A group of German nuns built their convent there, right next to the Templar's burial spot."

"We have ancestors buried there?"

"Not people, treasure."

Alex snapped her head up. "There's treasure?"

Lia laughed. "Calm down. Didn't Bree tell you?"

Alex narrowed her eyes as she punched her pillow. "No. But she told me something evil hides inside that place."

Lia's amusement died. "That's true. The Templars left a guardian. Some kind of demon. We're here to keep it from getting loose."

No way. Alex balked at the word *demon*. Her cousin was trying to scare her. "What? Like one of those TV shows about teenage vampire slayers?"

This time, Lia didn't laugh. In fact, her stony face reminded Alex of Aunt Bree. Even her voice was hard. "With everything you've seen, you doubt the supernatural?"

Alex wondered if the temperature in the room had plummeted. She imagined red eyes staring at her through the window and hugged herself to keep from shivering.

"Alex. Hey." Lia's snapping fingers brought her back to reality. "You're safe here."

"I can't believe you brought me over there. Are you insane? Why didn't you say anything?"

Lia muttered to herself, "Bree's going to kill me. She should be the one to explain."

"Well, she's not here. What's going on? What the hell do we have for a next-door neighbor?"

"Take it easy. There's no danger unless someone tries to steal the treasure. Our task is to prevent that from happening. That's why we're called Watchers."

"How do you know there's a demon?"

"It's struck before."

Alex almost choked. "Is that what happened to those people?"

Lia's body sagged. "I guess so. The Swensons were found murdered, slaughtered really."

"What about the nuns?"

Lia bent her head. "Same thing."

With a little screech, Alex swung her head toward the window. "Is it still loose in there?"

"God no. Our ancestors sent it back to its lair over a hundred years ago."

****

Lia didn't leave Alex until after midnight, but Alex had trouble falling asleep. When she did, terrible creatures peopled her dreams. She woke late. During the half hour before the curse ended, she stubbed her toe twice and banged her hip against the door. She'd never take her health for granted again.

The weather coincided with her feelings: bright and breezy. A nice day for lunch with Hunter, but first, she wanted to practice her shielding. As much as she hated to do it, she asked Bree, the most powerful mind reader, to help her.

Her aunt's eyes gleamed. "I'd love to work with you. Come into my office."

Bree had no trouble getting through Alex's barrier. Each successful invasion made Alex cringe, but she did learn to recognize the uncomfortable twisting associated with a mind probe.

"The minute you sense me in your head, put up your shield. I see you're using a stone wall."

"Yes. I wanted to have something big and sturdy."

"Good. When you set it, don't just picture a wall. Picture the stones slamming into place everywhere the probe tries to go. Your reaction will be slow at first, but, with practice, building your shield will become automatic."

Alex's ability to resist Bree's infiltrations grew with every new effort to read her.

Almost two hours later, her aunt congratulated her. "After a while, you should be able to identify the intruder. We can work on that another time."

Bolstered by her success, she thanked Bree and left to get ready for her date with Hunter. As she dressed, she noticed yesterday's wounds had all but disappeared. Those rotten gremlins. She was lucky to have a healer on call.

Hunter arrived a little after noon, and Alex hurried to beat Bree to the door. She couldn't help the quick, indrawn breath when she saw him. Blond streaks of hair swept across his forehead, and his dark eyes held a promise. She wasn't aware she'd been gaping until he started to grin. She almost choked in her hurry to speak. "You made it." *Damn, that sounded lame.*

Hunter looked around and lifted his eyebrow. "It's a very impressive address."

Alex led him into the house.

After the introductions to her aunts, Bree played the

"Who do you know that I know?" game, and Alex had time to enjoy an uninterrupted view of the guy. Today he wore navy slacks and an open-neck white shirt that set off his tan. She'd never been interested in blonds before, but she reserved the right to change her mind.

Following Bree's brief interrogation, Hunter turned to Alex. His appreciative stare traveled over her body. "You look lovely, but you might want to take a jacket with you and maybe wear more comfortable shoes."

Her smile dissolved as she looked down at her snappy red sandals.

"I don't want to spoil the surprise, but trust me, you'll be happy to have sneakers and a sweatshirt or jacket with you."

After a quick trip upstairs, she was ready. Her outfit now consisted of a coral blouse, white capris, and white canvas slip-ons. A navy windbreaker hung over her arm as they left.

Hunter's sensible car pulled out of the driveway without fanfare. And no spinning tires. "I like your aunts. You're lucky to have such great relatives. I have an aunt and uncle in Florida."

"No other family?"

"I'm afraid not. My parents died in a car crash when I was in high school. I was an only child. My aunt and uncle brought me up."

"That's terrible. My parents are both gone, too. My mother died a few months ago, and my father was killed last November by a drunk driver."

Hunter reached over and squeezed Alex's hand. "I'm so sorry."

"Thank you." She wanted more information about him. "So, were you an editor in Florida?"

Hunter lifted his eyebrows as he turned and grinned at her. "Worried about my bona fides?"

She shook her head. "No. Nothing like that. I'm just interested in why you decided to move such a huge distance and endure the severe climate shift."

"I didn't see much of an opportunity for advancement at the magazine in Florida. I was restless. Then an old friend of my father's offered me the chance to move here. My aunt and uncle said I was crazy to consider it, but I wanted a change. Now all I need is warm clothes. What about you? How do you like living here?"

She tilted her head. Her life in Newport? How to explain her gratitude for this family, people who had loved her mother? Or the pain caused by her mother's lies and secrets. Not to mention the danger she'd already experienced—along with fear of what the future might hold.

Hunter interrupted her musings. "You don't have to answer. It's probably too soon after your loss."

"No. I don't mind. It's just that there have been so many adjustments that it's difficult to answer. My family has been great, and now I'm excited at the prospect of working with you."

They arrived in downtown Newport, and he pulled into a parking area near a harbor-front restaurant. "This is it."

"Nice. On the water."

Hunter grinned. "Yep."

He helped her out of the car but steered her away from the building. "We're not going to the restaurant?"

He gave her an amused smile. "We'll be eating on the high seas."

Alex frowned and contemplated the water. "On a boat?"

"That's right."

She stopped and held up her hand. "Wait a minute." She dug through her purse. They had to be in there someplace. She never left without them. "Aah."

She pulled out two small cloth circles and slipped them on her wrists. "Okay. I'm ready to go."

At Hunter's quizzical expression, she explained that she needed the bands to stave off seasickness. She hated to flaunt her weakness, but he should have warned her. His smile dimmed, and his brows pulled together. "Do you want to forget this and go somewhere else?"

"No. I'm all set." She held up her wrists. "Where's the boat?"

"Yacht. We've been invited by my father's old friend who also happens to be one of the magazine's sponsors."

****

Alex's previous forays on the water had involved kayaks and small sailboats, never anything like this. As she walked up the ramp, she marveled at the length of the vessel. They followed the steward's sharp, white uniform along the deck, Hunter's hand warm against her back. Alex suppressed the urge to peek through the windows.

Hunter leaned down and whispered in her ear, "Ever been on a yacht before?"

When she shook her head, he said, "Neither have I. Pretty cool, huh?"

The steward opened the door to a large salon with several sofas and chairs in a stark black and white design. A few people sat, but most stood around a teak and brass bar. Tables filled with food held court at the opposite end. She tried to ignore the almost imperceptible dip and sway of the boat. Her stomach gave a slight lurch. She should have put the bands on earlier.

As they peeked around, a tall, distinguished gentleman came up to them. "Hunter, so glad you could make it." He turned to Alex. "And who is your charming companion?"

"Hi, Charles. I'd like you to meet Alex Ryan."

With a slight tip of his head, Charles extended his hand. "Charles Berenger. Welcome."

Alex found herself caught up in the man's rugged good looks and penetrating blue eyes. The silver sparks painting his dark hair added character to his demeanor. "Thank you for the invitation."

Charles placed her extended hand in both of his and held it for a moment. "My pleasure." A quizzical expression passed over his face. "I'm acquainted with quite a few people in Newport, but I don't believe I recognize the name Ryan."

"I just moved to town. I'm a freelance writer hoping to do some work for Hunter's magazine." She paused, indicated the room, and gave a little laugh. "When he asked me to lunch, I had no idea we'd be dining in such splendor."

Charles glanced around. "*Destiny* has been a great source of joy to me. I'm glad you like her." His eyes rested on Alex for a fraction. "I appreciate beauty."

The man had a devastating smile. When he asked her if she lived in Newport, the word, no, had been on her lips. Then she remembered with a pang that this was her new home.

Hunter broke in. "Perhaps you've heard of her

relatives. The Brendanis?"

Interest flickered across Charles' craggy features as he regarded Alex. "You wouldn't, by any chance, be related to Gabrielle Brendani?"

The name Gabrielle threw her for a minute. "Oh, you mean Aunt Bree."

Charles's layer of sophistication evaporated as he responded. "Yes, I guess that's what everyone calls her, but I always preferred her given name. I haven't seen her in years. How is she?"

"Good. She's fine."

"Please tell her I was asking for her. Wait a minute." He reached into his blazer pocket and produced a card, then a pen, and wrote on the back of the card. "Tell her I'd love to meet with her and ask her if she'd call my cell."

Alex accepted his card, but before she could put it in her purse, Charles lifted her hand, indicating the wristband. "You're afflicted with *mal de mer*?"

Alex recognized the French words for seasickness. "I'm afraid so."

Charles leaned in close and whispered, "Don't tell a soul, but I, too, suffer from that malady. Perhaps you'd let me share one of my special pills. It will take care of the problem without making you drowsy." He placed his hand on her arm. "Trust me, Alex. It works."

The movement of the boat and the sight of a plate full of mussels sent a wave of nausea through Alex's stomach. The bands weren't working. She nodded to Charles. "That sounds like an excellent idea. Thank you."

After taking the pill, Alex confessed to Hunter that she was unwell and needed to get some air. He took her out for a walk on the deck while the yacht pulled away from the pier into Newport Harbor. Whether relief came from the fresh breeze, Charles' remedy, or the faux bracelets around her wrists, something worked. She thought she was well enough to try some food.

When she bypassed the lobster, shrimp, and caviar and filled her plate with cheese, crackers, and fruit, Hunter was surprised. "Are you sure that's all you want?"

She wasn't about to tempt fate. "Better safe than sorry."

They sat down on a sofa and held their plates on their laps. She inspected the plush surroundings and wanted to pinch herself. She, Alex Ryan, was relaxing aboard a fancy yacht next to a gorgeous man.

When the waiter came by with a tray holding champagne, Alex decided to try one. As she lifted the glass to her lips, she remembered Bree's warning to stay away from alcohol. A few sips couldn't hurt. A short while later, she met some of Hunter's colleagues. Many of whom knew or were friendly with members of her family. She dared to imagine she belonged.

Empty flutes were replaced with more bubbly, and Hunter suggested they take another walk outside. The boat had moved into the harbor and was cruising along the waterfront. With the change in the ship's speed, Alex stumbled, but Hunter steadied her. Maybe she shouldn't have had champagne on top of that pill. She shook her head and followed Hunter out the door.

For a minute the moving landscape made her dizzy. She blinked a few times, but as her eyesight settled, another hazy sensation assailed her—a tiny twisting inside her head. She should never have had anything to drink. The feeling came again. Oh, God. She staggered toward the rail. Hunter grabbed her. The champagne spilled, and she didn't care. She shook her head and put up her shields. Too late. Someone had been in her mind.

Alarmed, she turned to the group in the cabin. No one looked suspicious. Maybe she was wrong. Maybe what she'd felt was just an alcohol buzz. Besides, what difference would it make? What could be in her mind that anyone would want? With a shrug, she tipped her glass over the rail. She'd had enough to drink.

"Are you all right?"

"Fine. Just getting my sea legs. I don't often travel by water." She smiled up at Hunter. He was so cute. "Make that ever."

Hunter, who still had his arm around her, pulled her close before releasing her. Alex stifled a giggle and wished she hadn't tossed her drink. Instead, she leaned on the rail and breathed in the salty spray flung up by the sleek bow cutting through the water. The sun and wind on her face restored her spirit. "Now I see why I needed something warm." A lingering worry about the mind probe concerned her, but Hunter's arm around her shoulder chased it away.

"Are you cold? You can have my jacket."

"No, I'm fine." She flashed him a smile. "Everything is perfect."

"I'm glad. I wish I could tell you more about the harbor, but I'm still learning my way around."

When the wind picked up, the waves did too. As Hunter squeezed her shoulder, her head began to spin. The minute she moved, her stomach gave an ominous flip. She clung to Hunter for support.

"What's wrong?"

"I don't feel well."

"Are you going to be sick?"

She put her hand over her mouth. "I think so."

"The head is inside. Come on."

"I won't make it." Horror enveloped her as she bent over and retched.

Hunter jumped out of the way as Alex's lunch splashed over the deck. Holding onto the rail, she waited for another bout, but the nausea subsided. She peered at the disgusting mess at her feet and wished she could jump overboard and disappear. When the deckhand arrived to hose down the area, she made a hasty escape into the bathroom. Her stomach still bothered her but no longer threatened to empty. Her only problem now was humiliation.

She'd embarrassed herself in front of Hunter, and she worried that Charles might be upset. Their host, however, took the whole incident in stride. As they were leaving, he said, "Don't worry, Alex. You're not the first, and I'm sure not the last to decorate our decks. I'm just sorry you were ill."

Alex knew her face was flaming. She wished she could be as blasé about the incident as her host.

Charles chuckled and squeezed her shoulder. "Remember, I've been in your shoes. Believe me, I know the feeling."

"Thank you."

"Don't forget to give Gabrielle my message."

****

Neither Hunter nor Alex spoke until they reached the car. She understood his reticence. He'd been privy to her disgrace. "Hunter, I'm so sorry. I ruined everything."

"Don't be silly. You heard Charles. No big deal."

Invisible bands squeezed her head, and the rest of

the conversation on the ride home was strained. When Hunter walked her to her door, she thanked him and apologized once more. She didn't expect to see him again. Earlier she'd hoped for a kiss at the end of the date. Now, she cringed, knowing even she wouldn't want to kiss her. Hunter surprised her, though, by lifting her hand to his lips. Despite her headache, the light touch of his mouth sent heat up her arm.

"I'd like to take you out again. What about Saturday night?" He grinned. "I promise no boats."

Oh, hell yes. Out loud, she said, "I'd love to. What time?"

Alex didn't get far down the hall before Bree's door opened. "How was your date?"

Alex put her hand to her head. "We went out on a boat, and I threw up all over the place."

"How awful for you." Bree leaned in toward her. "As a matter of fact, you don't look too good right now."

"I still have a headache."

"Maybe you should lie down for a while."

"I think I will." She started to turn and stopped. "It wasn't a total loss. He asked me out for Saturday night."

Bree's eyebrows rose. "You didn't accept?"

This woman was not going to run her life. "Of course I did. Why not?"

"Two days before your birthday? Have you forgotten that man with the knife? It's too dangerous."

Wonderful. *I'd been trying to put that out of my mind.*

Bree softened her tone. "Why don't we talk about this later when you're feeling better."

Alex kept quiet but bunched up her hand in the folded jacket on her arm. A card fell out. She picked it up and offered it to Bree. "I almost forgot. I met someone who wanted to be remembered to you. He gave me his card."

Bree's eyes widened as she read the name and turned the card over. A slight flush crept up her face. She straightened her shoulders and took a deep breath. "Where did you meet Charles?"

"On his yacht. You should see it. It's like a small ocean liner with staff dressed like navy officers."

"That's nice. What did Charles have to say?"

"He said he wanted you to please call him. Oh, and he also called you Gabrielle."

An almost smile appeared before her aunt could control her features. "Did he say how long he was staying?"

Alex lifted her shoulders. "No idea."

As Bree tapped the card against the fingers of her other hand, a faraway look crept into her eyes. She murmured to herself, "So, Charles is back." To Alex, she said, "What does he look like?"

Alex grinned and gave her aunt a thumbs-up. "He's hot, kind of a cross between George Clooney and Tom Cruise."

Bree allowed herself a slight chuckle. "He always was a handsome devil." She raised her arms over her head and stretched. "Have a good rest." Then she disappeared into her office.

On the way upstairs, Alex paused. She'd almost forgotten. A chill slid down her arms. Someone on that boat had invaded her mind. She knew her reaction time had been slowed by the alcohol, and Bree would be furious. Better not to mention it.

Chapter Sixteen

Alex had trouble falling asleep that night. When she did drift off, she dreamed she was standing at her bedroom window. Lights from the house next door glistened through the trees. She left her room and walked toward the eerie beacons. Tall oaks lined the way and crowded in on her as she passed. When she peeked behind her, she panicked. The path had disappeared. Instinct prompted her to turn and run, but an overwhelming force pulled her toward the lights. She had to follow. She reached the pitted gate that guarded the decaying edifice. An eerie quiet settled around her. The ordinary, comfortable evening sounds had evaporated. She could smell damp earth and mold. Vines and vegetation inside the gate stirred though there was no breeze. A sudden darkness enveloped her—the earlier lights vanished. Her body began to tremble. She couldn't understand why she'd come. Her heart pounded in her chest. Thank God she was on the outside of the iron barricade. Cold seeped through the metal bars and swirled around her. Time to leave. She forced her feet to move.

Alex. The soft voice slithered through her head. *Don't go. Come in.*

Unable to resist the lure of his voice, she turned back. Everything had changed. Music floated into the night, and the house glowed with welcome. As she began to smile, her inner guardian stirred, warning her. She had to leave.

Once more, the voice pleaded. She looked at the heavy metal barrier between her and the house and let out a relieved sigh. "I can't get through the gate."

She'd started on her way home when a sound sliced through the night air. It tore at her sanity. Her body tensed. Her heartbeat stuttered, and her legs lost all ability to move. The sharp creak of metal, straining against rust and age, echoed through the quiet night. Too terrified to look back, she prayed for help and cried out.

The voice, like invisible tentacles wrapping around her willpower, drew her in. *Come, Alex. Come visit me.*

Her treacherous body turned back, but a shout blasted through her mind. *Alex. Don't listen to him. Wake up. You have to wake up.*

"Mom?" About to walk through the gate, she spun around looking for her mother. Emptiness mocked her as she tried once more. "Mom?"

Running footsteps sounded behind her.

Alex. She recognized her mother's "take no prisoners" voice. *Picture your bedroom. Wake up. Now.*

Straining to comply, Alex blinked until her room came into focus. "Mom?" Her head twisted from side to side. "Where are you?"

With trembling hands, she rubbed the sleep from her eyes and sat up. Again, she checked her surroundings. This time her seeking gaze found what she was looking for. The silver urn. Her mother's resting place.

Mom hadn't called to her. She touched the soft silken sheets and scanned the wide expanse of the unfamiliar bed. No. This wasn't her home. Her mother wouldn't be there to comfort her. The scent of roses assailed her. "Oh Mom, I miss you so much."

As Alex's sad whisper hung in the air, a shaft of moonlight entered the room, and the dreadful memory of her nightmare slammed into her. She grabbed hold of her mother's teddy bear, Sashi, and heard a faint whisper in the air, "Take care, sweetheart."

****

Alex slept later than usual and, when she woke, found her aunts and Lia in the kitchen.

Bree wished her a good morning. "Did you sleep well?"

Alex leaned against the counter. "I'm having a little trouble adjusting. I woke up in the middle of the night thinking my mother was there. It always hurts when I remember she's gone."

Franki sat up. "Did she speak to you?"

"While I slept."

"What did she say?"

What difference did it make? "Um, be careful?"

"Alex, your mother was very powerful. When she left, she could sometimes see into our resting minds. Try to remember everything."

Her response sounded harsh, almost angry. "What are you talking about?"

Lia came to her defense. "Mother, stop. You're scaring her. Remember, this is all still new to her. Let her eat her breakfast in peace."

Pouting at her daughter, Franki said, "If my sister inherited that skill, she might be persuaded to visit the rest of us. It would be wonderful to see her again." To Alex, she said, "A dream walker has the ability to take an active part in a person's sleeping mind."

"You think my mother was trying to contact me?"

Franki nodded. "She may still be too weak. According to Kitty, the poison arrested her development in the spirit world, and then she expended what energy she'd acquired at the grave."

Alex's mind spun. The image of a popular Hollywood horror figure and his razored fingers flashed in her head. Her mother wasn't like that. She backed away, reached for the coffee, and hesitated. "I need to take a walk."

****

The more Alex learned about her mother, the higher her anxiety level rose. She couldn't correlate what she was hearing with the savvy, fun-loving woman who'd raised her. What had begun as an aimless walk somehow led to her mother's garden. She sat on the bench, closed her eyes, and let the heady scent of roses wash over her.

Although she'd participated in and observed the family's magical abilities, she still found it difficult to grasp. The idea of her mother waltzing through someone's dreams was too weird. Her temples began to throb. She needed space to think, to get away, even for a little bit. Aunt Bree had told Alex she was welcome to use any of the cars. The keys were always left in them. A trip to Newport would be perfect, someplace to hide out for a few hours. For a minute guilt surfaced, but if she told Bree, she'd never get out alone, and she planned to be back before anyone decided to look for her.

Minutes later, enveloped in the leather seat of the expensive silver sedan, she listened to the smooth hum of the motor. With the Newport Art Museum plugged into the car's satellite directional app, she gave a defiant toss of her head and backed out of the garage. The simple act of driving away from the house gave Alex a deep sense of independence. She hadn't realized how stifled she'd felt.

On Bellevue Avenue, she admired the fabled mansions along the way, but her interest lay at the other end. She parked the car and became one more anonymous tourist. The carefree stroll eased her anxiety and dissolved her headache. Her mood lightened farther as she spied a graceful waterfall of wisteria draped across a latticed enclosure. Finally, her goal appeared. The art museum whose decorative wood trim was an award-winning example of Styk-style architecture. The name referred to the linear stickwork that overlay the building.

Inside, the intricate designs of the walls, floors, and cabinetry vied for attention with the artwork. Alex, who'd expected to breeze through, found herself so enchanted with each room's hand-carved accents, each new floor design, that she had to remind herself to look at the paintings.

The unique character of the building and exhibits on the first floor had taken up so much of her time, Alex almost skipped the second floor. Curiosity propelled her forward, however, and she stepped onto the wide, ornate staircase. She relished the feel of the smooth wood railing under her fingers. With so much beauty crying for her attention, she had to watch her step.

At a curve halfway up the stairs, a whisper of cold teased her neck. She noticed a painting beside her. It appeared to be a study in gray. Ignoring a slight shiver, she moved closer. The slate-colored swirls represented heavy bands of fog. Smothered within its cloying mists she caught tantalizing glimpses of a turret. Her heart sped up. She moved even closer and wished she hadn't. The painting triggered vibes of danger. A quick check of the artist's name shocked her. *Diorama in Fog* had been done by her aunt, Francesca Brendani.

"Isn't that a chilling piece?"

Alex twisted around, almost losing her balance. The woman spoke again. "I find it somehow repellent, yet I keep coming back to it. I once tried to buy it, but it's not for sale."

Alex nodded in agreement. She looked at the canvas again and recognized parts of the house that had escaped the bands of fog, the house that haunted her. Her aunt had captured its disturbing essence, beautiful and unsettling at the same time. Alex understood the woman's fearful attraction.

Tearing her eyes away, she backed toward the railing as she experienced a moment of dizziness. She leaned as far from the picture as possible and decided she'd had enough art for one day.

By the time she reached the first floor, her head had cleared, but the chill remained. Despite her reaction to the painting, her chest swelled with an upwelling of pride. Aunt Franki must be an important artist.

Outside, she let the heat of the sun warm her. She had one more place she wanted to visit, the tower in the park across the street.

****

On their earlier tour of Newport, Nick had pointed out their ancestors' monument. A series of walkways cut through Touro Park. One led her to an impressive statue of Commodore Mathew Perry, a Newport native who had served in several wars. From there, she meandered to an impressive stone tower. Over twenty feet high, it dominated the area.

A group of tourists strolled around the wrought-iron

fence surrounding the structure. When Alex asked someone about it, she learned it was called the *Old Stone Mill*. The woman said it was believed to have been built around 1660 by Benedict Arnold, the first governor of Rhode Island. Another voice piped up saying that it might have been constructed by the Norsemen long before that.

This was the spot Uncle Sal had described. He'd called it mysterious, then confirmed their ancestors had built it. Were there Norsemen in their family tree?

She recalled her uncle's concern about rumors of lights being spotted in the vicinity, but no one else had seemed too concerned. For a moment, she studied the area. No houses close. She wouldn't be surprised if people worshiped here. Stranger things had happened.

Thinking she might have found the perfect subject for a magazine article, Alex walked around the cylindrical attraction. Eight fieldstone pillars formed arched doorways with a few smaller square openings above. As she circled, she felt an odd pull from within the mill. She wished she could get inside the stone pillars to take pictures, but the barrier prevented her.

During a lull in the activity around her, Alex peered through the arches and felt something stir in her chest. With an intuition she couldn't describe, she focused her gaze on a spot in the middle of the tower. To her surprise, she detected a faint residue. Using her new skills, she phased out the surrounding noise, honed in on that piece of ground, and attempted to decipher what kind of traces she'd discovered.

As she continued to watch the spot, a veil seemed to descend around her. The noise of the day receded, and the light changed. Her head felt strange, not quite dizzy, but off-kilter as if she had a cold. Then a low murmur filled her mind.

Her perception changed, and she blinked to re-establish her bearings. She saw movement within the mill and tried to focus on it. A filmy mist shimmered over the setting in front of her. It was evening. A full moon lit the scene. Inside, the light from torches highlighted a group of men as they stood around a fire. One of them held up what looked like a piece of wood and chanted something while striking his breast with a closed fist. The others then followed suit. They were performing some type of ceremony. The noise she'd heard had been the sound of their voices. Their light-colored shifts had large crosses on them, suggesting they might belong to the crusades. Huge swords hung by their sides. She tried to hear what they were saying but couldn't understand the language.

When one of the men threw something into the fire, the rich smell of incense tickled her nose, and she reached up to stifle a sneeze. Immediately, he snapped his head in her direction. Swallowing a gasp, her hand stilled. Her body began to shake as she waited to be discovered. His stare pinned her. She opened her mouth to speak, apologize, but his head swiveled away. He looked all around, finally coming back again to where Alex stood, but he did nothing. Afraid to move, Alex held her breath until he turned away again. Apparently satisfied that there was no threat, he concentrated once more on the ceremony.

She eased out a breath. *Oh God, what was happening? Who were these people? That man had sensed the motion of her hand, but how?* She had to get away. With slow, steady movements, she slid one foot backward, waited, and then moved the other. It seemed to take an eternity. Her mind screamed at her to run, but she ignored it. When no one looked up, she repeated her tentative steps. This time, however, she crashed into something.

As she started to fall, she saw his head swing back to her and his hand come up. Everything went dark then, and she felt pain. She closed her eyes against the voices. She was done for.

"Hey, lady. Are you okay? You took a nasty fall."

Alex opened her eyes to bright sunshine and the concerned visage of a pimply-faced teenager peering down at her. She lay on the ground. "Wha . . .?" She was back in the real world, sprawled on the grass in Touro Park, with a bunch of interested faces gawking at her.

The young man with the *I heart Newport* tee shirt who'd spoken to her, grabbed her hands to pull her to her feet. "You looked like you were having some kind of seizure. Are you sure you're okay?"

Aware of people gathering around her, she nodded. "Thank you. I'm fine now."

Her eyes kept straying to the stone structure, afraid to see an angry knight vaulting the fence. Oh, she thought, that's who they were, knights. Thankfully, she didn't have to face their wrath. The impact with the hard ground had broken whatever spell she'd been under. Just in case, though, she stepped farther away from the tower.

She brushed off the back of her shorts, reassured her would-be savior she'd sustained no damage, and turned to leave. A growl from her stomach reminded her of the time.

She'd planned to have lunch out, but now she thought she'd better get back. She didn't know where she'd been a few minutes ago, but it wasn't in this century. Though the incident bothered her, it wasn't the first time she'd experienced this strange phenomenon. Twice before, like today, the events she'd seen in her head reflected something from the past. At a museum in Arizona, she'd seen an Anasazi tribe preparing for a long journey. When she'd told her mother, Cecile had responded, "That's nice, honey. You've got quite an imagination."

At the time, that had made sense because the mysterious disappearance of the Anasazi was something she'd heard about all her life. Today, however, she'd been thinking about Governor Benedict Arnold in the 1600s. She was pretty sure that the men she'd seen in her vision weren't from that time. Those men had lived in an era a whole lot earlier. There was one other important detail that had made this vision different. Somehow, part of her had broken through the time barrier. Today, she'd been more than a spectator. She'd been a participant, and she didn't like it.

****

Unaware of her surroundings, Alex hurried back to the car. Her thoughts tumbled one on top of the next. What had just happened? It was like the library movie when the dinosaurs had seemed real. Was it a vision? How could someone see her if it was all in her mind? More important. Could she be hurt?

Halfway home, she almost went off the road when Bree's telepathic voice startled her. *Where are you? It's past lunch time.*

A twinge of guilt caused Alex to look over her shoulder before realizing her aunt couldn't observe her. Since she was sure Bree would catch any lie, she kept it simple. *I'll see you in a few minutes.*

She made it back to the house without incident, but she bumped into Franki as she left the garage. Her aunt's eyes brightened. "Were you looking for me?"

Alex dropped her gaze, staring at the bluestone under her feet. She'd forgotten that the garage and Franki's studio shared the same path. Fumbling for an excuse, she gave up and spit out the truth. "No. I borrowed one of the cars for a trip to Newport." A guilty heat crept up her face.

Franki's smile evaporated, and an eyebrow tipped up. "Did you need something?"

Alex couldn't hold it in any longer. "Actually, I did." She paused for a second, then plunged on. "I needed to get away and be by myself. It's as if I'm suffocated by everything that's happened. I had to go somewhere to breathe."

Franki looked hurt.

"Oh no, Aunty. It's nothing to do with you. It's just that—for the last six months, I've been on my own. Here, it's been close to impossible to achieve that. With the revelations, warnings, and magic, my head was ready to burst. I had to either run away for an hour or scream."

"All this must seem almost cruel, but, believe me, it's for your own protection. You shouldn't go anywhere by yourself." She pulled back and surveyed Alex. "Why don't you go to your room and freshen up before you see Bree? We'll meet you in the den."

"Okay."

On her way upstairs, she worried whether to tell her aunts about her vision.

Chapter Seventeen

When Alex walked into the den a short while later, Bree and Franki stopped talking. She knew they'd been discussing her. "Hello, dear, did you have a good time?" Bree said.

Dear? Uh-oh. "Yes, thank you."

"I trust the car worked well."

Alex had to swallow before she could answer. "It's a beautiful vehicle. Thank you for the offer to let me use it."

Bree's eyes rounded as her nostrils widened. "Where did you go?"

"The Newport Art Museum." Alex gave Franki a smile. "I was excited to find your work."

Franki nodded. "They have a couple of my paintings."

"I met a woman who was disappointed that your painting of the house in the fog wasn't for sale. She loved its haunting essence, but it upset me. I was drawn to it and repelled at the same time, almost as if it were the real thing."

The room went quiet—the lone sound, the metallic ring of Franki's bracelets as she fiddled with them. The explosion of Bree's voice made Alex flinch. "I told you those paintings should never leave your studio."

Worried that somehow she'd betrayed her aunt, Alex cringed beneath Bree's anger.

Franki's blue eyes sparked as she defended herself. "You can hardly see the house at all. No one would ever guess its location."

"You don't think they might wonder if the building was close to your own property?"

"No," she said as she crossed her arms and looked away from Bree.

Alex attempted to change the subject. "I also visited the Old Stone Mill in Touro Park. I may know what caused the lights there."

Both women turned to her. Her shoulders tensed, and she hesitated, recalling her close escape and wondering if her aunts would believe her. Seconds later, she remembered where she was. In this place, strange was normal.

After she described the scene she'd witnessed, Bree asked if she'd had visions before.

Alex nodded. "My mother called them daydreams, kind of like watching a movie, but I was never dizzy or disoriented like today. And no one ever reacted to me before."

"What?" Bree said as she snapped forward in her chair. "They knew you were there?"

"When I moved my arm, he looked right at me."

Franki's hand flew to her throat.

Alex hurried to quiet her aunts' concern. "Even though he sensed the movement, he couldn't actually see me."

"I don't like it," Franki said. "First the lights, now this."

Bree concurred. "They were Templars. Somehow she went back in time." She ran her fingers through her hair. "Whatever is going on is happening fast. We've got to figure this out. I'm calling Rosemary."

"I'll alert Sal," Franki said.

Alex tried to make sense of it. "Maybe I got so close today because I'm related to those men."

The worry never left Bree's face as she shook her head. "No. It's because we unbound your powers."

Alex started to say something else, but Bree held up her hand to stop her. She looked to her other aunt, but Franki, too, seemed lost in contemplation. Tension saturated the air, and Alex's inner guardian stirred. A small flutter of concern escalated to a steady hum in her chest.

Bree broke the silence. "Rosemary's contacting the Clan to see if anyone has experienced anything out of the ordinary."

"Good," Franki said. "Sal's coming over this evening after dinner and suggests that Rosemary and Nick do the same. He's certain that Alex's vision had to do with the strange lights there."

For the rest of the afternoon, Bree worked with Alex on her reaction time constructing her shield and the use of controlled energy bursts. "Your newly awakened gifts should make it easier to direct the force." Bree pointed to a pillow on the sofa. Alex gasped when it flew into the air.

"Now you try it. Just picture energy moving from your core to your finger and shoot it."

"Are you sure?"

"Try it."

Alex inhaled and tried to coax the energy from her core. She pictured the pillow sailing into the air and pointed. Nothing. She hunched her shoulders and looked down. "It didn't work."

Bree smiled. "It never works the first time."

Why did Bree always set her up for failure instead of explaining there was a learning curve?

Anger at her aunt's overbearing attitude bubbled up as she concentrated on the stupid pillow. Gritting her teeth, she pointed. A slight buzz alerted her, but it was too late. The pretty cushion exploded.

"Alex! What are you doing?" Bree said.

"I'm sorry. I didn't mean to do that. I was angry because I couldn't make it move."

"So, you killed it?" Bree shook her head, then smiled. "It seems your antipathy initiates a formidable reaction with more than electrical objects. You'll have to learn to manage the outbursts, which means controlling your mindset."

For the next hour, Bree worked with her niece on tempering her emotions. Finally, Bree called a halt. "I want you to take some time to relax. You'll need to rest before our meeting tonight. It will be late."

"What are you talking about?"

"Sal wants to check out the tower at night."

Alex backed away from her aunt shaking her head. "I'll wait for you here."

"Don't be silly. We'll need your perceptions. You're the only one who's been contacted."

She bit her lip. She didn't argue with Bree, but she had no intention of getting anywhere near that tower, especially at night.

****

The living room buzzed with voices: Alex, her aunts, uncle, cousins, and the Stuarts. Lia described it as a routine Clan meeting.

Excited to be part of the group, Alex sat next to her

cousin on the sofa. She tried to hide a yawn as she checked the clock; it was close to twelve thirty in the morning. Although Bree had suggested she nap after dinner, Alex had been too keyed up to relax.

When her gaze found Nick, he shot her a cheeky grin. He placed a carved wooden box on the table next to his grandmother who gestured at it. "I've brought some of our Templar records. I'm hoping to find something that we can use to reassure the knights at the tower that we mean no harm."

"Wait a minute," Bree said. "How do you plan to do that?"

Rosemary gave her a reassuring smile. "Sal and I discussed it and agreed that we will accompany Alex back to the tower tonight. We'd like her to attempt to contact the knights again."

Fear coiled in Alex's chest. She wanted nothing to do with those men. "No."

Agitated murmurs grew into objections. Nick turned to his grandmother. "You can't do that. It's too dangerous."

In a firm but quiet voice, Rosemary Stuart said, "As Clan leader I can and will do what I deem best for our well-being."

"What about Alexandra's safety?"

Sal spoke up. "She won't be alone. We'll be there with her. These are our ancestors. They won't harm one of their own."

Tony gave a rueful laugh. "How are they supposed to recognize her? They'll kill her first and ask questions later."

A lump formed in Alex's chest, and her hands shook. Lia clasped the trembling digits, and Alex felt a soothing wave of comfort spread through her.

Sal turned to glare at his son. "I believe the Templars are responsible for the strange lights reported in the area. If so, they'll be expecting communication."

Rosemary reached out and patted the air in a calm-down motion. "I believe if Alex gets through to them, she can reassure them in their own language. A phrase they'll recognize. *Pauperes commilitones Christi Templique Solomonici*."

Alex looked at the other faces, grateful she wasn't the only one confused.

Rosemary gave a lopsided grin. "It means *Poor fellow soldiers of Christ and the Temple Solomon*."

When the others grumbled, insisting they should all go along, Rosemary shook her head. "We don't want to attract attention."

"What if someone comes by?" Bree said. "If we spread out around the park and act as lookouts, I can persuade anyone who shows too much interest in us to leave."

"I'm going," Nick said.

When a few others echoed Bree's sentiments, Rosemary and Sal gave in. "Fine," Rosemary said, "let's lay out a plan."

In the end, they decided that Rosemary and Nick would accompany Alex as their particular gifts would offer the most help in case of trouble. The others would protect the outskirts, alerting Bree if her mind-manipulating skills were needed.

When Lia joined in the conversation, Alex slipped from the room. No one had asked for her input. They hadn't even considered her feelings. She was just a pawn in the larger game. She didn't want to go back. She wanted nothing to do with those wild, bearded men. One of their swords could slice her in two.

She'd gotten halfway to the kitchen when he called her name. "Alexandra. Wait a minute."

She paused, and Nick caught up to her. In the dim light, she couldn't make out his face, but concern filled his voice. Hers sounded pathetic. "I don't want to do it. I'm afraid they'll kill me."

"Don't listen to Tony." He put his hands on her shoulders. His voice soothed. "They can't force you to do this. If you decide to, I'll be there for you. I'll stand beside you and monitor your thoughts. If you get into trouble, I'll pull you away."

Though the words made sense, her insides were doing a tap dance. "But you can't imagine what they were like. They had these long, scuzzy beards and crazy eyes." She looked up at Nick's strong, clean chin. His hands on her shoulders conveyed a reassuring warmth. She wanted to believe in him, to accept that he'd take care of her.

"Why me? Why can't one of you try to contact them? If Uncle Sal's right about them signaling us, you all have much better skills."

"We don't have your unique gift."

Her chest tightened. She wanted to say no. She didn't owe them anything. She'd come to Newport because of her mother. But they were family. The only one she had. "I don't like it, but I'll do it. You'd better be there for me."

When Nick pulled her into his strong arms, she melted against him. His warm breath tickled her neck, and his hands caressed her back eliciting sensations deep in her belly. His scent wrapped around her. Maybe this wasn't such a bad idea.

****

The night air sent shivers along Alex's bare arms. She peered into the park. Streetlights stretched inward like ghostly fingers searching the darkness. She wanted to turn and run.

The group split up, leaving Alex with Rosemary and Nick.

Rosemary gripped Alex's hand and gave it a squeeze before disappearing into the park. When the night closed in on her, Alex swallowed and began to tremble. Nick put his arm around her and tucked her against his side. "Don't worry. She's scouting the area. We'll meet her there."

Could he hear the banging of her heart? She hated this fear. Maybe Nick could travel back with her if he held on tight. To the casual eye, Alex knew she and Nick would look like any other loving couple. She wished their presence was that innocent. Too soon they arrived at the tower. The sight of the arches brought back her earlier terror, the black glare of an angry knight. This was a bad idea.

She wasn't aware she'd begun to back away until Nick pulled her close. "Don't worry. Lia will help."

Her cousin rounded the fence. "You didn't think I'd abandon you, did you? You'll be fine." Lia took Alex's hand in both of hers. Her touch spread warmth and relaxation. Alex embraced the calm and squared her shoulders. "Thank you. I can do this."

Rosemary returned as Lia resumed her surveillance. She placed a piece of paper in Alex's hand. "Show them this document. It's part of a letter from Prince Henry the Navigator."

"Who's that?"

"Trust me. They will recognize his signature."

"Okay."

"Are you ready?"

She wasn't, but she nodded. She took a cleansing breath, leaned against the railing, and peered into the tower. A stray breeze tickled her neck. Night shadows flickered along the ground. Could she get through to them again? And if she did?

With a last glance toward Rosemary and Nick, she turned her attention to the center space, trying to will the men to appear. Nothing happened. The site felt different. What if she couldn't contact them? She tried again. Clearing her mind, she blocked out all outside influences and called on her inner power to reveal what lay within the stone enclosure. Still nothing. About to give up, she heard a noise—a low buzz that intensified into a hum. As it escalated, she felt Rosemary stiffen. Nick said something, but she missed it as the ever-increasing sound filled her head. She closed her eyes. A kind of vertigo threw her off balance. She tried to steady herself. Disoriented and scared, she felt as if she were being pulled away. She clutched the fence.

When the keening sound ended, unease replaced her dizziness. Incense filled her nostrils. Curious sounds assailed her. Animal calls? She snapped her eyes open and froze. Her reality had changed. Stone pillars now surrounded her. Dense foliage replaced the grass in the park. The city of Newport was gone. No lights, no streets, no family. A slight crackling distracted her. She turned and looked toward the noise. A small fire burned, still reeking of incense. Oh God. And a pair of leather boots.

Chapter Eighteen

Alex's resolve shattered as she looked at the man before her. A white shirt with a blood-red cross reached his knees. A crusader. She'd traveled to the fifteenth century.

She heard movement behind her. Before she could turn, someone grabbed and held her wrists. At her back, a gruff voice barked. She couldn't understand the language. She twisted around in a panic. "I don't understand you."

The man behind her squeezed. His grip so hard, she worried her bones might break. The pain increased, and a wave of despair enveloped her. She'd been transported to a distant time with no one to help her. No way to communicate, and they thought she was an enemy.

She turned to the man in front of her, hoping to find mercy. A mistake. His dark eyes held wildness. The rest of his face lay hidden behind black hair that fell to his shoulders. A knotted mat covered the lower part of his face. His hand rested on the hilt of an enormous sword. With one swipe, he could split her down the middle. Her breath caught in her throat. She almost wet herself. Trapped with no escape.

She sucked down the scream building in her throat. She didn't want to antagonize them further. Uncle Sal believed their ancestors wanted to communicate. Maybe if she said something. The man in front of her must be the leader. She lowered her gaze to show respect. Her voice came out in a squeak. "I come as a friend."

His voice thundered, startling her. She pulled back. The steely grip on her wrists disappeared. They'd freed her. Thank God.

Until the sharp bite of a sword bit into her throat. Her brief hope plummeted. Tony was right. They were going to kill her.

Rosemary's instructions deserted her. She held her breath, afraid to move. The huge warrior in front of her leaned in closer. She began to pray.

He spat out a sharp command that sounded like an ultimatum. Cold seeped into her bones. Her limbs trembled. He expected an answer, but she had no idea what he'd said. She tried to shake her head, but the edge of the blade stopped her.

His lips peeled away from yellowed teeth. Then he pulled his fist back, ready to strike.

She whipped her arms up to protect herself. Her eyes squeezed shut. Voices boomed around her. The sword sliced into her neck. This time she bellowed. Liquid dripped down her skin. Blood.

I'm going to die.

She braced herself and peeked through her arms. His raised fist opened. Words roared through her head. *Stop. Release her.*

What? The sharp point at her throat vanished. She'd understood his words. The leader thrust his head in her face. Sharp whiskers scratched her chin as he studied her. He shot his hand out and grabbed hers. Such a terrifying action, her legs almost buckled. *Look.* He lifted her arm above her head. Steel flashed to her left. Her knees knocked together.

Then she understood what he'd seen. The glowing cross on her wrist—the mark of the Templars. *She is one of us.* His features changed. Satisfaction replaced anger. His voice softened. *You've come.*

Was he welcoming her? A peek at the others reinforced the idea. Eyes clear, no rage, swords back in their sheaths. Relief flooded through her. She could understand him. Telepathy.

As she relaxed, her fist opened to the crinkle of paper. She'd forgotten the letter. She handed the rumpled sheet to her new friend. She was forgetting something else. What was it? Oh yes. The phrase Rosemary had taught her. She sent it to the leader.

A smile lit his face. *You heard our call.*

I... She looked at him in confusion. *You were expecting me?* Anger flared as she touched the cut on her neck. *Then why did you hurt me?*

His smile died. His eyebrows pulled together. Alarm filled his voice. *We must guard against the dark forces. Danger surrounds you. It's loose.*

What's loose? Alex said as anxiety returned.

The demon. The portal has opened. His eyes narrowed. *You've not seen it? No one has been killed?*

Her throat constricted. *No. The Convent House is deserted.*

Convent House? He looked at his fellows in confusion. *Of what do you speak?*

Of course. The house didn't exist during their time. *The structure that was built over your original encampment. Nothing horrible has happened.* Maybe he was wrong. *Are you sure this portal is open?*

He stood tall, planting his hand on the hilt of his sword. *The demon is loose. We've felt its hunger.*

Beware! You must protect the holy relic. It's up to you to sound the alert.

Confusion, then fear. A demon!

A voice in her ear. *Your Clan?*

My Clan?

Your family, girl.

B-Brendani.

A mist had begun to settle over them. Her vision blurred as someone whispered, *Take care, mia bella nipote. Destroy the fiend.* Then everything went dark.

****

"Alexandra, wake up." Nick's voice. "Talk to me."

She startled, then shook her head. As she attempted to sit up, she asked, "What's going on?"

"You fainted. Can you stand?"

"I think so."

"Let me help you."

Alex realized she'd been lying in Nick's arms. She was back and safe. Thank God. She'd done it. Rosemary hovered as Nick helped her to stand. "Did you see them? What happened?"

Sal's voice intervened. "Let's get out of here first. She's bleeding."

Nick picked her up and held her close to his chest. "I've got you, Alexandra."

****

In the car, while Rosemary cleaned the blood off Alex's neck, Lia used her healing powers. From his position of authority in the front seat, Uncle Sal bombarded her with questions, most of which she couldn't answer.

No, the warriors didn't identify themselves, but they looked like knights. Yes, they were worried about a demon on the loose. No, they didn't say what kind. *Were there different types of demons?* No, they hadn't told her how to defeat it. And, no, they hadn't identified the relic to be protected. Alex shook her head in wonder. How was she supposed to discover these things? Men like that didn't invite friendly chit-chat.

By the time they arrived home, sometime after two a.m., Alex was fighting to stay awake. The excited rush from the evening's success had drifted into a comforting numbness. She rubbed her eyes, hoping to escape to bed, but Rosemary wanted her to fill in the rest of the group gathered in the living room. Afraid she might fall asleep if she sat down, Alex stood, gripping the back of a chair.

As she dredged up memories of her bizarre encounter, her heart accelerated. When she finished, she unclenched her hands, and the letter Rosemary had given her floated to the floor.

A spate of questions vied for her attention. She was grateful when Rosemary intervened. "This young lady needs to go to bed. Tonight, for the sake of the Clan, she placed herself in a dangerous situation. She's earned her rest." With that, Rosemary put her arm around Alex. "We all thank you. We'll talk again tomorrow. You're exhausted. Go to bed."

Alex's mouth stretched in a huge yawn. The sound of restless conversation followed her into the hall. Uncle Sal repeated the words her ancestor had whispered in her ear.

Then, with a note of triumph, he said, "It means, Take care, my beautiful granddaughter."

****

After a short and fitful sleep, Alex began to second-guess herself about last night. If she'd really been with her ancestors, how had she done it? Could she go back in time? Or had the Templars somehow pulled her into their existence? She remembered her uncle talking about lights at the tower and the knight saying she'd answered their signal.

Her morning foray into her mother's sunlit garden should have calmed her. Instead, her mind churned as she played with the delicate rose in her hand. She didn't want to believe in demons, but while she sat there, Clan members searched the properties, hunting whatever had escaped from the Convent House. So much unnerving turmoil.

Bringing the rose to her face, she inhaled its sweet scent. She found it all confusing, but right now it didn't matter. She relished the fact that she'd impressed the whole Clan. She'd done something special. Even Aunt Bree congratulated her without adding one "but."

While basking in her importance, she received a message from Bree asking her to come to the study. A satisfied smile touched her lips. Nothing to worry about. This time she hadn't done anything wrong. As she left the garden, she noticed a drop of blood on her finger. She'd forgotten the thorns.

****

The slight murmur of voices made a comfortable hum as she walked through the hall. She entered the den and caught the scent of lemon from a cleaning solution. It smelled nice. "Good morning."

Franki looked up. "Good morning. I hope you slept well."

Alex remembered the nightmare she'd had the night before. Her face must have revealed concern because Bree caught it. "What?"

"Nothing." She didn't want to discuss the insane workings of her sleeping mind with her aunt, the psychologist.

Bree wouldn't let it go. "The sleeping unconscious can be important, even prophetic. Tell us what happened."

Alex experienced a chill as she remembered her terror. "I slept well last night, but the evening before—not so good."

Her aunts urged her to continue.

"I dreamed about the Convent House."

"Oh." Franki's voice rose as she fiddled with her hair and exchanged a look of concern with her sister.

Alex recounted what she remembered. "I was so grateful to wake up but disappointed that Mom wasn't there."

For a long moment, no one spoke. Franki recovered first. She clutched Alex's hand and said, "I have to paint her, Bree."

Whatever she'd expected from her aunts, it wasn't Franki's declaration. Odd, but Franki was an artist, after all.

It was Bree's expression that upset her. Her aunt's face paled, and her voice dropped to a whisper. "This is all happening too fast." She paused then cleared her throat. "You'd better get started."

Alex didn't understand what her portrait had to do with their problems, but she agreed to it, although her okay had a big question mark at the end.

Franki wanted to paint Alex on the bench in the center of the labyrinth. "Our gifts are much stronger there."

Alex, who'd been all set to go to the studio, kept

quiet.

"You go get your supplies, and we'll meet you there," Bree said.

Since there wasn't much room in the center of the labyrinth, Bree monitored her sister from the gazebo. Franki set up her easel and asked Alex to get comfortable on the stone seat.

Alex liked her aunts, but this whole setup was a little bizarre, especially with a demon on the loose. All because of a dream.

And then her grandmother's voice added to the absurdity. *How nice, visitors.*

Hi, Mother. I need to paint Alex. She's had some trouble.

Already?

Alex looked down, examining the ground that held Kitty's ashes, and wondered what her grandmother meant.

Well, dears, I won't bother you. You don't mind if I watch?

Fine with me. How about you, Alex?

Alex shook her head. *No problem here.*

Franki told Alex to relax and look out at the water. Then she began to paint.

The view held very little to capture Alex's interest, and she found it difficult to sit still. While she fidgeted, she thought about her strange new life and wondered what other family quirks she might discover. Her relatives had special gifts, as did she, but this afternoon didn't make sense. When she found herself dwelling on scenes from the Mad Hatter's tea party, a spark of guilt kicked in. How could she judge anyone when she'd spent part of the previous evening in the fifteenth century?

Alex chanced a peek at her aunt. A true artist, Franki painted with confidence. About fifteen minutes later, though, Franki's painting style changed. Her strokes were more erratic, and her pupils became huge, darkening her eyes. Alex looked on in fascination as her aunt's delicate hands sped up, faster and faster until at the end, her brush jerked about the canvas in frantic movements. Then she stopped, stood back, and pulled a cover over her work. She wiped the back of her hand across her brow. "That's it."

Kitty's voice had lost its flighty lilt as it drifted in. *Oh, Lord. You're right. It's begun.*

Franki looked pale and unsteady. Before Alex could go to her, Bree arrived and handed her sister a bottle of water. "Here. Drink up. You look exhausted."

"Thank you," Franki said and drank half in two gulps.

"Let's see what you've done." Bree moved to the easel, lifted the cover, and appraised the painting in silence.

Alex touched her chest to still the cold quivering there as the skin on her aunt's face grew slack and pale. Fear charged the air. The indomitable Bree seemed to deflate when she saw the canvas. "That's it then. We knew it would happen someday."

Icy fingers slithered down Alex's spine, keeping her in her seat. The sun warmed her skin, and fresh air from the river tousled her hair. Beyond the stone circles of the labyrinth, vibrant colors burst from the garden. Sweet birdsong trilled around them. How deceptive life could be and how unfair. Beauty and serenity shouldn't be the backdrop for encroaching evil.

All vitality seemed to have leached from Franki. In

a voice flat and toneless, she said, "It's times like this I wish I didn't have the sight."

Despite an inner warning, Alex moved toward the painting that had upset everyone. Bree's hand snapped out to stop her. "It's not a good idea for you to look at this yet. Not until you understand what's going on."

"But it's about me."

Franki answered with surprising authority, "You'll see it later," and forestalled further protest by recovering it.

At that moment, Alex blanched. Franki's tone of finality sounded exactly like Alex's mother.

Kitty spoke up. *This girl can do it. She can stand up to them. I can feel her strength. She's got Cece's gifts and some of her own. You must protect her until the Fourth.*

Privy to the conversation, Alex's mind swirled as Bree answered, *You're right, Mother. She's strong but such a novice. She knows nothing about the threat and even less about her powers. We don't have enough time.*

You have three days. Don't stand there whining. Teach the girl.

Bree's reaction to her mother's sharp taunts surprised Alex. Instead of standing her ground, she dropped her head. *Yes, Mother. I'll start now.*

Bree touched her niece's arm. "Come on, Alex, but watch your step. We need every bit of luck we can muster."

****

After lunch, Bree made Alex concentrate on her shield techniques and threat screening. "Danger will appear from where you least anticipate it. You need to develop the habit of protecting yourself on all sides."

"How do you expect me to detect a threat behind me?"

"Why did you react the night the car almost hit you?"

"What do you mean?"

"What impressions did you get just before your guardian warned you?"

Alex paused and recalled her feelings. "Danger. I sensed that first."

"That's what you want to work on. You have a built-in threat awareness. Learn to continually access it."

"But how?"

"Tune out distractions and tune in to the atmosphere about you. Right now, take a deep breath, close your eyes, and try to connect with the surrounding space. Sense the emptiness in the room except for my presence. Make yourself an object within a twenty-foot circumference and send out your probe. Picture it in your mind."

Alex tried to tune out the minutiae crowding her brain. The more she tried, the more her mind raced. This was a stupid test.

"Listen to me, Alex." Her aunt's voice was low and soothing. "I want you to delve within yourself. Reach for your serenity. You're protected here. All you need to do is concentrate on this room."

Alex slowed her breathing and visualized her safe place. At once her mind quieted. She focused on the empty area right there in front of her. Good. She was safe. She pushed her consciousness further out. Furniture posed no problem. Then she sought out all living things. Her search to either side yielded nothing, but, at her back, someone waited. A sense of caution rather than danger alerted her as she sought out the intruder. A wall appeared and dissolved into the presence of her aunt. Bree sent her congratulations.

Alex opened her eyes, puffed up with pride at her accomplishment. "It worked."

Bree placed her hand on Alex's shoulder. "You're good, but you need more practice. Your appraisal should take mere seconds to complete. Begin working on reining in your scattered thoughts. Your mind is a jumble of nonsense. When something unexpected happens, it runs amok. Don't examine each piece of information while you're out there and vulnerable. Focus on human motivation. Right now, you think it's impossible. Trust me. Continual awareness is not simply possible, it will become instinctive. But you must never stop practicing." Bree paused to look out the window. "From now on, we'll all need to assume a heightened consciousness."

She wandered over to her desk and sat down. "Rosemary has called a Clan meeting for tonight. Practice scanning your personal space and using your shields. I don't expect a malevolent presence. We've searched the grounds and found no sign of the demon, but it never hurts to be ready."

Alex gulped. She'd read stories about the occult. "But can't a demon materialize wherever it wants?"

"No. It's been programmed to attack when someone disturbs the burial site."

With a sigh of relief, Alex turned to leave.

"Before you go," her aunt called out, "there's something else I wanted to discuss. It's about your date tomorrow night."

Alex tensed.

Bree straightened her spine and pressed her lips

together. "With everything that's happened, maybe you should cancel."

Her nails bit into her palms at the challenge in Bree's voice. "Why? I'll be careful."

Bree leaned forward and rested her arms on the desk. "What about Hunter? He'd be no match for the people who are after you. He could get hurt."

Although the barb struck home, Alex vowed her aunt's scare tactics wouldn't work. Bree made it sound like Alex was being pursued by Ninja assassins, but Alex wasn't worried. Since the supposed demon never strayed from the relic buried near the Convent House, leaving the neighborhood should heighten her safety.

With her independence threatened, Alex's mind went on the offensive. She suspected Bree had an ulterior motive that had to do with Nick. Sure, he was cute, but half the time he treated her like a kid sister. Hunter, on the other hand, spoke to her as an equal. To him, her ideas mattered.

She remembered the velvety depth of his amber eyes and the feel of his lips against her skin. Saturday night promised even more. Bracing both legs, she thrust out her chin. "I haven't seen anything to suggest that I'm in danger. No one has bothered me." In a lower, more confident tone, she said, "Besides, I have powers now."

Bree shook her head. "I don't like frightening you, Alex, but you need to be worried. Look, why don't we talk about it after tonight's meeting? If you still insist on going, I can ask Lia or Nick to double-date with you. It might be a little awkward explaining it to Hunter, but at least you'd be able to go out with him."

Though she disliked the idea, Alex offered a limited concession. "Maybe. But not Nick."

The idea of him watching over her on a date made her very uncomfortable.

Chapter Nineteen

Preparations for the meeting had been going on all day. Rosemary sent her housekeeper Mattie to cook and serve the meal. When Alex worried about her outfit for the evening, Lia again offered her closet. She chose a filmy green dress that matched her eyes.

The family, gathered in the living room, centered their discussion on their hunt for a demon. That afternoon, while Franki painted Alex, others had continued their search around the Convent House. They'd found no indication of trouble.

Alex rubbed her arms as Lia spoke to her. "It doesn't make sense. In the past the demon went on a killing rampage. How can it be loose if we've found no evidence? It should have attacked us."

Alex tried to calm the flutters in her chest. "Maybe it's inside the Convent House."

"That place is locked up tight. They found no sign of demons or humans around it."

The arrival of Rosemary and Nick interrupted their conversation. He looked awesome. Alex tried not to stare, but in his dark, tailored jacket and close-fitting slacks, he owned the room.

He tipped his head in her direction, and a stray piece of dark hair slipped over one eye. His lips held a devilish grin as he strolled over. "You look lovely tonight, Alexandra."

Alex longed to brush the hair back from his forehead and slide her finger over those fresh lips. "So do you."

The words just popped out, but she meant them. Nick's grin broadened. She didn't know what to think of this man. When he didn't treat her like a little sister, he could be charming. But then Tony clapped Nick on the back, and Nick reverted to his teasing personality.

Rosemary, who'd followed her grandson, sent him a quelling glance. She took hold of Alex's hands. "You do look beautiful tonight. CeCe would be proud."

Mattie, Rosemary's housekeeper, announced dinner, and they moved to the dining room. Seated between Rosemary and Bree, Alex enjoyed Rosemary's reminiscences about CeCe's life in Newport. Their Clan leader portrayed Alex's mother as a light-hearted daredevil. Like a flower reaching toward the sun, Alex yearned for more. She'd only had glimpses of the carefree young girl Rosemary described.

Rosemary questioned Alex about her mother, father, and their lives in Phoenix. Alex sensed Rosemary's curiosity came from a loving interest and answered her questions with enthusiasm. Nick's grandmother made Alex feel like a cherished addition to the family rather than a new source of Clan power.

Engrossed in the stories about her mother, she'd missed the underlying tension building in the room. When Mattie brought in the dessert and Bree cleared her throat, an uneasy silence followed. "I've asked you all here to discuss some troubling events. I believe the rest of our Clan should have arrived by now. We'll join them in the living room in a moment. I've filled Rosemary in on the latest details. As Clan leader, she'll conduct the meeting."

Bree glanced at Alex, closed her eyes for a moment, and stood. "Ready?"

No one seemed inclined to touch their dessert. A chorus of scraping chairs followed her request.

As they approached the living room, Alex became aware of the distinctive music of Franki's bracelets. Her aunt's restless hands never stopped moving. First, she pulled at her hair, then played with her necklace, and then reached up to her hair again. The air thrummed with nervous strain. Alex's breathing quickened in anticipation. Something big was going down.

****

As Rosemary led Alex into the room where six strangers waited, she took Alex's hand, then directed her to a space on a sofa between herself and Franki. Alex surveyed the new group. She swallowed, her throat suddenly dry. The curious glances aimed her way only heightened her anxiety. The strangers appeared normal, casually dressed. She calculated their ages somewhere between thirty-five and fifty.

A few greetings were exchanged before everyone looked to Rosemary. "I'd like to say I'm glad to see the whole Clan tonight, but I'm not. Not under these circumstances." She paused and put her hand on Alex's shoulder. "Before I begin, let me introduce Cecile's daughter, Alex."

Alex ducked her head and wished she were invisible. She peeked up through her lashes at the strangers. No one had mentioned other Clan members. She hoped Rosemary wouldn't ask her to go through last night's events again.

Rosemary continued. "Cecile was murdered six months ago. We believe she can now work through her daughter to help us in this crisis. She's still with us in spirit." Rosemary turned to Franki, who held up CeCe's urn.

Loud chatter erupted. "Who killed her?" "Why was she murdered?" "What's the crisis?"

Rosemary raised her hand. "We have an emergency situation. We aren't certain how serious, but something has begun that could have lethal consequences."

At her words, all conversation ceased.

"The arrival of Alex may have precipitated it."

The statement, spoken in Rosemay's sensible tone, made Alex want to shrivel up and disappear. Instead, she straightened in her seat and ignored the calculating gazes turned toward her.

Rosemary clapped her hands. "Listen to me. We believe whatever began would have happened a long while ago if Cecile hadn't moved away. For some reason, the monster that lurks in that hellhole next door has targeted Alex, who turns twenty-five on the fourth of July."

Rosemary paused to let that sink in. Knowing looks passed between Clan members.

"Last night, events led us to the Newport Tower, our ancestor's legacy," she continued. "There, Alex came into contact with the ancients who built it. She received a warning."

Exclamations of "What?" and "How?" from the newcomers resounded in the room.

Rosemary curtailed their questions and gave them the Templar message. Alex squirmed at the disbelief and fear expressed on their faces. Trepidation led to argument.

Rosemary raised her voice. "I haven't finished. We

all wondered why Cecile left, why she abandoned her heritage. In hindsight, her departure may have been her guardian's method of protecting her." Rosemary lifted her hands in a gesture of helplessness and shook her head. "We'll never know. Our immediate concern is that something evil has marked her daughter."

Rosemary nodded to Franki. Her aunt walked to the other end of the room where a covered easel stood. Warning vibrations rippled through Alex; she moved one hand to her throat. Despite her guardian's alert, she needed to see her portrait, although she would have preferred to do so without an audience.

Rosemary held Alex's hand in a crushing grip as Franki prepared to unveil the canvas.

Before she could, however, one of the Clan members asked, "Rosemary, do you believe this girl? You think there's trouble in the house?"

A few other members echoed their concern. One woman shook her head. "It can't be. It hasn't been long enough since the last appearance."

The first man sounded a little more confident. He adjusted his glasses and cleared his throat. "The trouble must be because of the girl's inheritance. You said she'll receive her gifts on Monday. That must be it. If her powers will be as strong as you believe, they're probably sending out currents she can't control. No one else claims to have seen our ancestors. You can't assume that thing over there has awakened."

A few heads bobbed in agreement, grateful to accept a more comforting explanation.

Rosemary's words doused their obvious relief. "Enough, Adam. You can see for yourself." She flung her hand out in a gesture to Franki. "Uncover it."

As Franki reached out to expose her work, Alex closed her eyes and held her breath. She let it out in a rush when gasps echoed through the room. She squeezed her eyes tighter and tried to control her shaking. Her former curiosity was crushed by an elemental fear. Her one thought? Escape. She even considered making a run for it.

With all her concentration focused on how to remove herself from the room, it took her a moment to hear Rosemary whisper in her mind. *It will be painful, but you can do it. You must see how serious this is. Open your eyes.*

Alex tried to steady her fears. She eased her eyes open but gazed at the floor as she stood. Bracing herself, she looked up. No. Bile rose to her throat. She fought to keep it down.

How could her aunt have painted this?

Chapter Twenty

Rosemary had said that the painting would be bad, but Alex wasn't prepared for what she saw. Franki's small easel might have gone unnoticed in the large room, if not for the vibrant colors and bold brush strokes. Alex stared at the lifelike scene. She had no doubt she was the woman on the canvas. The face was hers. But she'd never looked like that.

Features contorted and mouth open in a silent scream, the image was a caricature of terror. Her painted twin—Alex didn't want it to be herself—lunged forward to escape some horror from behind. Her arms reached out as if trying to pull away, but something stopped her. Ground mist attempted to cover it. Bright, blood-colored light illuminated a writhing mass. Her skin tingled as if rough scales scraped around her ankle and slithered up to capture her leg. A scream rose in her mind.

She wanted to look away, but she couldn't. She tried to tell herself she was overreacting. It was a canvas covered with paint. The sensations were all in her head. She forced her eyes away from her terrible likeness to focus on the structure in the background—the house that tormented her.

Lia had shown her the place five days earlier. But this mansion bore no resemblance to that crumbling wreck. No longer old and decaying, it appeared strong and vital, suffused in a reddish-yellow light.

Alex wasn't aware of moving, yet she now stood within inches of the scene. A numbing silence embraced the room. The air tingled with anticipation, like the prelude to lightning. Over the drumbeat of her heart, she barely heard the whisper of her inner guardian. *Beware!*

Alex might have fallen then if strong hands hadn't steadied her. "Come on, Alexandra. Sit down."

She looked up at Nick's kind eyes and leaned into the strength of his arms as he led her to her seat. For a moment, she fled from her overwhelming fear to the safe place in her mind. Instinct screamed at her. She needed more than mental serenity. She needed physical distance. She never should have come here. She made a frantic plea to her mother.

The whisper of her mother's voice filled her head. *I'm here, baby.* A sense of warmth, like a soothing caress, enveloped her.

For a moment, Alex imagined her mother's sweet smile and a new strength swelled within her. She pulled herself upright and nodded to Rosemary. The meeting continued.

"As you all know, Franki can foresee the future through her work. This…" Rosemary gestured at the painting. "…came about after Alex experienced a worrisome nightmare. In it, she found herself in danger and awakened at her mother's warning. We'd always suspected Cecile's talents might include dream walking. It appears she has some of that ability still."

"Oh, come on," someone said. "That doesn't prove anything."

Ignoring the interruption, Rosemary continued. "As Alex stood before the gates of the Convent House, a voice tried to lure her inside. If Cecile hadn't intervened,

Alex might have been lost to us." She stopped to look them each in the eye. "We believe there is another out there who can stalk our sleep."

The room became still. Sensing the fear, Alex flinched at Rosemary's next words. "Good. You need to be afraid." She then clapped her hands in a demand for silence. "We must begin the *Watch*. Our Clan numbers eighteen. We'll double up and work a four-hour rotation with members on guard at the Convent House twenty-four seven. My grandson, Nick, will stay in this house to safeguard Alex's sleep. Once she comes into her full power, we will go after the entity together just as those first Templars did many years ago."

Alex saw negative headshakes as members looked around. From their faces, she understood they didn't like Rosemary's pronouncement. Some of the first Templars hadn't survived the demon's wrath.

Rosemary issued a challenge. "Do you think you'll live to see another day if it gets Alex? Look at that image. It's hungry. You'll be a tasty snack." She turned to Bree. "How are they taking it?"

Bree paused as she surveyed the group. "Oh, no, Sandi. You're wrong. You'll never get far enough away from it."

The pudgy brunette's mouth fell open. Bree scrutinized the rest of the group. "Sandi's not alone. You're all hoping to evade your responsibilities." In a harsh whisper, unlike her aunt's normal, rational tone, Bree finished, "It will hunt you down."

"Wait a minute," someone yelled. "Are you reading our minds?"

"You've got no right," another cried.

Amid anger and confusion, the pressure in the room

began to change. A scraping sound drew Alex's attention to the easel. It had moved backward on its own.

Rosemary raised her hand, and the painting moved to lean against the wall.

By this time, all the guests had left their seats, furious at the incursion into their thoughts. Nick and Tony moved in front of Rosemary. Alex, deciding this might be a suitable time to leave, leaned forward in her chair, but Rosemary's hand stopped her.

When one of the lights above the fireplace burst, Alex ducked and Rosemary leaped from her chair, pushing in front of Nick. Without saying a word, she raised her hands in the air, waving in a circular motion.

All noise dissolved. People still ranted, but Alex could no longer hear them. Alarmed, several Clan members reached out but immediately encountered the barrier Rosemary had erected around them.

Alex inhaled in disbelief and turned to Rosemary. Her protector had changed. Eyes burning black, legs planted wide, Rosemary issued a warning to the rebellious Clan members. *Enough! You would use your powers to destroy the Brendani home? You forget who I am, who we are.* Her tone became deceptively soft. *Perhaps you forget where your gifts originated. Perhaps you even forget why you were given these gifts.*

She turned to Bree and, with a chilling smile, continued. *Maybe we should all take a tour of the Convent House? I'm sure it will serve as an interesting reminder.*

As she said the last, all heads spun to the painting.

Rosemary waited another minute until she had their attention. *Are you ready to listen?*

Confusion mingled with fear on the faces of the

imprisoned Clan members as they digested the unpalatable truth. They each nodded to their leader.

Rosemary lifted her hands and erased the enclosure she'd created. She didn't need to raise her voice this time. "We've all fallen into complacency. We've accepted our special powers as our due. From this day forward, all that changes. As the original Templars were tasked with protecting the pilgrims, so too are we charged with safeguarding the innocent." She paused. "The Watcher Clan was created to contain the demon. Someone or something has awakened it. Trying to run is futile. We must act."

She raised her hands in a supplicating gesture. "Our heritage has caught up with us. It's time to pay for the gifts handed down from our ancestors." She took a deep breath. "After tonight, we have two more days. Two days to neutralize the threat. Until that's done, we're all marked individuals."

When no one spoke, Rosemary said, "Please believe me when I say I've had no desire to see this day. If there were any other way to manage the situation, I'd jump at it. We have no options."

The questions began.

"Who woke that thing up?"

"Why is it after Alex?"

Rosemary looked tired. "We believe she's targeted because of her forthcoming birthday. We're fairly certain the person who killed Cecile wants to get their hands on Alex and her powers. Instead of pointing fingers, we must come together to save not only Alex but the entire Clan."

The reminder of her mother's murder dug a fresh hole in Alex's heart.

After Rosemary's pronouncement, a few alternate plans of action flew around the room. Rosemary reminded them there was nowhere to run. "They reached Cecile in Arizona." The room quieted. "All right, this is how it will work. You'll be paired to enhance your strengths. We'll match you according to your powers: offensive with defensive, strong with weak. If something out of the ordinary happens on your patrol or anywhere else, you'll alert the rest of the Clan. We will face the threat as one."

The emotional current pulsing through the room left Alex breathless. What had she walked into?

Rosemary turned to Bree. "Please explain about the arrangements for Alex's birthday."

Bree, who'd been quiet while her peers voiced their concerns, positioned herself beside Alex. "We intend to have an Independence Day party with fireworks and music. The guests will be those in this room. Alex came into the world at 10:02 a.m., Eastern Time, on the fourth of July. If we've been successful in keeping her safe until that day, we can expect some kind of trouble then. We're hoping the birthday party will mask any loud noise. Best case scenario, the party will be a celebration of our success."

Rosemary punctuated her next words by pointing at each person. "Until then, each one of us has to keep on full alert, shields up, powers tuned. We can't trust anyone. It will have its minions out there. Protect yourselves and your children." She stopped and sighed. "We'll set up the round-the-clock guard on the Convent House tomorrow. In the meantime, we—" She gestured to the Stuarts and Brendanis. "—will continue to monitor the area. That gives you time to make arrangements at your own homes."

Before discussing the patrol rotation, Rosemary asked everyone to please refrain from using stimulants like coffee, alcohol, or drugs until after the crisis. "We need to be at our full power."

Alex sat wide-eyed as she listened to everyone groan. They all believed Alex had brought the trouble with her. And she had.

When Rosemary finished speaking, the guests circulated, studied the painting, and spoke in low voices. They all ignored Alex, treating her like a pariah. So much for the Clan working together. She'd like to tell them all to go to hell.

****

Nick handed her a glass of water. "I figured you might be thirsty." The look he gave her was one of pity. Damn, she could take his teasing but not his pity. She put down the water and walked out to the kitchen. Even Mattie gave her a wary glance as she paused in her cleaning duties.

Alex moved on through to the back porch and sat in one of the rockers. What she wanted to do was walk the labyrinth. Would her grandmother also blame her?

Nick threw himself in the chair next to her. "You shouldn't be outside by yourself at a time like this, Alexandra. You've had a nasty shock. If you want to talk, I'm here."

She craved solitude, not Nick and his left-handed sympathy. His grandmother must have put him up to it. Alex snapped, "If you must know, it occurred to me that the best solution to the problem for everyone in there would be to take me out of the equation. With me dead, whoever is after me will stop."

His voice hardened to granite. "Don't flatter yourself. Someone has awakened whatever is in that house. To deal with it, we need every Clan member."

Hell! When would she learn. Nick hadn't come out to be social. He was protecting one of the Clan's pawns. She stood and glared at him. "Am I allowed to take a walk in the labyrinth?" She turned and descended the steps.

"Suit yourself," he said and got up to follow her. "I'll wait for you at the entrance in case there's any trouble."

His words conjured up a picture of the monster. She stopped, peered through the shadows, and wrapped her arms around herself. "Is it around here?"

"I doubt it." In the moonlight, Alex caught a slight smirk on his face. "The demon's range should be limited to the area around the treasure. You'll be safe in the labyrinth, and I'll take care of you out here."

She stared out at the long, shadowy path to the labyrinth and almost reversed her decision. If it hadn't been for Nick's superior attitude, she might have turned around. Instead, she swallowed her fear and stepped into the garden. The call of a night bird startled her, and when a sudden breeze rustled the bushes, she jumped. By the time she reached her grandmother's sanctuary, her body hummed with tension.

The crescent moon's soft glow provided sufficient illumination to follow the rocks that bordered the swirling path. Alex slowed her footsteps trying to gain control of her fears. What should she do? A demon had singled her out, and all those people who joined them tonight hated her. In their position, she might despise herself, too.

She shuddered as she remembered Franki's painting

and twisted her head toward the Convent House, half expecting to glimpse a hungry snake.

No need to look over your shoulder. That devil's spawn couldn't breach this magic. You're perfectly safe with us.

Alex didn't know whether to be relieved by her grandmother's words or angry that Kitty was so dismissive of her feelings. Before she could decide, she detected the presence of another spirit. Hope filled her heart. "Mom? Is that you?"

Kitty snorted. *Of course not.*

"Who is it?"

A softer, kinder voice answered, *I'm Gabrielle, your great-grandmother.*

Kitty cut in. *I'm not alone. My mother and grandmother are here, too. We're the Keepers of the Labyrinth.*

"What about my mom?" Alex asked, close to begging for the comfort of her mother's voice. "Why isn't she with you?"

CeCe isn't a keeper. Then, of course, she's using her fledgling ghost energies to help you stay alive. Now, say hello to Gabrielle.

Chastened, Alex wondered at the proper etiquette and decided on formal. "I'm pleased to meet you."

You don't have to speak out loud, dear. We can hear your thoughts when they're directed at us.

Sorry, I forgot.

Kitty broke in. *What are you moping about?*

Why had she come? To find some comfort? To get assurance that the demon's awakening wasn't her fault? She looked around, hoping no one could hear her, then gave herself a mental head slap. She'd use telepathy. She blurted out her fear. *Everyone inside hates me. They say I'm the reason the monster, from that place (*she cocked her thumb in the direction of the Convent House*), is after them. And there's a humongous black snake that wants to kill me.*

Oh, yes, the painting. I don't blame you for being afraid of that thing, but for Heaven's sake, you're not defenseless.

What are you talking about?

Your powers.

Oh, right. I'm going to read its mind, so I'll know when to jump out of the way.

I don't appreciate your tone, young lady.

Sorry. She wasn't, though.

How did you handle that man at the cemetery?

In the chaos of the last few days, Alex had almost forgotten. The terrifying trip to the fifteenth century last night and Franki's artwork today had driven the kidnap attempt from her mind.

The sweet voice answered. *Cece told us what happened. You poor thing.*

But...I... That wasn't me. I can't do that.

Kitty broke in. *Of course, you can't do that, yet. Your mother guided you.*

Kitty's words struck a memory. Alex had called on her mother right before the heat had traveled into her hand.

For someone with so much talent, you can be awfully dense, Kitty said.

Alex couldn't believe she'd expected encouragement from her grandmother.

The sharp voice continued. *Until you receive your gifts, your mother can help you. She's still adjusting to her new circumstances, which means her own powers are unreliable. Call on her when you're in real trouble. In the meantime, before you use any magic, picture it in your mind, then do it. Forget all this useless self-doubt. Trust your gifts.*

Alex recognized sound advice, but Kitty's delivery left a lot to be desired.

You might as well know who your allies are, her grandmother said. *You don't have much time to get the hang of your skills. We're here for you.*

That's right, dear, Gabrielle added.

A noise like a snort from Kitty preceded her pronouncement. *CeCe believes your powers will be important. I'd guess so if they woke up that age-old demon. Trouble is, if you do get to your birthday, you won't have time to learn how to use your new gifts.*

Alex almost choked. Kitty was the antithesis of a doting grandmother.

A summons from Rosemary cut off Alex's sarcastic reply.

Chapter Twenty-One

Rosemary stood in the living room in front of the Clan to make her announcement. "I wanted to keep you all apprised of the latest plans. Everyone stays together. We'll announce the Fourth of July party in honor of Alex and tell everyone that our relatives will be arriving. You will each bring your family. We've decided it's best to keep those with our blood close. There's plenty of room if we use both houses. We've designated the Brendani home as headquarters, so Mattie will oversee the main meals here.

"From now on, no one roams these grounds alone. Though the demon's mandate is to protect the relic buried near the Convent House, we must stay on guard. We will take no chances. Let me make this crystal clear. We do not know what or who we're up against. This thing has no compunction about killing."

Nick's blue-eyed grandmother, a sixty-something well-dressed woman, spoke in matter-of-fact tones about war with a demon. Alex wrapped her arms around herself and dug her fingernails into her skin, hoping to wake from this nightmare. Instead, the pain just added to her discomfort. Maybe she should hop on the next plane home. Then a familiar ache reminded her. She had no home. Even if she did, what good would it do? That man had found her, and running away hadn't saved her mom.

A commotion stirred the room as Lia took

Rosemary's place. Her cousin's appearance surprised Alex. Instead of her usual self-assured charm, she appeared subdued and distracted as she surveyed the room. This was the first time Alex had seen Lia without a smile. Lia twined a finger around a curl against her shoulder while her other hand pointed to a chart with the sleeping arrangements.

The distribution of bedroom assignments didn't interest Alex until she saw Nick's name in the slot next to her. She wondered why Lia had put him there and went up to question her.

Her cousin's eyebrows rose. "You want your bodyguard nearby."

Alex didn't think she needed someone to watch over her, although if she had to have a personal guard, she'd like him to be cute. Nick was definitely hot, but she knew he'd try to take over her life. That wasn't going to happen.

Determined to speak to someone about it, she had to suppress a grin when she realized that she'd rather talk to her tough Aunt Bree than sweet Rosemary, who'd taken on the personality of a military general.

She found a tired-looking Bree in the kitchen making tea. Her aunt managed to give her a lopsided smile. "Quite a night. I'm afraid we weren't prepared for this."

"I'm so sorry."

"It's not your fault. Someone out there covets both the Templar treasure and your impending gifts."

"Aunt Bree?"

"Yes?"

"Don't you think I'd be better off with someone from our family protecting me instead of Nick?"

Bree's eyes filled with sympathy. "It's difficult for you to understand all this, Alex, but you have to accept that we know what's best for you. Nick's talents make him the only person able to do the job."

"He can *persuade* the snake to leave me alone?"

A tiny chuckle escaped. "Of course not. That's just one of his gifts."

"Huh?"

"We're certain someone has targeted you in your sleep. If that's true, you're in grave danger. You can be manipulated or even killed. You need another with those abilities to protect you. Two nights ago, your mother was able to wake you before you were harmed, but she's weak, and the next time, your attacker will be ready for her. That's where Nick comes in. He'll be able to guard your sleep."

"Nick's a dream walker?"

Bree poured hot water into her cup, releasing the scent of mint into the air. "He is."

"You mean he can enter my mind when I sleep?"

"That's right."

For a minute, Alex marveled at the scope of Nick's powers. He was like a superhero. On the back of that awareness, another surfaced. Nick would be able to see all her nighttime fantasies. Heat surged to her face. She stood tall, gave an emphatic headshake, and raised her voice. "No way. I'm not comfortable having him in my mind, let alone my dreams."

Bree's pursed lips told her she'd made a mistake. Any fragility she'd attributed to Bree vanished. Her aunt's expression froze. Red crept up her cheeks, and her eyes blazed. Alex took a step backward. "You have no say in this whatsoever. If you think we'll stand for childish tantrums when our lives are in danger, you are sadly mistaken. Nick will watch over you in your dreams, your mind, or *any* place he deems necessary to ensure the safety of everybody in this Clan. Is that understood?"

Alex wasn't sure that she got the whole picture, but she knew when to back off. She dropped her gaze and gave a curt, "Fine."

The door slammed on Bree's exit as her tea steamed on the counter. Alex craved space and fresh air. She spun, headed for the back door, but stopped when she heard the low buzz of conversation.

Lia's voice filtered through the screen. "With everything that's going on, shouldn't Alex cancel the date with Hunter tomorrow night?"

Exasperation filled Nick's voice as he answered. Alex imagined him brushing his hand through his hair. "Of course she should, but we can't do anything about it unless Bree changes her mind."

Lia sounded peeved. "You'd think, after seeing that painting, Alex would be happy to stay where it's safe. It's irresponsible for her to insist on keeping that date even if she does have a crush on the guy."

How dare they talk this way behind her back? Alex leaned in to hear better.

"Tell me about it," Nick said. "God, she's stubborn. She told me we'd be better off if she was dead."

"Oh, no."

"Right. At least she won't be alone tomorrow night. I'm glad you'll be with her. I'll stay nearby. If anything at all seems off, call me."

"I'm sure Bree knows what she's doing, but if someone released that beast and is still alive . . ."

"That's what I'm afraid of. Anyone who could control a demon would have tremendous power."

"With Alex's birthday less than three days away, her nemesis is sure to have a plan."

Nick sounded grim. "Rosemary expects Alex's gifts to be significant. We can't let him get those powers."

A loud bang on the outside wall made Alex jump and back up. "Damn," Nick said, "I wish I knew how the dream walker plans to do this."

A brief silence followed, and Alex checked behind her to make sure she was alone.

When Lia spoke again, she sounded scared. "I'm worried, Nick. What if he comes after Alex and we can't protect her?"

Alex had to strain to hear Nick's answer.

"I think Bree and Rosemary are working on a plan."

"For tomorrow night?"

"Right. Whoever wants Alex won't be expecting bodyguards."

"You mean a trap?"

"Look, don't say anything. It's not finalized. I wish we had some kind of clue about who or what we're fighting."

"I know."

"At least Alex is taking care of herself. I tried to get into her mind, and her shields were up. She's accepted the reality of her situation, and she doesn't like it or the people who've gotten her involved. I'm certain she'll try to stay awake tonight so I can't protect her."

Alex, listening in the kitchen, gave an emphatic nod.

"I'm sure you're right," Lia said. "I'll talk to her later. If she wants to stay up, I'll keep her company and let you know when she sleeps. Nick?"

"Yeah."

"This thing has me frightened."

"Me too."

The sound of movement on the porch had Alex scurrying to the other side of the kitchen. She grabbed a soda from the refrigerator and almost dropped it when she heard Bree's clipped voice behind her. "What are you going to do about your date?"

When had Bree come in? Had she caught her eavesdropping? "What do you mean?"

"You need to call it off."

"I . . ." Alex's mind whirled. An image of Franki's creation filled her head, and she almost dropped the can. Then she remembered the demon only cared about the treasure, and she wouldn't be anywhere near it. She'd be safe in Newport with Hunter.

Everyone here was against her. The hell with them all. She couldn't wait to get away from people who didn't value her. She remembered the promise in Hunter's soft, brown eyes, the hard strength in his arms. Her body heated as she reacted to the memory. She wished he was with her now.

What was the big fuss, anyway? Lia would be along as their protection. She tuned out her intuition and the uncomfortable inner voice that said she was being childish. Instead, she raised her chin in defiance. "I'm going."

****

Leaving no room for discussion, Alex swept out of the kitchen and escaped to her room. Tired but afraid to sleep, she walked to the window. Worries stampeded through her brain, leaving behind a chaotic mess—demons, Clans, crazy psychic relatives. As she tried to rein in those images, she sensed someone. Spikes of cold invaded her body, and she hugged herself. The sound of her name sent her into a panic. She ducked away from the window.

"Alex?"

A light tap accompanied the voice. Not the demon. Someone at her door. She released her breath. "Come in."

Lia poked her head in. "Am I disturbing you?"

The sting from the overheard conversation in the kitchen was fresh in her mind, and Alex reacted. "You here to babysit?"

Although she'd tried to make it a joke, she could see Lia caught her mood. "What's wrong?" she asked. "I mean other than the whole end of the world thing."

Alex liked Lia and hated to lose the one friend she'd made in Newport. Maybe she should 'fess up about snooping. They'd moved to the sofa. Summer sounds—the rapid chirp of crickets and the faint murmur of wind chimes—drifted in through the window.

She avoided Lia's gaze and contemplated her twisting hands. "I heard you and Nick." She looked up in time to see Lia's eyebrows rise in a question. "Outside on the porch a little while ago."

"Oh," Lia said. "We were talking about your date with Hunter. It's none of our business, but we're both worried about you."

Alex rolled her eyes and tipped her head. "Oh, right. I'm too *irresponsible* to know what's good for me."

Lia blinked and then burst out laughing.

Her cousin thought their intrusion into her life was funny?

Before Alex could explode, Lia touched her

shoulder. "I'm sorry, Alex. I'm not laughing at you. I mean, I sort of am, but are you serious? You're worried about me calling you irresponsible?"

Alex felt betrayed but tried not to show it. "I don't see the humor."

"Come on, Alex. I didn't mean it. I made a poor choice of words. But after all that's happened to you tonight, I'm surprised that word is all you're upset about."

"I guess you're right, but I hate having someone tell me what to do, and going to Kitty for sympathy didn't help."

"Oh, big mistake," her cousin said with a grin. "What did she say?"

"That I wouldn't have time to learn my powers to be of any help."

"Tact was never Kitty's strong suit."

"She also called herself a keeper. What did she mean?"

"Every generation, someone is born in the Clan who's destined to protect the labyrinth and its magic. When they die, they're buried there. The keeper is always a woman."

"How do you know who's next?"

Lia lifted one shoulder. "You'll have to ask Kitty."

Her cousin's green eyes held nothing but sympathy. She took a deep breath. Lia wasn't the enemy. She confided to her cousin, "After seeing your mother's painting tonight, I'm afraid Hunter might be my last chance to have fun."

Lia nodded in understanding. "Let's get comfortable."

Alex turned sideways to face Lia, crossed her legs, and clutched a pillow in front of her. Lia pulled up her knees and hugged them. Since the topic of men was Lia's favorite, they spent the next half hour discussing old boyfriends, favorite movie stars, and their wish lists for the future.

Lia yawned and said, "I'm sure you don't want to hear this, but the best thing for you right now would be to rest. You've had shock after shock, and your system needs to replenish itself." As she spoke, Lia placed her hand on Alex's shoulder.

Denial leaped to Alex's lips, but a strange lethargy silenced her. Lia now held both of Alex's shoulders as she led her to the bed. "Lay down for a minute. I'll stay with you."

Alex knew she shouldn't sleep but forgot why. As Lia brushed her hand across her cousin's forehead, Alex closed her eyes.

Chapter Twenty-Two

Alex woke to a beautiful field filled with wildflowers accompanied by the contented hum of insects. Beside her, a sparkling stream made little splashing noises as it meandered by. The rock at her back had captured the heat of the sun, and she leaned into its warmth. Upstream, a lone fisherman cast his line. Her body relaxed to the soothing sounds around her as she let her eyes close. Somewhere in her mind, she remembered Lia had sent her there, but she didn't care. She embraced the comfortable nest and relaxed.

Sometime later, a prickling sensation along the back of her neck disturbed her. She strained her senses, trying to discover the cause. Silence. That was it. The absence of sound—no birds, no insects. Even the warmth from her rock had died. When she heard a soft, scraping noise, a warning flashed through her head. She began to shiver. Afraid to move until she could find the source of the danger, she raked her gaze around the area. The angler hadn't moved. She was safe there. The stream, too, was innocent. But the field... She focused on the tall grass at the edge of the wildflowers. An almost hypnotic swaying held her attention. The undulations moved closer.

Pounding footsteps jarred her into motion, and she leaped up. The fisherman was speeding toward her, yelling. She ran from him toward the field.

"Alexandra, no."

Nick? She stopped. What was he doing fishing?

"Get out of here, Alexandra."

Confused and frightened, she said, "Where can I go?"

"Get out of the dream!"

The urgency in his voice startled her. She shook her head and blinked her eyes trying to wake up. It didn't work. She looked at the rocks behind her and the water in front of her and froze.

"Dammit! Wake yourself up!"

Afraid to stay there any longer, Alex leaped into the stream, stumbled on the stones, and flailed in the water.

"Keep going. Don't look back."

Alex tried, but she couldn't help herself. She turned. What she saw stole her breath. And then she screamed. Backpedaling, she tripped and fell into the icy stream. Still yelling, she swallowed water and had a fit of coughing. She gave a panicky look back at the monster, whose huge, black triangular head had emerged from the grass. As its body slithered into the open, the enormous snake paused and lifted itself to a man's height. Her heart stopped for a moment, and her bladder released. The beast flicked its tongue in all directions. Then the head stilled. Its glowing, red eyes found Alex. Giant fangs sprang from its mouth. Her breath seized. Above the banging of her heart, she heard a voice call to her.

"Over here, Alex, quick. You'll be safe."

She turned toward the opposite bank. A man dressed in fishing garb stood there. His hand reached toward her ready to help. The sun in her eyes marred her vision, and she moved to shade the glare. A large hat hid his face. Before she could react, a strange whirring noise and a piercing shriek pulled her attention back to the demon.

The serpent rose in the air. Nick had snagged it with his fishing line. He tried to pull it away from her. His voice choked with the strain. "For God's sake, wake up. Get out. Now!"

"I can't. But I'm okay. This man's going to help me."

"No, don't. It's him."

Alex slogged toward the opposite shore. She reached for the offered hand. A familiar voice stopped her. "No, Alex."

Her mother stood next to her. "Mom?"

The man grabbed for her, his fingers scraping her hand. CeCe pulled her daughter back, and an angry roar battered her ears. When he jumped in the water, her mother said, "Picture yourself sitting up in bed. Now."

****

The scent of lavender greeted her as she opened her eyes. Though her heart still slammed inside her chest, relief overrode the fear. She was safe in her bed. Her sense of comfort disappeared when she heard a commotion on the floor. Lia knelt over someone who lay there. Alex pulled her sheet to cover up and stared aghast at Nick. His eyes snapped open with a sudden jerk. Why was he on the floor of her room?

Lia grabbed his shoulders. "Hold still, Nick, you're hurt." She wrapped her hands around Nick's arm. Blood dripped between her fingers. "Did it bite you?"

"No. That's from the fishing line." He stopped thrashing and glared at Alex. "Why didn't you wake up? Why were you running right into his arms?"

Alex had trouble speaking, the memory of the salivating viper still strong. Her hands dug into the safety of her bed as she shook her head.

"Calm down, Nick." Lia soothed him.

Nick gestured toward Alex. "Take care of her. She's the one who needs calming."

Before Lia could react, the bedroom door opened, and Bree walked in. "What happened?"

Nick's arm had stopped bleeding, and Lia sat beside Alex, holding her hands.

Nick answered. "He was there. A black monstrosity waiting to pounce. I didn't see him until he was right on her. She tried to get away in the stream, but the snake had her in his sights. I kept telling her to wake up, but she wouldn't. Then she headed right into the arms of that bastard."

Under Nick's accusing stare, it took Alex a second to find her voice. "I tried to wake up, but it didn't work. If my mother hadn't taken my hand, I'd still be there." She turned to explain to Bree. "That man promised me safety."

Bree raised her eyebrows. "What man?" She looked at Nick. "That monster was there?"

"Oh, yeah. That son of a bitch didn't count on me being around, so he used the snake to take me out and scare Alex into his arms." He scowled at Alex. "And she was ready to go with him."

Alex glared back. "Better him than the snake. But my mother saved me."

Bree raised a calming hand to Nick. "Your mother was with you? What did she do?"

Alex relayed her mother's instructions, and Nick snorted in disgust. "Damn. That's on me. I was so certain I'd be able to get her out that I never told her how to wake up."

"Don't blame yourself, Nicky," Bree said. "None of

us had any idea that this would happen. We had no time to prepare. Isn't it enough that you saved her life?"

Bree reached out to Lia. "And you, my dear, have done enough tonight. You're exhausted. Get to bed. Rest. It's almost four in the morning. I'll call in to your work and tell them you're not feeling well." She turned. "That goes for you, too, Nicky. You need to replenish your energy. I'll take care of Alex."

After they left, Bree sat down next to Alex on the bed. "What a horrible ordeal."

Alex wrapped her arms around her shaking body. "You have no idea."

"Don't worry. Whoever is behind this will also have to rest. You'll be safe until tonight," Bree murmured. "Though your enemy is strong enough to guide the demon into your dreams, he is but a single entity."

Chapter Twenty-Three

After Nick and Lia left the bedroom, Alex asked Bree, "Why was Nick here?"

"It's easier for the walker to control a scene the closer he is to the subject, and we can observe you both in case of trouble."

Alex supposed that made sense in a world of ghosts, gifts, and demons. That fact didn't help her nerves, though. "What if I fall asleep and he isn't around?" She was aware of the whine in her voice but couldn't stop. "How can I fight a monster in my dreams?" She swung her legs off the bed and almost fell. "Oh!"

Bree caught her arm and held her up. "Careful. You've had quite a shock with only two hours of sleep. Let's go downstairs and get something warm into you."

Alex checked the clock, surprised so much had happened in such a short time. She kept reliving her frenzied flight from the serpent. Memories of the frigid water made her shiver, and she scrunched her toes against the pain of the sharp rocks that had bitten into her feet.

The quiet in the kitchen unnerved her. Bree made them both a cup of tea. Alex couldn't sit still and jumped at the least sound. To keep busy, she grabbed the teacups to clean. Her aunt, who hadn't said much, touched Alex's shoulder. "You need sleep."

The cup in Alex's hand slipped and smashed on the

floor. Panic edged her voice. "I can't. He'll get me if I do."

Bree's tone softened. "It won't be dangerous. I told you he must sleep, too. Now is the perfect time to rest. I'm going to stay with you."

Alex's voice bordered on a scream. "But you can't come into my dream."

Bree reached for her niece's hands. "If you relax your shields, I can see into your mind. The minute I see any threat, I'll have Nick come to you, and you can always call on your mother."

Alex didn't like the idea but agreed. After Bree cleaned up the cup fragments, they went upstairs. The minute Alex walked into the room she froze. "No."

"You need to rest." Bree coaxed Alex to the bed.

"Sit. I want you to look at my necklace."

Alex locked her gaze on the shiny gold coin Bree lifted in the air. It twisted back and forth, catching the light. She became fascinated as Bree's fingers twisted the bright circle.

"Watch the medallion as it turns. Think of happy times."

Lost in the whirling coin and the soft cadence of her aunt's voice, sweet memories of her mom and the laughter they'd shared comforted her. She touched the special locket hanging near her heart, a gift from her mom that held a Navajo protection charm.

The sphere spun faster. A warm glow spread out toward Alex, and her fears eased. When Bree suggested she close her eyes, it seemed like a great idea. Images of her mother morphed into a quiet stretch of beach. She sat on a blanket and leaned back to enjoy the peaceful scene. Gentle waves lapped the shore, gulls squawked overhead, and the sun caressed her body.

"May I join you?"

Surprised to see Nick but pleased, Alex patted the spot next to her. "This deserted stretch of sand is beautiful. Do you come here often?"

Nick sat down and put his bag beside him. "When I want to get away from everyone. It's a great place to meditate."

"What do you have in the bag?"

He lifted his shoulders. "Beach stuff."

"Want to go for a swim?"

Nick had the cutest grin. "Not today. The water's pretty cold."

Alex stood up and grabbed his hand. "Come on, you sissy."

The minute he started to get up, she ran to the water.

"Wait a minute." Nick hurried after her.

Too late. She started to scream.

Nick plunged into the water and pulled her to him and swung all around. "Where is it?"

Crushed up against Nick's chest, Alex found it difficult to breathe. She choked out, "Where's what?"

"Why were you screaming?" he yelled.

No longer enjoying herself, she said, "The water. It's freezing."

Nick released his pent-up breath and his death hold on her. He kept his arm around her waist as he pulled her out of the water. Alex had to take quick steps to match his gait as they marched up the beach.

She bristled. "You don't have to be so mean. I wanted a quick swim."

Nick's grip on Alex tightened. The hard muscles of his arm bit into her. "When you screamed, I was sure he had you. I didn't think I could get there in time."

He took a long breath. "This isn't a game, Alexandra. We're not going to wake up and laugh about our crazy experience. That snake is real, and so is his bite."

"I-I'm sorry, Nick."

His voice lost some of its gruffness. "Don't take off like that again."

She became hyper-aware of the pounding of his heart and the taut muscles of his body. When she looked up at him, she caught her breath. His eyes burned into hers, and for a minute, she imagined what it would be like to have those delicious lips teasing hers. She dared to relax in his embrace.

With the tips of his fingers, he brushed the hair out of her eyes. Her lips parted as she lifted her face to his. The abrupt emptiness when he let her go made her stagger. With ragged breaths, he said, "Sit."

Her face began to flame as she threw herself down on the blanket. Ooh, she hated him.

They sat there in silence for a while. Nick spoke first. "I always seem to blame you for something you can't help. Sorry. Let's try to relax and enjoy the beach. You saw for yourself that the water is too cold."

He stopped talking, then, and lay back on the blanket with his hands behind his head.

Since his apology sounded sincere, Alex let some of her anger dissolve and lay back next to him. As the salt air washed over her, she enjoyed the sound of the waves and the pungent aroma of seaweed. She trailed soft sand through her fingers as she pondered the many sides of the man next to her. After a while, she broke the silence. "You know all about me, but how about you? You own the pub and live with your grandmother. What else? What do you do for fun?"

Nick chuckled. "I save damsels in distress."

Alex turned on her side to face him. His profile emphasized his hawk-like nose. The biceps on his arms stood out as he cradled his head. She gazed at his strong body and cleared her throat. "Don't you have anyone special in your life?"

"Special like how?"

"Special like a girlfriend."

Nick hesitated. "Rosemary is my girlfriend."

"Your grandmother?"

Nick turned and raised his eyebrow. "Yeah, you got a problem with that?"

Alex experienced a little skip in the vicinity of her heart. No girlfriend. She uttered her next question almost in a whisper.

"What happened to your mother?"

"She died."

Alex sensed his pain and didn't push. For once, she kept her mouth shut.

After a while, Nick spoke again. "She left us when I was twelve. Moved to New York City. I visited her there once. She died in a freak accident." The muscles in his jaw twitched. "A building crane collapsed."

Alex kept her voice low. "You lived with your grandmother?"

"My grandmother took over whenever my father had to go on a mission."

"Ooh, was he a spy?"

Nick's eyes sparkled as he grinned. "Navy Seal. They go when and where they're called."

"Oh."

More silence.

"What was your mother like?"

A long pause. "She was beautiful and selfish." He sat up. "I'd rather not talk about her. She's gone."

"Oh, Nick, I'm so sorry."

"It's no worse than you losing your mother."

But his situation was much worse. Alex had enjoyed her mother's love for her whole life. Nick had been abandoned as a young boy and then, again, when fate took her forever. Her death, so far away and in such a tragic manner, must have been devastating.

Their talk turned to likes and dislikes, favorite movies, books, songs, sports, and other interests. They were both enjoying themselves until the sky darkened. Nick, who was arguing the superiority of his New York team, stopped in mid-sentence and stood up. Alex hadn't noticed the storm creep in. A crack of thunder rumbled in the air, and she flinched, looking around in a panic.

"Where is it?"

"It's okay, Alexandra. It's not the snake." He reached down to take her hand. "It's time to get back. Picture yourself waking up in your bed. You go first."

Alex cringed as another clap of thunder rolled in. She squeezed Nick's hand and fought to focus on sitting in the middle of her bed.

Bree's voice greeted her before she opened her eyes. "I was afraid you'd never get my message. How are you doing?"

Alex took in the creamy walls of her room and the stern face of the woman in the chair across from her. Then she hugged herself. She'd done it. She'd woken herself up. "Hi, Aunt Bree."

"You've been asleep for six hours."

Alex yawned and stretched. "That must be why I feel so great."

"Good. I'm leaving. Come down when you're ready."

Alex got up to fix her hair and smiled as she remembered the look in Nick's eyes before he let go of her. Mmm, she could get used to having a bodyguard.

****

When Alex joined the family in the living room, she arrived in time to hear Bree questioning Nick. "Did you find someone to cover for you at the pub over the weekend?"

"My manager will do it. He's taken over for me before, and he's willing to work the busy holiday. I've hired two extra bartenders to help."

Guilt ate into Alex. She wanted to apologize. Nick had to abandon his business to watch over her at night.

Then, Lia poked her in the arm. "Did you call Hunter yet?"

"Rats." Alex couldn't believe she'd forgotten. "I haven't. I hate to do this to him. What am I going to say?"

"Just ask him if he's up for a double date with your cousin."

Uncle Sal moved his gaze between Nick and Alex. "I take it nothing untoward occurred while you slept?"

Nick ignored a stare from Alex and shook his head.

Alex glanced at her aunt. "Not until the thunderstorm."

One side of Sal's mouth quirked up as he looked at his sister. "A little dramatic, don't you think?"

Bree's reaction to her brother's teasing amused Alex. Her aunt's back straightened, and she spoke in a defensive tone. "It was the quickest way to get their attention."

"And, it worked," Nick said as he reached over and squeezed Bree's hand.

Franki, whose aqua outfit was covered by a large apron, poked her head into the room. "I just took a fresh blueberry pie out of the oven, if anyone's interested."

Everyone followed Franki into the kitchen.

Her aunt had confided to Alex that baking helped to calm her when she was anxious. Looking at the kitchen, Alex worried that her aunt might be close to a breakdown. The room, redolent with the smells of fresh blueberry pie, had baked goods on every available surface.

Bree stopped short and blinked at the crowded counters. "My God, Franki!"

Franki ignored her sister. "Someone will have to come to the store with me today. I'll never be able to carry all the food we'll need for the rest of the weekend."

Bree swatted her sister's back. "For Heaven's sake, have it delivered."

Franki's shoulders drooped. "You're right. I'm not thinking straight."

Lia walked over to give her mother a hug. "You're doing fine."

Sal ignored the conversation and cut himself a piece of pie. "Anyone else want some?"

Franki wrung her hands. "Is it too hot? Did it fall apart?"

"Calm down, KiKi," he said. "Everyone's on edge today, and it will get worse with all the people in the house. Let's try to get through it." He blew on the purple berries covering his fork and took a bite. "It's delicious."

Alex's lips twitched into a grin. She found it

difficult to imagine her suave, sophisticated aunt as KiKi.

Her humor dissolved, however, as she envisioned her sweet aunt in another more sinister role—prophetess through art. Suppressing a shiver, she remembered the depiction of the snake trying to drag her into the Convent House.

Chapter Twenty-Four

Alex licked a tasty piece of blueberry from her lip and followed Bree to her office. Today's agenda included the manipulation of small objects, moving and stopping them. Alex fared better this time. Nothing broke.

"Come on," Bree said. "Let's go outside. The entire Clan will be there, polishing their skills. The *Watch* begins tonight. Our gifts need to be strong."

Bree carried her training supplies in a canvas bag to the gazebo.

They stepped inside the ivory pavilion, and Alex paused to take in the view. To her left, varying tones of green with bright multicolored splashes, like paint on an artist's palette. On her right, restless blue-gray waters against a creamy stretch of beach. Such a beautiful place to relax, but her aunt was all business. She pulled a tennis ball from her bag and placed it on the floor. "Float this around us."

Alex blinked. Levitation? The last time she'd tried it, she'd annihilated Bree's pillow. "I can't do that."

"Not with that defeatist attitude. Now, clear your mind. Let go of the negative energy." She punctuated her order with a slap to the bench. The resounding smack shattered Alex's moment of tranquility and scared a small bird into noisy flight.

Alex followed the bird's path, wishing she could

join him. Instead, she nodded to Bree.

"Okay," Bree said, "reach deep inside. Seek your power. Command it to obey."

Alex didn't have the kind of magic Bree described. The whole idea was foolish, but she tried. Her aunt whispered, "The heat will radiate from your core. Embrace it."

Alex stilled, closed her eyes, and sought a fiery depth within her. She sensed a pulse deep in her chest. A spark of warmth emerged and began to grow. Her confidence increased. As she held her hands toward the ball, her fingers tingled. She envisioned holding it in her hands. Nothing. She blocked out everything else as she concentrated on the warmth in her hands and willed the object to come to her. An instant later, she embraced the fuzzy sphere. She stretched her lips in a huge smile, then opened her hands and imagined the ball sailing around the gazebo. Though it took three tries before the ball remained in the air, and then only for a few seconds, she puffed up with pride at her success.

"About time," Bree said, but she was grinning.

Weary from her effort, Alex leaned back.

"All right. On to self-protection."

Alex objected, but Bree was gone. When Alex followed, Bree said, "No. Stay there. I want you to close your eyes and sense my position as I move around. At the same time, I'll try to penetrate your wall. Stop me."

The strain of keeping track of her aunt and trying to maintain her shield proved too much. Bree broke into her mind three times. With sweat trickling into her eyes, Alex put her hands to her head and dropped to the bench. "I need to stop."

"Perfect time to take a short break," Bree said.

Alex leaned back, tired after her exertions. From her position on the raised platform, she saw two Clan members from last night's meeting maneuvering on the beach at the river's edge. The men faced each other with what looked like a soccer ball hanging in the air between them. She stared in fascination as the ball shot toward one of the men, then, when the ball exploded in the air, she gasped and clutched her throat. The noise and violence of the power display left her shaking. These were the same people who had been so angry at her presence last night.

A movement to her left caught her eye—a small dust storm near the greenhouse. She watched in horror as it changed into a funnel cloud. "A tornado!" she screamed and grabbed her aunt.

Bree chuckled. "That's Lia."

"What?"

"Your cousin can control the wind."

Alex stared at the small twister. Impossible. Lia was a healer. She shook her head. "How can she do that?"

"It's one of her gifts."

Everywhere Alex looked she saw the unbelievable. The sound of a motorboat on the river caught her attention. "What about the neighbors and people out on the water? What will they think?"

Bree grinned and brushed her hand in the air. "Nothing to worry about. We've put a shielding spell on the property."

Alex wondered again if she'd lost her mind after Mom's death, and all this was a hallucination. She shivered. That scenario might be preferable to one involving psychic powers and a hungry demon. Her gaze slid to the trees concealing the Convent House. A light buzzing stirred in her ears. The sound reminded her of the emergency broadcast system on the TV or radio, but softer.

"Alex!"

She blinked and pulled away from Bree's fingers snapping in her face. "What?"

"Are you okay? I know you're tired, but you can nap in the house."

"I'm sorry. I . . ." Trying to focus, she said, "I was somewhere else. Another time."

Bree furrowed her brows. "What now?"

"I had a vision. A young woman with dark hair fashioned in a bun at the nape of her neck. Her red gown looked like a creation from the 1800s."

"Where was she?"

"In a room with a massive fireplace." Alex paused. "Gold drapes covered the windows, and beautiful objects surrounded her."

"What was she doing?"

Alex placed her fingers on her forehead as she remembered. "Staring at a table with some cards on it." Her voice dropped to a whisper. "Then it got weird."

"What do you mean?"

"All of a sudden she turned toward me and glared as if I'd caught her in the act of doing something wrong."

"She saw you?"

Alex nodded.

"Are you certain?"

She wrapped her arms around herself. "Positive."

"Whoa. I don't understand this power you have, but it's worrying. It's as if you have a foot in each world." Bree stood up. "Let's go. You've done enough for today."

On her way to the house, Alex kept glancing behind her, unable to shake the feeling of hostile scrutiny.

****

Silence greeted them when they entered the house. Most of the Clan were outside practicing. Not so in the den where Bree led her. Franki, Sal, and Nick turned expectant gazes as she walked in.

"I told them about your vision," Bree said.

Franki asked, "Can you try to place the vision in your mind and send it to us?"

These personal intrusions made her crazy. They had no perception of the word, privacy. She grimaced but said, "Fine."

First, she called on the magic inside her. Once the comforting heat answered, she summoned the image of the woman she'd seen and relayed it to those in the room.

"Oh!" Franki stepped back. "She knew you were there."

Bree nodded. "I agree."

Alex pursed her lips. "That's what I thought. Do you have any idea who she is?"

Nick answered. "We're hoping my grandmother will be able to figure it out."

"Yes, Nicky, I'm glad you called me." Rosemary sailed through the door. With a smile in Alex's direction, she said, "I'm the oldest in the group and may have come across a photo from that time. May I see the vision?"

"Why not. Just call me the Oracle of Brendani."

Rosemary's lips twitched in amusement. "I'm glad you've still got your sense of humor."

The Clan leader studied the projected scene. Only the widening of her eyes indicated her concern. "I may have an idea as to her identity. And, if I'm right, it answers a lot of questions. What else do you remember about the room?"

Alex closed her eyes. Her one clear memory was the anger on the woman's face. Then she noticed something else. "A harp, painted gold."

"Thank you, Alex. I believe the woman in your vision was Madelaine Swenson."

Alex ignored the interest Rosemary's announcement had engendered, dropped down into a chair, and shut her eyes.

Two more days, Alexandra. You can handle it.

Despite her current state of confusion and the crowded room, Nick's presence in her mind reassured her. His words, telegraphed for Alex alone, eased her anxiety. She thanked him in kind, peeked up, and tilted her head to give him a tired smile.

Then Lia walked in. "Hey, Cuz, let's get ready for our date."

Alex slapped her forehead. "I forgot to call him."

"Don't worry," Lia said. "We'll surprise him." She tugged Alex out of the chair and led her from the room. When Alex looked back, she caught an angry frown on Nick's lips.

Had she made a mistake about tonight? She turned to Lia. "I do want to see Hunter again. He's nice, and we had so much fun, but I hate letting you all down."

"I thought you said this guy was gorgeous?"

Alex found it so difficult to follow the convoluted reasoning of these people. "What's that got to do with anything?"

Lia poked her. "You focus on the color of his eyes and the size of his biceps, and I guarantee you'll forget all about the problems at home. Besides, there's nothing else to do right now, so we might as well enjoy ourselves while we can. Come on. I'll help you choose an outfit."

Alex insisted on wearing something from her closet and Lia helped. "This skirt and top of yours will look dynamite together. Add gold earrings and a necklace, and he'll be your slave."

Alex laughed. "You're so bad."

"Listen, I know what excites a man."

The outfit was one Alex had bought before her mother became ill. They'd planned to attend a festive art gala. The memory awakened a gnawing ache.

"Alex." Lia's voice snapped her out of her funk. "Get ready. He's due in an hour."

As Alex headed for the shower, she recalled the woman's angry face in her vision. It sparked a terrible insight. What if someone could look in on Alex the way she'd eavesdropped on that woman?

****

The identity of Lia's date surprised Alex.

"You remember Rich from last night," her cousin said.

She'd seen those broad shoulders and dirty blond hair at the Clan meeting the night before. His presence brought back some of the angst she'd experienced when so much resentment had been directed at her. His smile seemed genuine, though. "Right. Hi, Rich. Nice to see you again."

Was Lia dating this guy? She shot Lia a quizzical look.

"Rosemary wanted extra muscle with us tonight."

A few minutes later, Hunter arrived. Alex couldn't suppress the knot in her stomach as she introduced him to Lia and Rich. He seemed pleased to meet them until

Lia said, "Hope you don't mind us barging in on your date?"

Eyes narrowed, he peered at Alex. She could feel her face heat up as words tripped from her mouth. "I meant to tell you, but I . . .there was so much . . ."

Lia cut in. "We're having a family reunion, and poor Alex has been bombarded with all the new faces. It's been crazy here for all of us, so I pushed to horn in on your date. You don't mind, do you?" she asked with an innocent smile.

Hunter's gaze swung to Alex, confusion in his eyes. He moved from one foot to the other as he tried to explain. "Unfortunately, I've made reservations for two at the Bayview Inn. They're so difficult to get. I'm afraid I can't change them."

"Oh, don't worry. That's perfect," Lia said. Her honey-colored mane of hair bounced around her beautiful face. "The owner is a friend of Daddy's. We won't have any trouble."

Hunter's face reddened, but he said, "Great!"

The restaurant sat on a cliff overlooking Narragansett Bay. Hunter led the group out to the spacious lawn bordered by a glorious blue span of water. Tables, set up for cocktails and relaxation, dotted the grass. Alex stood, enchanted by the view. A hint of salt caught on her tongue as the wind teased her skin. She turned to Hunter. "Could we stay out here for a few minutes?"

His eyes gleamed, and he stood a little taller. "That was the plan. Our reservation isn't until seven." He located a table and signaled the waiter. "We have plenty of time to have a drink and enjoy the scenery."

Alex blinked and shot a panicky look toward Lia.

None of them were supposed to drink alcohol. How could they explain that? Her worry turned to shock when Rich held up his hands in front of Hunter and said, "We won't be drinking alcohol tonight, but you won't mind. You won't question it because you'll believe it's normal."

Alex opened her mouth in shock and snapped her head toward Hunter. He never even raised his eyebrows. He nodded as if people said things like that all the time.

She gave her cousin a "what just happened?" stare and received an amused wink in return.

Lia proceeded to compliment Hunter on his excellent dining choice and asked, "How do you like working in Newport?"

"What's not to love? I get to meet loads of interesting people and live in a writer's paradise." He turned a soft smile on Alex. "Now that I've found your beautiful cousin, I can't imagine being anywhere else."

Alex managed to smile at the compliment while her mind churned. Had Rich just used magic? Could he do that? Foolish question. He had, and it worked since Hunter's expression never changed when they all ordered a soda.

By the time their table was ready, Alex's mood had brightened. She'd enjoyed the light-hearted conversation, and Hunter made her feel special. When he looked her way, and that was most of the time, she saw desire. Alex exercised a little partner appreciation, herself. Hunter, attentive, buff, and adorable, made her pulse race. She was glad Rich's good looks had discouraged any competition from Lia.

The building, steeped in history, intrigued her. Its original flavor was evident in the sweeping wooden staircase leading to the second-floor dining area. Here, wide oak floorboards contrasted with impeccable white tablecloths. The wait staff, in formal black and white, made Alex imagine she was a guest of the Vanderbilts during Newport's Gilded Age.

Hunter had reserved a table next to one of the windows. As predicted, the maître d' had no trouble tweaking the reservation. In the cozy atmosphere, the conversation turned to more personal topics. Hunter asked Lia what she did for work.

"I'm the concierge at the Chandler Regency Arms."

"Nice. That's an exclusive place. I'll have to see if I can get some advertising from you."

"Remind me, Alex. I'll put him in touch with the marketing director."

"Thanks, Lia. What about you, Rich?"

Lia leaned into Rich in a playful manner, making his blue eyes crinkle and a lopsided smile soften his square jaw. "Rich is a big, tough cop."

Alex caught herself before her mouth fell open. She was sure that Lia and Rich didn't know each other that well. Either Lia was a consummate actress, or she really dug the guy.

"Newport Police?" Hunter said.

"State police. Out of the Portsmouth barracks."

"Right. I've driven by there. You do a lot of traffic stops?"

"I'm part of the Tactical Operations team. We respond to crisis situations all over New England."

Alex stifled a smile as she noticed her cousin's eyes glow with interest while Rich described his work.

During dessert, the setting sun produced a spectacular display of orange and purple light. Alex stared out the window. "Oh, look. It's beautiful."

Hunter leaned in close and put his lips to her ear. "I ordered it just for you." The warmth of his lips on her neck sent electricity along her nerves. He put his hand on her shoulder. "I have the perfect end to a perfect evening."

She grinned at him. "And that is?"

"Dancing in Newport."

"Oh, let's," Alex said as she gave Lia a hopeful look.

Her cousin nodded. "Great idea. It's time we worked off some of that marvelous meal."

****

Newport's main drag throbbed with life. Bright lights spilling from busy establishments, the constant flow of headlights on the streets, and the excited babble of hundreds of moving partygoers melded into a scene that resembled a psychedelic beehive. Alex walked along with Hunter's protective arm at her waist, reveling in the festive atmosphere.

Before the foursome went into the bar, Lia contacted Alex. *Be on high alert. A closed-in crowd could mean trouble.*

The telepathy startled Alex. She'd forgotten the threat to her safety. How could she have become so involved with Hunter that she'd distanced herself from the horror of the last two days? With a mental pinch, she went on alert. On the way to the bar, she sent out a scan in a close circle around her. Not to read minds, but to open herself to her guardian, the one who'd saved her from the speeding car. Shields up and strong, Alex followed Hunter.

Movement proved difficult. As Hunter held Alex close to him and worked his way through the crowd, her

232

soft curves yielded to the hard muscles under his shirt. She liked the sensation. She wished she could give in to the feeling and melt against him but forced herself to continue her vigilance.

Hunter gazed down at her. "Ready to dance?"

She nodded her head, not trusting her voice. As she concentrated on the music, she relaxed into the safety of Hunter's arm. His shoulder was so comfortable.

Lia's telepathy jolted her. *Alex!*

Okay, Lia. I'll stop enjoying myself.

The dance ended, and Hunter led her to the bar. While Alex sipped her coke, he asked, "Are you having a good time?"

If she didn't have to be on constant guard, she'd be having a blast. Otherwise, she was golden. She gazed up at Hunter through her lashes. "What's not to like with good music and a handsome partner?"

During their next dance, Alex recognized the edges of trouble. Her skin began to tingle, and her guardian sent out a warning. Someone near her was sending out aggressive vibes.

When she saw Lia and Rich close in, her caution ramped up to full-blown fear. She flashed back to the demon, and she stumbled. Hunter caught her, and she felt her face flame. *He must think I'm the world's most graceless female.*

Having to hide the possible danger from Hunter seemed wrong, but it was for his own good. As she looked over to Lia and Rich, the atmosphere around her cleared. Her guardian quieted. She hadn't been the target. Her muscles relaxed, and, trusting that Lia and Rich would protect her, she managed to enjoy herself.

Both couples met up at the bar. Hunter and Rich

were discussing Newport restaurants when Alex noticed a familiar face. In a voice heavy with sarcasm, she whispered in Lia's ear. "How many people did Bree send to spy on me?"

"What are you talking about?"

"Don't look so innocent. I saw another member of the Clan over by the door."

Lia's lazy expression sharpened as she peered around the room. "Where?"

Alex started to point to the place where he'd been. "He's gone now."

"Who was it?"

"I can't remember his name, but he was the dude doing all the bitching last night."

"Adam?"

"Yeah, that might be the guy. Tall, slim, glasses?"

"That's him." Under her breath, she said, "What's he doing here tonight?" She alerted Rich and turned to Alex. "Don't go anywhere. I'll be right back."

A hand slid around Alex's waist. Hunter smiled down at her. "Everything all right?"

"Absolutely."

"Ready to dance?"

"Hold that thought while I take a trip to the ladies' room. I'll be back in a sec." She made sure to scope out those around her as she walked toward the back of the club. Lia would have a hissy, but she wasn't going far. She sent her cousin a message. *I'm in the ladies' room. Be a few minutes. They're crowded.*

No, Alex. Wait for me.

For crying out loud, I'm within screaming distance.

With too many people waiting to relieve themselves, Alex waited in the dingy hall that connected to the kitchen and the back door the waitstaff used for breaks. The dark green paint had outlived its shelf life. Grease and other unpleasant odors made her nose twitch. Despite all the turmoil, though, she was having a great time with Hunter.

When the back door opened, she assumed another busboy was back from a cigarette break. The cool air hit her at the same time as her guardian's warning. Before she could run, he had her. A hand clamped over her mouth, and her feet left the floor. He'd pinned her arms, but she was free to kick. And she did, as hard as she could. She sent out a silent scream for help and prayed Lia and Rich would hear her.

Chapter Twenty-Five

Alex's captor rammed his way out the door. He yelled, "Get the stuff," as he dragged her toward a parked car.

A whiny voice cut in. "Told ya. You should a done her in there."

"Hurry up. She's strong." He grabbed her upper arm and pinched. "Cut it out, bitch."

Alex screamed against the slimy hand attached to her face. The stink of sweat and cigarettes gagged her. She kicked so hard at his legs that one of her shoes flew off. Lia had warned her. Why hadn't she listened?

"Shit, hold her still. I have to get this over her nose."

"Hurry up."

Lia's voice came into her head. *Where are you?*

Out back.

The man moved his hand long enough for the second one to shove something at her. Terrified, Alex squealed and drove her feet into him. He went down and came up swearing. Before she could holler again, the first guy covered her mouth. His friend moved behind him, and together, they managed to clamp the cloth over her face. She stopped trying to scream and concentrated on holding her breath. She wrenched her head back and forth trying to get away from the noxious smelling rag. Her chest burned with the need to breathe. She held out as long as she could, but her starving lungs won the battle. A sickening sweet fog crept into her mouth. At the same moment, the vise around her arms disappeared, and she fell. Disoriented and in pain, she sucked in the fresh air.

"Are you okay?"

"Lia?"

"I've got you."

"My head hurts."

"You banged it when he dropped you."

The fog still lingered. As she tried to clear it, she asked, "What happened?"

"They ran toward the street when we arrived. Rich went after them. Let's see if you can stand."

Lia helped her up. Alex's head ached, and she had to fight nausea. While she clung to her cousin, whistles, bangs, and excited voices added to her discomfort. "You'll be all right in a minute." As Lia's soft hands touched Alex's head, the pain diminished.

A slurring voice interrupted them. "Oh man, too much partying? Need some help, honey?" Two young men, unsteady on their feet, headed toward them.

Lia flashed a smile. "Thanks, but we're fine."

Undeterred, they moved closer. One of them had a bottle of vodka in his hand. He held it up like a trophy. "We got a boat. Wanna go for a ride?"

Lia shook her head. "No than…"

An angry voice broke in. "Take a hike while you still can." Alex turned to see Nick square his shoulders and gesture with his thumb toward the street.

The men lumbered off.

Nick strode to Alex. "Are you hurt?"

"A little dizzy, but otherwise good."

She flinched as a loud firework went off near them,

and Nick put his arm around her. "It's all right. You're safe now."

Still a little woozy, Alex leaned into his embrace.

Rich returned a few minutes later, disgust in his voice. "Those bastards. I couldn't use my gifts with everyone around. They got away in the crowd."

"We've got to get back to Hunter," Lia said.

Nick dropped his arm from Alex. "Right. See you later."

Alex missed his warmth. Before she could thank him, he was gone.

Lia smoothed Alex's hair. "We'll tell Hunter you had an accident, and you need to go home. Rich can convince Hunter everything's fine."

****

Rich reentered the club from the front. The women planned to arrive after he met up with Hunter. Alex apologized over and over to Lia while Lia checked for trouble. When they went inside and the door closed in the small, dark corridor, Alex started to tremble.

"Wait a sec." Lia smoothed down Alex's skirt and rubbed her arms.

Alex's limbs stopped shaking and her confidence returned. She hugged her cousin. "Thank you. What will I tell Hunter?"

"Tell him you slipped, fell, and hit your head. You've got a terrible headache and need to go home."

Alex and Lia walked toward their dates at the bar in time to hear Rich say, "Hey, Hunter, what's up? I had to get a little fresh air. This place is intense." He ignored Alex and Lia as he said, "Where are the girls?"

"No idea. I was beginning to think I'd been dumped."

Lia's bright voice cut into his lament. "Hi, guys. Sorry we're late. Alex had an accident."

Hunter hurried over to her. "What happened?"

"I'm not sure. There must have been grease on the floor. I slipped and hit my head." She put her hand on Hunter's arm and looked up into his dark eyes. "Do you mind taking me home? My head is pounding."

"Of course not."

On the way home, Alex tried to stay focused on Hunter to assure him she'd had a wonderful time while she tucked away the quiet terror that threatened to burst from every pore. The couple in the back seat kept to themselves until the car pulled up to the house. They said their goodbyes and disappeared inside. Hunter stopped Alex at the front door. His passionate gaze shook her. "I want to go out with you again. Come with me tomorrow night to the fireworks. They're supposed to be spectacular. You'll love them."

His voice and the pressure of his hand against her waist produced a rush of heat. She imagined what it would be like to have him hold her in the dark as explosions of light shattered the sky. Too bad she couldn't go. But tonight's attack had convinced her that whether insulated by a crowd of people, or flanked by guardians, she wasn't safe. "I'd love to go with you, but my aunt has made plans for the next two days. Relatives will be coming to meet me. I can't leave."

Hunter's face echoed his disappointment. "Are you sure? I guarantee satisfaction." He leaned in, his kiss soft and sweet.

Alex smiled and reached for the door handle. "Good night, Hunter."

"Wait a minute. Isn't there any time we can get

together tomorrow? For lunch or coffee? You must be able to take a break sometime."

The wounded look in his eyes cut into her. She couldn't leave him like that. A quick get-together in the light of day wouldn't hurt. "Why don't we plan to meet in the middle of the morning, around ten? That way I won't spoil any luncheon plans my aunt might have. Call me."

As she turned to the door, his arm circled her waist and his lips found hers. Pulling her against him, he deepened the kiss. Although this was what she'd hoped for earlier, she felt no excitement. She pulled away and avoided his eyes. "Good night."

****

At ten past twelve, Alex didn't expect to find anyone up. The people in the kitchen who stared in her direction surprised and irritated her. She hoped her recent romantic exploits weren't obvious. But when Nick's ironic "Have a good time?" made her blush, she went on the offensive. "What are you all doing up at this hour?"

Bree slammed her cup down on the table. "Have you not been paying attention? In less than two days, you'll inherit your gifts. Someone doesn't want that to happen."

"I know . . ."

"And what about tonight? How did they overpower you? Why didn't you use your gifts?"

Alex remembered her terror. "I didn't sense him until he grabbed me. He had my arms pinned. What could I do?"

"Did you call on your mother?"

Alex dropped her gaze. She couldn't believe Bree blamed her for panicking. "I didn't think of it."

"What about controlling his mind?"

Alex jerked her head back and stared at her aunt. "I can't do that."

Disgust filled Bree's voice. "Of course you can. You've been persuading people to do your bidding your whole life."

Alex sighed. Bree was on a roll. "We're all trying to protect your life, not to mention our own, while you're out mooning around a stranger."

Alex's embarrassment lessened as her anger took hold. "You told me it would be fine to go out tonight if I took someone with me. Well, I did."

"And look how that worked out. What's the matter with you? Are you infatuated with him?"

That last bit had been so unfair that Alex lost it. "What difference would it make if I was? Since when is my love life anyone else's business?" She couldn't take anymore and turned to go. "Don't I have the right to some privacy?" Heat singed her cheeks. She noticed Nick's face was also red but, from the angry set of his jaw, not from embarrassment.

Bree put her arm around Alex's shoulders and led her out of the room. "We don't know who he is."

Alex tried to pull away, but Bree held fast. "Listen to me for a minute. In two days, you'll be safe from outside interference." She twisted her lips. "God willing. In any case, you can date Hunter all you want after the fourth. But, until then, stay away from him."

Alex looked down, unable to make eye contact.

"Do you understand?"

Alex hoped her aunt wouldn't see the lie in her eyes as she said, "Yes," and walked off. Being treated like a child didn't sit well with her. She wondered if she'd ever fit in with this family.

****

When Lia knocked on her door, she yelled, "Go away."

"Come on, Alex. Give me a break. You knew we'd have to tell Bree."

She did understand. Bree was the leader. But, dammit, she hated the fact that her life was out there, a topic to be dissected by everyone.

She opened the door and managed a grudging, "I know," before Lia hooked her arm through Alex's. "Come on. Let's have some girl talk."

Alex had to admit Lia wasn't the enemy, and Alex missed having a friend. "Why not?"

Once they got comfortable on the sofa, Lia said, "I told Bree you saw Adam at the club, and no one here has seen him tonight. It's kind of strange."

"He could have had a date."

"Maybe." But Lia didn't look convinced.

"Do you think he had something to do with the attack tonight?"

"Right now, he's a possibility," Lia said. "Someone in our Clan is in on this. We've got to stay alert."

Alex rubbed her arms. "Are you sure?"

"Yeah. It bites." Lia shook her head and flashed an impish grin. "So, he's a good kisser?"

Alex couldn't stay mad at Lia. Besides, she needed to tell someone. It had been a long time since she'd been on a date that ended in a kiss. Her face heated as she said, "I guess."

"What do you mean?"

"When we were dancing at the club, everything felt right. I enjoyed his strong body and sexy voice and expected our lips to meet with fireworks or, at least, some heat, but it didn't happen."

"What did you tell him when he asked you out again?"

"How . . ."

"He's smitten."

"I told him that the next two days would be crammed with relatives I'd never met."

"I'll bet your reaction had more to do with the assault tonight than Hunter." Lia's voice became serious. "For the next two days, why don't we concentrate on security? After that"—she grinned—"nothing but fun."

Guilt at her promise to meet Hunter tomorrow morning welled up, but Alex kept quiet. She turned the conversation around to Lia and Rich. "How long have you known him?"

Lia examined her nails. "Since last night."

"You looked pretty comfortable with each other."

Lia looked up from beneath her lashes and chuckled. "We're having lunch together, tomorrow. He's so hot. I hated to say good night."

"Why did you?"

Lia rolled her eyes. "Bree would have pitched a fit."

They discussed men for a while, and then Lia said, "Okay. Time to sleep. Bree and Nick are on their way."

"But I'm not tired." She swallowed as her pulse quickened.

"Calm down. You'll be fine."

A quick knock on the door announced the rest of her nighttime contingent. Alex stood and backed away.

Bree strode in taking charge. "Nick should sleep first in case someone's waiting for Alex."

Alex gasped. "You think he's there?"

Nick frowned at Bree as he answered Alex. "No. He

can't find you unless you're already in a dream." Nick's usual warm tone had changed, becoming more clinical as he continued, "At any time, if you suspect you're in trouble, wake yourself up. Picture yourself sitting in this bed. If you see me in trouble, wake up. You can't do anything to help me, and I can't wake up until you do. Don't hesitate. Get out of there. If you can't do it, call on your mother. She should be hidden somewhere near."

"Why would she be hidden?" Alex wanted to connect with her mother.

Bree answered. "Her powers are weak. It's too dangerous for her to be seen."

She didn't get it. How could you hurt a ghost?

Nick's voice brought her back to the uncomfortable present. "Are you ready?"

She shook her head. Lia took her arm. "Breathe."

Lia's gift produced the usual calm. Alex nodded. "Okay."

Bree turned to Nick. "Nicky, I want you on the bed this time." She scowled at Alex before she could object. "There's plenty of room there. He must be close, and I need to watch you both."

Alex caught the fresh grin on Nick's face as he lay down on his side of the bed and said, "Good night, Alexandra."

She couldn't understand why Nick's brief return to an irritating tease made her so happy, but she savored the moment.

Lia moved over to Nick and put her hand on his forehead. In a matter of minutes, he was asleep. She gestured to Alex. "Come on. Your turn."

Chapter Twenty-Six

Alex shivered on the deserted beach as gusty winds nipped at her skin. Clouds scudded across the gray sky like dirty puffs of smoke, blotting out any hope of sunlight. She rubbed her arms to warm them. This wasn't her idea of a great scenario. Then she recognized the shape of the dune to her left and its solitary scrub pine. Her mood lightened. The same place she and Nick had met for their last slumbering rendezvous.

Buoyed by that thought, she lifted her face to the elements and breathed in the scent of seaweed. The beat of the pounding surf echoed inside her chest as she contemplated the beauty of this isolated strip of sand.

"Here. Put this on."

"Whoa. You scared me." Alex came back to the present with a start.

Nick rolled his eyes but held out a blue zip-front sweatshirt.

She slid her arms in, grateful for the warmth. "Thanks, did you read my mind?"

Before she could secure the zipper, he'd come around in front of her and taken the ends out of her hands. She held her breath as his fingers inched upwards, past her abdomen, her waist, and her breasts. He paused as he reached her chin. She tipped her head up, unable to move. With his eyes locked on hers, his voice softened. "Better?"

Heat, that had nothing to do with the sweatshirt, spread through her body. The intensity of her reaction to him surprised her. She'd been sure she wanted Hunter, but somehow Nick unearthed stronger emotions. She licked her lips in unconscious invitation.

He took a deep breath, grinned, and dropped his hands.

What? Damn him! That was a deliberate tease. Oh no. He wasn't getting away with that. Before he could move, Alex grabbed the collar of his jacket and pulled him to her. The astonishment on his face was satisfying.

Inches away, she watched his blue eyes turn dark and dangerous. A wave of need swept through her, and she claimed his mouth. At that moment everything changed.

Her touch seemed to ignite a fire. He growled and pulled her in, taking control as he deepened the kiss.

She tasted the salt on his lips and inhaled his spicy scent. As his hands moved lower against her back, her senses reeled. She ran her fingers through his hair. Heat consumed her body. Her breath caught in her throat.

Lost in the heady sensation of Nick, she almost fell when he released her. She blinked and peered at him, trying to understand. His hair was mussed. Passion still clouded his eyes. What was wrong?

"Alexandra, we can't. Not now. Not here. It's too dangerous. I have to stay alert. No distractions." He gave a rueful smile. "No matter how beautiful."

While Alex fought to control her frazzled breathing, she considered her reaction to him. She'd never lost herself so completely to any boy or man.

The wind tugged at Nick's hair as he scanned the area. Head tilted in a listening pose, and legs planted ready for trouble, he resembled a warrior. *Her warrior.*

While she pondered her chaotic emotions, she realized he was staring at her. His handsome face showed nothing of his former lust. She saw only curiosity. Was he going to ignore the attraction? Once again, she didn't know what to think about this man.

Despite a little ache in the vicinity of her heart, she sucked in her breath. If he wanted to play like it never happened, she could too. When a fresh burst of cool air made her rub her arms, she went on the offensive. "Why didn't you bring us to someplace warm?"

As he spoke, his attention turned to the water. "Lia sent us here. She must have been distracted."

Dread squeezed her chest. "What do you see?"

He knelt and gripped her arm. "Stay with me."

She swallowed, her throat suddenly dry, and dropped down beside him.

He lowered his voice. "It's a seal playing in the waves."

A little way out in the water a dark body skimmed across the swells. "Oh, look it's surfing. How cute."

Nick's head continually moved in all directions as he viewed their surroundings. "It might be a diversion."

The flutters in her chest turned into a fist-sized lump. She fought the desire to crawl into his lap. "The snake?"

"Easy. Calm down. You're safe." He opened his beach bag and took out what looked like a toy gun. The short silver barrel and black grip were almost lost in his large hand. He slid a black rectangle into the handle with a snap. "I'm prepared this time."

A cry from the ocean seized their attention. Making horrific sounds, the same seal flopped in the water. Then, the sudden flash of a black fin cut through the foam; the seal shrieked again. A shark.

Alex choked. "Oh no. He's killing it."

"He's toying with it."

Alex sat, staring in horrified fascination until a loud click caught her attention. Nick had cocked the gun. It was pointed behind her. She whipped her head around. A couple of hundred feet away, a flat black triangle moved over the top of the dune. Her heart began to pound. The snake's head lifted and swayed as its tongue darted around.

She knew the moment it found her. The swaying stopped, and its eyes became red slits. She caught its stare. It had found its prey. A slow ripple swelled along its length, and it moved toward her. Her skin tingled, and her bladder craved release. She wanted to run, but her limbs wouldn't obey.

"Alexandra. Wake up." Mesmerized by the serpent, she'd forgotten Nick.

"*Now!*"

The desperation in his voice brought her out of her daze. She shut her eyes and pictured herself in her bed. The sound of a gunshot echoed in her head as she woke up. She turned to Nick. His eyes remained closed, but his body twisted in desperate contortions.

"Aunt Bree, wake him up. He's with the snake."

Her aunt looked ill. "I can't. He has to come out of it himself."

"I heard a gunshot. Maybe he killed it." The image of Nick alone with that monster made her ill. "We've got to do something!"

She looked around for anything that might help and spied her mother's urn. *Mom.*

She grabbed it and sent out a silent plea. With her whole heart, she willed her mother to help Nick. Seconds later, the mattress shook. He was back. Lia hovered over him.

Alex tried to see what Lia was doing. "Is he hurt?"

Bree patted her shoulder. "Lia will take care of him."

Lia's touch calmed Nick's frantic spasms. "Easy, Nick."

Alex longed to comfort him. "Nick. I'm so sorry. When I saw that thing, I froze."

A grunt and a whispered "It's okay," didn't ease Alex's conscience. As she scooted off the bed, she filled Lia and Bree in on the situation. "Nick guessed the seal was a diversion, but its agony was so awful we couldn't take our eyes off it until that thing snuck up on us."

Guilt ate at her. If she hadn't hesitated... She jumped when he whispered, "Thanks, Alexandra." Blue eyes blazed in his colorless face. Alex turned to Lia. "Can you help him?"

"I'll do my best. He's been bitten. There's snake venom, and I can sense the presence of dark magic."

Bree's voice filled with alarm. "Can you determine what it is?"

"I'll have to take some blood and test it." Lia smoothed Nick's forehead. "I'll be right back."

Her cousin ran to the door, and Alex moved to Nick's side. She held his hand in both of hers. "Did you kill it?"

"No." He managed to squeeze her fingers. "She saved me."

Bree broke in. "Who, Nicky?"

"Alexandra's. . ." He coughed and waited to catch

his breath. "Mother."

"My . . ." She'd begged her mother to save him. "Did she come?"

"Surprised it." He closed his eyes and dragged in a breath. "From behind."

Lia returned. "That's enough. Nick needs to rest." She prepared to draw his blood.

Alex wanted to stay with him. If she hadn't hesitated to wake, he might be fine. He got hurt protecting her.

Bree leaned over to kiss Nick's cheek then shooed her out. "There's nothing you can do for him now. It's up to Lia."

"She can fix him, though, right?" A couple of tears slipped down her cheeks before she could blink them back.

Bree ran a hand over her face. "Don't worry." The words, meant to be soothing, held no confidence.

As fingers of doubt squeezed Alex's chest, Franki burst into the bedroom, rushed over to Nick, and stroked his forehead. "It's all right honey, Lia will find the antidote." Her panic-stricken look at her sister, though, was anything but self-assured.

Alex wanted to scream, "Lia can do it." She had to. A sharp sting of fear bit into her, and she clutched Nick's hand. She couldn't lose him now.

Bree captured her arm. "Let's go. Franki will keep us informed. Right now, we need to update the others."

Forced to relinquish their brief contact, she committed his handsome face to memory.

Chapter Twenty-Seven

Bits of conversation greeted Alex and Bree as they walked into the kitchen. People sat at the table munching on cake and cookies. The smell of coffee hung in the air. Cups and food crumbs cluttered the table. Their discussion died off when Bree cleared her throat. All eyes fastened on her. "We've had a new development."

Alex gaped at her aunt. *Development? More like a catastrophe. Nick had been poisoned.*

Instantly, the mood in the room changed. Tired camaraderie evolved into edgy awareness as Bree described the attack and Nick's condition. Already nervous about the looming confrontation, the news hit them hard. A few stares swung in Alex's direction. She braced herself. This group already blamed her for the resurgence of the demon. Now they'd discovered one of their own was gravely injured. Heat rushed to her face. No way would she accept responsibility for what was going on.

A balding, thickset man erupted from his chair. His cold eyes and stance reminded Alex of a jungle cat about to pounce. "Should we just let it pick us off one by one?" His eyes tightened, and he pointed at Alex. "She's the one it wants."

Anger replaced fear as she took a step toward him. A fiery streak traveled down both arms; her fingers were already buzzing.

When the light in the kitchen blinked and smoke began to rise from the toaster, Bree grabbed one of her niece's clenched fists and stabbed her finger at the speaker. Her voice slashed like a razor as she pointed to the door. "Somewhere out there a dark force, powerful enough to free the demon and live, waits. Our ancestors who watch over what is theirs sent us a warning. Do you feel comfortable enough to defy them?"

The dissenter sat down. Rich gave him a hard poke before smiling at Alex. "We've got your back."

The rest of the group nodded.

"Good," Bree said. "As for our adversary, he can't enter your dreams without personal information about you and your habits. Vigilance is imperative. There's a real person behind all of this, and we have to find him."

She put her hands up to forestall any more questions. "Right now, someone needs to pick up Rosemary so she can be with her grandson."

Nick. For a moment, Alex had forgotten her savior was upstairs, fighting for his life. Rosemary would be devastated if anything happened to him. Even Bree had changed in the last hour, her shoulders bowed, and pieces of hair thrust at odd angles where she'd run her hands through it.

Rich slid into trooper mode. "Do we have any idea of the origin of this threat?"

Bree answered with a heavy sigh, "No."

"Today is the third," he said. "We've got one day. We'll have to take extra care. No one goes anywhere alone."

"What about Lia?" Alex said. "Is she alone?"

"Where is she?" Rich said as he shot out of his seat.

Bree's voice held panic. "The greenhouse. She's

testing Nicky's blood."

The kitchen door banged before she finished the sentence. Bree dropped to a chair, her hand against her forehead. "Who's on sentry duty?"

"Tony replaced me," someone said.

"I'll check in with him." Moments later, Alex watched her aunt's eyes tighten. Not a good sign. "Who's his partner?"

One of the men consulted a list on the counter. "Looks like Adam."

Bree closed her eyes for a few seconds, before whipping them open again. "You need to look for Adam. I can't reach him, and Tony's drunk."

"Oh, Lord." Rosemary appeared in the doorway. The Clan's unwavering leader looked tired and frail. She placed her hand on Bree's shoulder. "Take care of this. I have information about the snake, but right now I must go to my grandson. I'll meet you in the den."

****

Worry spurred Alex's steps as she paced the floor of the den. For some reason, Rich hadn't gotten back to them yet. *Please let Lia be all right.* A small ache began at her temples as she realized how much she cared for her cousin, and without Lia, Nick didn't have a chance.

Her aunt, who'd remained silent, gave an audible sigh. "Lia's safe, working hard on a cure."

"Thank God." Alex's relief was short-lived. How long could Nick hang on?

It seemed like hours until Rosemary returned from Nick's side. Alex pounced before the woman could sit down. "How is he?"

"Still fighting. He's tough." Rosemary looked her age as she eased into a chair and released a long breath.

She closed her eyes and began to massage both temples with her fingertips. "We have to believe that Lia will succeed."

A painful lump lodged in Alex's chest. Nick had to survive. She didn't think she could stay in Newport without him.

"What did you want to talk to us about?" Bree asked.

Rosemary took a moment to compose herself. "First, I did some research on the young woman with the red gown in Alex's vision."

"How could she see me?" Alex said.

"I believe, in her loneliness, she turned to magic. Those were Tarot cards on her table. Please stay very still if you have any more visions. I'm afraid your gift allows you to step into another time."

Alex wanted to throw her hands in the air and scream. Now her *good* powers might be harmful. She knew there was no way to control the spectral images any more than the disastrous heat in her hands. She hoped she didn't inherit any more unstable gifts tomorrow.

Lost in her worries, she almost missed Bree's head tilt in a listening pose. When her aunt's features crumpled, a ball of dread lodged in Alex's chest. *Please God, not Nick.*

Bree faced Rosemary. "They can't find Adam."

"It's escalating," Rosemary said as her shoulders sagged.

Adam was the guy Alex had seen at the club. The same one who'd railed against her at the Clan meeting. Now he'd disappeared.

Rosemary continued. "There's something else we must discuss. I searched our archives for information about the demon. In a thick wooden box with the Grand

Master's seal, I found a document with the word *daemonium* in it."

Bree's sharp inhalation of breath was audible. "Demon."

Rosemary nodded. "There appears to be a chant in what I believe is ancient Latin or, as it was known before 75 BC, Archaic. I've asked my son, Duncan, to contact a linguist."

In response to Alex's raised eyebrows, Rosemary said, "Duncan is Nick's father. He teaches at the Naval War college."

Alex nodded. "Right. Uncle Sal mentioned him before."

"I can check the Internet for a translation," Bree said, "but we need to hurry. We have less than thirty hours to go."

Chapter Twenty-Eight

Rosemary and Bree didn't need Alex, so she hurried upstairs. The scratch of Franki's pencil caught her attention as she walked in the door. Her aunt, absorbed in her work, didn't look up, so Alex slipped over to the bed. She brushed her hand across Nick's face. He didn't move. With his eyes closed and his mouth half-open, he looked so vulnerable. Memories swamped her. A different room. Another loved one struggling to survive.

Her mother had lost that fight. Alex closed her eyes and prayed that Nick's strength and Lia's magic would prevail.

Franki still hadn't lifted her head from the page, and Alex realized why. Her aunt's frenzied movements and disconnect from her surroundings signaled spectral art. Alex remembered the last example of Franki's work and hesitated, but curiosity pulled her forward. She peeked over her aunt's shoulder and gasped. Nick's handsome face, almost unrecognizable, stared back at her—pasty cheeks and lips pinched together in pain. But he wasn't alone. A raven-colored serpent coiled itself around Nick's body to eliminate any chance of escape.

Alex winced and grabbed her aunt's shoulder. "We've got to wake him up."

Franki snapped out of her daze, looked at Alex, and peered at the drawing in her lap. "This isn't what you think. The image represents the incursion of the poison, not a demon attack." Her aunt closed her eyes for a minute, her voice weary when she spoke. "He's fighting, but his strength is waning."

Alex had trouble breathing as she spun around and faced the bed. "We have to help. What good are all our powers if we can't save him?"

An argument downstairs interrupted them, not the first squabble to break out today. Alex recognized Bree's indignant tone and Tony's anger. She followed her aunt to the landing.

Tony sounded like a petulant child. "Leave me alone. I'm fine."

Outrage colored Bree's tone. "How could you?"

"Get off my case. I had a couple of drinks. So what?"

"*So what?*" she demanded. "We can't find Adam. You were supposed to stay together."

"For Christ's sake, I needed to take a leak. We're not joined at the hip."

"Enough," Rosemary said. "Both of you meet me in the living room."

Conversation ceased as they walked away.

Franki started back toward the bedroom, but her steps paused. "I have to join them, Alex. I'll bring my drawing. Please stay with Nick."

"Of course," Alex said. "I'll tell Lia where you'll be."

After Franki left with the distressing sketch still clutched in her hand, Alex crossed to the unconscious figure on the four-poster bed. Nick's ashen features made a macabre contrast to the red duvet. His hair, sticking up in tufts, reminded her of the day in Nick's convertible when the state of their hair led to so much laughter. Her throat constricted as she remembered the times they'd shared since her move here. How his teasing had irritated her. The last beach dream. His touch. The taste of his lips. She reached out to him to push a stray lock back into place. At that moment, they connected.

Alexandra.

Alex cradled his cheek and probed his mind. *I'm here.*

Don't sleep.

That brought a slight smile to her lips. *Like I could in this madhouse.* She detected his heavy sigh. *Nick, don't tire yourself out. I'll sit with you. You just rest. Lia's working on an antidote.*

Okay. He sounded so frail. Then, as the voice in her head faded, she heard a final whisper, *Stay close.*

She squeezed his hand, but his pale lips called to her. As she leaned down to kiss him, invisible claws dug at her chest. The loss of another loved one would be too much. She used her free hand to wipe away tears as she contacted Lia. *He communicated with me. He's very weak.*

Don't leave him alone. I've got Rich watching my back.

Lia?

Yes?

Hurry.

****

Rosemary arrived at Nick's bedside with a man whom she introduced as her son, Duncan. Alex stood and offered him her chair.

"Has he spoken?" Duncan asked as he sat down.

"He told me to stay awake."

Rosemary swiped at her eyes before giving her

grandson a kiss. "I'll be downstairs if you need me."

Alex stood behind the chair and watched as Duncan trailed his fingers along his son's cheek. "Oh God, Nick, what's happened to you?"

At the sound of his anguish, Alex almost wept. "You can talk to him, but he's very weak."

As he covered Nick's hand, Duncan looked at Alex. "Okay, tell me the whole story."

She studied the man who clutched his son. He could never deny his parentage. He had the same hair with an added touch of gray. The worried blue eyes that pleaded with Alex to explain why his son lay there were identical to Nick's. And the physical similarities—strong chin, captivating dimple, wide shoulders, and regal stature— were remarkable. It was the similarities that made the comparison so painful. Duncan's strength dominated the room as Nick's once had. Nick's aura had changed from the clear red of his powerful, passionate nature to a dark, muddy gray. As his strength diminished, he looked less and less like his father.

She found it difficult to explain the series of events because she didn't understand it all herself, but she tried. When she finished telling Duncan the story, anger sparked in his eyes.

He straightened his shoulders, then spoke with a hard edge to his voice. "He should never have gone back in with that snake. I don't care what your powers will be."

Alex blinked and backed away from his pain, but Duncan's gaze swung to his son. He covered Nick's hand with both of his. "No, no, Nicky. Don't try to speak. It's fine. I don't blame her. I'm just so worried about you. Rest, son. I'll take care of you both."

Tears streamed down Duncan's cheeks as he turned

to Alex. "I'm sorry…Alexandra, is it?"

Through the lump in her throat, she said, "Nick insists on using my full name. Everyone else calls me Alex."

"Please excuse my outburst. It isn't directed toward you. I want to help my son, but I'm so powerless here."

Alex concentrated on her hands as she crushed the cushioned top of the leather chair. When she first came to this home, she'd found pleasure in the opulence around her. Now she realized she'd be happy to spend the rest of her days in a hovel, if it would bring Nick back.

Duncan gave his son's hand a last squeeze before he rose. "I have to see where I'm needed. Take care of my boy."

Alex nodded and moved to retake her seat in the chair. She grasped Nick's hand and sent out another plea to Lia.

Her cousin's answer conveyed exhaustion. *I'm on my way over. I may have found something. I'll be there soon.*

Hope surged, and Alex told Nick, *Hang on. Lia thinks she's found the answer.*

Chapter Twenty-Nine

The antidote for Nick arrived at the same time the search team found Adam, alive, but in bad shape. Bree sent Alex to the kitchen. "Franki has something for you."

On her way downstairs, she overheard part of a conversation from the living room but didn't recognize the voices. "She must be special if the guy killed her mother to get to her."

Her steps faltered. She grabbed the banister as the thought cut into her. *What kind of monster could do this?*

The scent of warm chocolate greeted her in the kitchen. Her mouth watered. Mattie made the best brownies. Franki handed Alex a small orange pill and a glass of water. "We don't like to use stimulants, but, in your case, it's necessary."

"Thank you. I'm so tired." She popped the pill in her mouth, guzzled the water, then sat at the table and stretched, waiting for relief.

Franki grinned. "It takes a while to kick in. I'll be upstairs if you need anything."

A while later, the hitch in her breathing alerted her to something happening. A weird rush of energy. She blinked and tapped her fingers against the table. Her nerve endings zinged. Wow! Powerful stuff. She bounced on the chair and looked around for something to do, then remembered Nick. Had the serum worked? She jogged upstairs and heard his voice in her bedroom.

Relief and joy filled her heart as she swung through the door. "You're awake."

Someone had combed his hair and propped him up against the pillow. Though he still looked like an invalid, he sent her a huge grin. A lump formed in her throat, and it took all her willpower not to blubber. Lia slept beside him on the bed while Bree and Rosemary hovered over them both.

No longer worried Nick might die, Alex's sense of humor kicked in. "You know, Aunt Bree, if I'd had any idea how crowded my bedroom would be, I'd never have consented to come."

Instead of rolling her eyes, Bree smiled at Alex's bad joke. "I'm glad you're taking care of yourself. How are you doing?"

Alex popped out her answer with alacrity. "I feel pretty good."

Nick's deep voice interjected, "A little too good, Alexandra?"

She couldn't believe how well he knew her. Embarrassment gave her voice a little edge. "I might have taken a pill."

He laughed. "You needed it."

Alex turned to her sleeping cousin. "What about Lia?"

Franki brushed her hand across her daughter's forehead. "She got up to check on Nick and Adam before she crashed."

Alex had trouble standing still and couldn't stop rubbing her hands. "I guess you don't need me. I'll see you later."

"Be careful, Alex," Rosemary said. "If you're not used to this medication, it can do quite a number on you.

You're liable to run yourself ragged and then collapse. Whatever you do, promise you won't do it alone."

Alex made a face, the same one she saved for her mother's lectures, but she agreed.

When she said goodbye to Nick, he grinned. "What? No more tears for me?"

Heat shot into her face.

As she hurried from the room, Rosemary said, "Stop teasing her, Nicky."

Alex sprinted down the steps and into the kitchen. Her gaze strayed to the cups left on the table. She'd have to take care of that. After she'd washed, dried, and put them away, she cleaned the table and counters. She was sweeping the floor when Bree walked in.

"I'm afraid those pills are too strong for you."

"I'd like to take a walk."

"I'll go with you."

****

Bree accompanied Alex on a brisk trek to the beach. By the time they'd reached the water, Alex had given her aunt a nonstop recital of her college experience and part-time writing career. When she finally took a breath, she said, "I can't seem to stop talking."

With an amused smile, Bree congratulated Alex on her accomplishments.

The blue-green chop of the river captured Alex's attention. She enjoyed the lively song of waves splashing against the rocks and inhaled its salty essence before turning to go back.

"It won't be long before this mess is over," Bree said, "and you can begin your new life."

The reminder of tomorrow's encounter sent a rush of fear to her belly. *What if the Clan lost the battle?*

Bree left her on the porch where she challenged the stamina of a rocking chair. A buzzing on her hip startled her and halted her momentum. She tugged the cell out of her pocket. "Hello?"

"Alex, it's Hunter."

His voice surprised her. "Hi, Hunter. What's up."

"I've been waiting for you. We had a date. Remember?"

"Oh, no. What time is it?" She'd forgotten all about it. She must have thought the phone's vibration was part of the pill's energy rush.

"Almost noon. I called when you didn't show, but there was no answer. I decided you might have trouble getting out, so I waited. I can be parked up the street from your drive in twenty minutes. Can you ditch the family and get down there?" His voice softened. "I miss you. It would just be for a short while."

An image of Nick's blue eyes dark with hunger captured her thoughts. Though she'd enjoyed her date with Hunter, she didn't want a relationship with him.

When she didn't reply, he said, "I also have a contract for you to sign. I told my boss about your pitch, and he loved it. What do you say? It won't take long. Then I'll be able to get through the Fourth alone."

Alex perked up at the word, contract. After this mess was over, she wanted to write. Hunter's magazine would be perfect. Besides, it was daylight. There were Clan members all over the place. She could run down and get back with no trouble at all. "Sounds good. I'll be there."

She hung up and planned her strategy. She wanted to sign that contract before the publisher changed his mind. For the next ten minutes, Alex paced along the patio then slipped around the side of the house to the driveway.

Chapter Thirty

Nick surprised Bree when he walked into the kitchen.

"You're better? Shouldn't you rest? I can bring some food up to you."

"I'm fine. Lia's serum knocked the poison out of my body, and her healing took care of the rest." He looked around the spacious room. "Where did Alexandra go?"

"Out on the porch."

"Thanks." He poked his head out the back door, then went outside. "Alexandra?" He checked the patio and then spoke to her mind. *Alexandra. It's me. Where are you?*

You're feeling better? Good. I'll be up to see you.

Where are you?

Give me ten minutes, and I'll be there.

Her evasion alerted him, and when he insisted she disclose her whereabouts, he got no answer. He knew something was wrong and felt no compulsion about infiltrating her thoughts. The name, Hunter, sent him running after her.

****

A twisting worm slid into her mind. She slammed down her shield. Too late. Nick's voice burst into Alex's head. *Alexandra. Don't be stupid. You don't know this guy. It isn't safe to be out there alone. Where are you?*

How had he found out? Damn, this wasn't working

the way she planned. She'd tried to saunter down the long driveway to escape attention. Now, she panicked when she heard a car behind her. She'd never make it unless she could find a hiding place. She swiveled her head all around—trees, no low bushes. She looked back. Too late. Nick's red car roared up beside her. He slammed on his brakes.

Alex gave him her most daunting glare. "What?"

She flinched when she saw Nick's cold eyes and the thin line of his lips. "Get in."

She tried once more. "I'm taking a walk."

Nick never changed his expression, and the timbre of his voice was frightening. "Do I have to get out and drag you to the car?"

Alex wouldn't have been surprised to see fire come out of his nostrils. She had nowhere to go, so she flounced over to the passenger side of the car.

The drive back to the house passed in uncomfortable silence.

Nick walked behind her into the house where Rosemary and Bree waited.

The ice in Bree's voice could have frozen the river. "I'm sure I made it plain that your well-being was intricately entwined with the Clan's. We pulled people from their posts to search for you. Nick almost died to save you. Your mother risked her very existence, and Adam may never be the same. Yet, you have no compunction about taking off for a tryst with a perfect stranger while everyone else expends their energy trying to keep us alive. How could you?"

The richly appointed hall resonated with anger and disappointment from people who, moments ago, had feared for her life. Guilt burned inside her. She knew

Bree was correct in her assessment. She also understood that she'd lost her aunt's trust. The depth of the hurt Alex felt surprised her.

No one would believe her now, but she meant it with all her heart when she said, "I'm sorry."

****

The group in the hall dispersed, and Alex, unsure of what to do, started for the stairs. The effects of the pill were wearing off, and she wanted to get away from everyone.

Rosemary moved to stand in front of her. "Wait a minute."

This was a different female from the affable woman who'd spoken to her in the bedroom. The neutral expression on her face, as if she and Alex were strangers, hurt Alex more than anger would have done. She paused, waiting for more.

"Come out to the kitchen with me and help Mattie get lunch ready." Rosemary turned and walked away. Alex followed. Her shoulders slumped as the pill's effects waned.

The housekeeper had platters of food ready for Alex to take into the dining room. When Mattie smiled at her, Alex choked up. Someone in the house didn't hate her.

The Clan arrived to eat, but Alex stayed in the kitchen. She wasn't hungry and didn't want to face anyone. Besides, no one cared unless she fell asleep without Nick to protect her from the dream walker.

"Och, lass. You need to eat something. Here you go." Mattie placed a sandwich, brownie, and an apple in front of her along with a glass of lemonade.

"Thank you, Mattie." Alex took a long drink and yawned.

"Now don't be goin' to sleep. Stay awake and eat your food."

Mattie must be the designated babysitter. Alex took a bite of her sandwich and stifled another yawn. A seductive lassitude crept over her. "Do you have any coffee, Mattie?"

"I'll get a pot going."

Mattie puttered around, and Alex drank her lemonade. It tasted good. Another yawn and Alex shook herself. She found it difficult to hold up her head.

"Eat up, lassie. I'll be right back."

Alex's eyelids kept closing. Blink. Blink.

****

She opened her eyes to a strange room with modern lines and light furnishings, nothing like the Brendani home. She approved of the white walls and the thick beige carpet. Both blended nicely with overstuffed furniture done in light earth tones. The whole room screamed money and comfort.

Outside, green lawns peppered with shrubs and trees gave way to an endless expanse of ocean, alive with sparks of sunlight.

She walked to the terrace doors to get a better view.

"I'm glad you enjoy it."

Recognizing the voice from her boat trip with Hunter, Alex turned to find Bree's former boyfriend. "Charles?"

He joined her at the door. "Welcome to my home, Alex."

She was confused. "It's magnificent, but what am I doing here?"

"I have a birthday present for you."

Chapter Thirty-One

Franki's yell brought Nick rushing into the kitchen. When he saw the sleeping girl, frustrated anger filled his voice. "How did this happen? Who was supposed to be with her?"

"I left her with Mattie," Rosemary said.

Mattie had just hurried in from the hall. "What's the matter?"

He pointed to Alex.

The housekeeper's hand went to her mouth; her eyes became huge. "I-I was only gone for a minute. She was fine when I left. I'm so sorry."

His grandmother put her arm around Mattie's shoulders and closed her eyes with a sigh. "It's all right. We should have kept a better watch on her."

Franki's face crumpled. "The poor thing. We ostracized her and made her eat out here all by herself. No wonder she was afraid to call for help."

"It's the middle of the day," Nick said. "There's no way the dream walker can know she'd fall asleep. I'll find her. Lia?"

He moved Alex to the floor, then lay down beside her. Lia placed one hand on his head and the other over his eyes. Though he went to sleep, he woke moments later. "I need help. How can we contact Cecile?"

Lia ran out and returned almost immediately with her aunt's urn. She placed it on the floor at Nick's side.

270

He squeezed Alex's arm and rubbed his cheek against her face. "I can't find her anywhere."

Bree's eyes were wild. "We must find her. I'll send a team to check out Hunter's place."

"That bastard," Nick said. "If I get my hands on him, I'll kill him."

Since communicating with the dead was one of her gifts, Rosemary crouched down beside him, placed her hands on the smooth surface of the urn, and closed her eyes.

While Rosemary contacted Cecile, Lia helped Nick sleep once more. He returned to the dream world to search for Alexandra.

****

Nick woke on the beach and found a woman who looked a lot like Bree—but even more like Alexandra. He put out his hand. "I'm happy to meet you, Cecile."

A sad smile flickered across her face. "I'm afraid it isn't a happy time. I can't sense my daughter. Are you sure she's asleep?"

The corner of Nick's mouth lifted. "She's resting in my arms."

"It means she doesn't know she needs help. How close is she to my remains?"

"Your urn is right next to her, but we believe that bastard Hunter Davis has her in his thrall."

Cecile closed her eyes for a moment. "I'm afraid you're right." With a sigh, she said, "At least he hasn't killed her. I'd know the minute she entered my realm. For now, Alex is alive. We have to wait until she calls."

"Can't you sense her, try to contact her?"

"There's no way to break through the spell surrounding her. She has to reach out. If she's unaware of the danger, she won't seek escape."

Nick marched back and forth, rubbing his hands over his face. "There must be something we can do."

She shook her head. "All we can do is wait."

A spiral of dread coiled in Nick's stomach. What would happen to her if his efforts failed?

****

The thick carpet swallowed their footsteps as Charles slid his arm around Alex's waist to lead her on a tour of his home. After the angry glares and ugly comments she'd been subjected to in the Brendani house, Charles's interest in her well-being soothed her. She relished his attention.

Each new room brought one more thing for Alex to appreciate. Two of the second-floor bedrooms were suites. Their decor followed the light and airy muted tones of the living room. Charles' study, however, was a different story. It could have been ripped out of a nineteenth-century novel. Alex stood in front of a heavy mahogany desk that matched the bookcases around the room. Deep crimson drapes added to the somber mood. A painting hung above the stone fireplace. It portrayed a large manor house totally engulfed in flames. Alex didn't like the vibe and shivered.

"Ah, Alex. This isn't quite to your taste," Charles murmured. "No matter. I believe you'll enjoy the last one."

An uncomfortable twinge had begun in her chest, but before she could analyze it, Charles led her back into the bright hall and positioned her in front of another door. "Go ahead, open it." As she wrapped her fingers around the doorknob, he whispered, "Happy birthday!"

Alex couldn't help a quick intake of breath as she

stepped into the room. He chuckled. "I can see you like this one."

The sandy-colored carpet at her feet resembled the earth around her home in Arizona. The drapes, duvet, and sofa pillows had variations of the deep purple shades of the distant mountains. A southwest landscape hung above the bed—a canyon scene with blue skies, spiky cacti, and a multicolored range in the background. Hints of Phoenix were everywhere from the huge pillows tossed on the bed to the colorful Hopi Kachinas, Indian spirit dolls, on the bureau. He even had a small potted saguaro cactus in the corner.

The whole room was bathed in light from the floor-to-ceiling windows that overlooked the same ocean view she'd admired in the living room. "It's Phoenix," she murmured. "I feel like I'm back there."

"One never forgets a place like that."

"You've been there?"

"I enjoyed a month with a friend of mine there a few years ago. When I returned, I had this room refurbished. It reminds me of that fantastic area. All my visitors enjoyed it. I hoped it might encourage you to stay with me for a little while."

The pieces of art in the room captured Alex's attention. All accessories to remind her of her home: wood carvings, pottery, and wonderful paintings. "That's so nice of you, Charles. I can't imagine a lovelier place to stay, but I have to get back home. I wasn't supposed to fall asleep."

"You're fine here."

"No," she said, starting to tremble. "I forgot. There's a huge snake. I've got to wake up."

Charles went over to Alex and put his arms around

her. "Don't worry, my dear. I won't let anything harm you. My home is protected against any evil. You'll be safe." As he spoke, he flicked his fingers at her, and she was pulled into his deep blue eyes. "You can trust me. Your happiness is important to me."

Alex forgot her worries and beamed at Charles. "In that case, thank you. I'd love to stay."

"I'm so glad. Remember I can protect you from anything. Call me, and I'll come immediately."

"Charles?"

"Yes, my dear."

"How did you know about my birthday?"

****

It was close to an hour since Alex had fallen asleep. Rosemary realized their vigil might be a long one. People drifted in and out of the kitchen after checking on the two sleeping Clansmen in the other room.

A couple of hours later, Rich returned.

Happy for any diversion from her vigil, Rosemary smiled up at him. "Did you find Hunter?"

At his grimace, Rosemary feared the worst. "Nobody's seen the guy since Friday morning. They checked with the phone company. The last time he used his cell was to call Alex today. They're getting his records for the past couple of weeks. I told them it was a matter of life and death, so they've put it on a fast track."

Rosemary didn't like it. Why would Hunter disappear unless he was complicit? "Rich, if you need to apply some persuasion anywhere, Bree can help."

He nodded. "Thanks, but I have that covered." As he spoke, his eyes scanned the room.

She took pity on him. "Lia's in Bree's office, checking on Adam."

When he left, she leaned back in her chair. What more could she do to protect the Clan? If they couldn't get Alex back before tomorrow morning, she was certain the battle would be vicious and equally as sure many wouldn't survive. She hoped the poison Lia had derived from the demon's venom would help prevent unnecessary deaths.

Worry for Nicky, vulnerable not only in his dream world but in his real life, tormented her. She knew he was falling in love. If something happened to his Alexandra, how well would he perform in the battle?

It was time to talk to him. She sent a message to Cecile.

When Nick's eyes opened, he held up his hand to his grandmother. "Before you speak, we have to move Alex and her mother's urn to a more comfortable spot."

"Fine, but I have to talk to you."

She tried not to fidget as she instructed two men to move a mattress down from the third floor and place it in the living room. Nick wrapped a blanket over the top, lifted Alex, and placed her on the soft surface. Rosemary wanted to speak to her grandson in the kitchen, but he went no farther than the dining room door so that he could still see Alex. "This is far enough," he said.

"All right." Rosemary's breath came out in an upward stream of air that lifted blonde tendrils from her forehead. "We'll do it here."

Steeling herself for Nick's reaction, Rosemary outlined her plan. "If our efforts fail, we have to stop this man from gaining Alex's powers." Nick's face hardened. Rosemary's hair again lifted as she blew air from her mouth. "At the last minute," she warned, "if we can't reach Alex, we have to stop her from drawing down her powers. Any way we can."

Nick's eyes flashed. His tone signaled a threat. "What do you mean?"

Duncan walked in as his mother backed away. "Nick!"

Rosemary touched her son's arm. "I'm fine." She continued to speak to Nick. "You understand the danger of those powers in the wrong hands. At the very least, our lives will be forfeit. At worst, that madman will find a way to use that power against innocents. We have to make sure that doesn't happen."

Duncan wrapped his arm around his son's shoulders. "No one wants to hurt Alex. It's a last-ditch plan to be considered if everything else fails."

Nick tried to shrug out of his father's embrace, but Duncan held tight. The anger never left Nick's face, but he conceded. "We wait until the very last minute." He glared at his father. "And I give the order."

Rosemary nodded once. "Agreed."

Rich, who'd been waiting until the discussion ended, stepped in to speak to Rosemary. "I have news about Hunter. His phone calls in the last couple of weeks show the number of some millionaire who's got a house on Ten Mile Drive. My friends are headed out there now to see if they can find him."

"Thank you, Rich. Do you have the man's name?"

"Yeah." Rich checked his notes. "Last name's Berenger."

Rosemary didn't recognize the name and sent it on to the rest of the Clan. "Maybe one of the others has heard of him."

Rich looked at his watch. "My shift will start in a couple minutes. I'll see you later." He grabbed some cookies in the kitchen and started out the door.

Rosemary stopped him. "One more thing, Rich."

"Yeah?"

"What is Berenger's first name? Bree may know him."

He pulled out his notebook. "Charles. Charles Berenger."

****

Rosemary relayed the information to Bree and heard an immediate gasp. "Bree. What is it?"

After a minute, Bree said, "Would you mind sending a replacement for me?"

"Of course. Someone will be right there."

The fact that Bree would leave her post spoke volumes. She must be very upset. The moment she walked in the door, her pain was evident. Her shoulders slumped, and her steps were uncertain. Rosemary beckoned to her. "Let's go to the den."

Bree gave a resigned sigh and followed her.

Once the door closed and they sat down, Rosemary said, "What is this all about? Who is Charles Berenger?"

Bree closed her eyes for a moment, then shook her head. "He can't be the same one."

Rosemary sat back and waited for the story.

"We were young and in love. He had a healthy ego and was a bit controlling." She smiled. "We clashed a lot but had fun making up. He never had any powers. He certainly wasn't a dream walker." She furrowed her brows and reached into her pants pocket for a card. Her voice dropped to a whisper. "He's in town now." She came out of her seat with a jolt. "How could he be behind this horror? Oh, God. That would mean in addition to ensnaring Alex, he killed CeCe."

Rosemary took his card. As she looked at it, she received more information on the man. With a pitying look at her friend, she said, "I'm sorry, Bree, but I just found out that Charles Berenger recently sold a home in Phoenix where CeCe and Alex lived."

Chapter Thirty-Two

Charles went to a great deal of trouble in the dreamscape to make this room look like Phoenix so that Alex would be comfortable until the receipt of her powers on her birthday. Now, she was frowning. He suppressed his anger and said, "What's the matter?"

"I celebrated all my birthdays in Phoenix with my parents. Mom always insisted on a party. This is the first year she won't be with me. I miss her."

Charles reinserted the magic into his tone. "Which of Gabrielle's sisters is your dear mother? I remember they were all beautiful."

"CeCe." Alex's face crumpled. "She died a few months ago."

"I'm so sorry." Charles placed his hand on her forehead. "You're fine. The pain is gone."

He wanted Alex clueless and happy until the time arrived. At that exact moment, Charles planned to divert Alex's powers to himself. First, however, he had to find a way to secure her body at the Convent House.

"You're a lucky young lady to be a descendant of the Templars. All those years ago, I knew Gabrielle was different."

It had taken him close to a decade to discover the secret. While he researched and plotted, he'd perfected his own arts with the help of black magic. The discovery of a summoning spell for the demon had been a lucky break. He'd used his own powers to trap Najash, then secure its submission. Najash turned into a very useful pet.

Alex frowned. "You know about our gifts?"

"Yes. Isn't it exciting? You'll receive yours tomorrow morning." He'd looked up her birth certificate, Alexandra Ryan, born in Arizona at 8:02 a.m. on July 4th, 10:02 a.m., Rhode Island time.

Alex sent him a vacuous smile. The spell clouded her mind. He congratulated himself on his selection of Cecile, the bird who'd left the nest. Away from her powerful home base, she was vulnerable.

With a fond smile for her daughter, he said, "I should have had you in Phoenix. Never mind. I'll have you with me tomorrow morning, and all will be well."

Alex wrinkled her forehead, but then her face cleared. "Good."

"No thanks to that imbecile, Adam, who refused to finish the job after the failed attack in Newport. Now, I'll have to rely on someone else."

"What?"

He patted Alex's shoulder. "You look confused, my dear. Why don't you lay down and rest?"

"Okay."

The compliance spell he'd invoked worked nicely. He'd grown fond of the pretty young thing. Too bad she'd have to be eliminated. Ah well. He sighed. That was the price one had to pay if one wanted control over the Watcher Clan. With Alex's powers added to his own, and his hungry snake, he should have very little resistance. He gave Alex a kiss on her forehead and walked out.

****

After Charles left the dream world and awakened in his actual home, he sensed Hunter's agitation. The fool should be in the living room where he'd left him, but he'd gone outside. Charles found him near the water and hurried after him. "You imbecile. Get in the house before someone sees you."

Hunter gaped at Charles and headed for the house at a half-run. Back inside, Charles smiled to himself. Hunter was a useful pawn. Without another word, Charles walked away, and like a repentant puppy, Hunter followed.

In the study, he briefed Charles on the plans at the Brendani house. "A lot has been happening. They're all nervous about losing Alex. Nick and her mother's ghost are searching for her right now."

Charles flared his nostrils and folded his arms. "He survived the attack. What else?"

"Lia saved him with some kind of antidote."

"Hasn't she been a busy little bee?"

"And get this. If they can't wake Alex before her birthday, they'll kill her."

"I was afraid of that. You'll have to protect her until I can finish the spell."

"Me? How can I protect her?"

"Use the abilities I gave you."

"Against all those people?"

"I'll put you under a protection spell. Alex has to survive to draw down those powers. Once that's done, she'll no longer be needed. Now, listen. I want you to relay my instructions for tomorrow morning. We need a distraction to get her inside that mausoleum. They guard it around the clock. The four a.m. shift change would be the best time to do it. The replacements will leave the house, and the returning guards will be tired."

"Right."

"Isn't that idiot, Adam, the one I punished, still in bad shape?"

"I guess so."

"Well, find out!"

Charles looked at the painting behind his desk. With a twist of his lips, he said, "A little diversion might be in order. Find out where they keep him, and make sure our friend on the inside is ready."

"They've got dogs on the property."

"Poison them."

"How will we carry her to the Convent House?"

The smile Charles turned on Hunter made him ill. "I'll wake her up."

"What about the snake?"

Charles flattened his lips and glared at Hunter. Then he mumbled a few words and snapped his fingers.

Hunter immediately grabbed his head and began to keen, "No. Oh, no. Please stop. Pleeeeease."

Charles clicked his digits again and growled at Hunter. "Keep your mouth shut unless I ask you something."

****

No longer tired, Alex got up to wander around the room Charles created based on his travels to Arizona. At the window, she stood captivated for a moment by the continuous flow of the waves. When her attention waned, she went to study the bright painting over the bed. Her mother had loved Phoenix. She'd have enjoyed this room. Alex missed her mother so much that she unconsciously reached out for her. The door opened, and Charles appeared. "Hi, Charles. My mother would love it here."

He seemed to be beside her without ever having moved and placed his hand on her forehead. "You're fine by yourself, Alex. You're comfortable and happy. You don't want to be anywhere else, and you're tired."

Alex smiled. She was so lucky to be with this kind man. It came as no surprise that Aunt Bree had once dated him. She lay down on the bed but, before she closed her eyes, wondered at the dark expression that slid over her new friend's face.

When he paused at the door, she heard him whisper. "Little bitch, calling out to your mother. You should have stayed compliant for hours. I'll have to keep a closer eye on you."

For a moment she was confused, but then her eyelids fluttered, and she eased into sleep.

Chapter Thirty-Three

The moment Charles awakened and entered the living room, Hunter hurried up to him. "They've tracked you," he said in a breathless voice. "The police are on the way."

Charles, who'd expected something like this, had a bag packed with everything he needed in the car. "Let's go."

"What about Alex?" Hunter said.

"She'll be fine in the dreamscape for a couple more hours. I can monitor her from any place nearby. Now be quiet and drive. I'm expecting an important call." Charles looked pleased as he extracted his cell. "Let's see how long it takes her."

Hunter shot a brief glance at his master but didn't ask any questions.

They'd made it all the way into downtown Newport before the phone beeped. Charles's lips twisted as he checked the screen. "Ah, my dear Gabrielle. Now, you want me."

His face cleared, and he put on a smile before he answered. "Good evening, Gabrielle. How nice to hear from you. I was hoping you'd call."

"Charles. What have you done?"

"What's wrong? Why are you so angry?"

Her tone became more reasonable. "I don't understand. What do you hope to gain?"

"I'm confused, Gabrielle. What are you talking about?"

"Let my niece go."

Charles gave a surprised laugh. "Your niece? You mean that sweet young lady who visited me on my yacht? I haven't seen her since that luncheon."

He heard her release a long breath before she spoke, and he grinned. He could picture her reining in her temper. "Charles, please. I need to talk to you. Where can we meet?"

"As much as I'd like that, I'm a little busy right now. Perhaps we can get together next week."

"How can you be so heartless? You've got money and power. What more do you want?"

"Heartless? Me?" Anger tinged his voice. "As I recall, it's you who was without heart. I gave you mine, and you crushed it."

Bree's tone softened. "I've regretted it more times than you can imagine. Help me to understand this, and together we can arrive at some kind of solution."

"Ah. There's the woman I loved, soft and seductive. Do you remember our last Fourth of July? In the boat in the harbor?" Knowing his Gabrielle, he suppressed a chuckle. By now, she'd be ready to throttle him.

"How could I forget, Charles? You were wonderful. The man I remember wouldn't want to harm my niece. Meet me. Anywhere you want."

"What a pretty speech. I wish I could believe it. But I've fallen for your wiles too many times. You always managed to get your way. Not today. I do wish I had time to be with you, though. You're still as beautiful as ever."

"But... How... When did you see me?"

"Ah. Let's see. It must have been in Phoenix."

"What? You—you son of a bitch."

Charles grinned. After he took over the Clan, she'd change that tone. An image of a compliant Gabrielle flashed through his mind. She was still exciting.

"Language, Gabrielle. Such a fiery temper. I wish I could continue this conversation, but I have too much to do. I've so enjoyed our little talk. Goodbye for now."

****

"Charles! Charles!" Bree threw the phone down on the table. "He's gone."

Nick had awakened in the Brendani living room to check the progress in the hunt for Berenger. After witnessing Bree's defeat, he slammed his hand against the wall. "That son of a bitch was so close."

Rosemary touched her grandson's shoulder. "Wait a minute. CeCe needs you again."

Nick glanced at the urn and back at his grandmother. "You can communicate with CeCe without using a spell now?"

"No. But CeCe can speak to Kitty, who relayed the information to me."

Nick hurried to Alex and tried to fall asleep to no avail. "It's not working. I need Lia."

"She's on guard duty at the house," Rosemary said. "It will take too long for her to get here. Maybe CeCe can reach out and pull you in. Try to relax."

Rosemary closed her eyes and touched the urn to contact Alex's mom. "She says she'll try to use your previous connection to draw you in."

When Nick opened his mind to Cecile, he heard a slight whisper. *Nick?*

I'm here.

A deep sigh followed his response. *Thank God.*

Now, listen to my voice. Focus on me. I'll guide you. Embrace the warmth of my light. Follow my psychic trail. I'm waiting for you. Come to me.

With eyes closed, Nick concentrated on the magic of Cecile's voice and basked in her comforting heat. The sight of her roadmap teased out a grin. Stretched in front of him—a line of sparkling fireflies led him into her sphere.

When he arrived, the smile died on his face. Cecile was there with her daughter, but Alexandra couldn't leave the room. Cecile paced outside. "The spell on Alex is wearing off. She called to me."

"Nick," Alex said. "This is my mother." Frustration edged her voice. "But I'm trapped here."

"Don't worry, Alexandra," he said. "We'll take care of that."

Reassured, Alex gave up poking at the doorway. Cecile stopped her frantic movement and held her hands up in defeat. She stepped aside for Nick to take over. "He's constructed wards to guard the room."

"You mean like a spell?"

"Yes. He's used a few bands of magic to block the door, but they're complicated."

"Okay. Let me see what I can do. Step back from the door, Alexandra."

When she moved, Nick lifted his right hand and sent a blast of energy at the door. The loud crack had Alex covering her ears.

"Did it work, Mom?"

"Not yet, honey. Try again, Nick, but hurry. He'll be back when he senses Alex is alert."

"I'm trying. Get away from the door."

This time, he lifted both hands. A flash preceded the

sharp sound of the bolt that slammed into what looked like space. The room shook, but Cecile confirmed the wards were still in place.

Nick banged his hand against the barrier in frustration. "It should have shattered."

"Not even a dent."

He groaned again.

"Wait a minute," Cecile said. "I've been studying these wards. The configuration looks familiar. I may be able to undo them, but I need more strength. I need your help, Nick."

"What can I do?"

"Let me hook into your powers."

"What? How?"

"I learned this trick from an old tribal shaman. It won't take long, a few minutes." She took a big breath. "But you'll be vulnerable during that time."

Nick narrowed his eyes as he regarded Cecile. For an instant, he hesitated. Then he glanced at Alexandra. He'd do anything for her. "What do I have to do?"

"Good man. Hold my hands and give me access to your mind."

He did as she asked, and immediately felt a loss of energy, a heaviness in his limbs, and a terrifying sense of fatigue and vulnerability swept over him.

"I learned this incantation a short while after I received my powers," CeCe said. "Southwest mysticism is very potent. I availed myself of various protective spells and counter-spells to black magic." She paused and then whispered foreign words using strange hand movements around the door. "One down, three to go."

Nick's attention shifted from Cecile to Alexandra, and then the empty hall. "How are you doing?"

"I'm almost finished, but he's coming."

The air wavered, and Berenger appeared. Nick knew he was defenseless. If Charles attacked now, Nick would die. Fury filled Charles' face as he looked from Nick to Cecile.

When Cecile whispered, "Almost," Nick knew he had to do something. Before Berenger could act, Nick caught him with an uppercut. Though fire seared his fist, it felt so good to smash the bastard's face. Charles went down but came back up roaring. The two men locked eyes. Rage suffused Charles' features, and he began to utter a spell.

Cecile squeezed Nick's hand, released his powers, and disappeared with her daughter.

****

"Let me go."

When Alex awoke on the floor of the Brendani living room, her arms pinned to her sides, she panicked and started to squirm. A small chuckle echoed behind her back. "Nick?"

He squeezed a little tighter before he released her and helped her stand. She shook her head in confusion. She'd just been a prisoner in Charles' house. Then she remembered she and her mother had left Nick to face Charles alone. "You got away?"

He held his arms out from his body as if to say, "Here I am."

She was so happy; she gave him a big hug. Then she noticed the mattress. "What were we doing on the living room floor?"

He flashed her a wicked grin that worried her. Then she peeked at the people in the room. No one seemed shocked.

"We were dreaming," he said.

One hand over her heart, Rosemary interrupted. "Thank God you're back."

Franki hurried over and pulled her niece into a tight embrace. "It's so good to see you safe, honey. We were all sick with worry."

Alex lifted an eyebrow. A few hours ago, everyone but the cook couldn't have cared less about her. Her family had all but shunned her. "Do you mind if I get some food? I never finished my lunch, and I'm starving."

Bree tucked Alex under her arm. "I'll fix a meal for you. I'm sorry I was so harsh this afternoon. It seems I don't do well in crises." She squeezed Alex's shoulder. "It's good to have you home again. Now, all we need to do is keep everyone alive until you receive your gifts."

Chapter Thirty-Four

Tony was grateful his patrol partner for tonight was Lia, especially since Rosemary had decreed no alcohol. His nerves were on fire, and he was acting twitchy, but Lia never mentioned it. He paced for a while before sitting down. Lia strolled over and sat on the ground next to him. "How ya doing, Cuz?"

He laughed. "I'm sure you know. You've always understood me."

She punched his arm. "That's because I love you, brat."

"Even though my powers are weak?"

"Your gifts have nothing to do with it. You're a good man."

He couldn't stand it any longer. He had to tell someone. He grabbed his head. "I've been partying too much—booze and drugs. Even though they reduce my powers, I can't help myself."

Lia leaned over and hugged him. "It'll be all right. I can help you. Together we can win."

"Forget it. I'm a lost cause."

She smacked him. "Are not."

He smiled.

She took his hand. "Remember Purgatory Chasm?"

With a chuckle, he said, "What were you, ten years old? You had to get that damn bird."

An image of her crawling to the edge of the cliff to

rescue the stupid thing flashed in his mind. It had been no use trying to deter her. She was determined. When she was almost there, she'd slipped, and his heart nearly stopped. If she hadn't caught on to that small sapling, the rocky surf below would have chopped her up for fish food.

"But you were my hero. You saved me."

Some hero. His stomach had churned, and he'd nearly wet himself as he inched out to get her. At the last minute, he sent out a fervent prayer, grabbed her wrist, and hauled her toward him.

She giggled. "And then you went back and saved the baby tern."

He'd never understand what prompted him to go back for that scrawny sack of feathers. Probably the pathetic look on Lia's face. A half-laugh, half-snort escaped him. "And then you named him Tony Bird."

In her sweetest voice, she said, "After his savior."

He shook his head. "You and your damned sick animals."

For a minute they shared a treasured memory, then a message came in and Tony broke the silence. "Alex is okay. Great. Everyone must be happy. They'll all forgive her for this afternoon's screw-up, but I take a little drink on duty…."

"Stop it. Everyone loves you."

"Don't worry. You don't have to stroke my ego. I'm good."

But he wasn't.

****

The sharp whistles and cracks of fireworks added to Tony's increasing discomfort. He finished checking the perimeter and sent Lia a message. *Our replacements should arrive soon.*

After another loud boom, Lia replied, *I wonder when our own fireworks will start.*

Tony's stomach tightened. He didn't think he could face what was coming without a drink.

They joined the others in the kitchen for a bite to eat. Tony couldn't keep still. He picked up a cookie, put it down, then tapped his fingers on the counter. His eyes drifted toward the liquor cabinet. Not an option right now. He ripped the top off a soda can, took a swig, and grabbed a sandwich out of the refrigerator.

"Damn," Rich said as he leaned against the counter, "this feels like the longest night ever logged through the universe. It beats any stakeout I've ever experienced by years."

Tony yawned. "You got that right. What's the countdown now?"

Franki slid an arm around her daughter. "A little under ten hours. The anticipation is the most difficult."

Lia kissed the top of her mother's head. "We'll get through it as long as we all pull together."

Tony stood up, finished his drink, and stretched. A great big yawn widened his mouth before he said, "I'm beat. See you in a couple of hours."

He stumbled as he moved up the stairs. "Whoa!" He was a little dizzy and uncoordinated like he'd been drugged.

He took off his shoes and lay down on the bed in his clothes. As soon as his head hit the pillow, he began to dream. His sleeping mind looked around in confusion at an exclusive Newport pier and the well-dressed man in front of him.

What was he doing at a Newport pier, and who was

this guy?

"Tony, my boy, good to see you."

He scrutinized the man in front of him. Craggy face, gray-streaked hair, and dark blue eyes. He was certain he'd never met him. "Who are you?"

"Let's talk on my yacht."

Tony followed the man to a large vessel moored at the dock and whistled. Nice digs. He might as well see what the guy wanted.

He examined the opulent surroundings as he followed his host. *This little boat must be worth a bundle.*

"Make yourself comfortable. Would you like a drink?"

"Why not?"

The man motioned to his steward to fix himself and his guest a drink.

A few short minutes later, Tony took a long sip of his scotch and leaned back in the soft leather chair. "So…I don't know your name."

"Charles."

"So, Charles." He swept his hand around to include the room. "To what do I owe the pleasure?"

Charles, with a small, perceptive grin, put down his drink. "I wanted to talk to you about money."

Hmm, this excursion might turn out to be quite profitable. He could use an infusion of cash right now. He'd lost a lot more money in the last few months than he cared to remember. With a slight nod to his host, he said, "I'm all ears, Charles."

"Then I'll get right to the point. I own quite a few concerns in Newport. I believe you're familiar with them." He went on to name some of the places where Tony liked to party.

Tony's good humor crumbled as Charles listed not only the establishments but the names of his bookies. He took a deep gulp of his drink.

Then Charles adopted a heavier, more threatening tone. "That's right, Tony. You owe me quite a bit of money." He paused, took a sip of his drink, and waited.

A tight band squeezed Tony's chest, and he eyed the door. Before he could move, though, Charles' expression lightened, and he leaned forward with a smile. "I'm aware you've had some bad luck, and you've got a family who doesn't understand."

Relieved, Tony spilled out his frustration. "You don't know the half of it."

"What I propose is that you do some work for me. I'll pay you well, and you can take care of your debt at the same time. Interested?"

Tony almost leaped out of his chair. "Sure. What do you have in mind? I'm a good lawyer, you know."

Charles gestured to the steward. While he refilled Tony's glass, Charles lifted his hand to encompass their palatial surroundings. "As you can see, Tony, I like wealth and power. Given the chance, any one of us would, don't you agree?"

Tony couldn't believe his luck. "Absolutely."

"I have a problem I need your help with."

"Anything."

Charles preened like a satisfied cat and almost purred his response. "Good. Your cousin Alex had lunch here a few days ago."

Tony couldn't hide his less-than-happy reaction to that bit of news. "She gets around, doesn't she?"

"She seemed like a smart young lady."

"Oh, she is that. She's been here two weeks, and

she's the darling of the household."

"Sounds like she's not your favorite."

Tony backpedaled in a hurry. This guy might be a fan of Alex. "No. No. I like her. She's a nice kid."

Charles chuckled at his response. "Don't worry about it. I'd like to help you out." He leaned forward. "How would you like me to take her off your hands for a while?"

Chapter Thirty-Five

Alex followed her aunt to the kitchen. It had been a long time since her meal this morning, and she wanted food. The room was deserted except for the housekeeper.

"For Heaven's sake, Mattie, you've been hard at work all day." Bree made a shooing gesture with her hands. "Go lay down and rest."

Alex touched Mattie's shoulder. "I'll clean up. It's the least I can do for all your kindness." She wouldn't forget the compassion Mattie had shown when the others shunned her.

The housekeeper looked a little embarrassed but finished cleaning the counter and left.

"How about a hot cup of tea?" Bree said as she turned the heat on under the kettle. She took something from the refrigerator and zapped it in the microwave.

"Real tea?"

"Decaf. Now tell me, Alex, can you remember anything that Charles might have said that would help us?"

Alex shook her head. "He talked about the house and his possessions. The place is awesome."

"Think back. Anything that might give us an idea?"

Alex took a bite from the bowl of tasty beef stew Bree had nuked. Her stomach growled in response, and she had to make herself slow down. "There was one room I didn't like. His study. It looked like one of those old Gothic movies. Everything was blood red except for the mahogany furniture." Alex shivered. "It was so disturbing. He had a ghoulish painting over his desk of a house being consumed by fire. The brightest colors in the room came from the orange and yellow of the flames ripping through the house."

"An unsettling choice, but I'm not surprised," Bree murmured. "I remember him hurrying us to go look at a fire in Newport. I was appalled. I backed away from the heat and noise of the inferno, but Charles edged in closer." Bree's eyes narrowed before she spoke. "I guess that sick interest carried through the rest of his life."

Looking refreshed and comfortable in clean clothes, Nick came into the kitchen. Alex liked the way his dark, wet hair curled around his ears. She braced herself, though, as she met the mischief in his eyes and the determined set of his freshly shaved jaw. She found it surprising that a man wearing a tee shirt and jeans could affect such a swagger.

"What are you up to?" she asked.

"Me?" Nick's innocent act wouldn't fly if he had a trapeze.

"Come on, Nicky," Bree said. "Let Alex eat her dinner."

He held up both hands in surrender. "I'm just doing my job as Alexandra's guardian." He sat down and stole a couple of her chips.

"Hey! There's plenty on the counter. Get your own."

"Ow. That's cold."

"Oh. You want to talk about cold? How about your behavior toward me this afternoon?"

Nick stopped smiling and ducked his head. "I'm sorry about that. I might have been a jerk, but sneaking off to meet Hunter wasn't your finest hour, either."

Alex wanted to forgive and forget, but the pain of his rejection had cut deep. She mumbled, "I only wanted the contract."

"Okay, Alexandra. Let's call a truce. In a few hours, we'll be fighting for our lives. Let's not die despising each other."

Nick's unsettling reminder made Alex's resentment seem petty. She admitted she didn't loathe him.

A grin slid over his face. "And I definitely don't hate you."

Alex squelched a smile as she finished her food. She refused to reveal her delight in his words.

"Wonderful," Bree said. "Everyone's happy. Now, can we talk about tomorrow?" She pointed to Alex. "While you were having your *nap*, Rosemary finished making plans. She'd like us to be at the Convent House when you receive your gifts. That way, we can protect you and then use your new powers to help defeat that monster."

"The snake?" Alex gulped as she remembered those fat, black coils.

The expression on Bree's face hardened. "Both monsters." She touched Alex's hand. "This must all sound scary, but you'll be ready once you have your gifts."

Nick hurried to reassure Alex. "Lia has developed a poison to use on the snake. We'll use that along with our powers to defeat the demon." He turned his gaze to Bree and deepened his voice. "And its handler."

The idea of having to face her nightmare once more made her ill. "Why can't I get my powers here at the Brendani house?"

As if it were the most reasonable answer in the world, Bree said, "He won't try to get you here."

Alex dropped her spoon and glared at Bree. "I'm bait?"

"You won't be alone. We'll all be there."

"Easy for you to say. You haven't seen that vicious beast."

Bree patted her shoulder. "We'll prevail. Why don't you go up and take a shower? I promise it'll brighten your outlook."

No longer hungry, Alex pushed away her food. "There's no way I'm going to feel better until this thing is over." When she considered Bree's suggestion, she realized her aunt was right. She needed to scrub off the slimy essence of Charles Berenger.

She stood up, and so did Nick.

"Where do you think you're going?"

"With you."

"With me? While I shower?" With an emphatic headshake, she said, "No way."

Nick's eyes gleamed. "I don't intend to get in the shower with you, Alexandra."

She gave him her best glare. A sharp retort sprang to her lips, but Nick beat her to it. "Unless you want me to?"

Alex's chin shot into the air. Trying to ignore the thrill of heat singeing her insides, she said, "Dream on, Mr. Stuart."

Bree clapped her hands. "Stop. I've got to get some sleep. The other women are sleeping or on duty. Nick will be a perfect gentleman or"—Bree pointed her finger at him—"answer to me."

Amusement suffused his face, but he answered,

"Yes, ma'am."

"Oh, and before you leave, Rosemary came across an ancient incantation we hope will work against the demon. It must be delivered into the demon's mind and needs at least three to send it. Clan members with that ability are Rosemary, you two, and me. We'll need to be physically linked for the spell to work." She handed them each a piece of paper.

Two short lines, but the foreign words confused Alex. Bree went over the pronunciation with them a few times. "Practice until the phrase is etched in your brain."

"What do the words mean?" Alex asked.

"Najash, demon serpent, in the name of God, depart this realm."

"That's it?" Alex said.

"There was more, but we deleted the bit about returning it to protect the treasure. Rosemary and I decided we'd rather have demon-free property in the future."

Nick snorted. "Good call." He turned to Alex. "Ready?"

Left with no other choice, she headed for the stairs.

****

The hot spray of the shower pummeled away the pain of her captivity. Realizing she had no control over the imminent confrontation with her enemies, she reveled in her present freedom. These precious hours might be all she'd have, and she intended to enjoy them.

Unbidden, a dangerous thought entered her head. Did that include the aggravating, adorable man sitting in her bedroom? Having Nick so near made her skin tingle. If they wanted to succeed tomorrow, though, they couldn't have distractions clouding their judgment. And for Alex, Nick was one enormous distraction. Best if she didn't let her hormones run away with her now.

A knock on the door snapped her back to reality. "Everything good in there?"

Ooh, he drove her crazy. "I'm fine. Leave me alone."

She turned off the water and reached for the big fluffy green towels on the warming rack. One to dry off and the other for her hair. She'd never experienced the decadence of warm towels after a shower. Wrapping one around her was Heaven! The soft, green warmth begged her to stay cuddled in it forever. Too bad her watchdog was so impatient. She looked around for her clothes. "Oh, hell!"

She'd left them in the bedroom. She was going to have to parade in front of Nick in a towel. Desire welled up, and her lips curved into a coy smile. *Serves him right. He insisted on coming with me.* This should be interesting. She smoothed her damp hair back and opened the door. Nick, who'd been looking out the window, turned with an impish grin, saying, "Now, don't you feel bet..." Unable to finish his sentence, he stared open-mouthed at Alex.

She adopted a sweet smile. "I do." A pout followed. "But I forgot my clothes."

While she took her time walking to the bureau for her things, Nick found his voice, a shade deeper than usual. "I wouldn't worry about that, Alexandra. I quite like the towel. The green matches your eyes."

As he spoke, he moved in behind her and put his hands on her bare shoulders.

Alex couldn't help the sensuous shiver that shook her body. It took all her willpower not to lean into him.

She closed her eyes as he kneaded her skin.

The timbre of his low growl sent sparks along her body. "Your towel is still warm."

Somehow Alex found herself resting against his hard chest, arching her neck, and hoping for more. His warm breath caressed her as he said, "Are you sure this is what you want?" His ragged whisper against her skin ignited her blood.

Oh damn, it so was. Then a voice inside her head warned. *Not now.* She sighed as she reached back to touch his cheek. "It's not a great time with everything hanging over our heads."

Her words turned into a tiny gasp as the stubble on Nick's chin tickled her neck. Her mind screamed she should stop him now, but her body begged for more.

With a gentle nip, he tugged on her earlobe. "But that's just it, Alexandra." His lips moved lower, and she tilted her head to give him room.

"This might be the last chance we have to be together." His velvety voice and the slow, sensuous, downward trail of his hands along her arms sent a shock of heat to her belly and below. Beneath the towel, her body shivered in anticipation. One small tug was all he'd need.

His teeth grazed her ear as he whispered, "I'd hate to die without ever having loved you." He ended the sentence by sliding his tongue along her cheek.

Heat shot through her. Feelings she'd refused to acknowledge emerged. No matter what happened, Nick was the one. "I want you, too."

He turned her around to face him and leaned down to savor her lips. The tender kiss wasn't enough. She reached up to tangle her fingers in his hair and pull him closer. He deepened the kiss and dragged her against him.

As her fingers massaged his still-damp scalp, his spicy, masculine scent spurred her desire. The taste of coffee lingered on his tongue. A fiery need coursed through her, and she clung to him as he carried her to the bed.

Her towel disappeared. Then his clothes. She drank in the sight of this gorgeous man and welcomed him to her.

His eyes turned dark with passion. "I've pictured you like this ever since those damn gremlins tripped you into the kitchen." He kissed her eyes, nose, and lips, while his hands made her moan with delight. As she squirmed beneath him, his voice entered her head. *You like that?*

Oh God, yes. She arched up.

You're beautiful, Alexandra.

His words made her heart swell. Lost in his embrace, she forgot about their problems. All she cared about was Nick.

His lovemaking became more urgent. Breath thundered in her chest. She raked his back and moaned. She couldn't get close enough to him. He was devouring her, and she loved it. Then he opened his mind to show her how much he cared. Seeing his true feelings was so seductive she nearly lost it. She tore down her own barrier to reveal her heart's truth. She loved him.

When the final explosion came, she cried out his name.

****

Alex listened to the noise of the midnight contingent leaving for their posts as she cuddled into Nick. He tightened his arms around her and yawned. "I could use a little more sleep, and you need to be rested and ready for this morning. Why don't we try another dream?"

Her muscles tensed. His words triggered all her "fight or flight" reflexes, and she snapped at him. "I couldn't fall asleep right now."

"Easy sweetheart. You'll be safe. I'll help you."

"You?" She sat up and glared at him. "How can you help me?" They'd always needed Lia to ease them into sleep.

He traced his finger down the length of her arm. Despite her fear, his touch stirred her senses. "Come down here."

The low rumble of his voice reverberated in her stomach. She lay back, and he held her so close, the heat from his body became part of her own. With a tender touch, he stroked her face. "Stop worrying. You're tired. Relax. I'm with you. Open your mind."

How could she not listen to this man who had shared his inner being? Although fear bubbled up, she realized Nick had always protected her. He'd earned her trust. With a quick visit to her mind's place of serenity, she dropped her shields.

One minute she was lost in Nick's gaze, the next, warmed by the heat of the sun. Nearby tufts of grass danced to the tune of wayward currents of air. Beyond the grassy field, tree-lined hills rose to paint a delightful scene, but something wasn't right. The smell. She scrunched up her nose.

The sound of a loud snort startled her. She spun around, then grinned. Horses. A beautiful roan stallion by the fence tossed his head at her. "Hi there, handsome. What are you doing in my dream?"

"Guarding your body."

Nick's arms wrapped around her, and she chuckled. "I was talking to the horse." Twisting her head for a kiss, she said, "But, seriously, why here?" She'd expected to be at the beach.

"Horses hate snakes. They'll react right away if one is near, and we'll have plenty of time to wake up."

Beautiful equine bodies grazed near them. Alex sighed and experienced a small sense of peace. When she saw Nick smile at something behind her, she turned and cried out, "Mom?" Her heart swelled. "You're here." She launched herself at her mother, threw her arms around her, and cried. In this reality, CeCe was as substantial as she and Nick. Between sobs, she said, "I've missed you so much."

"I've missed you, too, sweetheart."

While the women hugged, Nick scanned the vast acreage.

Alex bombarded her mother with questions. "Why couldn't you visit me while I slept before?"

"It's taken me some time to get used to my new existence. For a while, I floated in the background of your mind, struggling to warn you, but now I've gained some strength. I can dream walk again, use telepathy, and Mother's helped me learn a few ghostly tricks."

"You mean Kitty? She's a trip. Which reminds me, I thought I was crazy when I arrived. Why did you hide everything from me?"

"Sweetheart, I wanted a normal life for you and Daddy. He had no idea I was different. He'd never have been comfortable with our gifts. I didn't want to lose him, so I convinced him to run away with me." She smiled. "I told him he was my knight in shining armor."

"What about me? Did you think I wouldn't notice anything strange on my twenty-fifth birthday?"

Cecile squeezed Alex's shoulder. "I'm so sorry, my love. I'd planned to explain months before that day, but then your father died, and simple things like getting out of bed in the morning became difficult."

Nick's head snapped up. "Something's wrong at the house. Time to go. Sorry, Cecile." He reached out to Alex, and they both woke up.

"What's going on?" The smell of horses lingered in her nostrils as she blinked at her bedroom. The jump to reality still unsettled her.

"Get dressed. There's a fire."

Chapter Thirty-Six

Alex and Nick raced from the bedroom and down the stairs toward Mattie's screams.

Alex grabbed the housekeeper's arm. "What is it?"

"Bree's office is on fire. Adam's in there, but I can't open the door."

Nick grabbed the knob. Locked. He threw himself at the heavy wood with no luck. "I'll have to get in through the window." He grabbed Alex by her shoulders. "You stay here where you're safe. I'll be right back."

Outside, the glow from the fire blended with the sharp light of sunrise. Nick put his hand up to block the strong rays. From the corner of his eye, he saw movement, then a sharp pain ripped through his head, and he crumpled to the ground.

****

Alex panicked when Tony's voice entered her mind. *Nick's hurt. I can't wake him.*

As fear stabbed her heart, she screamed out Nick's name. *I'm on my way.*

She forgot all about safety and ran out the front door into the deep shade created by the house. The minute she jumped off the bottom step, a shadowy figure reached out and put an arm around her. She tried to twist out of his grip. "Let me go. Nick's in trouble."

She never suspected the threat until she turned and saw his face, hard and calculating. Hunter? He was part of this? How could she have fallen for his lies? "Why are you doing this? Please let me go."

"Stop struggling. You'll be fine."

Before she could react, he shoved a cloth over her nose and mouth. She fought and tried to hold her breath, but this time, she lost. Aware she had seconds of consciousness left, she sent out a last, silent scream to the Clan.

****

Alex's psychic scream invaded the murk in Nick's mind. It hurt to open his eyes. Why was he staring at the bottom of a rhododendron bush? He struggled to his feet, fighting against the incessant throbbing in his head. He didn't understand why he was in pain, but he recognized Alexandra's cry for help. Still shaky, he moved to go to her.

The flickering light in Bree's office stopped him. A fire? Then he remembered Adam. He'd burn to death if Nick didn't go after him now. With a roar, Nick used an energy blast to knock the glass out of the window. He crawled in, tripped over the window seat, and landed on the floor, re-aggravating the pain in his head. *Son of a bitch!*

He called out to Adam. No response. The curling patches of smoke in the room made it impossible to see. Shards of glass crunched underneath him, but he concentrated on locating Adam. To avoid the fumes, he stayed close to the floor. Hacking sounds came from his left, and he moved in that direction. The crackle of flames as they consumed Bree's possessions made him sick. Intense heat bore into him, and his own coughs drowned out any noise from his injured comrade. Nick prayed the man was still alive. Then his knee hit something soft. He'd found him.

Nick alerted the rest of the family and dragged the unconscious man over to the door. It took precious minutes to unlock it. Before he could get out of the way, the heavy door slammed into them. "Hold it. Let us get out of the way."

"Okay," Franki said. "Hurry."

He dragged Adam around the door and handed him out to Franki and Mattie who hauled Adam into the corridor. Nick staggered out after them and slammed the office door closed against the blaze.

The women half carried, half dragged Adam down the hall while Nick stumbled behind. All he could think of was the psychic scream from the woman he loved. "They have Alexandra. I've got to find her."

Franki grabbed Nick's arm and forced him to sit while Lia tended to Adam. By that time, Rosemary had arrived. "What's going on? I heard Alex. My God! The place is burning."

Franki had sent someone out into the yard to spray water into the room. "The fire department is on the way." She knelt in front of Nick and made a cursory inspection of his head and face. "He's bleeding, Lia."

Lia reached her hand out and held his head. "He'll be fine until I can get this one stabilized. Adam needs immediate help. His lungs are filled with smoke."

Rosemary tried to see Nick's injury, but he pushed her probing fingers away. "I'm fine. I'm going after Alexandra."

His grandmother slapped his hands. "Nicholas! You're not all right until Lia says you are. Besides, everyone is already searching for Alex. There's nothing more you can do."

A coughing spasm kept him in place. He sent out a blast to Clan members for information on their search. By the time Lia got to him, he'd accepted that he could do nothing to help his precious Alexandra.

Bree arrived on the scene, breathless from hurrying back to the house. Franki asked how the fire started, then turned to her sister. "Was the fireplace lit?"

"Of course not," Bree spat out. "It's July, for God's sake."

Nick spoke up. "The fire didn't begin in the fireplace, and it wasn't an accident. That bastard used Adam as a decoy. He didn't care if anyone died or the house burned down. He wanted to take me out so he could kidnap Alexandra."

Defeat laced Rosemary's voice. "I was aware we had a traitor in our midst, but I never imagined they'd be willing to commit murder."

Nick's gut clenched as if a fist squeezed it. "Time is running out for Alexandra."

Chapter Thirty-Seven

Nick ran out in front of the Brendani House, hoping for any sign of the kidnapping. Nothing. No trace. *Why did she leave the house after he'd told her to stay safe?* His heart ached. Only a few hours ago, she'd been in his arms, so giving, so trusting. He had to find her.

A familiar voice entered his head. Cecile. *He has her, Nick. She's caught in his web, again.*

A coughing spasm shook his chest just as he slammed his hand against a nearby tree. *I have no idea where she is, and we've got less than five hours left.*

We have to save her, CeCe said. *I'm afraid her survival isn't part of his plans. Contact me the minute you discover anything.*

Cecile's words penetrated his chest like a jagged knife. He promised to keep her informed. Searchers still combed the grounds, some with dogs. The thought of Alexandra in the clutches of that madman made him crazy. Where would he have taken her? A spark of light off to his left caught his eye. A reflection of the sun. The sole object in that direction was the mausoleum they'd been guarding. Everyone had left their posts there to search for Alexandra and help with the fire.

Damn! A perfect diversion if Charles wanted to sneak into the mansion.

No sooner had he thought about that hellhole, than Rich sent him a message. *Meet me at the Convent House.*

I've found the door he's been using, but I can't get in. Something's blocking me.

Nick broke into a run and sent the information to Rosemary. She told him she'd have everyone meet at the Brendani home before they joined him at the cursed ruin next door.

****

The sweet, yeasty scent of cinnamon buns permeated the Brendani kitchen. One of Rosemary's favorites, but she wasn't tempted. The weight of the upcoming battle had her stomach in knots.

When the returning searchers arrived, she asked them to meet her in the living room. Her words put them on edge, but they agreed and talked and munched their way in to see her. Their eyes widened at the sight of weapons piled on a side table, and all conversation stopped. A few threw nervous glances at the clock. Only four hours remained until Alex's birthday and the confrontation. With the excitement of the search, some might have forgotten the countdown.

Ignoring the flutters in her stomach, she straightened her shoulders. "It's time. Rich and Nick are waiting for us at the Convent House. Take a weapon but be careful. Each gun has six darts loaded with a special poison infused with the snake's own venom."

She paused. "This is important. When we find the snake, we must attack it in unison. Multiple assaults will frustrate the serpent and let the poison work." She turned to Lia. "Please show them how to use the guns."

A few people were missing from the gathering, her son being one of them. After a message to Duncan went unanswered, the twisting in her chest became an icy coil. Something was wrong.

"I didn't see him come downstairs during the fire," Franki said.

Dread filled her soul. "Where are the others? Has anyone seen them?" A collection of negative headshakes greeted her question. The cold mass inside her expanded. "This isn't good. Someone, please check upstairs."

Lia ran up. Rosemary watched fear infect the faces of those grouped in the living room. Then someone rubbed his eyes, yawned, and sat on the floor. Another one followed.

Lia's voice entered her head. *Duncan and the rest of the crew have been drugged. I can't bring them around. They'll be out of it for hours.*

The living room now resembled a teenage sleepover. More bodies hit the floor as others slept.

"The cinnamon buns!" Franki screamed. She threw away the one she'd just bitten into. "Don't eat them."

A finger of fear twisted in Rosemary's gut as she tried to understand what was happening. She'd lost half her Clan. The only members still standing beside herself were Bree, Lia, Tony, and two others.

She listened to Bree's frantic cries to her sister. "Can you throw up? Try to get it out of your system."

Rosemary sighed. It wouldn't help. Franki weighed next to nothing, and she'd already absorbed the drug. Her eyes were losing their battle to stay open.

"Bree," Rosemary said, "put her on the sofa."

A sudden urge to join Franki almost overwhelmed her. She didn't think she could handle much more. Her heart broke as Bree kissed her sister and said, "Lie down and rest. We'll be back later to wake you up. I love you."

Lia wiped tears from her eyes. "Mommy, we'll see you in a little while."

As Franki lost consciousness, Rosemary reeled from the final blow. "Mattie. She made the buns." She clutched her chest. "Why would she do it?"

Bree placed a steadying hand on Rosemary's shoulder. "Don't worry about that now. It's time to leave."

Rosemary blinked her eyes but continued, "She's been with me for over twenty years."

"Rosemary," Bree said, her voice sharp. "Come on. It's time to join Nick at the Convent House."

Rosemary's head drooped for a moment as she sent a message to her grandson. *Half the Clan have been drugged. Six of us are on our way. I need you or Rich to pick up the extra guns.*

With a heavy heart, she remembered her heritage, straightened her shoulders, and shook off the betrayal. "Okay. Let's go eliminate a couple of snakes."

****

Nick followed Rich's directions to the trail he'd found but detected no clear path until he pushed through the bushes and saw tamped-down vegetation. "Damn! I should have seen this days ago."

Rosemary's news had hit him hard. Now, he only had half his Clan to help rescue Alexandra and take down Charles and the snake.

Nick took a deep breath and twisted his lips into a grim smile. Didn't matter. He'd take eight Templars against a madman and his pet demon any day. The Watcher Clan would prevail once he figured out how to get them inside.

He contacted Cecile to let her know where Charles had taken Alexandra.

Okay, Nick. I'll meet you there, but hurry. We don't

have much time. If he's spun one of his webs, I'll need your help to undo the magic. We're not in a dream now. You'll have to do the spell.

Irritation sharpened his voice. *I would, Cecile, but we've run into trouble out here. He's put some kind of ward over the entrance. We're searching for another way in, but it doesn't look good.*

He turned to Rich. "Go back to the house and get the extra rifles. I'll keep trying here. I'll check for any crack he forgot."

After Rich sped off, Nick scooped up a fist-size rock and threw it at an upstairs window. He barely dodged the ricochet after it hit an invisible wall.

Cecile had arrived. *It won't work, Nick. He's got the whole place covered.*

We've got to get in.

Calm down. We can do it. Take me back to his entry point. He'd have wanted to make access there easier.

He raced back to meet Cecile. She stayed quiet for a minute, and his patience dissolved. *Can you see it?*

Yes. Now, let me study this. It's complicated, a little different from the one at his house.

While Cecile surveyed the door, he paced and tried not to think of the time. Alexandra needed them.

At last, she spoke. *I believe I've got it. You'll have to do the incantations and the hand motions exactly as I instruct you. If not, it won't work. Are you ready?*

"Let's do it."

All right. Here goes. Wave your right hand in a half circle clockwise from nine to three as you say, Al-na-as-dzoh. Nick flubbed the wording a few times before he got it right.

Good. One down. Now extend your right pointer and

middle finger to make a V-shape and twist to the right as if turning a key and say, Na-jih-co-nah-ya.

Together, Cecile and Nick unbound the wards until they hit a snag. *It didn't work, Nick. The strand is still there. Your hand was off. Try moving just your thumb at the end.*

Nick's mouth hurt from trying to pronounce the strange sounds, and the tendons in his hands ached as he tried to duplicate the moves Cecile described. He sighed, wiped the sweat off his forehead, and rubbed his hands against his pants. *Okay, let's do this again.*

Cecile repeated the incantation and this time it worked. *You're doing great. One more to go.*

He began the hand movement.

"We're here, Nick."

His grandmother. Her words ruined his concentration, and his hand slipped. "Dammit!"

He turned pleading eyes on the group. "I need quiet. Cecile's directing me."

They nodded, and Nick began again, achingly aware of the time. It was almost seven a.m., three hours until Alex received her powers.

He'd almost finished the last spell when Rich ran up. "I got most of the guns. We're all set."

"God!" Nick said as he threw his hands in the air. "I almost had it."

Lia took Rich aside, shushing him, and explained what was happening. Nick and Cecile started on the last band again.

Nick feared his tongue would be forever tangled by the archaic language he was spouting. He forced himself to concentrate on Cecile's instructions, freed the last strand, and opened the door.

Cecile congratulated him. *Good work. I'll find Alex.*

As he scrambled forward, Rosemary clutched his arm. Stress brought out a hint of her Scottish burr as she demanded caution. "You'll be no help to the lass if you're dead."

She handed him a rifle, and they all crept through the door into the demon's den.

Chapter Thirty-Eight

Alex came to, lying on a hard surface in a dark, cold room. It smelled old and musty, like an abandoned cellar. She raised herself onto her hands and knees trying to stand. The room started to spin, and bile climbed to the back of her throat. She was just able to crawl toward the corner before she threw up. She wiped her mouth with her sleeve and dragged herself away from the mess. The effort proved too much for her, and she lay back on the floor. When she tried again, she was less dizzy, and her stomach only threatened to heave. If she wanted to get out, she'd have to slow down. Her fingernails bit into her palms as she squeezed her hands. How long did she have left?

Still woozy from the drugs, Alex tried to force the chaos from her head. She wanted to get clear enough to read Charles' thoughts and alert the Clan to his plans. Every time she tried, though, her mind fractured into tiny pieces running in all directions. She found it difficult to concentrate, and her stomach kept promising trouble.

Alex wrapped her hands around her head, hating the dizzying ache. She relived all the stupid mistakes she'd made in the past few days that brought her to this place. Hunter. He must have been the one who'd invaded her mind on the yacht.

And Nick. Why hadn't she listened to him when he told her to stay inside? Oh, God! She'd forgotten. She sent up a fervent prayer that Nick was all right. Thanks to her massive stupidity, she was back in the madman's clutches. She harbored no illusions about her chances with Charles. He'd had no compunction about killing her mother.

Alex tried once more to move. This time, she dragged herself into a sitting position and peered at her surroundings. She had to shift her head in small increments, stopping often in order to focus her eyes.

Whoa. What she saw surprised her. She'd gotten the *old* part right, but this was no cellar. The mold under her nose? Not clammy stones or rotting wood, but a filthy carpet.

After another cautious turn of her head, Alex curled her lip. "Well, well. Looks like my aunt's painting was right on."

She recognized the dilapidated replica of the room she'd seen in her vision. The one place she'd tried so hard to avoid. The Convent House had captured her after all.

Charles had dumped her in a corner near the dirty but still impressive brick fireplace. Peering around the massive room, she saw the remnants of its gloried past. Intricate ceiling designs and lavish furnishings lay buried beneath the grime. The rotted piece of material beneath her had probably been yellow in its day. She shivered as she remembered the bloodied carpet in her dream.

The ultimate proof she'd awakened in the Convent House sat about ten feet away from her. Although time and neglect had done their best to destroy it, a once magnificent harp stood tall and proud near the fireplace. Alex closed her eyes against an attack of vertigo. Too much concentration. She'd have to pull herself together if she wanted to help. Once more, she scanned the room. Alone. Charles must think she was still out.

She took a few deep breaths and decided, *I can do this.*

After two failed attempts, she finally made it to her feet and staggered against the wall, upsetting her still-iffy stomach. Praying that the cobwebs near her head held no spiders, she leaned there for another minute, trying to quiet her insides and gather her courage. She had to get out of there.

When she felt stronger, she braced herself and lunged toward the far door. Seconds later, she smashed into an invisible barrier that knocked her to the ground. Sharp pain radiated down her shoulder to her arm. "Damn!"

She banged her fists against the floor, swallowing against the sudden rise of bile. Tears pricked her eyes, but she brushed them away. She couldn't give up now. She couldn't let him win. Charles had bound her into this corner, the same as he'd done at his home, but she'd gotten out of that.

Closing her eyes, she sent out a plea to her mother. *Help! I'm in the Convent House, bound by a spell.*

Like the warmth of a soft hug, her mother's voice soothed her anxiety. *Sweetheart, Clan members have broken into the house. They'll be here in a few minutes.*

Mom? I'm awake, I think. How can I hear you?

I'm stronger now, but, honey, I need to prepare you for the change.

I don't care about that. She didn't want to hear anything more about her powers. She wished she could wipe the past few months from her brain.

I know you're tired. It's just a little longer. Can you

do it?

Alex took a steadying breath. *Okay, Mom.*

I wish you were in better shape, but you'll be fine. First, sweetheart, there is nothing to fear. Your gifts are a part of you. They've always been dormant in your body, and this spark will ignite them. When it happens, you'll feel strange. Don't worry. That's normal. Accept the change and go with it.

Alex hoped she'd live to receive the powers her mother spoke about. *How much longer?*

It's close, my love. Trust me when I say you'll be fine.

What about Charles? He's going to take the powers before I can get them.

Don't worry, Alex. He won't steal your gifts. Can you sense me with you?

Yes.

I'll be with you through the change as well. You won't be alone.

She could do this. No matter what she had to face, Mom would be with her. While she'd been listening to her mother, she managed to stand.

Charles had entered the room. "You seem to be much better, my dear. I'm glad. We want to make sure you attract your powers at the proper time. You should be perfect in—" He checked his watch. "—a little over two hours." He grinned. "If you'll excuse me, Alex, I have to get ready."

Charles had brought some things with him. An enormous book, an iron pot, and a bunch of herbs. Then Alex noticed he'd already set up candles in a circular pattern on the other side of her prison. Somehow, she'd missed those in her previous sweep of the room.

When her gaze moved toward the fireplace, an involuntary scream escaped her. Coiled there like a huge, tar-blackened rope was the snake. At the sound of her scream, its massive head spun in her direction, and it moved. Alex backed up to the wall.

The interruption caused Charles to swear. His features twisted into a grimace, and he stopped his preparations to spit out a quick incantation. The snake paused, sending its tongue in Alex's direction. A rank smell reached her nose at the same time she heard its loud warning hiss. Her stomach turned to mush, and her strength dissolved. With the snake's fiery gaze boring into her, Alex slid down the wall. More mumblings from Charles sent the snake back to its original position by the fireplace.

Alex stilled and swallowed. It took all her control not to be sick again.

You're safe, honey. He can't get you behind this barrier. The Clan is close. I'm going to inform Nick that Charles and the snake are here. Nick will come in to help me with these wards. There aren't many.

But the snake.

The Clan will set up a diversion. You'll be fine. Everything will work out. Once you're free of this spell, you can receive your gifts.

Chapter Thirty-Nine

CeCe asked her daughter to distract Charles and take his attention away from the door to the hall. Still trembling from her encounter with the demon, Alex had to force herself to stand and face her captor. It took her a few tries to find her voice. "Charles?"

He looked up from his task.

"How did you know about the snake?"

He stood there, almost preening, and laughed. "Let's just say I have friends in high places." Then his voice filled with disdain. "Your precious Clan members. All those gifts squandered over the years. I'll teach them what power can do." He swept his hand through the air. "They had this place available to them for their whole lives, but no one dared enter. The answer was right here the whole time. The Swenson woman must have found the spell. She brought Najash into her fancy mansion without understanding she had to protect herself. Stupid cow! This is where Najash took them all out. Look," he said pointing to the floor. "You can still see the blood stains."

At the mention of Madelaine Swenson's name, Alex noticed a dip in the room temperature. The hair at the back of her neck rose. A spirit had joined them. "She's here now."

Charles recoiled. "What?"

"Madelaine. She's in this room."

Charles swiveled his head up and all around him. "Don't give me that crap. There's no one here."

Just then, the snake lifted its head, tasting the air with its tongue. For a minute Charles flinched. A flash of fear crossed his face. His head swung around in a frantic search. He paused and turned his attention to the door. Looking at his watch in disgust, he said, "It seems they've gotten in early. I had no idea they had someone talented enough to disengage my wards."

The countenance Alex had once regarded as handsome turned ugly. "Don't get your hopes up, Alex. Most of Gabrielle's little posse should be dead by now."

"What? What do you mean?"

His evil countenance twisted in a half laugh, half snort. "One of your precious Clan members works for me." At Alex's look of shock, he said, "I'm not heartless. I told her to save a few. After all, I do need some talent when I take over the Clan."

He turned, dismissing Alex, and spit out some indistinguishable words causing the snake to move toward the doorway. A satisfied expression covered his face. "I believe Najash should be able to hold the stragglers."

Alex didn't hear him. Her mind had shut down after the word, dead. A crushing emptiness depleted her strength, and she staggered. Her rebellious stomach had nothing left in it, but, still, she gagged. *Mom? Mom? Who's dead?*

****

A chill swept over Nick as he stepped into the Convent House. He remembered the demon had been here over a century ago and slaughtered an entire family. How much blood would it shed today?

The seven Clan members who were left followed him along a trail carved through century-old grime into a massive entrance hall, three stories high. A sweeping staircase dominated the space. Above them hung an extravagant chandelier, once a salute to opulence, now a tarnished epitaph written in the dust of time. The pungent scent of decay surrounded them.

The last time Nick had been in these rooms, he and Tony had been brave knights conquering the keep for their king. With all the enthusiasm of ten-year-olds, they'd run up and down the staircase, brandishing sticks and yelling things like "Huzzah!" and "Take that, you villain."

Everything was different today. The hall was filled with family and friends fighting for their lives against a deadly foe. An enemy who wanted to kill the woman he loved. He wasn't about to let that happen. He'd give his life for Alexandra.

A telepathic message from Rosemary reminded everyone to use their dart guns. *We need to get as much poison as possible into the snake.*

They crept forward, weapons clutched in their hands, scanning the darkened room for trouble. A faint light spilled out from the living room door. Alexandra must be there. He hurried across the hall but paused when he felt a shift in the atmosphere. He sent a quick message to the others for silence.

His nose quivered at the foul smell it encountered. In the stillness, he heard a scraping noise and cringed. The telltale sound of a snake on the move. He sent out a warning seconds before a huge black head appeared at the top of the doorway.

Although he'd known what to expect, the sight

chilled him. He'd almost died of its bite. Horror clouded the faces of his clansmen, and panicky shots flew wide of their mark. The hissing giant lunged at the intruders who resorted to energy blasts. His grandmother's sharp command pierced his thoughts. *Use the poison to weaken the monster.*

Their next multipronged attack rattled the demon. His head swiveled with each hit, unsure of which direction to attack. That small respite gave the Clan enough time to overcome their initial terror and hit their planned targets.

Missiles flew, and the snake reared back. It hissed and rose some ten feet in the air. Shafts hung from its dirty, black scales like lonely needles on a grotesque Christmas tree. The serpent wove back and forth in a frenzy, making false starts as it spotted each movement. Clan members leaped away from the fangs. Then, the hell-spawn spat a stream of venom at Nick. He barely dodged it and alerted the others to the new tactic.

Those who'd run out of ammunition focused on their magic. When a clansman got knocked across the floor, Lia dropped her gun to play medic. The others kept the demon busy while she worked.

A few people tried flinging objects at the serpent. One large, wooden table crashed against the snake's head. Rotted with age, it broke on contact, sending shards flying in all directions. Tony jumped as one sharp piece slashed the side of his arm. When a fragment narrowly missed Rosemary, she sent out an order to stop hurling furniture.

Nick needed to get to Alexandra. She didn't have much time, and he didn't trust Charles not to hurt her. He asked Lia for help. She made her way over to him, while the Clan kept the snake busy. Lia closed her eyes, threw her head back, and lifted her arm. She spun her hand in a circular motion, and a spurt of air moved through the room. Bit by bit, a swirling dusty spiral formed. The twisting wind morphed into a dirt devil. The demon backed away from the turbulence, swinging its head to evade the grit.

It was enough for Nick to slip into the room, where he ducked behind pieces of discarded furniture. Charles was busy with his potions in front of the fireplace. Nick held his breath until he located Alexandra, then let out a sigh. She was alive, but she looked so forlorn. He wanted to rush over, wrap her in his arms, and kiss away all her pain.

Unfortunately, the solution wasn't that easy. First, he had to sneak over there, undetected, then undo the wards without alerting Charles, and finally, keep her safe until the Mutata. Oh yes. Kill the demon. A yell from the other room reminded him he'd have to hurry.

Chapter Forty

With every loud crash or yell, Alex cringed. Her mother had promised her no one was dead, but it sounded like that could change any minute. The Clan was in this lethal battle because of her, and she could do nothing to help them.

The noise of the fight didn't impact Charles. He remained focused on his task other than the occasional, "Good boy, Najash," when someone screamed. He never noticed Nick sneak in, but Alex caught the movement and stared. Nick ducked around discarded pieces of furniture to get to her.

He was alive. Despite the circumstances, she felt her heart swell. She opened her mouth to speak, but he signaled her to be quiet.

CeCe let Alex listen in to the spell-reversal instructions. Alex blinked in amazement as her mom spouted foreign words. She was so proud of Nick, but she worried as he whispered the alien language. She hoped the background chaos would mask his voice. Somehow, though, Charles heard. He snapped his head around, pointed his hands toward Nick, and chanted.

"Nick," she yelled, "duck!"

He wasn't fast enough, and a part of the bolt caught his leg, taking him down. Alex panicked. She saw Charles prepare for another attack but could do nothing to prevent it. "Mom, help him." As a ghost, CeCe was powerless.

Alex didn't see Nick move, but he somehow sent a searing shot of energy at Charles, who dove for the floor.

She peered at Nick. "You're okay?"

He smiled and continued removing the wards. He'd eliminated one more when Alex warned him again. He leaped away seconds before Charles' shot flew by him.

Unable to help him, she fixed her gaze on Charles. He'd murdered her mother and intended to kill the man she loved. Another bolt just missed Nick. She tried to get into her enemy's head, but he had an iron shield. A ball of anger churned in her gut. Pushing against the bounds of her prison, she let out all her pain and frustration. Heat built in her core, funneled through her arms, and slid into her hands. Her fingers crackled as blue flames leaped out.

Charles looked at her in horror. A burning stench filled the air, and her hands no longer encountered an invisible wall. Her chest heaved, and her fingers itched. Before she could wonder what had happened, her mother said, *Well done, sweetheart. You broke his spell.*

"How? Did I get my powers?"

No, honey. You've been building up a magnetic field for the past few months, although it was out of control.

"Oh, my God." The power that ruined her life back home saved her today.

Nick took her hand. "What was that?"

"Watch out for Charles."

Nick pushed her out of the way, ducked, and returned fire. He then tossed his gun to her. "This is the poison for the snake. There are only two shots left. Make them count."

When Alex walked out of her prison, Charles'

features distorted into an ugly glare. His loss of concentration allowed Nick's next bolt to catch him on the side of his arm. He went down, but only for a moment.

Alex saw Bree slip into the room. As Charles shook off Nick's hit and prepared his retaliation, Bree spoke. "Give up Charles. You're going to lose."

He swiveled toward her in astonishment. "Gabrielle?" For a long moment, he gazed at her. A brief smile creased his lips. A minute later, his expression turned to horror. The snake slid in right after her.

"Gabrielle, behind you." As Najash moved toward Bree, Charles hurled the blast he'd meant for Nick at the snake's head.

Bree dashed out of the way as the missile connected. Najash reared back, making an unearthly noise. Its eyes blazed as it shook off the attack.

Nick took advantage of the confusion and tried to sneak Alex out of the room, but the demon saw them. Bree yelled out a warning. Alex clutched Nick's arm and panicked. They were pinned in the corner.

Worry contorted Charles's face. Alex knew he didn't care about them. He must be worried about his imminent source of power. Pointing at the serpent, he began reciting a spell. He had to jump out of the way of the snake's thrashing tail, but the incantation worked. It stopped moving forward.

By that time, Alex had emptied the gun. Both shots went wild. She dropped the weapon and leaned into Nick. They were safe for a moment.

****

And then they weren't. With a flick of its tongue, the demon's eye slits widened. It refocused its attention on

Alex and Nick. She uttered a low moan. They had no place to go.

Nick tried to defend them, but Alex was aware of his weakened state. If only she could help. She peeked into the snake's mind. No coherent thoughts. Just bloodlust. In the end, she clutched Nick's back and prayed for a quick death.

Then time seemed to stop, and the room began to shimmer. A tingling began in her fingers and traveled throughout her body. Surrounded by a cocoon of heat, her vision clouded. A strange whistling noise filled her head. Her ears became blocked as if there had been a change in the air pressure, and sounds in the room around her dimmed. Her heart banged so hard she was afraid she might die.

Her mother's voice calmed her. *Don't be afraid, sweetheart. It's your gift. You're receiving your powers. Save yourself. Concentrate on shields!*

As Alex experienced the changes in her body, she recognized the emergence of her gift. The special power that had waited for this moment. A huge surge of energy rushed through her. Instinct took over. She visualized a large protective barrier, wrapped it tight around herself and Nick, and made it solid and impenetrable.

When she looked up, though, her breathing hitched. Huge fangs already dripped venom. He lunged. She closed her eyes, squeezed Nick, and prayed.

Instead of the anticipated stab of pain, however, there was a loud smack, and the ground shook. The sensation was followed by a huge crash. Her eyes popped open. The snake had bounced off her shield and slammed against the wall. "Oh, my God!" The words came out in a croak.

Nick turned to her, eyes wide and mouth open. Alex's own mouth was so dry, words choked out of her. "It worked. My shield."

Charles, who'd been trying to stop the snake from killing the source of his expected power, gaped at Alex in disbelief. "You can't have received your powers. It's too soon."

Anger seemed to seethe from his pores. He waved his hands in the air. "It's impossible. I planned for everything. Your father, your mother, that sniveling brat, Hunter. I beat the Brendanis and their Clan. You're mine!" His manic denial echoed through the room.

The high-pitched scream also alerted the snake. Turning toward the sound, the frenzied beast tried once more to exact its punishment. Charles might have made it, but, as he backpedaled spouting his spell, he tripped. He was able to get off a small energy blast, but it grazed the snake. Najash hissed and kept on going.

Everyone's attention had been on Alex and Nick, but Charles's terrified shriek changed that. Alex watched in horror as the demon opened its jaws and dove for Charles. As he yelled for help, she tried to insert a shield in front of him, but the snake was too quick. Fangs sliced into him, and Charles gave out one last, pain-filled screech. Blood pooled around his body. Najash had finally succeeded in eliminating one of his enemies.

Before the demon could further savage the body, Alex and the others sent multiple blasts at it. The hurting monster swayed as he moved away from Charles, giving Alex a full view of the remains. The sight made her gag. She noticed Bree staring at the body of her former lover and wished she could shield her aunt from the terrible sight.

A sudden shout snapped Bree out of her reverie. The snake began moving toward her. She aimed her gun. Nothing happened. She was out of darts. Alex started to fashion a barrier when Tony rushed up.

"Aunty, move." Aiming his gun, he hit the serpent twice. The beast reared and charged, snapping in every direction. Thanks to Tony, Bree got away, but the thrashing tail caught him and slammed him against the wall.

Alex, ready to turn her new powers on the snake, called to Nick and Bree, *The spell.* They had each memorized the words.

Holding hands, they began the ancient Latin invocation while the others tried to keep the serpent from slithering down its hole. The spell was working. Najash paused his attack.

Their individual gifts united as though woven together in an age-old tapestry. With their combined strength, they concentrated on defeating the demon. The writhing viper began to move toward the fireplace. Alex dug into its mind and worked to wipe out the escape plan. Najash stopped its forward momentum and swung around looking confused.

Alex tightened her hold on Nick, and they continued the spell, repeating it over and over. Najash's back-and-forth movements slowed as its strength diminished. The poison from the darts had finally begun to work, but the demon still fought.

Fatigue threatened Alex, and she could sense the exhaustion of her comrades. They couldn't keep up the pressure much longer. The heavy drain from their prolonged attack would soon deplete their strength. The demon sensed their weakness, hissed, and slid toward them. The rest of the Clan had also expended most of their stamina. Nick gave her hand a reassuring squeeze, but she feared the demon would win.

A movement to her left startled her. What she saw made her doubt her senses. Then, she felt the crush of another Templar hand. The three bearded knights she'd met in the tower stood next to her. In battle dress, blood red cross on a white tunic, they peered at her. The leader dipped his heavy brows and spoke to her mind, *We'll help.* As his huge, callused fingers gripped her own, her ancestors joined in the incantation.

An enormous bolt of power surged through her. She turned it on the demon. Nick and Bree stood taller with the renewed strength of the knights. Najash also reacted. It reared up, bared its fangs, and began to writhe as if in pain. Alex and her group jumped out of the way as the serpent slumped to the ground, its head hitting where they had been standing. The monster twitched and hissed but couldn't move.

She sagged with relief. They'd done it. The knights who'd created this menace had come back to help destroy it. When she turned to thank her ancient brethren, the leader winked at her and grinned. *We heard the ancient spell and felt your need. Your gifts are strong. A true daughter of the Knights Templar.*

As she expressed gratitude to her invisible ancestors, she realized her Clan must think she'd lost it. She'd explain it all later. For now, she smiled as all three executed a deep bow and faded away.

With the snake immobilized, Clan members hurried in and used knives to detach its head. Alex had to look away from the still-twitching body. As her adrenaline waned, her head began to ache, and she staggered. A strong arm reached out to steady her. She marveled at Nick, who supported her as well as Aunt Bree. He dredged up a tiny smile. "We did it."

Then, they noticed two bodies crumpled on the floor. Lia bent over Rich, felt for a pulse, and touched his heart. Her head shook back and forth as her shocked gaze moved to Tony.

Alex's heart broke for Lia as she ran toward her cousin and cradled his head in her lap. She put her hands over Tony's heart and leaned in. Then made a muffled sound like keening. When she sat up, caramel tresses covered her face, and her body convulsed with sobs.

Alex listened to Lia's unguarded agony. "Oh, God. It's too late. I can't save either of you."

Bree hurried over but could do nothing. She stood there looking at Lia and Tony. Tears streaked down her cheeks.

From beside Alex, Nick jerked. His voice filled with anguish as he cried, "Tony."

After a while, Bree left Lia and walked past the snake. She stood over the blood-soaked carnage that had been Charles Berenger. Her whispered words of sorrow echoed in the room. "What happened to you, Charles?" Sounding like a lost little girl, she said, "What became of the handsome young boy who stole my heart? I did love you, but you wanted too much from me."

She covered her face for a moment, then straightened up. Passing her hand over her forehead, she spoke again, steel in her voice. "You may have saved my life today, but you killed my sister and nephew. Enjoy hell, you bastard." She spun around and walked away.

Alex felt sick and helpless as she watched her family: Lia rocking Tony's lifeless body and Rosemary consoling Bree. Slipping an arm around her waist, Nick pulled Alex tight against his side.

She turned her face up to him. "Tony treated me like one of the family from the start. If I'd received my powers a little earlier, he and Rich might still be alive."

Nick swallowed before he spoke, his voice ragged with pain. "Don't blame yourself. Charles was the one who set the demon loose. He's the one who killed them."

Chapter Forty-One

Nick held on to Alexandra. His heart ached for Tony and Rich, and his body cried out for rest. A movement near the door caught his attention. Someone scuttling out. "I have to go."

He gave Alex a kiss and slipped out the front door in time to see his prey run toward the street. He gave chase toward a car idling at the end of the overgrown drive. Afraid the runner might get away, Nick sent out an energy blast that knocked the man to the ground.

Seconds later, a woman leaped out of the car and ran to the prone body. "Hunter. Baby, wake up."

Nick had to pry the woman away and got the brunt of her rage. She punched and scratched him as she screamed, "What did you do to my baby? Get Lia."

Busy protecting himself, it took a minute for Nick to recognize the face under the hat. He felt something inside him break. Mattie. The woman who'd always let him sneak into the kitchen for cookies when he was a boy. The woman he'd regarded as family. Mattie was the traitor.

"What did you do to him? He needs help. Get Lia."

When she launched another attack, Nick pulled her hands behind her back. "He's fine. It was just a blast of air."

She gave him more trouble than Hunter did when he came to.

****

Once the adrenaline rush from the receipt of Alex's powers faded, exhaustion crept in. The sight of her *new* family amid their fallen loved ones broke her heart. Wonderful people who would never be the same again. Bree looked like a broken woman, shoulders bowed and tears streaming down her face. Lia, dry-eyed, moved like a robot as she shuffled between the two bodies.

Alex left them to their grief and walked outside. She craved fresh air.

A chill swept through her as she walked by the gate. She turned to stare at the source of her nightmares. Alive and menacing in her dreams, the reality, nothing but a disintegrating pile of stones and timber. The centuries-old evil that overshadowed her family hadn't originated in the rotting mansion, but in the sinister magic executed on that spot all those years ago.

Noisy chirps distracted her, and she sought out the vocalist. Though hidden in the leaves, she had no trouble locating the mockingbird's plumage. Her vision had sharpened as well as her hearing. What else had changed? A fallen branch caught her eye. With a sweep of her hand, she sent it skittering across the ground and did the same to a large stone next to it. She uttered a cry of delight, and her self-confidence soared. A few more objects along the way bent to her powers.

At the edge of the tree line, though, the sight of the Brendani house made her pause. She ignored the familiar cry of gulls overhead as her heart constricted. All these wonderful new gifts had come at a terrible price. She closed her eyes and remembered. Tony. The sweet and fun-loving man who'd made her laugh with his ridiculous stories. Although he'd also been the voice in her head that said Nick was injured, she knew her cousin had done it under threat from Charles. She didn't care what his crime had been. In the end, Tony proved himself, fighting and dying for his family. His secret was safe with her.

And Rich, the tough cop with a soft spot for Lia. He'd stood up for Alex against the bullies and been struck down defending his Clan. His loyalty and bravery couldn't be questioned.

In the past two weeks, Alex had become accustomed to her strange, new existence, but the result of today's violence would live with her for a long time.

****

Before Alex surrendered to the lure of her bed, she wanted to visit her grandmothers.

The minute she stepped onto the labyrinth's winding path, its magic enveloped her. She embraced its psychic strength. A streak of movement flashed along the ground. She stood still and waited. There. She saw it again. This time, she caught sight of a tiny being with a large head, sharp chin, and wrinkled forehead. When he realized she could see him, his eyes widened, and she read the panic in his mind.

Using her gifts to hold him in place, she said, "That's right, little man. I'm looking at you, and if I can see you, I can punish you."

After all the pain and humiliation these gremlins had caused her, the idea of payback sounded good. She could cover the troublesome being with a shield and gloat as his terror mounted. Maybe it would be more fun to lift him up by his feet and let him dangle until he cried for mercy. More ideas flitted through her mind, but as she watched his distress, her throat tightened. What was she doing?

With a sigh, she pointed to the trembling figure and said, "If I find you harassing anyone else in my family the way you tortured me, I will come after you. Understand?"

The terrified creature nodded, and she allowed him to disappear. For a minute, she savored her power, enjoying the feeling of omnipotence. She'd never have to grovel to anyone again. Her excitement dissolved as a picture of Charles and his "pet" flashed through her mind. His urge for dominance had resulted in the death of Tony, Rich, and her parents.

The idea of what she'd almost done to the little gremlin shook her. She'd have to be careful. She hadn't grown up learning how to use her gifts. They called to her now, a strong and insidious craving. She'd need help from the Clan to understand and use them properly before her gifts could become an addiction.

The outside noise and confusion faded as she continued to the center of the labyrinth. She saw Kitty and her great-grandmother, Gabrielle.

Hi, ladies. She'd remembered to use telepathy.

The spirits spoke at the same time, but Kitty's voice overrode Gabrielle. *You did good, granddaughter. We're very proud of you. Of course, my CeCe saved the day. It's wonderful to have her back.*

Thank you, Kitty. What a pretty dress you have on.

Kitty fluffed up her skirt. *I'm glad you like it. It's my fav. . .* She stopped and poked the other woman. *Get up, Mother. She can see us.*

When Gabrielle stood and smoothed down her dress, Alex noted the family resemblance in the women. *It's so nice to see you, great-grandmother. You look beautiful.*

And may I say that you're also lovely today. Your new gifts radiate from you. Very impressive. Happy Birthday.

Kitty concurred. *I wouldn't be surprised if you joined us here one day. You'd make an excellent keeper.*

Alex tried not to grimace at her grandmother's words. She could think of few things worse than an eternity in the labyrinth with Kitty. *I better get going. Aunt Bree needs help.*

A deep voice stopped her. *Just a minute.*

Alex flinched at the booming tone. Kitty spun around and gasped at the towering figure in Templar raiment resting his hand on his sword.

The sight of the bearded giant made Alex nervous, too. *What are you doing here?* Was he now part of the labyrinth ghosts?

His beard twitched as he twisted his lips into a grimace that may have been intended as a smile. When his features hardened, his next words allayed one fear but ignited another. *The future harbors betrayal. Take care, daughter of the Templars.*

What? But we found the traitors.

Before she could ask any questions, his figure dissolved, leaving a brief impression of the Templar Cross. A look of awe spread across Kitty's face. *You can summon the knights?*

After a couple of swallows, Alex said, *No. I-I don't think so.* A thread of worry nudged her. *Could they pop in on her whenever they wanted?*

Chapter Forty-Two

When she entered the living room, she heard Bree's cry, something between a moan and a sob. The floor was littered with remnants of the morning's horror: pieces of cinnamon buns, darts, and a couple of Clan members still asleep. A groggy Franki roused herself from the couch.

The sisters reunited, and Bree broke the heartbreaking news about Tony and Rich to Franki. When the phone rang, Alex offered to answer it, but Bree waved her off.

After a minute, Bree hung up and rolled her eyes. "The caterers will be here in an hour." She checked the messages. "Oh, Lord. Donny and the Light Machine plan to arrive at four to set up the fireworks."

When she saw the last one, she slumped into a chair and cradled her head in her hands. "The band. Tony's friends. He told me I'd love them." She sat up, tears cascading down her cheeks, and said to Franki, "I can't believe he's gone. He saved my life. Now Sal and his family must go over and claim his body. We can't let anyone else in there."

Alex fought the headache that threatened and summoned the willpower to take command. "We'll cancel the party. The companies won't mind as long as they get paid. We'll give them extra for their trouble."

Bree straightened her shoulders and shook her head. "No. Today is your birthday, and, dammit, we're going to have a party. It doesn't matter if the house smells like burnt wood, if half the guests will be yawning, or if one of the rooms on the third floor holds two prisoners."

When Franki gave her a panicked look, she explained that Nick had secured Hunter and his mother, Mattie, upstairs. "Poor Mattie. Charles made her work for him by threatening her son, Hunter. At least she didn't follow his orders to poison the men. He intended to add Alex's powers to his own and rule the Clan. He would have been unstoppable."

Bree rubbed her eyes. "Never mind. Tonight, the Brendanis are having a Fourth of July bash in honor of Alexandra Ryan's birthday, and Tony's favorite band will be playing." She choked out the last.

Alex nodded and sent up a prayer of gratitude that most of their Clan was alive to celebrate.

****

Alex helped Franki and Bree clean up the living room, then headed off to crash. The winding staircase looked like an obstacle course threatening to overcome her.

She'd taken a few steps up when she heard his voice. "Alexandra, wait."

Nick ran after her, hair askew and clothes in shreds, but to her, he looked wonderful. When she'd feared Charles had killed him, she'd felt like a black hole had swallowed her. Nothing mattered.

Now, as she gazed at the man she loved, hope brightened her soul, but she needed to touch him, confirm his reality. She brushed her hand across his cheek, and the soft caress in his eyes started a warm fluttering in her chest. She grinned. He was the genuine article, all right.

"I thought I'd never be able to hold you again," he said as he pulled her to him.

Images from the morning assailed her: venom dripping from the demon's fangs, Charles attacking Nick, Nick shielding her from the serpent. She clung to him. When he finally relaxed his arms, she staggered.

"I know you're tired, Alexandra. So am I." He gathered her close again and captured her in a deep kiss. Heat spread to her abdomen. His voice deepened. "Why don't we rest together?"

Despite her fatigue, she ached to be in his arms and whispered, "I'd like that."

As they walked into her bedroom, she flicked her hand behind her and heard the door close. Then she realized what she'd done. She had powers. Before she could dwell on her new abilities, Nick wrapped his arms around her and drew her in. He nuzzled her neck and sighed. "You're safe. I thought I'd lose you."

His words awakened a sense of freedom she hadn't felt since she'd arrived. She could sleep whenever she wanted. Thoughts of independence fled as she abandoned herself to Nick's hungry mouth. She ran her fingers through his hair and scraped her nails against his shoulders. He groaned and lifted her onto the bed. For a moment, he simply gazed at her. "The thought of that monster hurting you made me sick."

He cupped her face in his hands. His gentle touch, the brush of his lips along her forehead, eyes, and nose, aroused ripples of love. Lying next to Nick felt so right. This was the man she wanted to spend the rest of her life with, but when he got around to her lips, she yawned in his face. "Oh no. I'm so sorry."

He lifted his head, drew in a ragged breath, and

grinned. "That's what I get for trying to seduce a woman who's emotionally and physically drained."

He gave her a soft kiss and whispered, "Come here." As he cuddled her in his arms, an enormous yawn stretched his face. "What do you say we rest first."

In answer, she snuggled into him and closed her eyes. Scattered images plagued her. Pieces of the morning's horror and suffering crept in.

Then, everything changed, as if a curtain had lifted. A sense of comfort and safety settled over her. She inspected her surroundings. A luxurious patio with plush furniture and a view of bright flowers and palm trees. She wore a simple peasant blouse and skirt. With a sigh, she relaxed into the comfortable outdoor bed.

"May I join you, Alexandra?"

Her pulse quickened as she looked at him. Gone was the evidence of their terrible battle. Nick's handsome face gazed down at her. Dark hair curled around his ears. The set of his jaw and the cleft in his chin held purpose, and mischief dwelt in those dark blue orbs.

She batted her eyes. "I don't know. What will we do with no snake to threaten us?"

He leaned down and stroked her face. "I guess we'll have to improvise."

"Mm. I like the sound of that." She inhaled his scent and licked her lips. "You smell so good."

He grinned.

His fingers slid along her shoulders and back while he removed her blouse. Her breathing hitched. Heat spread down her body as she undid the buttons of his shirt.

His eyes became almost black when she slowly shimmied out of her skirt. "So beautiful." He breathed.

He stripped off his shorts, and the sight of his taut body stirred her senses. He teased her with tiny, tormenting kisses to her forehead, cheeks, and lips. Her need intensified as she stroked his arms and massaged his chest. He tangled his hands in her hair and licked the tender skin along the side of her neck. Each touch sent waves of pleasure through her. As his tongue moved lower, she gasped, wanting more.

His voice deepened. "I love how you taste."

Heat pooled between her thighs. She kissed and licked his skin as her hands moved lower. He moaned and captured her mouth. Deep, hungry kisses made her arch against him. Sighs of pleasure became cries of desire. She wanted him.

Yes, Alexandra. Now!

"Oh my God," she gasped when he entered her. Sexual lightning bolts took her breath away. Exquisite. Torture. She arched into him. Heat and need threatened to consume her. Her heart pounded, and her body begged for release.

He captured her mouth. *I love you.* His explosion sent her over the edge, and she shattered into streams of ecstasy.

When her breathing finally calmed, she said, "I've never… That was…"

He grinned. "Your first time with your new powers?"

"You mean…"

"That's right, sweetheart. Get used to it." His arms tightened around her as he kissed her. "That's how it's going to be for the rest of our lives."

A word about the author...

Margo is the author of the award-winning novel, Trace of Evil, set in Salem, Massachusetts. A delicious ghostly adventure.

After relocating to Rhode Island, she discovered the Newport Tower whose origin harks back to the Knights Templar. Curiosity and imagination sparked this first story in the Watcher Clan trilogy. Stay tuned for the next two. Today, she, her husband Paul, and two spoiled cats live in Florida where inspiration may lead her to gator-infested swamps!

MargoCarey.com

The Convent House is a work of fiction. Characters and various locations are products of Margo's imagination.